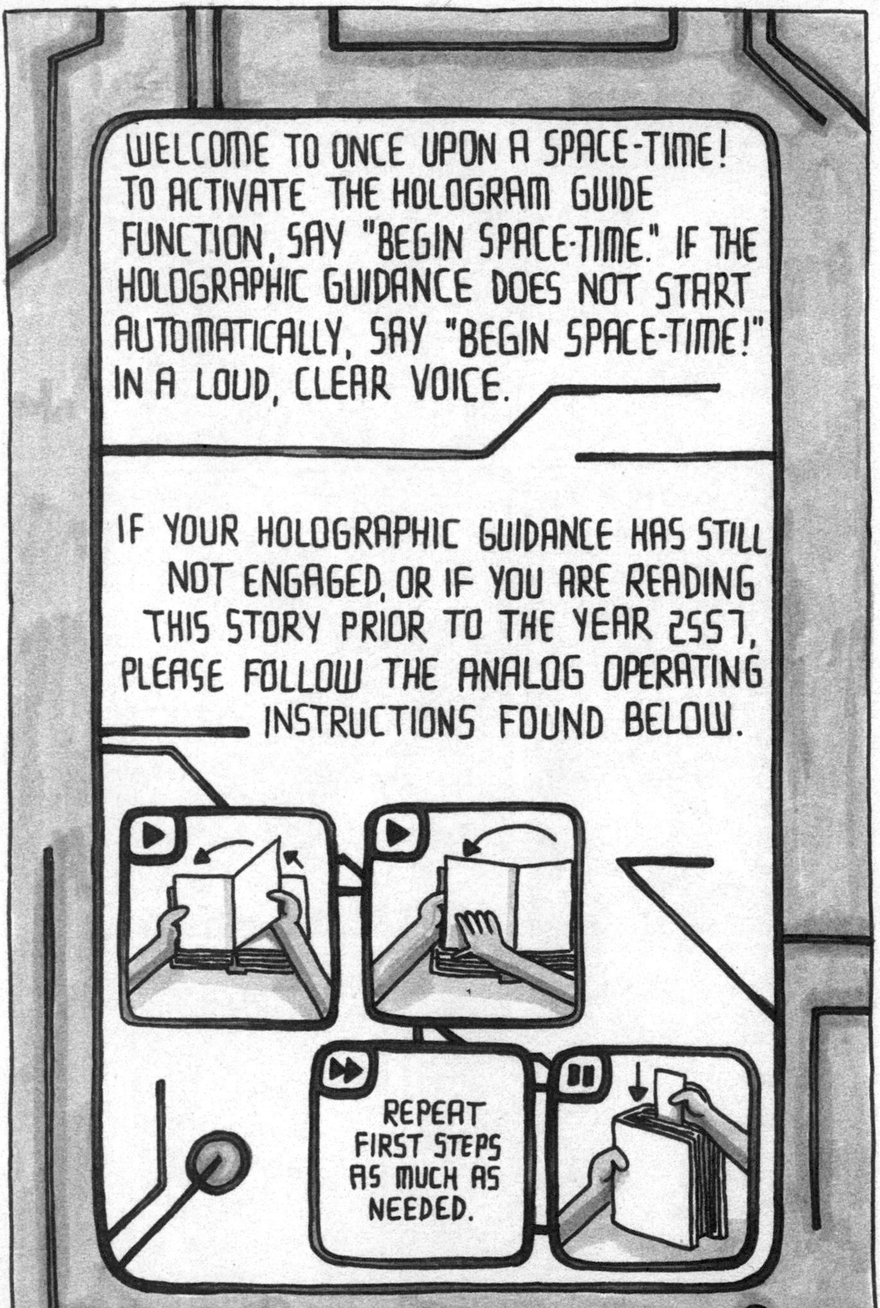
WELCOME TO ONCE UPON A SPACE-TIME! TO ACTIVATE THE HOLOGRAM GUIDE FUNCTION, SAY "BEGIN SPACE-TIME." IF THE HOLOGRAPHIC GUIDANCE DOES NOT START AUTOMATICALLY, SAY "BEGIN SPACE-TIME!" IN A LOUD, CLEAR VOICE.
IF YOUR HOLOGRAPHIC GUIDANCE HAS STILL NOT ENGAGED, OR IF YOU ARE READING THIS STORY PRIOR TO THE YEAR 2557, PLEASE FOLLOW THE ANALOG OPERATING INSTRUCTIONS FOUND BELOW.
REPEAT FIRST STEPS AS MUCH AS NEEDED.

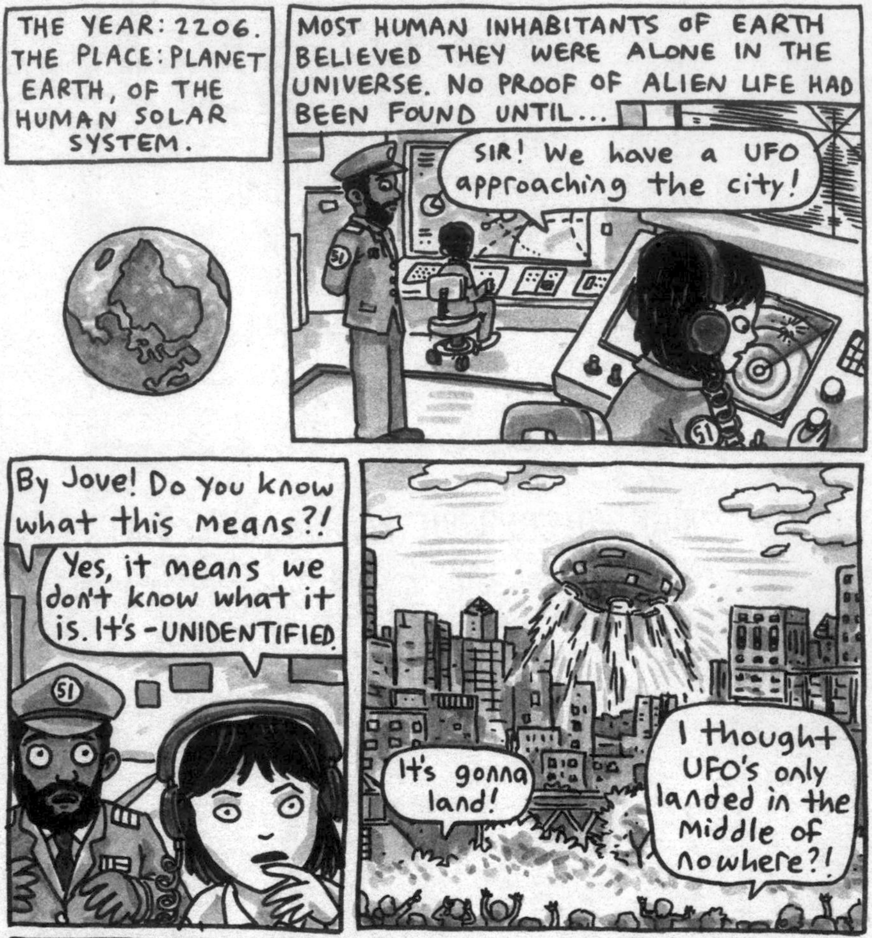
THE YEAR: 2206. THE PLACE: PLANET EARTH, OF THE HUMAN SOLAR SYSTEM.
MOST HUMAN INHABITANTS OF EARTH BELIEVED THEY WERE ALONE IN THE UNIVERSE. NO PROOF OF ALIEN LIFE HAD BEEN FOUND UNTIL...
SIR! We have a UFO approaching the city!
51
51
By Jove! Do you know what this means?!
Yes, it means we don't know what it is. It's -UNIDENTIFIED.
51
It's gonna land!
I thought UFO's only landed in the middle of nowhere?!
Someone... someTHING is coming out!

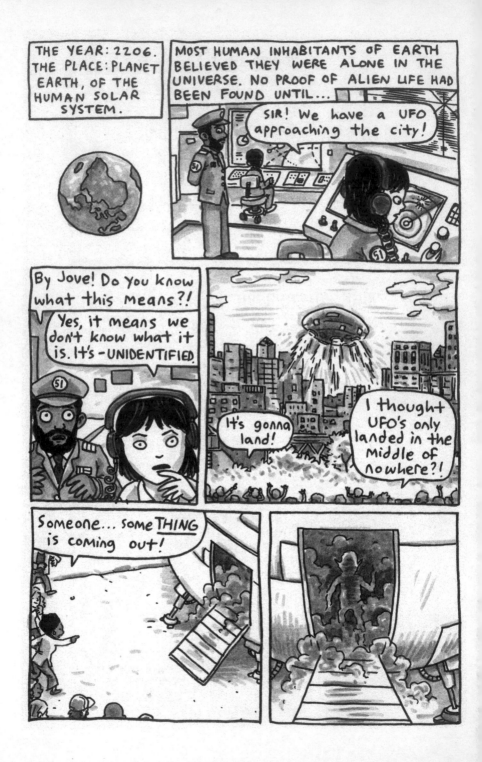

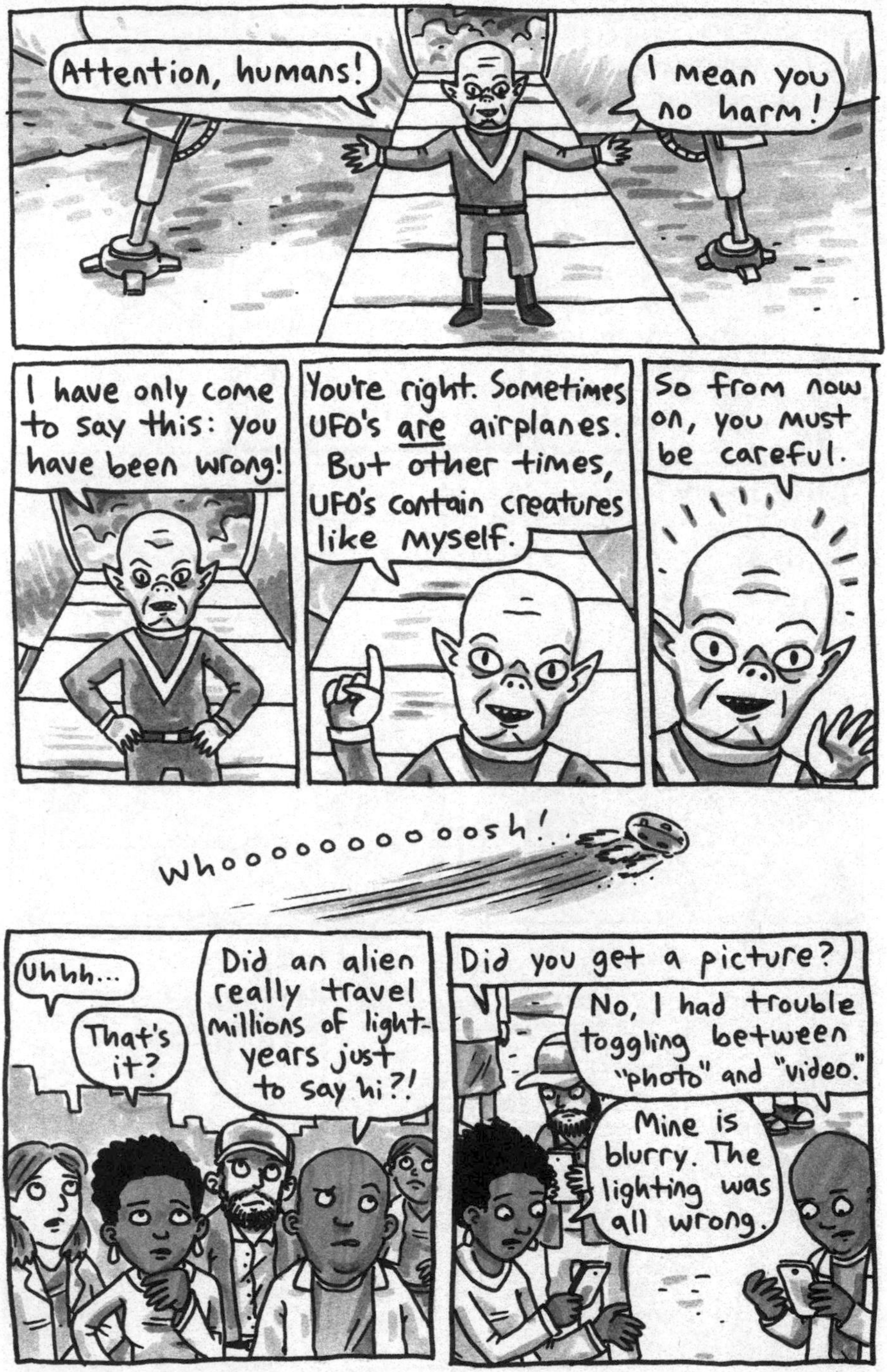
Attention, humans!
I mean you no harm!
I have only come to say this: you have been wrong!
You're right. Sometimes UFO's are airplanes. But other times, UFO's contain creatures like myself.
So from now on, you must be careful.
Whooooooooooosh!
Uhhh...
That's it?
Did an alien really travel millions of light-years just to say hi?!
Did you get a picture?
No, I had trouble toggling between "photo" and "video."
Mine is blurry. The lighting was all wrong.

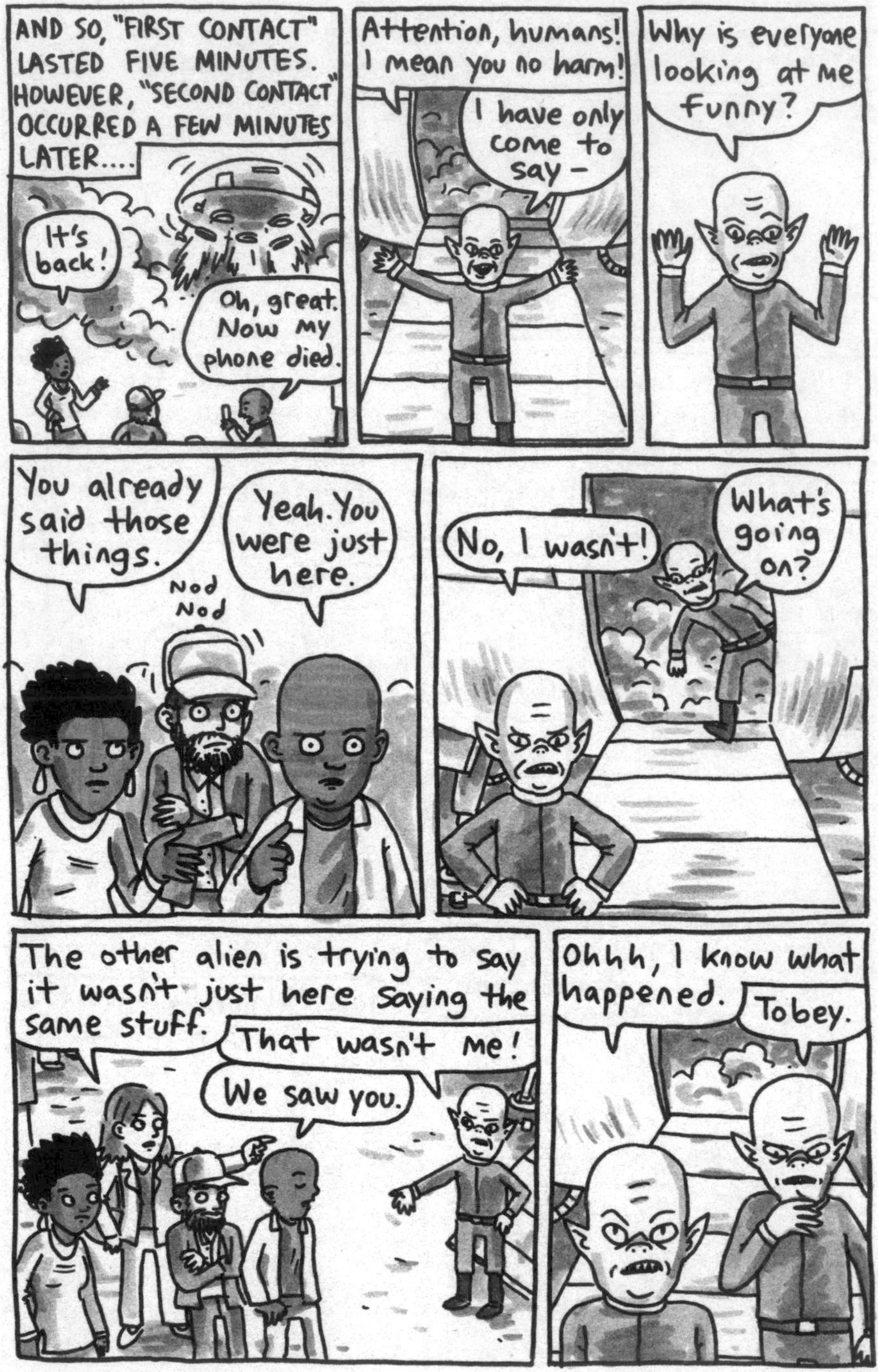

AND SO, "FIRST CONTACT" LASTED FIVE MINUTES. HOWEVER, "SECOND CONTACT" OCCURRED A FEW MINUTES LATER....
It's back!
Oh, great. Now my phone died.
Attention, humans! I mean you no harm!
I have only come to say -
Why is everyone looking at me funny?
You already said those things.
Nod Nod
Yeah. You were just here.
No, I wasn't!
What's going on?
The other alien is trying to say it wasn't just here saying the same stuff.
That wasn't me!
We saw you.
Ohhh, I know what happened.
Tobey.

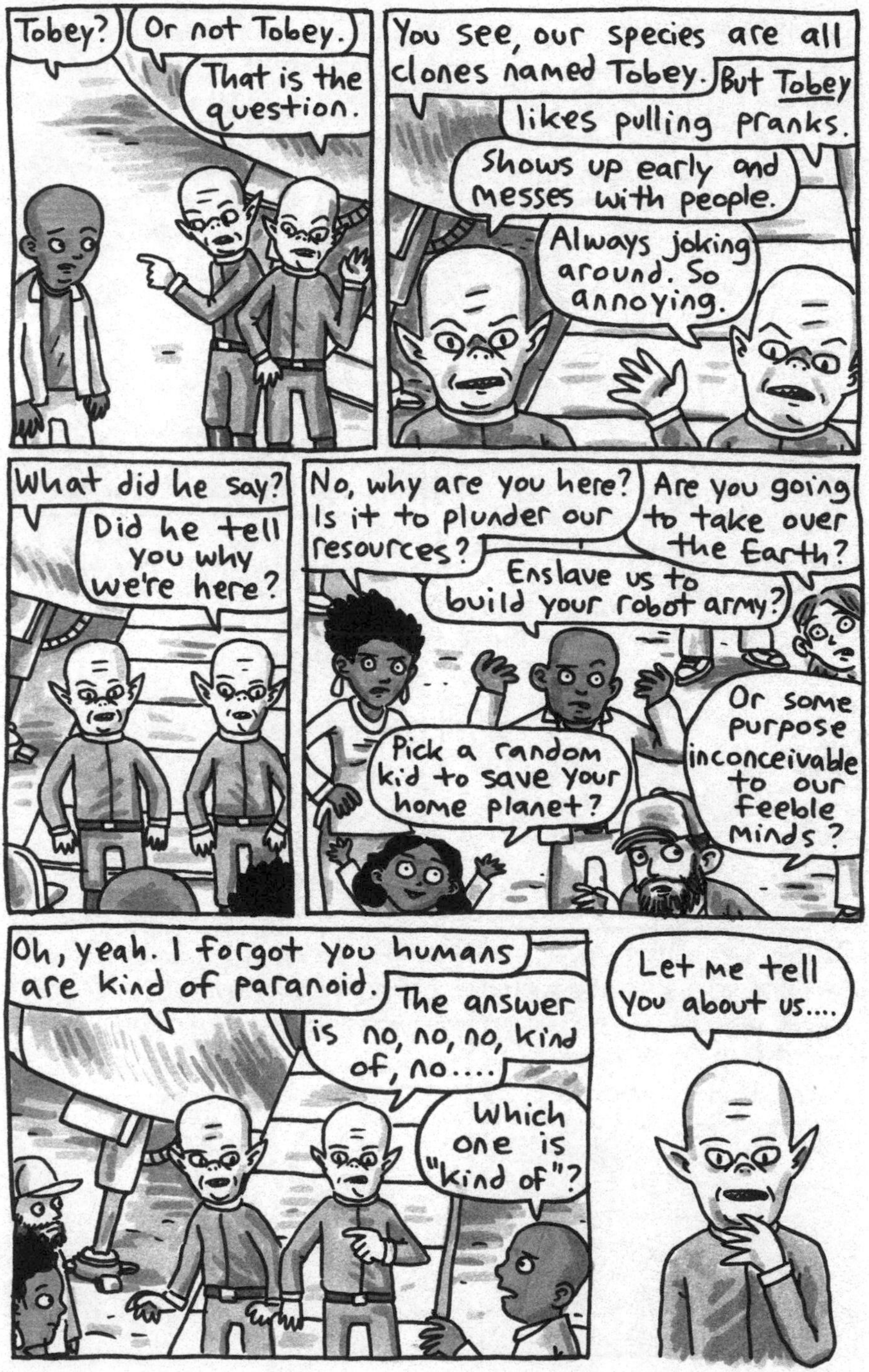
Tobey?
Or not Tobey.
That is the question.
You see, our species are all clones named Tobey.
But Tobey likes pulling pranks.
Shows up early and messes with people.
Always joking around. So annoying.
What did he say?
Did he tell you why we're here?
No, why are you here? Is it to plunder our resources?
Are you going to take over the Earth?
Enslave us to build your robot army?
Pick a random kid to save your home planet?
Or some purpose inconceivable to our feeble minds?
Oh, yeah. I forgot you humans are kind of paranoid.
The answer is no, no, no, kind of, no....
Which one is "kind of"?
Let me tell you about us....

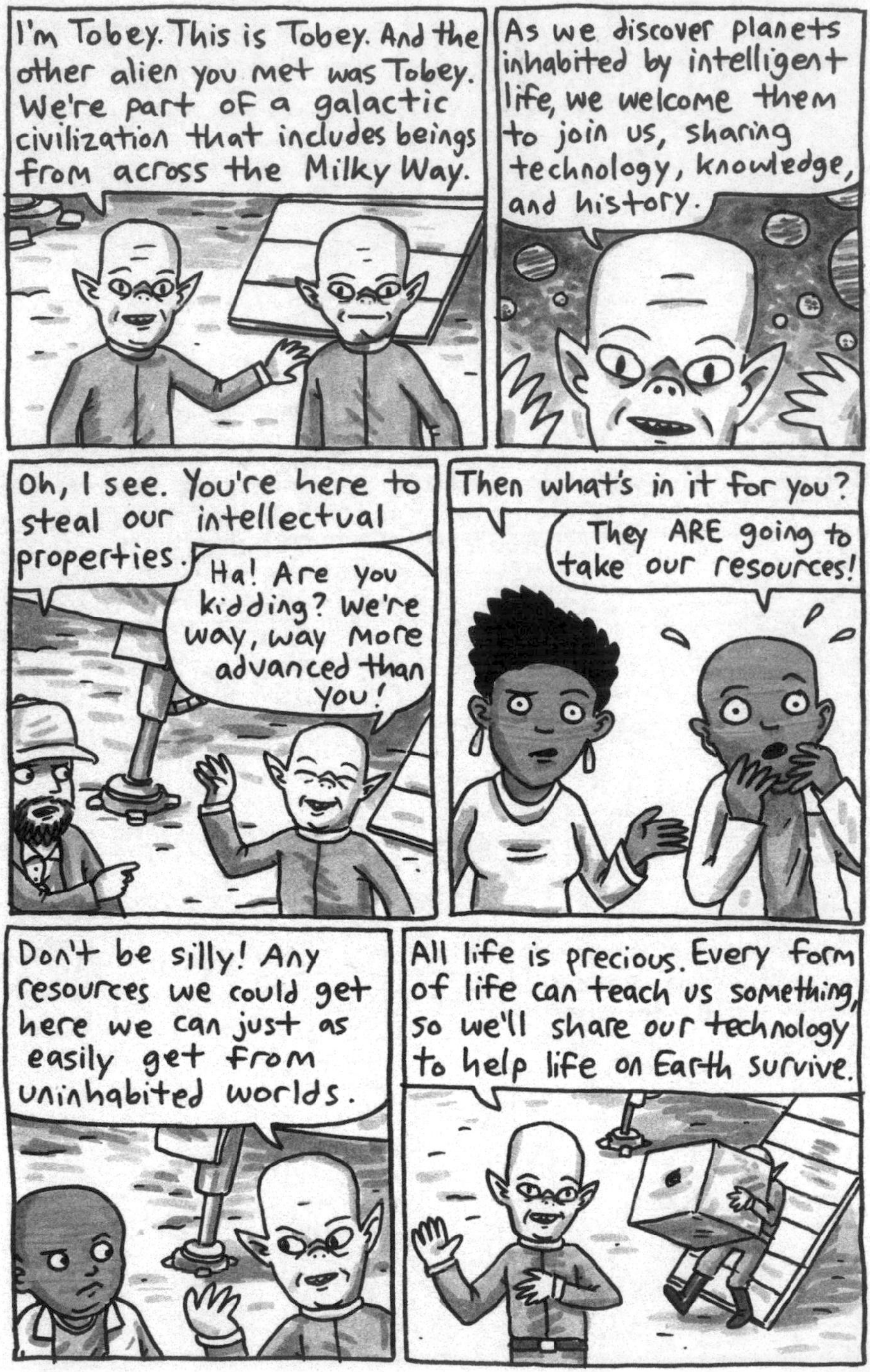
I'm Tobey. This is Tobey. And the other alien you met was Tobey. We're part of a galactic civilization that includes beings from across the Milky Way.
As we discover planets inhabited by intelligent life, we welcome them to join us, sharing technology, knowledge, and history.
Oh, I see. You're here to steal our intellectual properties.
Ha! Are you kidding? We're way, way more advanced than you!
Then what's in it for you?
They ARE going to take our resources!
Don't be silly! Any resources we could get here we can just as easily get from uninhabited worlds.
All life is precious. Every form of life can teach us something, so we'll share our technology to help life on Earth survive.

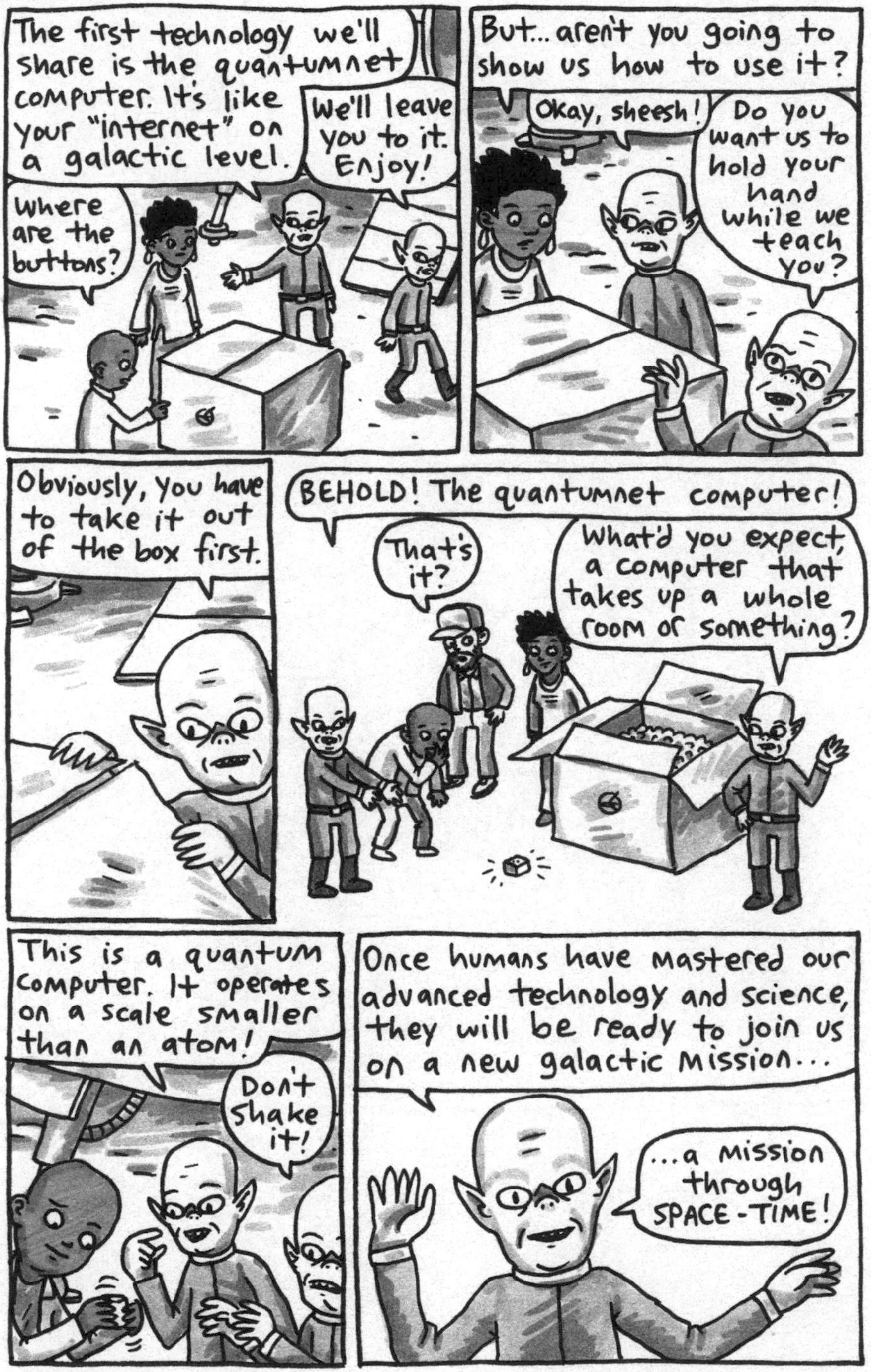
The first technology we'll share is the quantumnet computer. It's like your "internet" on a galactic level.
We'll leave you to it. Enjoy!
Where are the buttons?
But... aren't you going to show us how to use it?
Okay, sheesh!
Do you want us to hold your hand while we teach you?
Obviously, you have to take it out of the box first.
BEHOLD! The quantumnet computer!
That's it?
What'd you expect, a computer that takes up a whole room or something?
This is a quantum computer. It operates on a scale smaller than an atom!
Don't shake it!
Once humans have mastered our advanced technology and science, they will be ready to join us on a new galactic mission...
...a mission through SPACE-TIME!

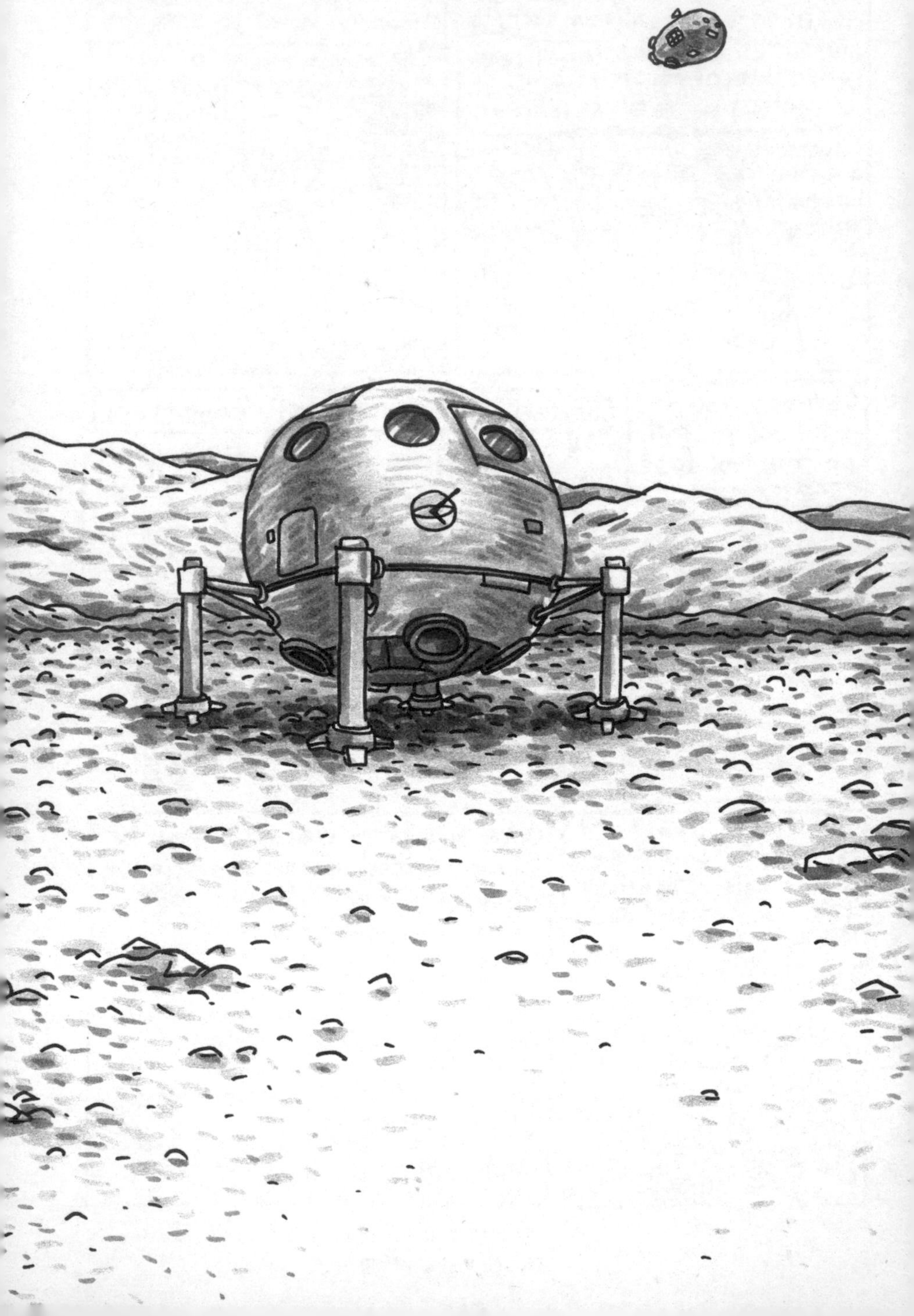

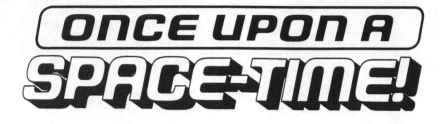

ONCE UPON A SPACE-TIME!

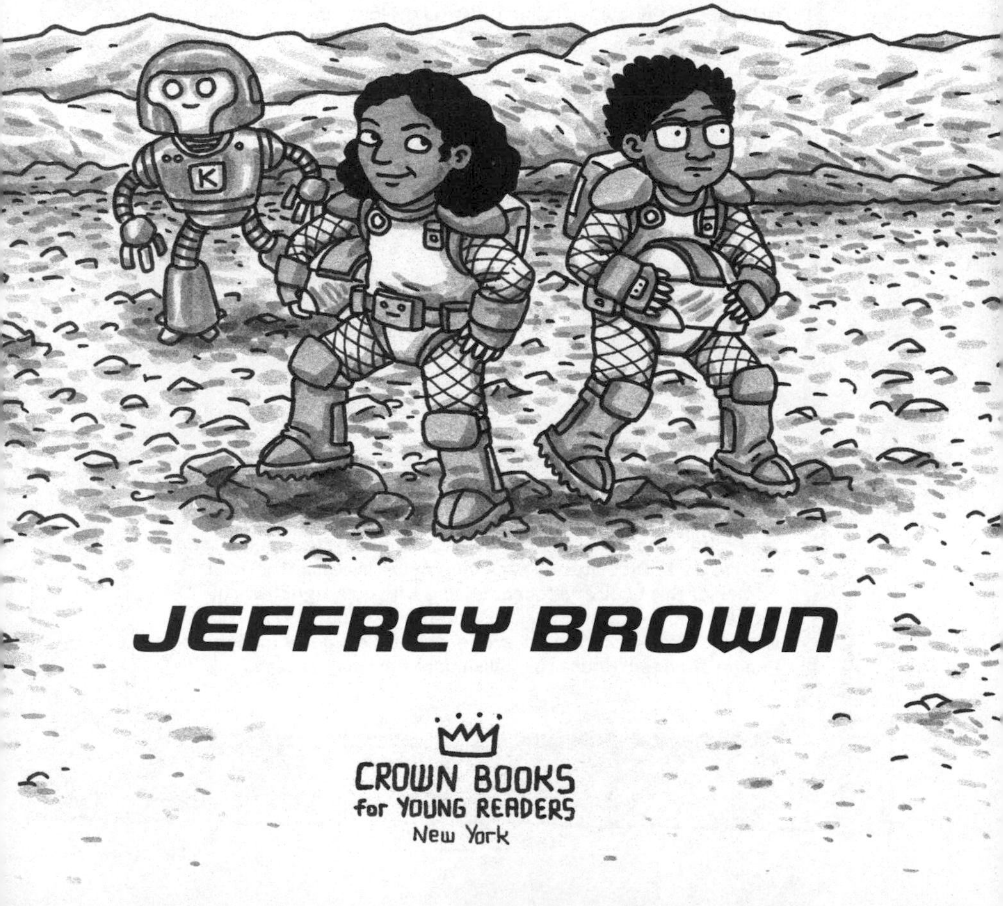

K

JEFFREY BROWN

CROWN BOOKS
for YOUNG READERS
New York

THE FOLLOWING TECHNICAL DATA CAN BE USED TO IDENTIFY THE CURRENT ANALOG VOLUME OF SPACE-TIME! WITHIN HUMAN INFORMATION SYSTEMS.

This is a work of fiction. Names, characters, places, and incidents either are the product of the author's imagination or are used fictitiously. Any resemblance to actual persons, living or dead, events, or locales is entirely coincidental.

 Published in the United States by Crown Books for Young Readers, an imprint of Random House Children's Books, a division of Penguin Random House LLC, New York.

Crown and the colophon are registered trademarks of Penguin Random House LLC.

Visit us on the Web! rhcbooks.com

Educators and librarians, for a variety of teaching tools, visit us at RHTeachersLibrarians.com

Library of Congress Cataloging-in-Publication Data is available upon request.

ISBN 978-0-553-53435-1 (trade)
ISBN 978-0-553-53436-8 (lib. bdg.)
ISBN 978-0-553-53437-5 (ebook)

Printed in the United States of America

10 9 8 7 6 5 4 3 2 1

First Edition

NOT QUITE THE RIGHT STUFF

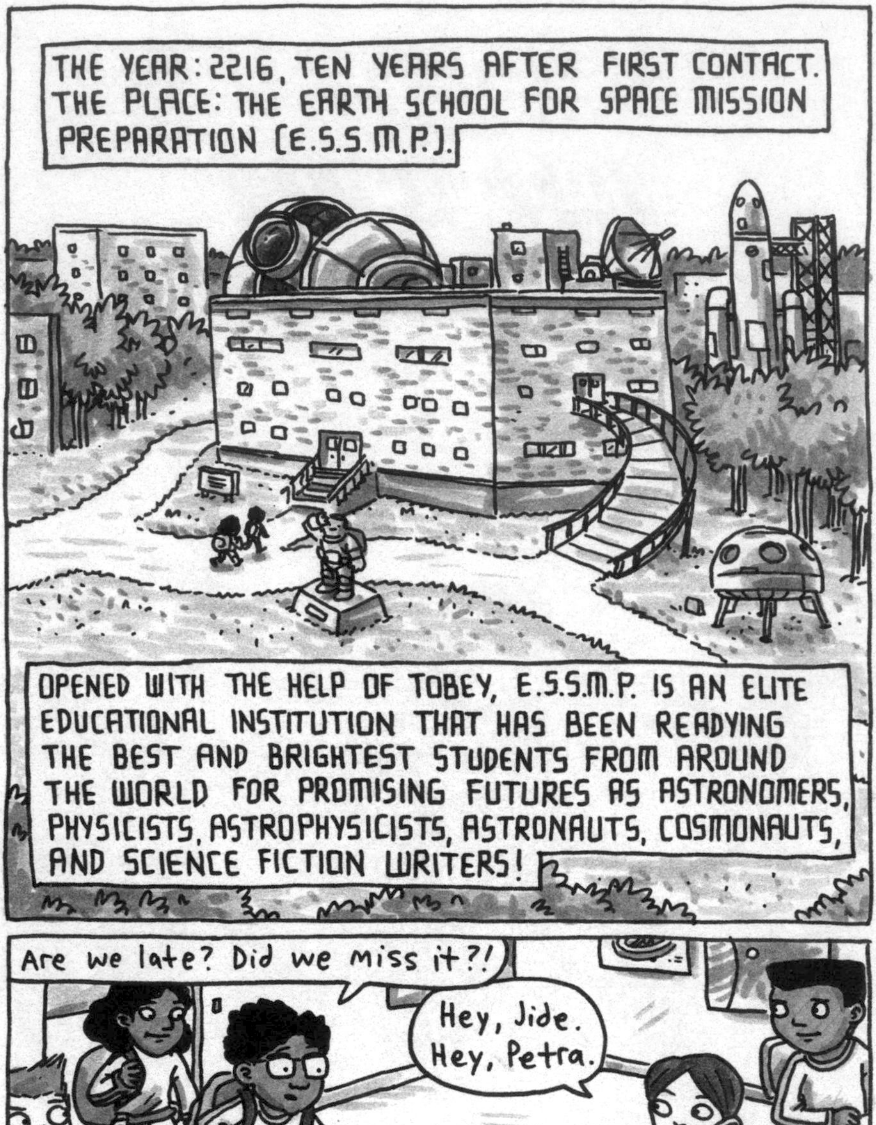
THE YEAR: 2216, TEN YEARS AFTER FIRST CONTACT. THE PLACE: THE EARTH SCHOOL FOR SPACE MISSION PREPARATION (E.S.S.M.P.).
OPENED WITH THE HELP OF TOBEY, E.S.S.M.P. IS AN ELITE EDUCATIONAL INSTITUTION THAT HAS BEEN READYING THE BEST AND BRIGHTEST STUDENTS FROM AROUND THE WORLD FOR PROMISING FUTURES AS ASTRONOMERS, PHYSICISTS, ASTROPHYSICISTS, ASTRONAUTS, COSMONAUTS, AND SCIENCE FICTION WRITERS!

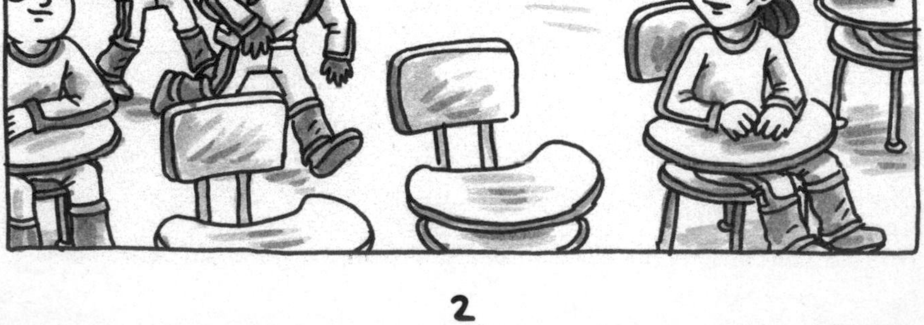
Are we late? Did we miss it?!
Hey, Jide. Hey, Petra.

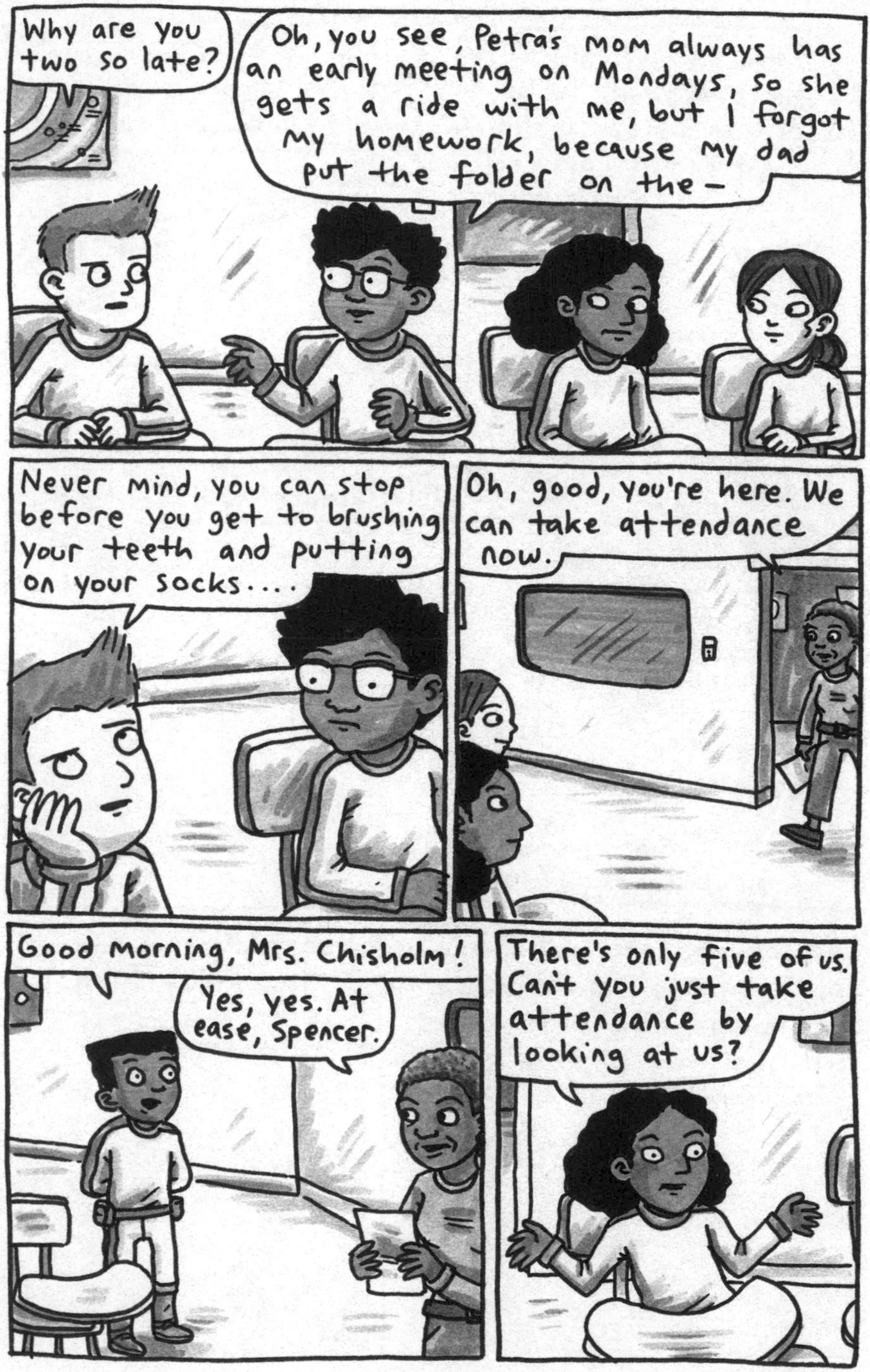
Why are you two so late?
Oh, you see, Petra's mom always has an early meeting on Mondays, so she gets a ride with me, but I forgot my homework, because my dad put the folder on the—
Never mind, you can stop before you get to brushing your teeth and putting on your socks....
Oh, good, you're here. We can take attendance now.
Good morning, Mrs. Chisholm!
Yes, yes. At ease, Spencer.
There's only five of us. Can't you just take attendance by looking at us?

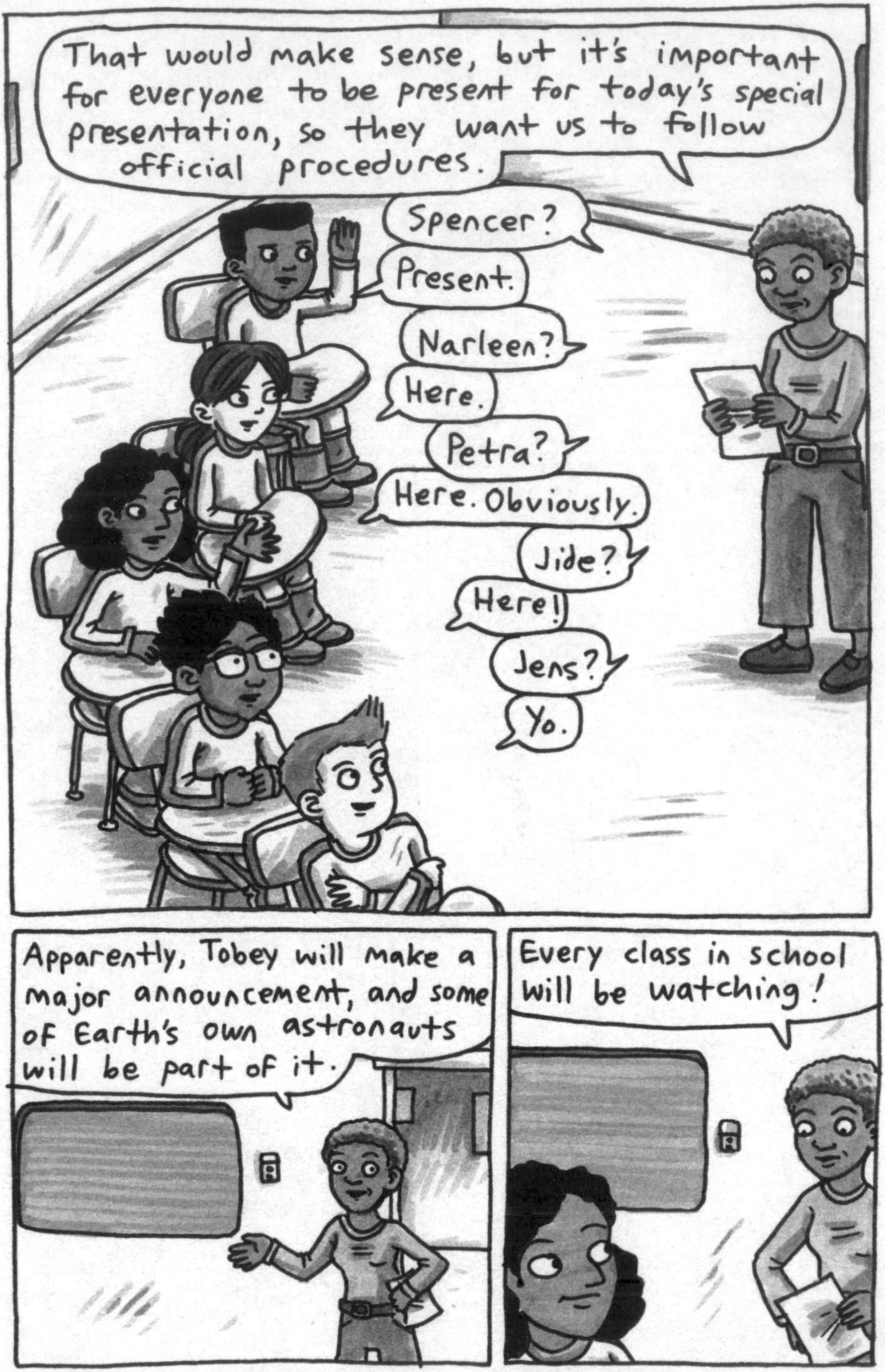
That would make sense, but it's important for everyone to be present for today's special presentation, so they want us to follow official procedures.
Spencer?
Present.
Narleen?
Here.
Petra?
Here. Obviously.
Jide?
Here!
Jens?
Yo.
Apparently, Tobey will make a major announcement, and some of Earth's own astronauts will be part of it.
Every class in school will be watching!

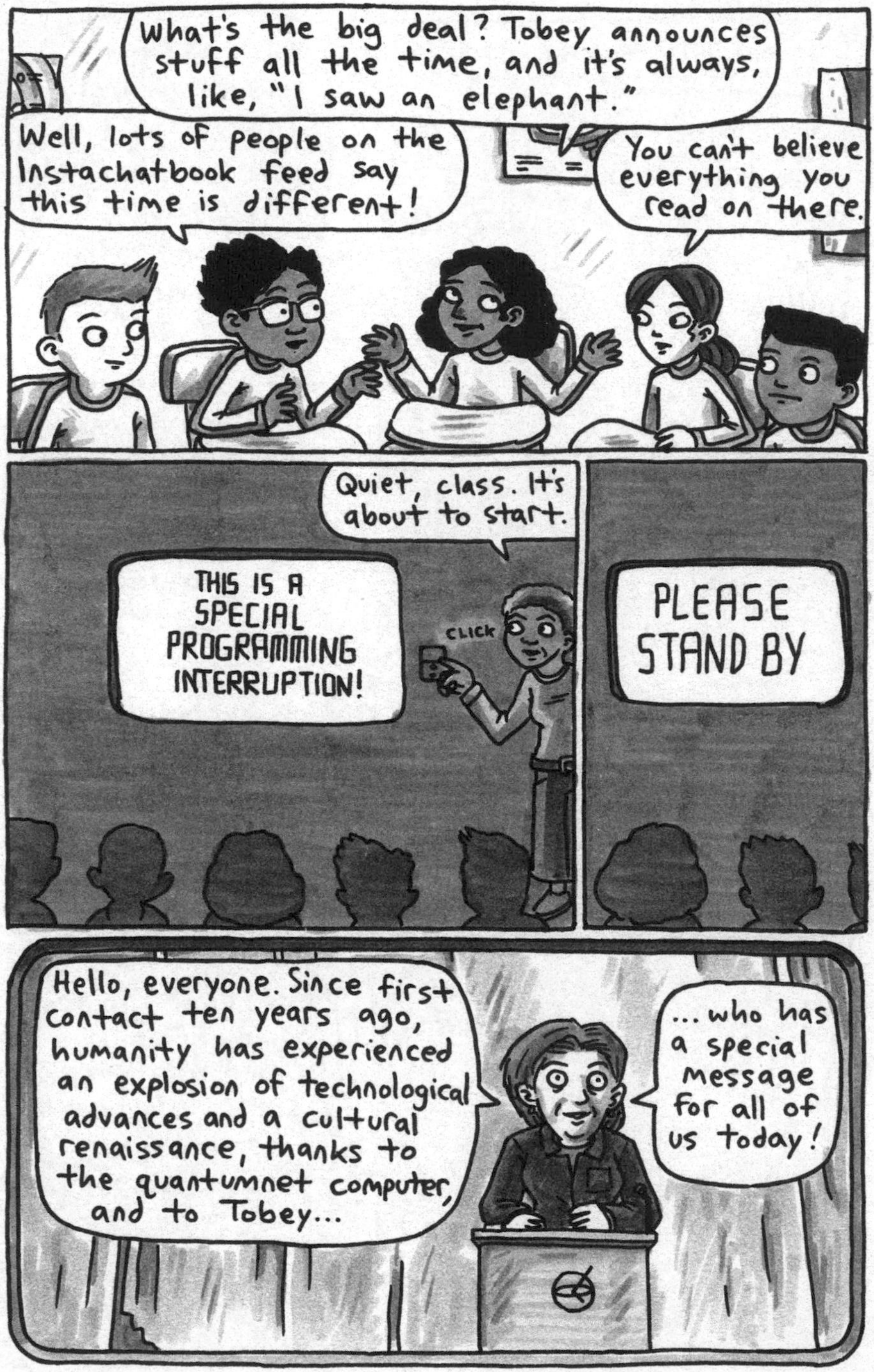
What's the big deal? Tobey announces stuff all the time, and it's always, like, "I saw an elephant."
Well, lots of people on the Instachatbook feed say this time is different!
You can't believe everything you read on there.
Quiet, class. It's about to start.
THIS IS A SPECIAL PROGRAMMING INTERRUPTION!
CLICK
PLEASE STAND BY
Hello, everyone. Since first contact ten years ago, humanity has experienced an explosion of technological advances and a cultural renaissance, thanks to the quantumnet computer, and to Tobey...
...who has a special message for all of us today!

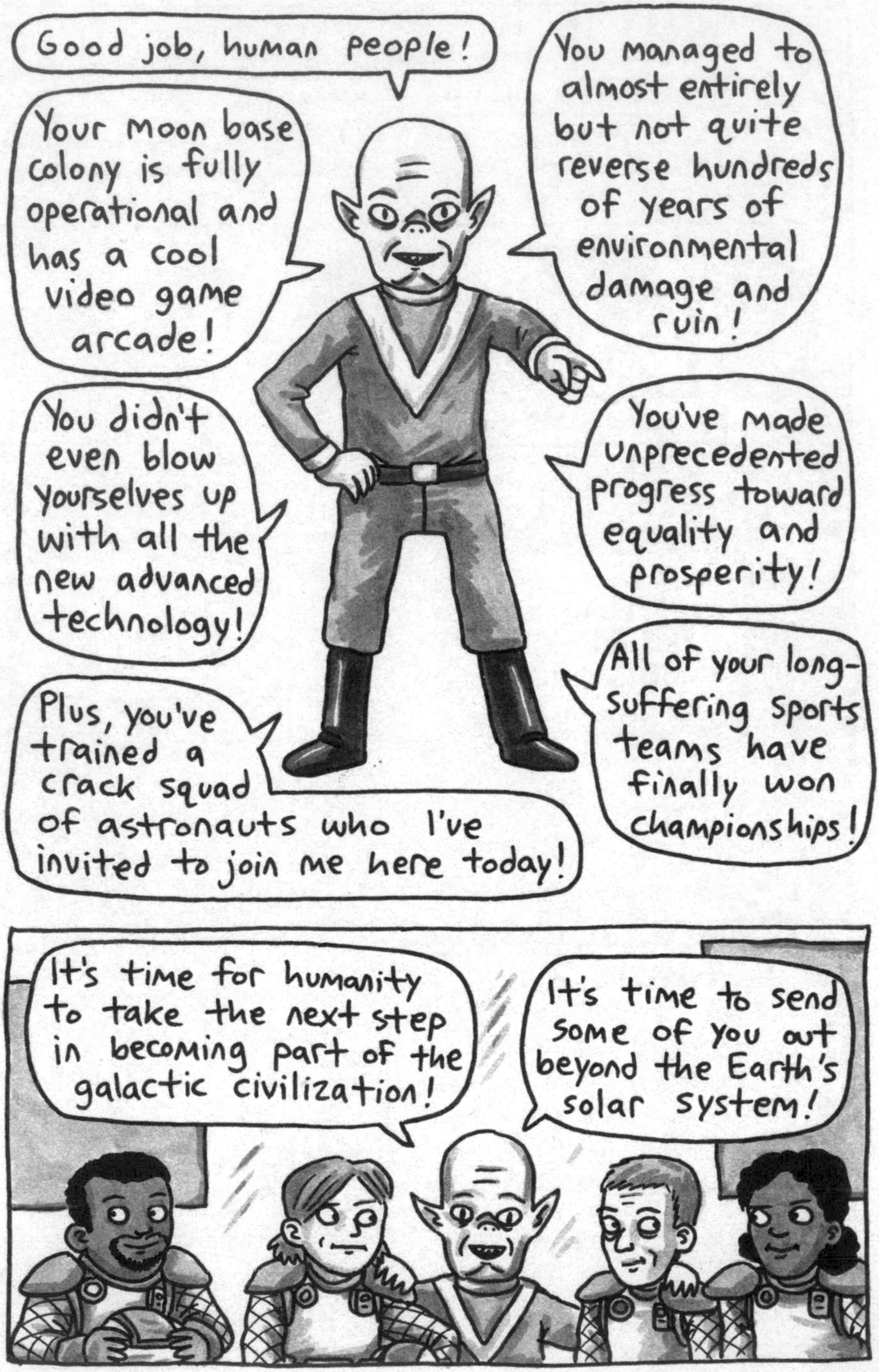
Good job, human people!
Your moon base colony is fully operational and has a cool video game arcade!
You managed to almost entirely but not quite reverse hundreds of years of environmental damage and ruin!
You didn't even blow yourselves up with all the new advanced technology!
You've made unprecedented progress toward equality and prosperity!
All of your long-suffering sports teams have finally won championships!
Plus, you've trained a crack squad of astronauts who I've invited to join me here today!
It's time for humanity to take the next step in becoming part of the galactic civilization!
It's time to send some of you out beyond the Earth's solar system!

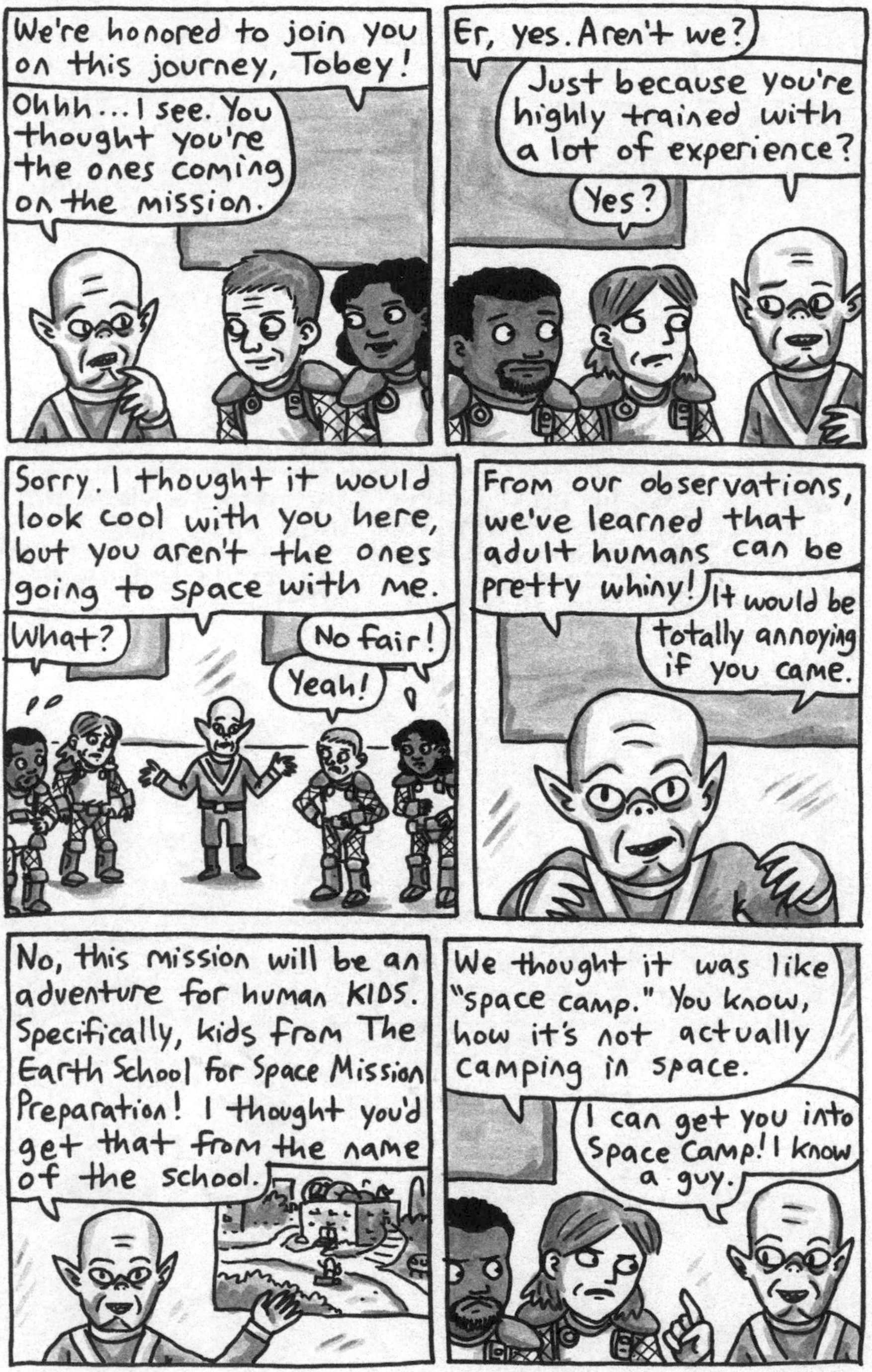

We're honored to join you on this journey, Tobey!
Ohhh... I see. You thought you're the ones coming on the mission.
Er, yes. Aren't we?
Just because you're highly trained with a lot of experience?
Yes?
Sorry. I thought it would look cool with you here, but you aren't the ones going to space with me.
What?
No fair!
Yeah!
From our observations, we've learned that adult humans can be pretty whiny!
It would be totally annoying if you came.
No, this mission will be an adventure for human KIDS. Specifically, kids from The Earth School for Space Mission Preparation! I thought you'd get that from the name of the school.
We thought it was like "space camp." You know, how it's not actually camping in space.
I can get you into Space Camp! I know a guy.

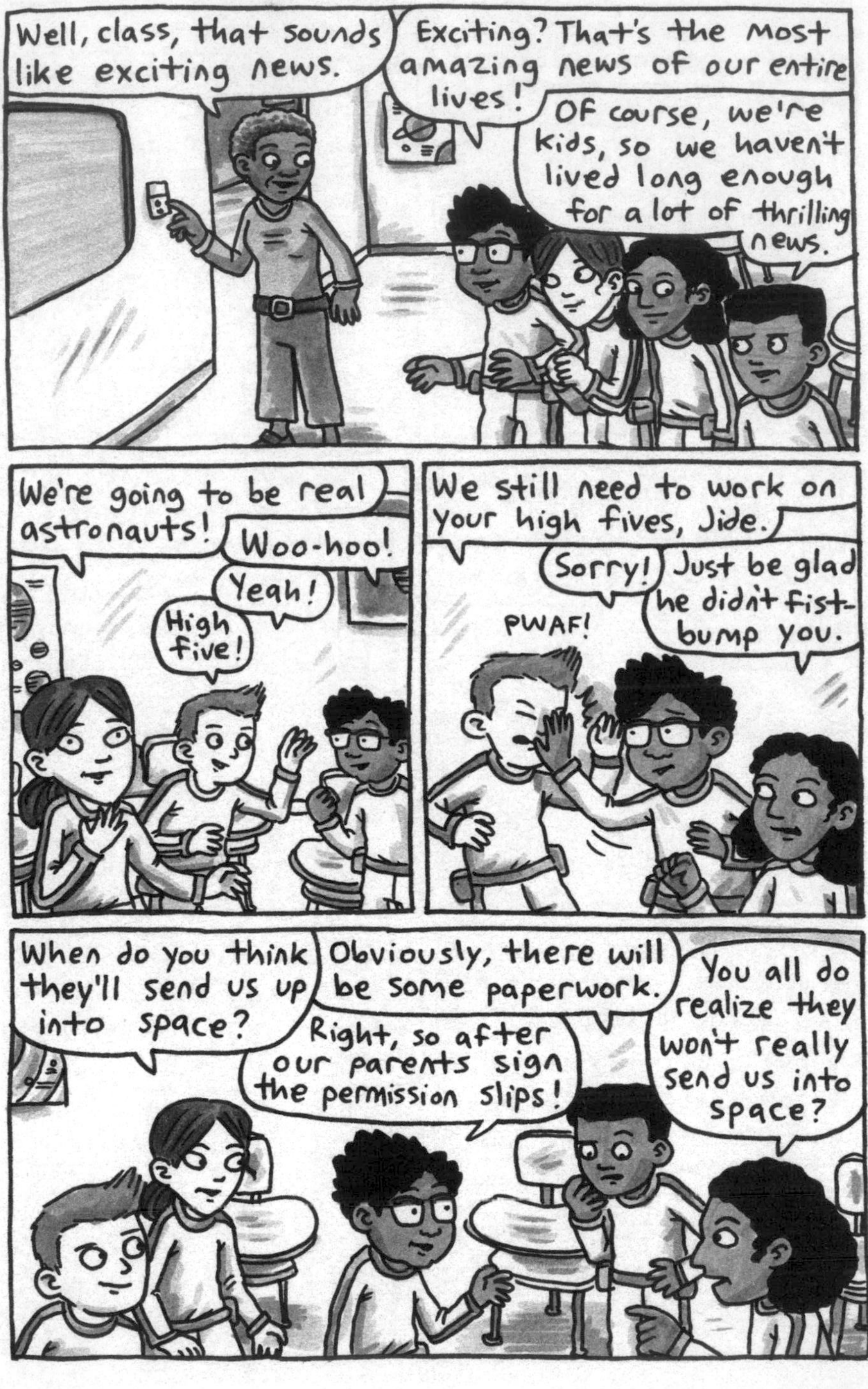
Well, class, that sounds like exciting news.
Exciting? That's the most amazing news of our entire lives!
Of course, we're kids, so we haven't lived long enough for a lot of thrilling news.
We're going to be real astronauts!
Woo-hoo!
Yeah!
High five!
We still need to work on your high fives, Jide.
Sorry!
Just be glad he didn't fist-bump you.
PWAF!
When do you think they'll send us up into space?
Obviously, there will be some paperwork.
Right, so after our parents sign the permission slips!
You all do realize they won't really send us into space?

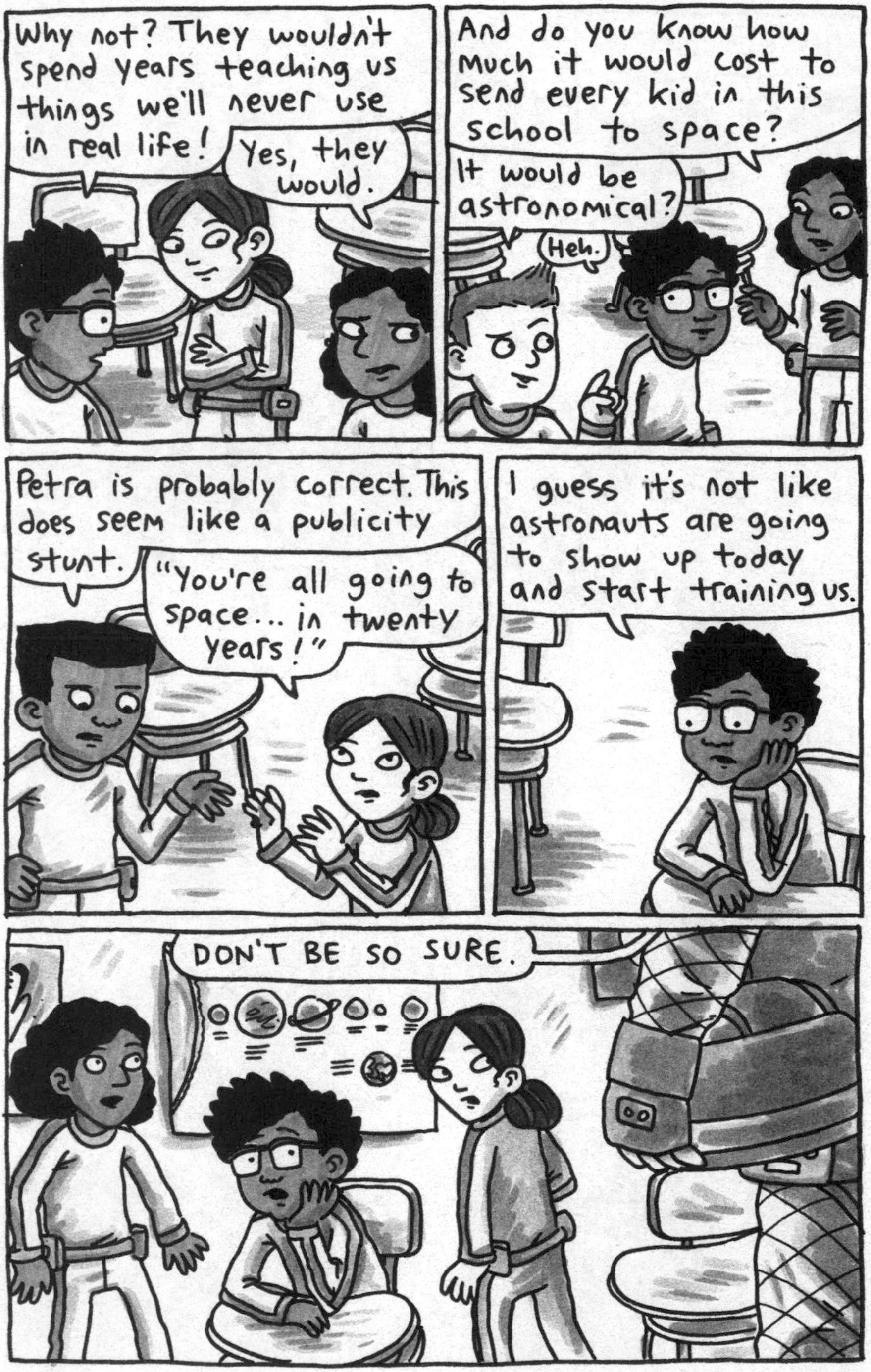
Why not? They wouldn't spend years teaching us things we'll never use in real life!
Yes, they would.
And do you know how much it would cost to send every kid in this school to space?
It would be astronomical?
Heh.
Petra is probably correct. This does seem like a publicity stunt.
"You're all going to space... in twenty years!"
I guess it's not like astronauts are going to show up today and start training us.
DON'T BE SO SURE.

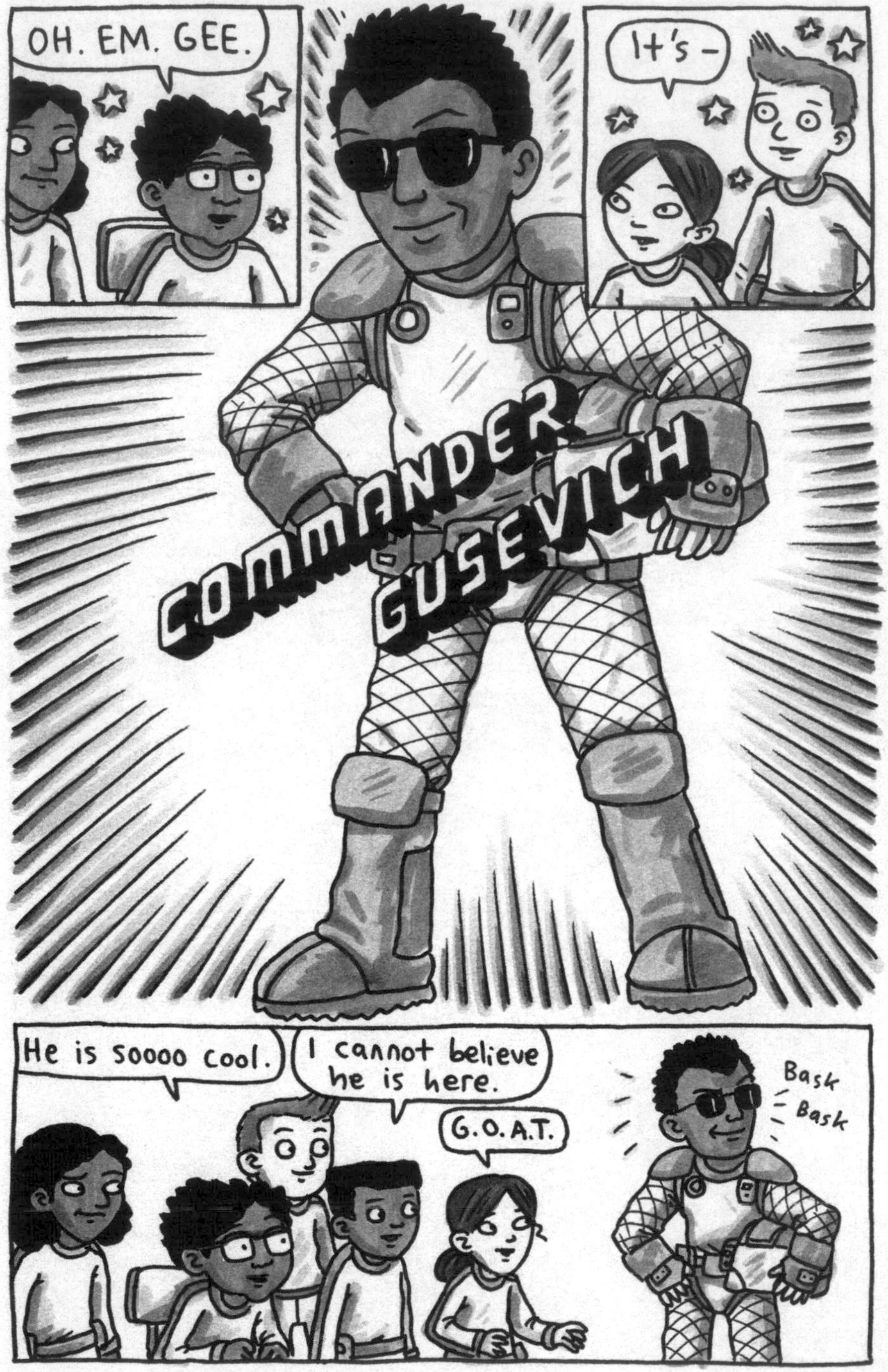
OH. EM. GEE.
It's –
COMMANDER GUSEVICH
He is soooo cool.
I cannot believe he is here.
G.O.A.T.
Bask
Bask

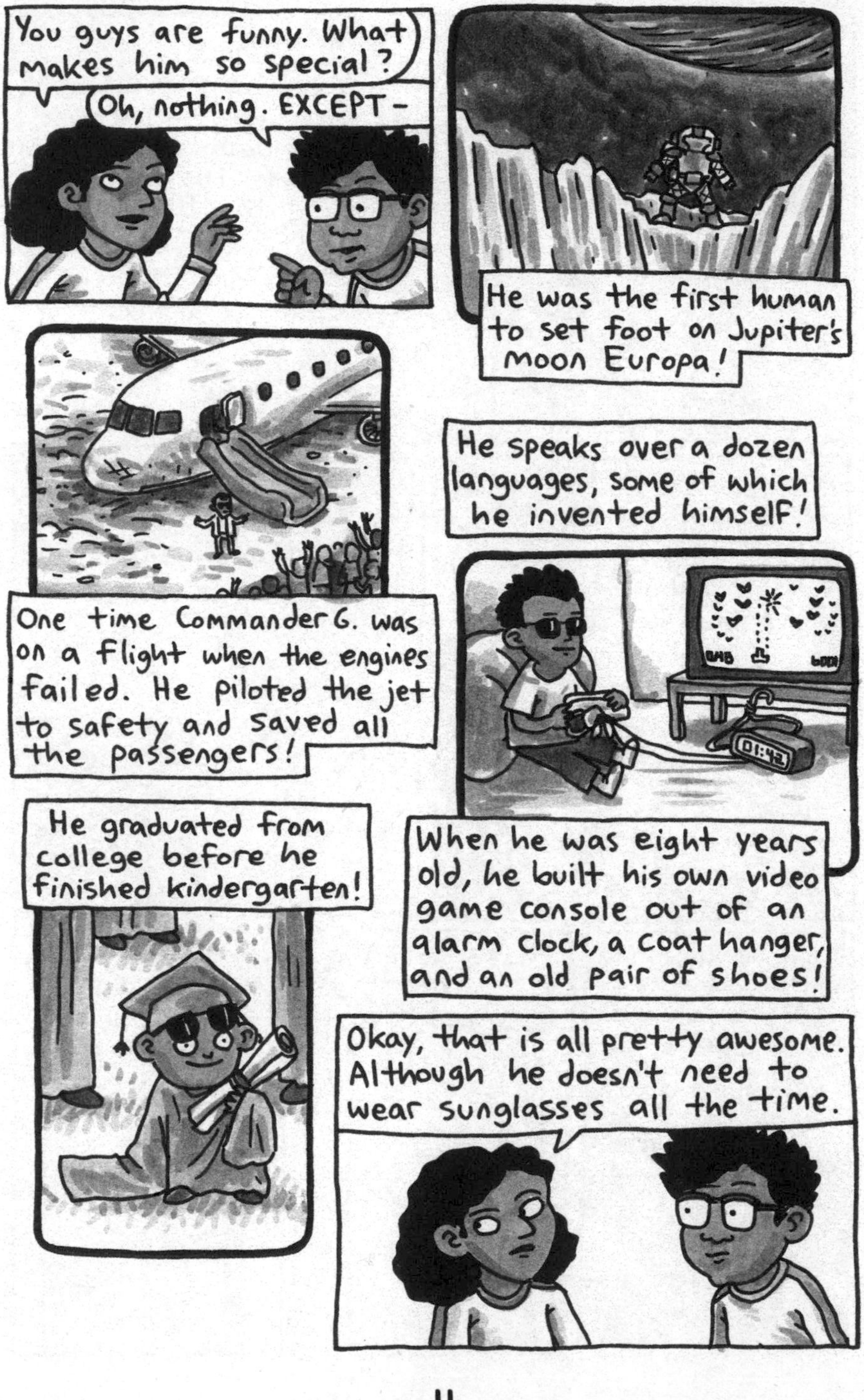
You guys are funny. What makes him so special?
Oh, nothing. EXCEPT-
He was the first human to set foot on Jupiter's moon Europa!
One time Commander G. was on a flight when the engines failed. He piloted the jet to safety and saved all the passengers!
He speaks over a dozen languages, some of which he invented himself!
When he was eight years old, he built his own video game console out of an alarm clock, a coat hanger, and an old pair of shoes!
01:42
He graduated from college before he finished kindergarten!
Okay, that is all pretty awesome. Although he doesn't need to wear sunglasses all the time.

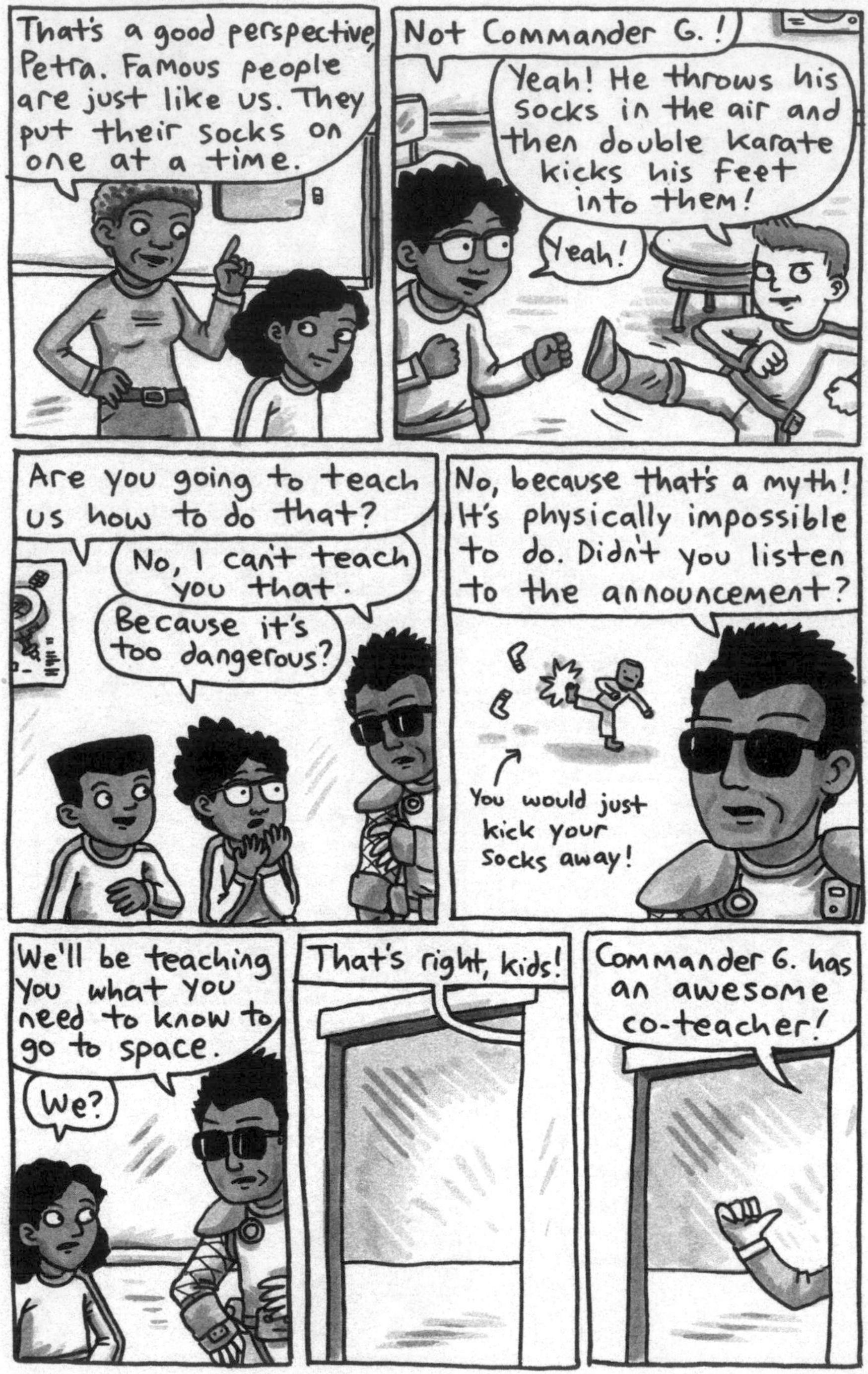

That's a good perspective, Petra. Famous people are just like us. They put their socks on one at a time.
Not Commander G.!
Yeah! He throws his socks in the air and then double karate kicks his feet into them!
Yeah!
Are you going to teach us how to do that?
No, I can't teach you that.
Because it's too dangerous?
No, because that's a myth! It's physically impossible to do. Didn't you listen to the announcement?
You would just kick your socks away!
We'll be teaching you what you need to know to go to space.
We?
That's right, kids!
Commander G. has an awesome co-teacher!

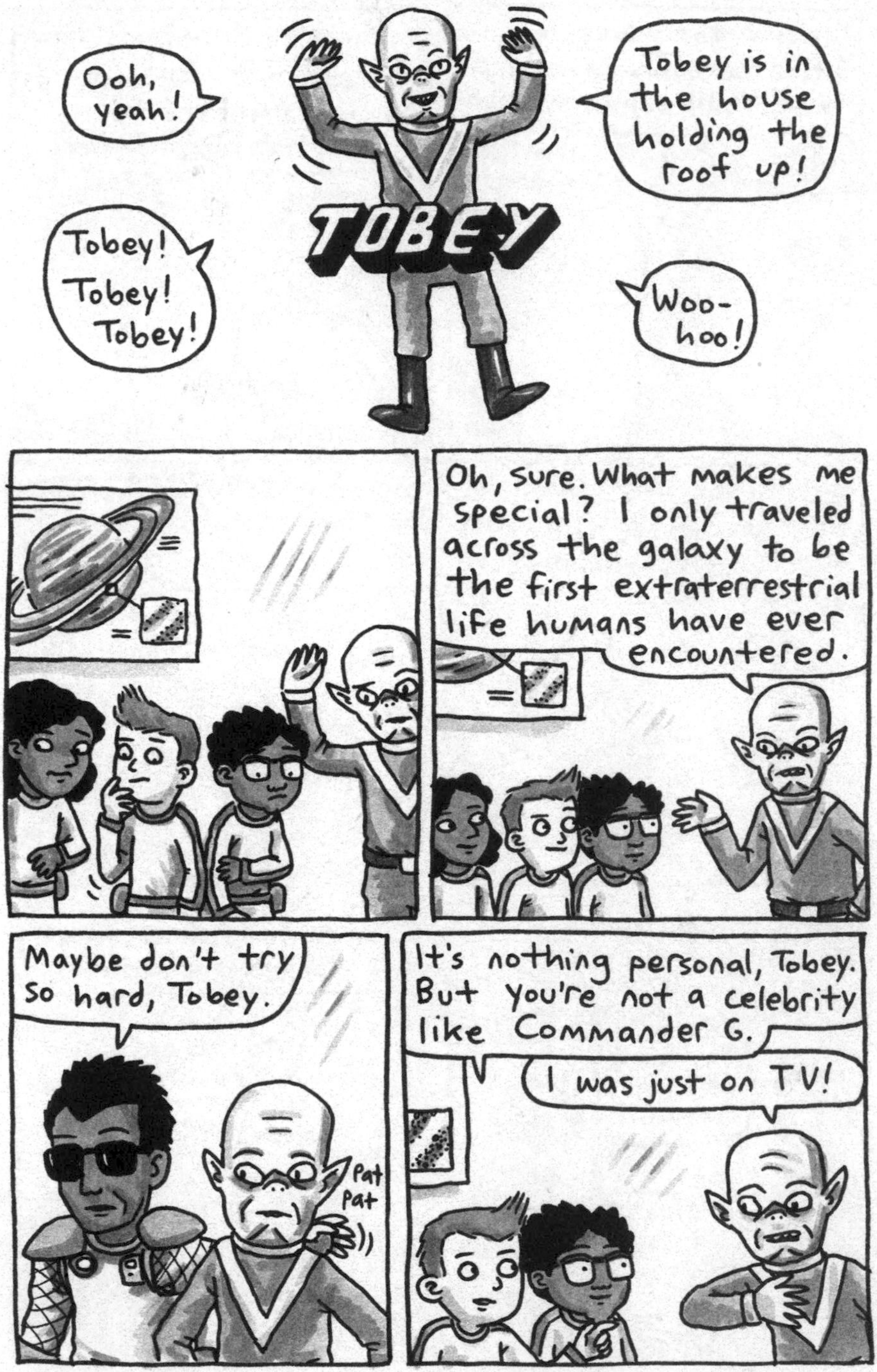
Ooh, yeah!
Tobey is in the house holding the roof up!
TOBEY
Tobey! Tobey! Tobey!
Woo-hoo!
Oh, sure. What makes me special? I only traveled across the galaxy to be the first extraterrestrial life humans have ever encountered.
Maybe don't try so hard, Tobey.
Pat pat
It's nothing personal, Tobey. But you're not a celebrity like Commander G.
I was just on TV!

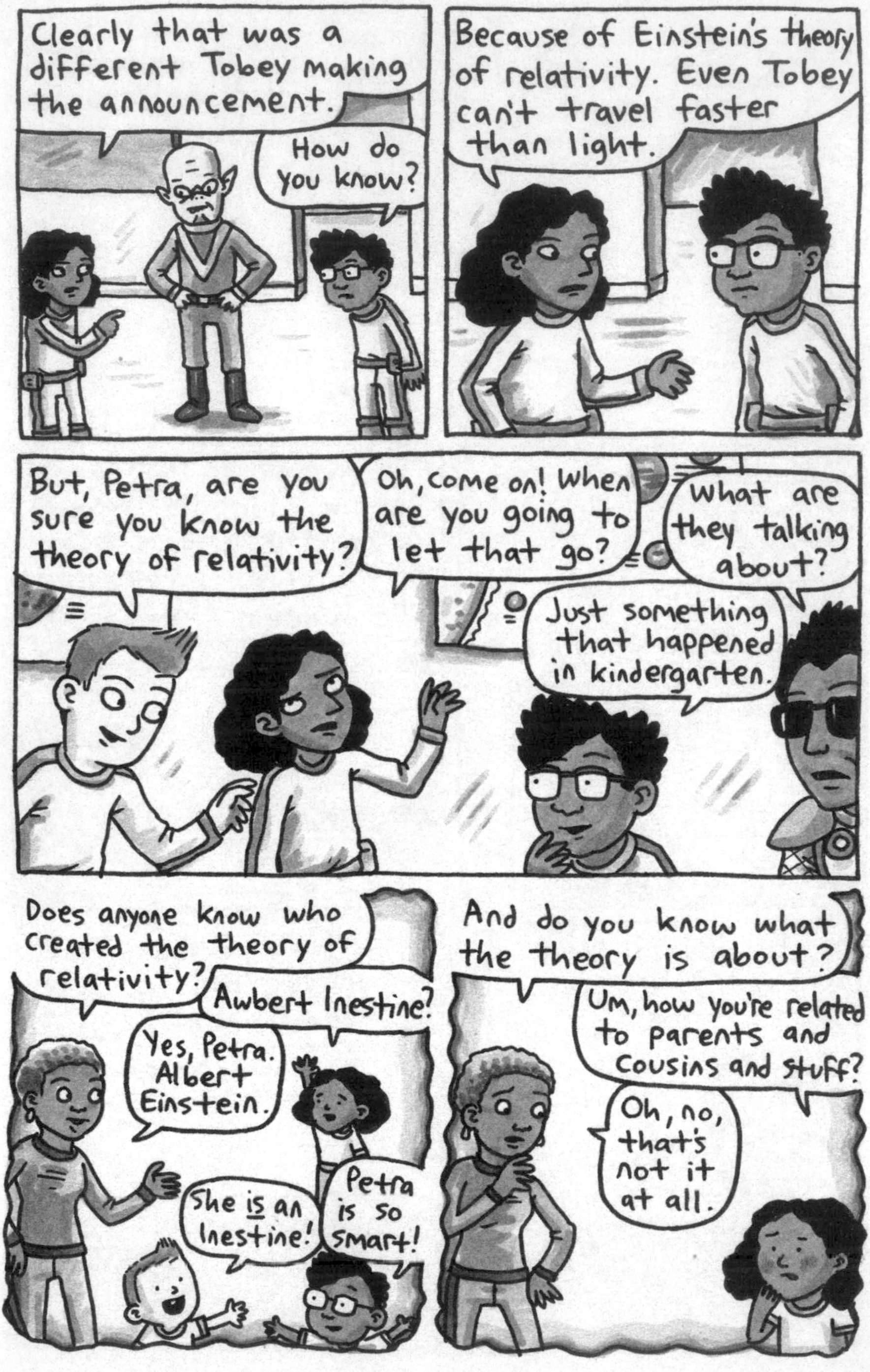
Clearly that was a different Tobey making the announcement.
How do you know?
Because of Einstein's theory of relativity. Even Tobey can't travel faster than light.
But, Petra, are you sure you know the theory of relativity?
Oh, come on! When are you going to let that go?
What are they talking about?
Just something that happened in kindergarten.
Does anyone know who created the theory of relativity?
Awbert Inestine?
Yes, Petra. Albert Einstein.
She is an Inestine!
Petra is so smart!
And do you know what the theory is about?
Um, how you're related to parents and cousins and stuff?
Oh, no, that's not it at all.

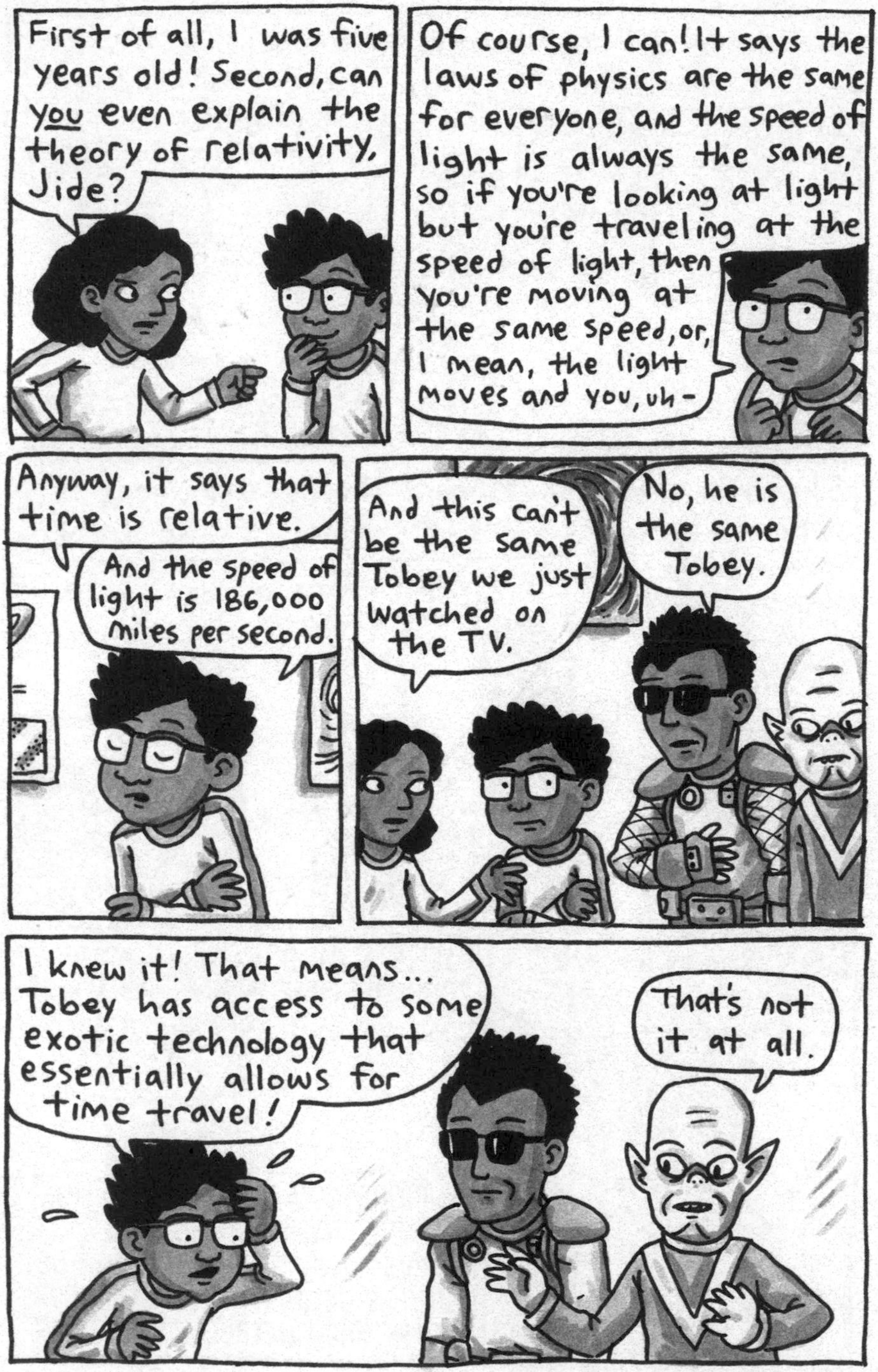
First of all, I was five years old! Second, can you even explain the theory of relativity, Jide?
Of course, I can! It says the laws of physics are the same for everyone, and the speed of light is always the same, so if you're looking at light but you're traveling at the speed of light, then you're moving at the same speed, or, I mean, the light moves and you, uh-
Anyway, it says that time is relative.
And the speed of light is 186,000 miles per second.
And this can't be the same Tobey we just watched on the TV.
No, he is the same Tobey.
I knew it! That means... Tobey has access to some exotic technology that essentially allows for time travel!
That's not it at all.

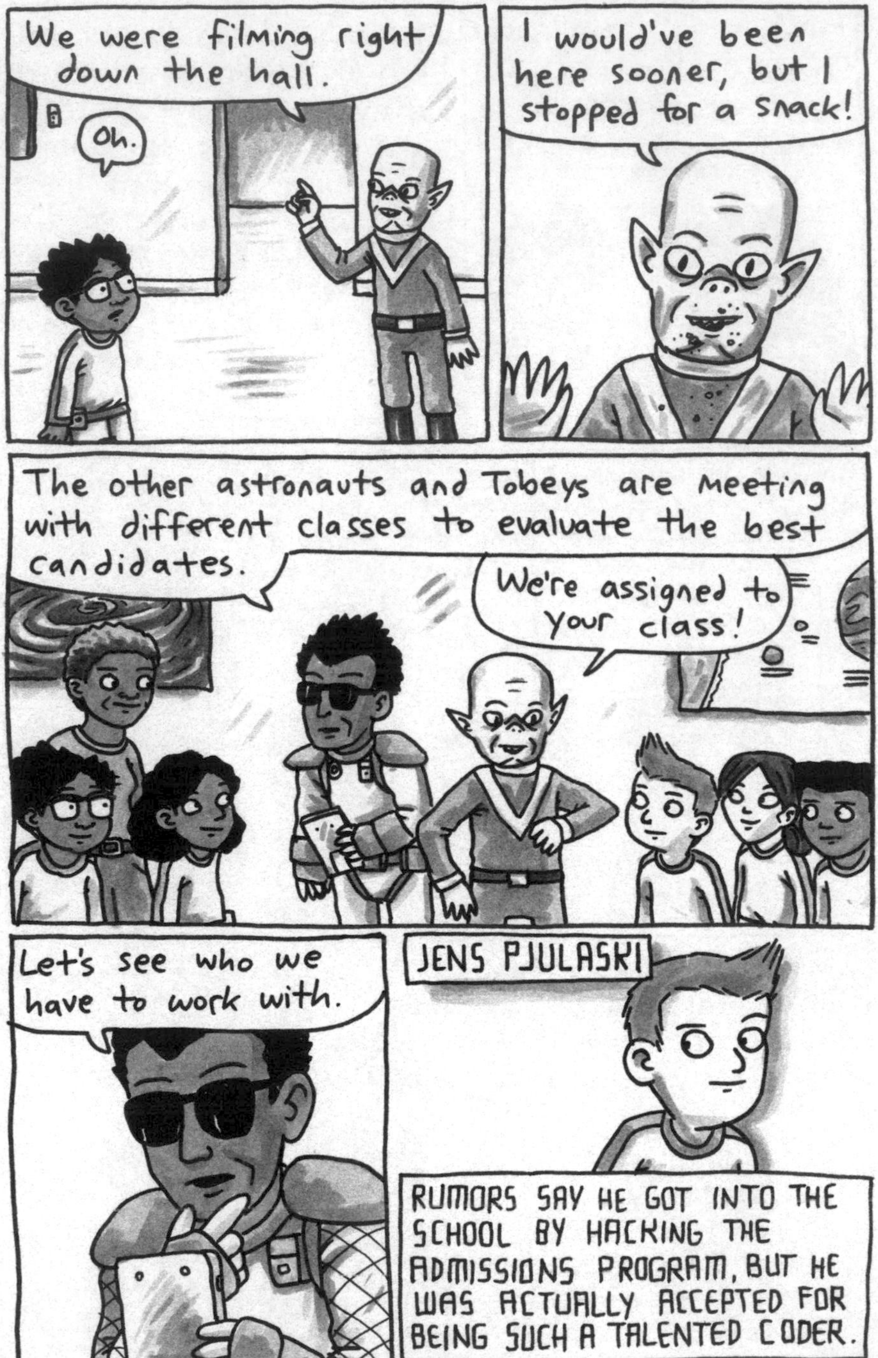
We were filming right down the hall.
Oh.
I would've been here sooner, but I stopped for a snack!
The other astronauts and Tobeys are meeting with different classes to evaluate the best candidates.
We're assigned to your class!
Let's see who we have to work with.
JENS PJULASKI
RUMORS SAY HE GOT INTO THE SCHOOL BY HACKING THE ADMISSIONS PROGRAM, BUT HE WAS ACTUALLY ACCEPTED FOR BEING SUCH A TALENTED CODER.

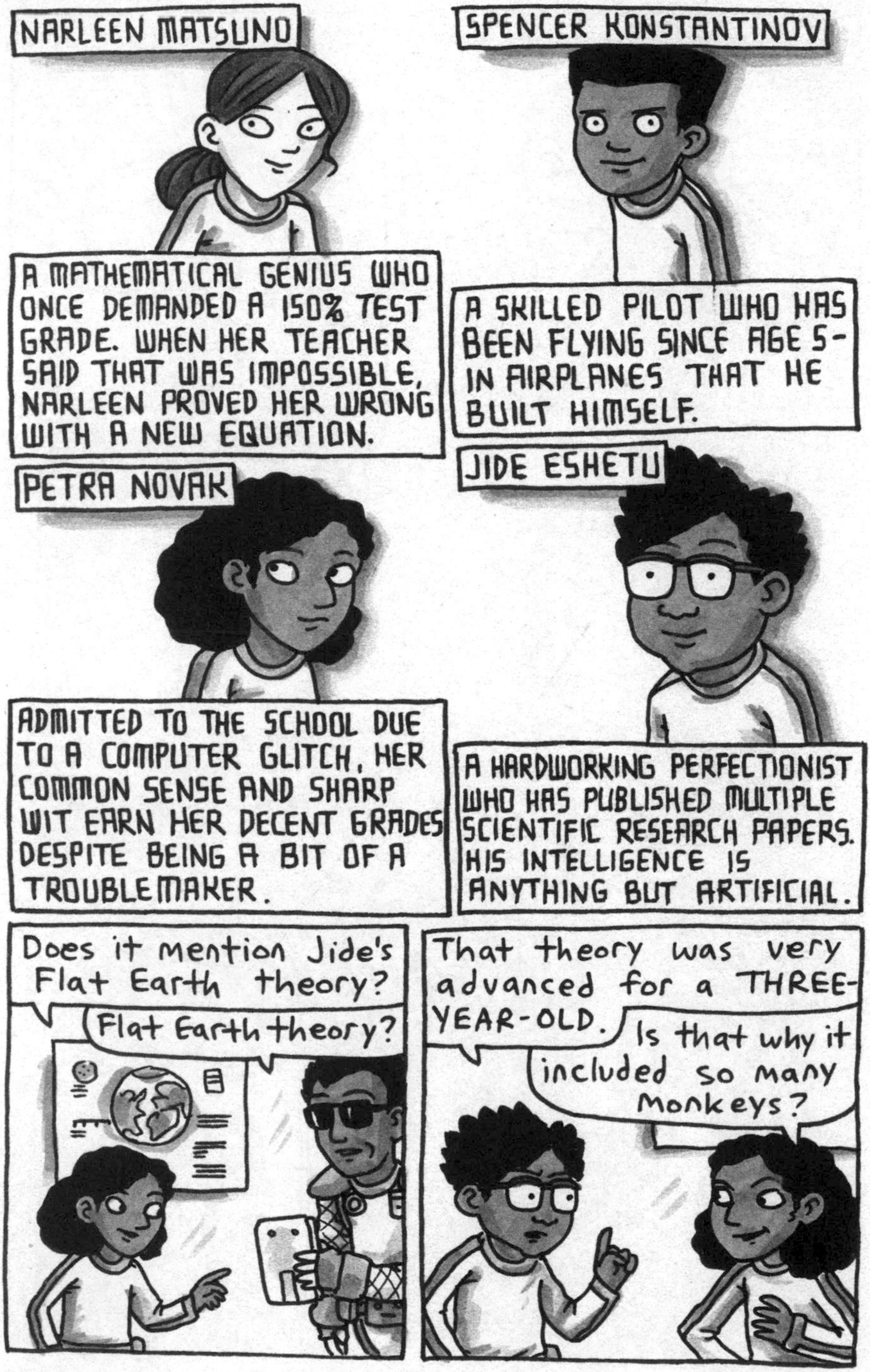

NARLEEN MATSUNO
A MATHEMATICAL GENIUS WHO ONCE DEMANDED A 150% TEST GRADE. WHEN HER TEACHER SAID THAT WAS IMPOSSIBLE, NARLEEN PROVED HER WRONG WITH A NEW EQUATION.
SPENCER KONSTANTINOV
A SKILLED PILOT WHO HAS BEEN FLYING SINCE AGE 5- IN AIRPLANES THAT HE BUILT HIMSELF.
PETRA NOVAK
ADMITTED TO THE SCHOOL DUE TO A COMPUTER GLITCH, HER COMMON SENSE AND SHARP WIT EARN HER DECENT GRADES DESPITE BEING A BIT OF A TROUBLEMAKER.
JIDE ESHETU
A HARDWORKING PERFECTIONIST WHO HAS PUBLISHED MULTIPLE SCIENTIFIC RESEARCH PAPERS. HIS INTELLIGENCE IS ANYTHING BUT ARTIFICIAL.
Does it mention Jide's Flat Earth theory?
Flat Earth theory?
That theory was very advanced for a THREE-YEAR-OLD.
Is that why it included so many Monkeys?

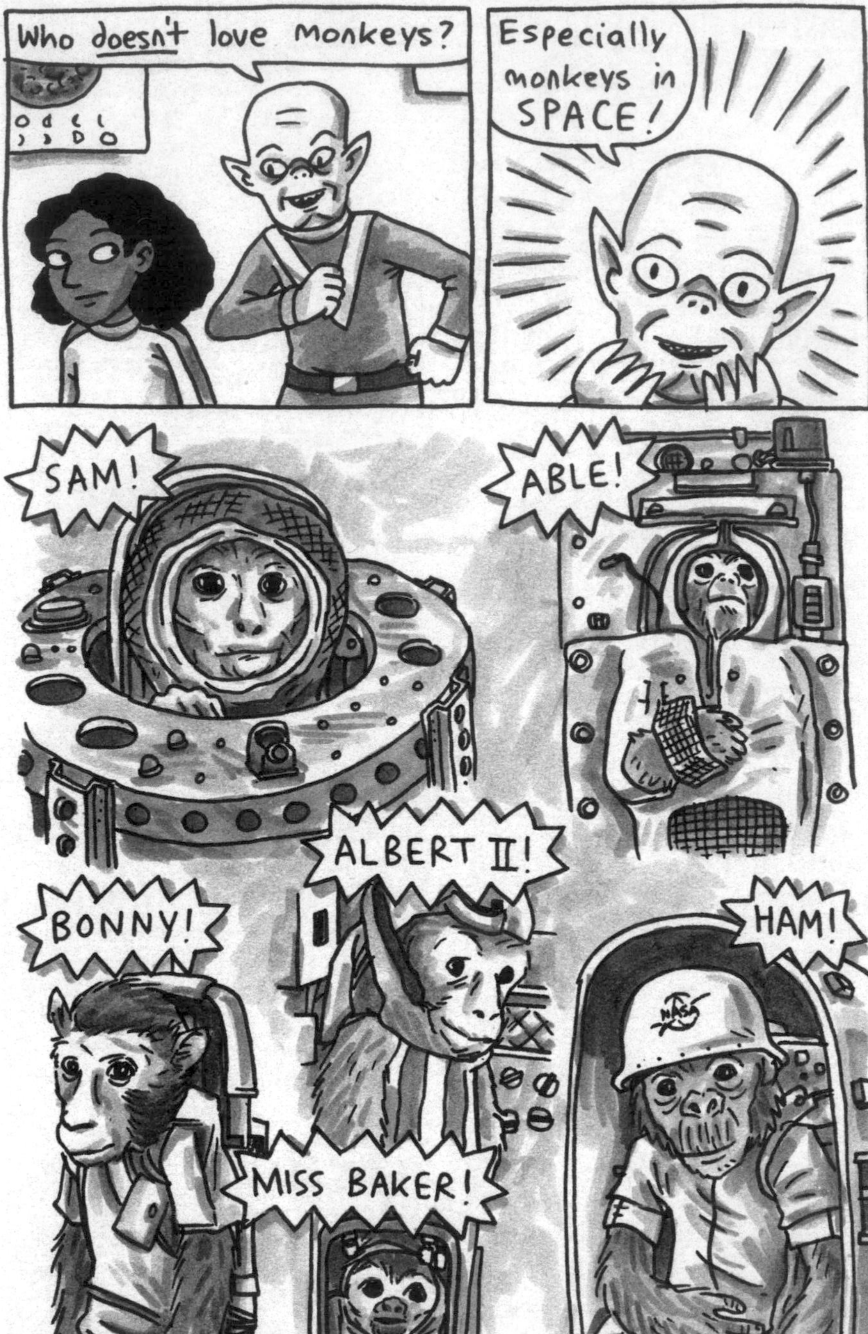
Who doesn't love monkeys?
Especially monkeys in SPACE!
SAM!
ABLE!
ALBERT II!
BONNY!
HAM!
MISS BAKER!

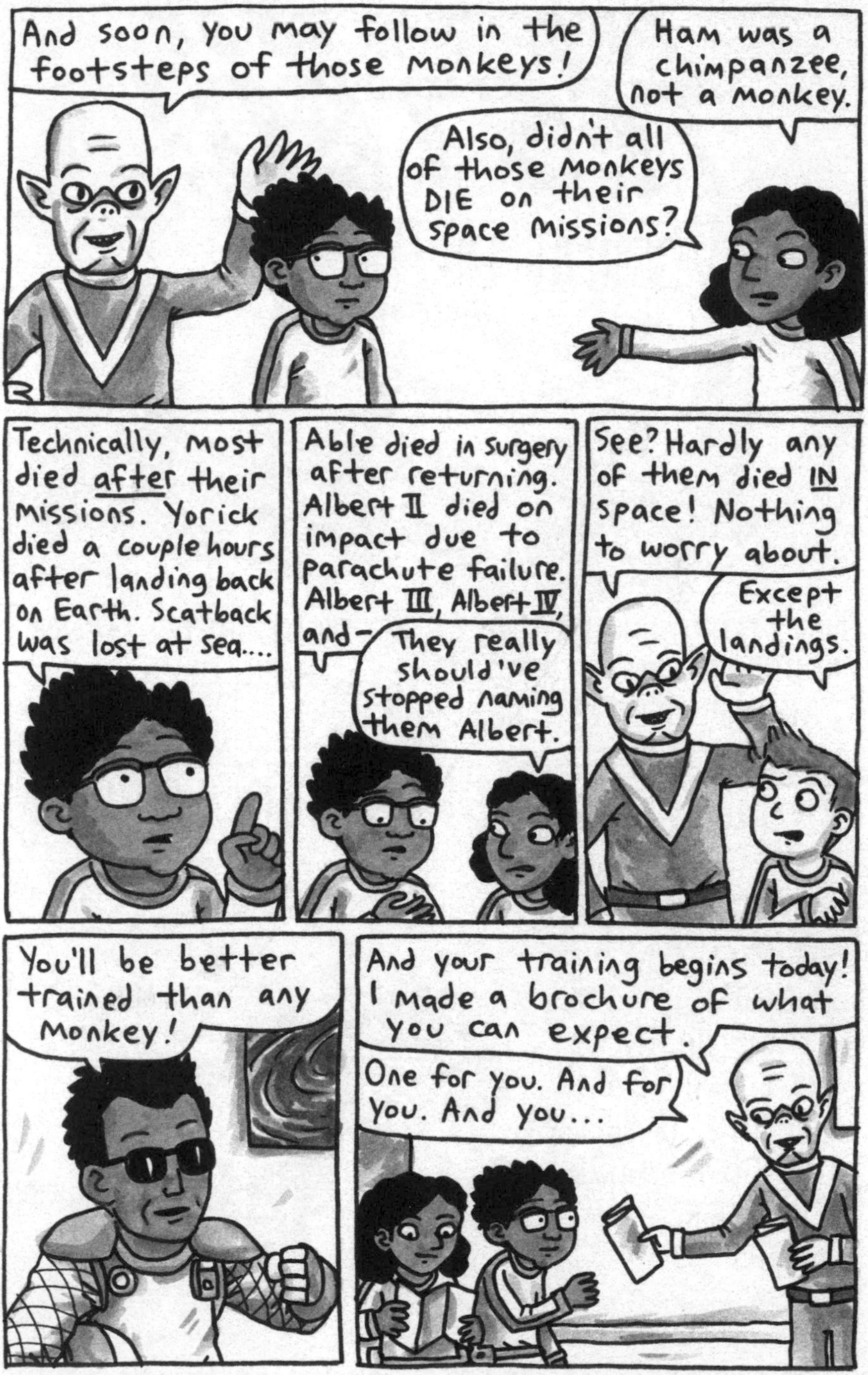
And soon, you may follow in the footsteps of those monkeys!
Ham was a chimpanzee, not a monkey.
Also, didn't all of those monkeys DIE on their space missions?
Technically, most died after their missions. Yorick died a couple hours after landing back on Earth. Scatback was lost at sea....
Able died in surgery after returning. Albert II died on impact due to parachute failure. Albert III, Albert IV, and–
They really should've stopped naming them Albert.
See? Hardly any of them died IN space! Nothing to worry about.
Except the landings.
You'll be better trained than any monkey!
And your training begins today! I made a brochure of what you can expect.
One for you. And for you. And you...

PREPARE TO BE TESTED!

THE VOMINATOR!

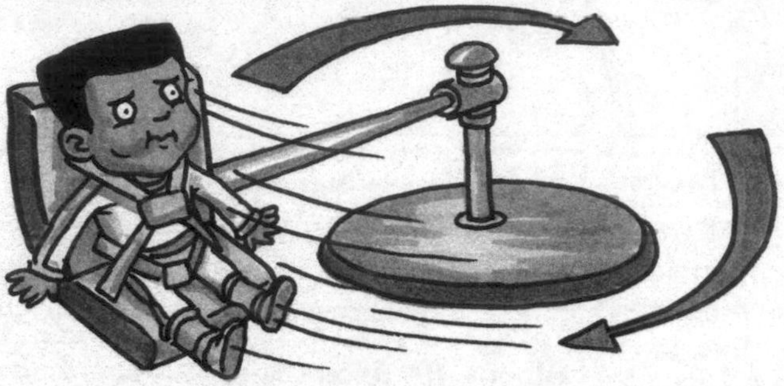

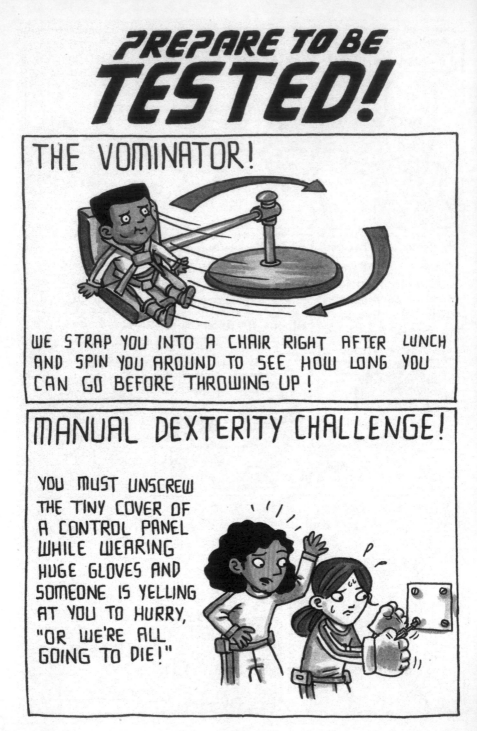

WE STRAP YOU INTO A CHAIR RIGHT AFTER LUNCH AND SPIN YOU AROUND TO SEE HOW LONG YOU CAN GO BEFORE THROWING UP!

MANUAL DEXTERITY CHALLENGE!

YOU MUST UNSCREW THE TINY COVER OF A CONTROL PANEL WHILE WEARING HUGE GLOVES AND SOMEONE IS YELLING AT YOU TO HURRY, "OR WE'RE ALL GOING TO DIE!"

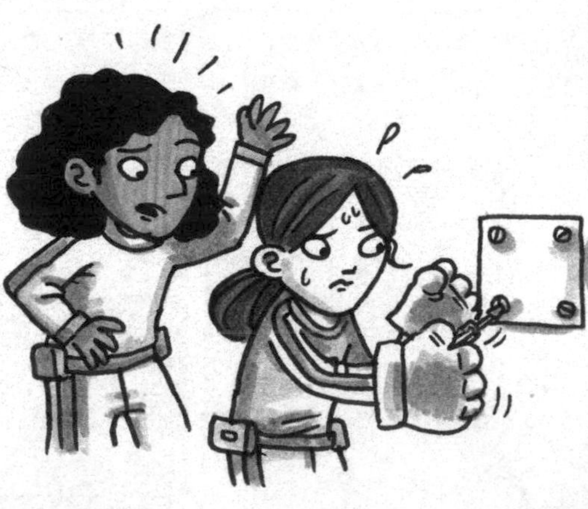

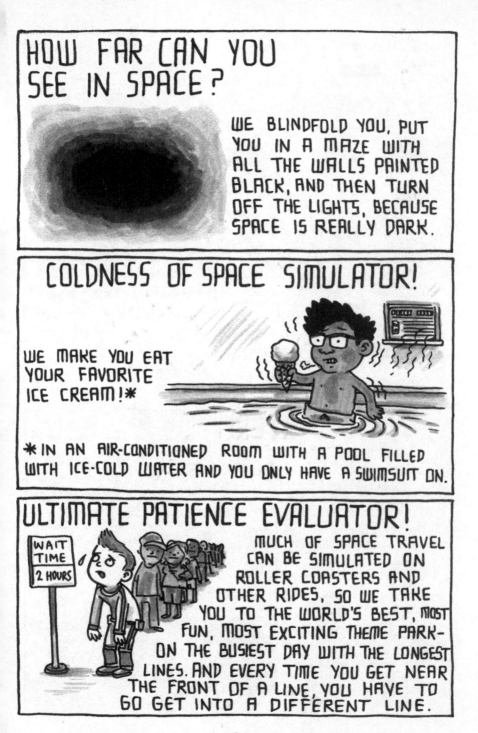

HOW FAR CAN YOU SEE IN SPACE?

WE BLINDFOLD YOU, PUT YOU IN A MAZE WITH ALL THE WALLS PAINTED BLACK, AND THEN TURN OFF THE LIGHTS, BECAUSE SPACE IS REALLY DARK.

COLDNESS OF SPACE SIMULATOR!

WE MAKE YOU EAT YOUR FAVORITE ICE CREAM!*

*IN AN AIR-CONDITIONED ROOM WITH A POOL FILLED WITH ICE-COLD WATER AND YOU ONLY HAVE A SWIMSUIT ON.

ULTIMATE PATIENCE EVALUATOR!

WAIT TIME 2 HOURS

MUCH OF SPACE TRAVEL CAN BE SIMULATED ON ROLLER COASTERS AND OTHER RIDES, SO WE TAKE YOU TO THE WORLD'S BEST, MOST FUN, MOST EXCITING THEME PARK—ON THE BUSIEST DAY WITH THE LONGEST LINES. AND EVERY TIME YOU GET NEAR THE FRONT OF A LINE, YOU HAVE TO GO GET INTO A DIFFERENT LINE.

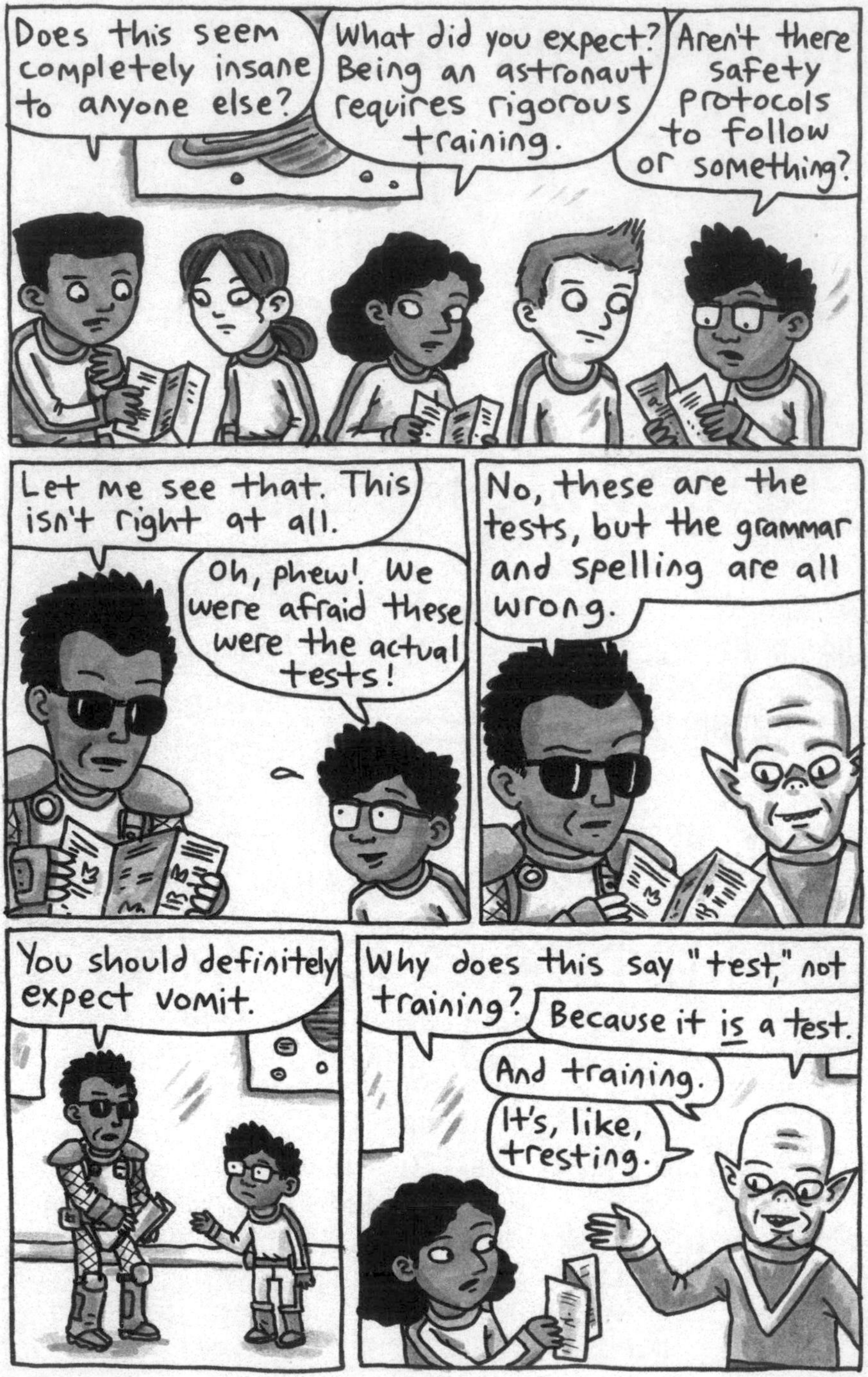
Does this seem completely insane to anyone else?
What did you expect? Being an astronaut requires rigorous training.
Aren't there safety protocols to follow or something?
Let me see that. This isn't right at all.
Oh, phew! We were afraid these were the actual tests!
No, these are the tests, but the grammar and spelling are all wrong.
You should definitely expect vomit.
Why does this say "test," not training?
Because it is a test.
And training.
It's, like, tresting.

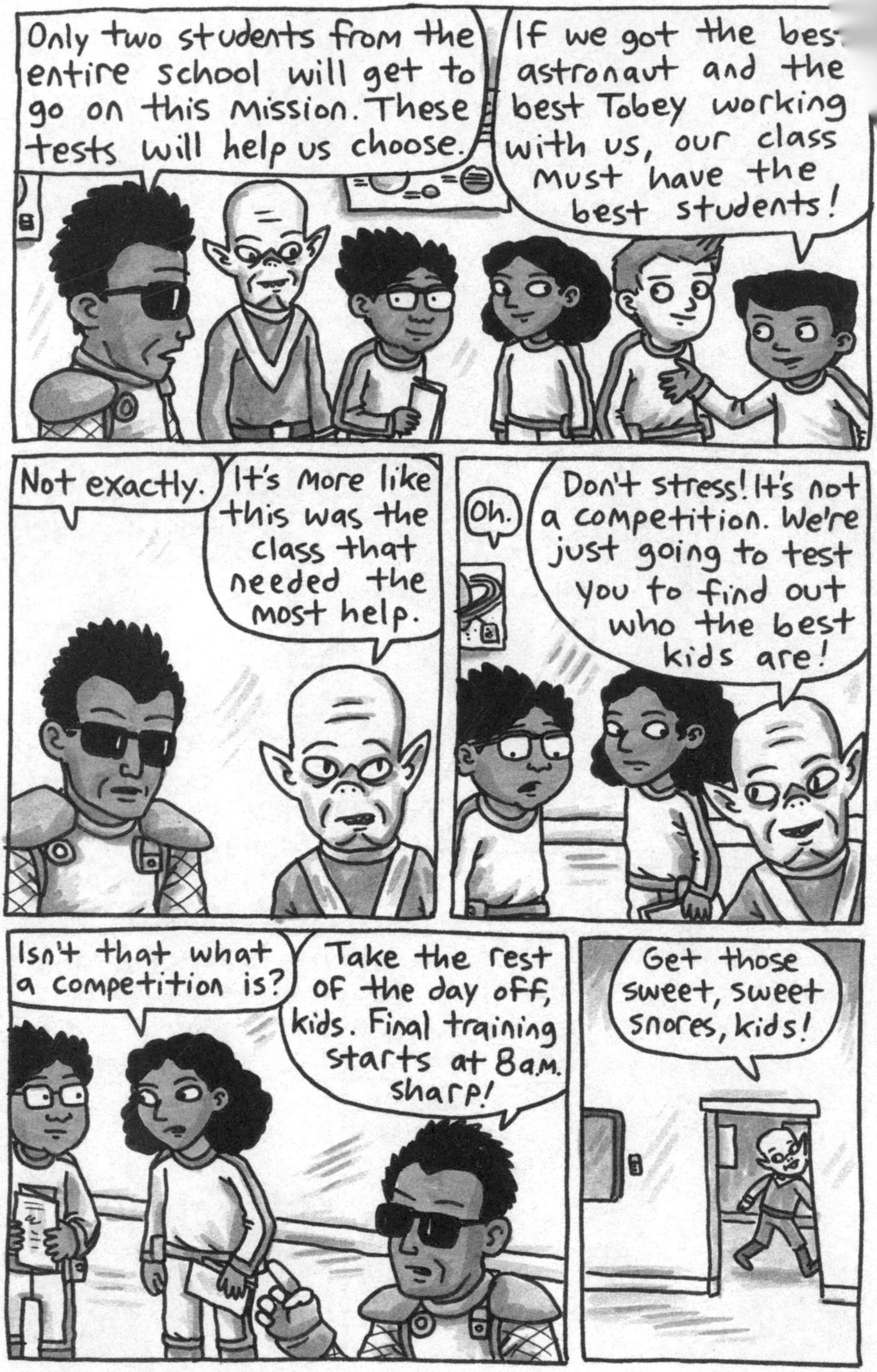
Only two students from the entire school will get to go on this mission. These tests will help us choose.
If we got the best astronaut and the best Tobey working with us, our class must have the best students!
Not exactly.
It's more like this was the class that needed the most help.
Oh.
Don't stress! It's not a competition. We're just going to test you to find out who the best kids are!
Isn't that what a competition is?
Take the rest of the day off, kids. Final training starts at 8 A.M. sharp!
Get those sweet, sweet snores, kids!

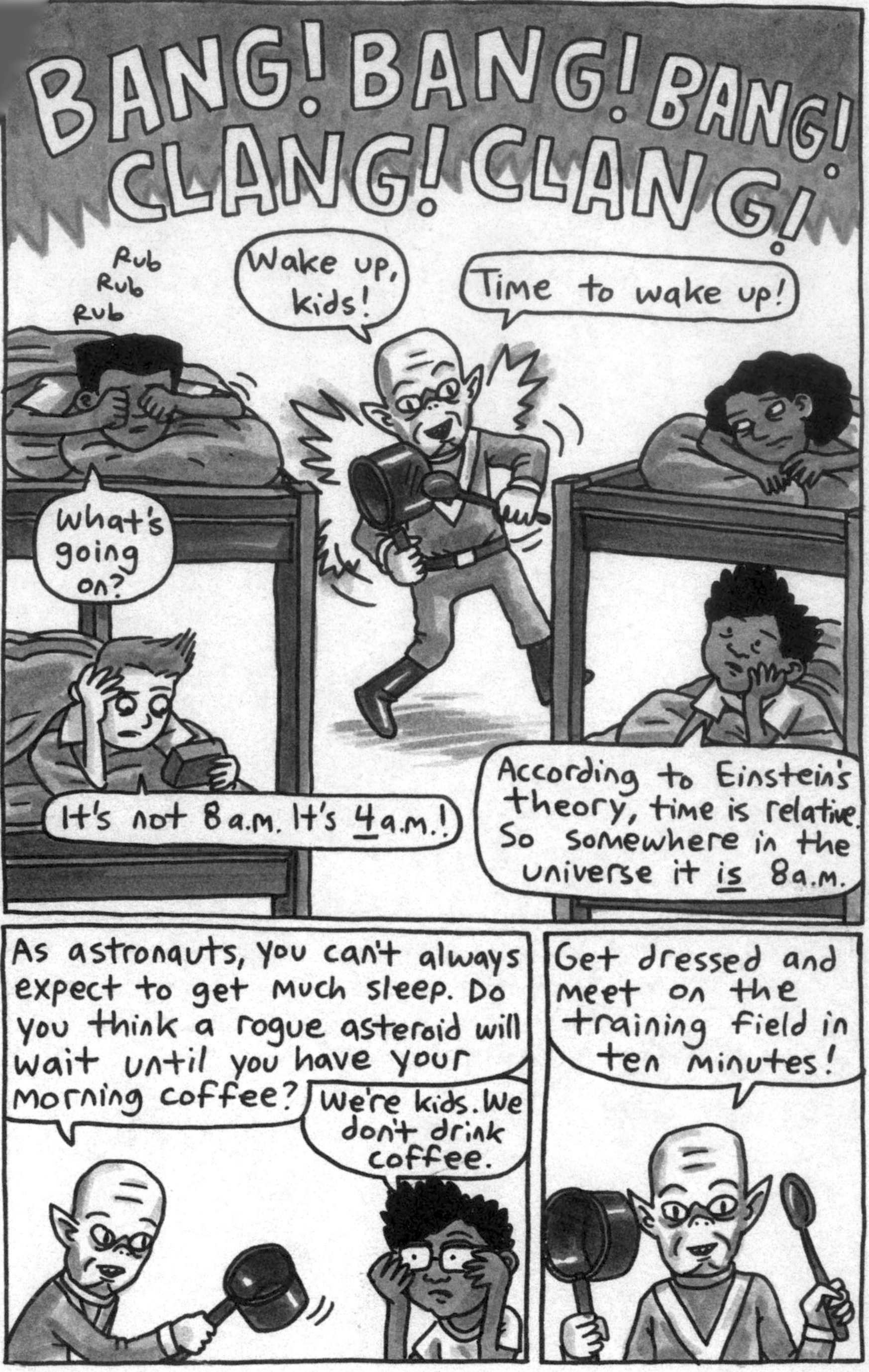
BANG! BANG! BANG!
CLANG! CLANG!
Rub Rub Rub
Wake up, kids!
Time to wake up!
What's going on?
It's not 8 a.m. It's 4 a.m.!
According to Einstein's theory, time is relative. So somewhere in the universe it is 8 a.m.
As astronauts, you can't always expect to get much sleep. Do you think a rogue asteroid will wait until you have your morning coffee?
We're kids. We don't drink coffee.
Get dressed and meet on the training field in ten minutes!

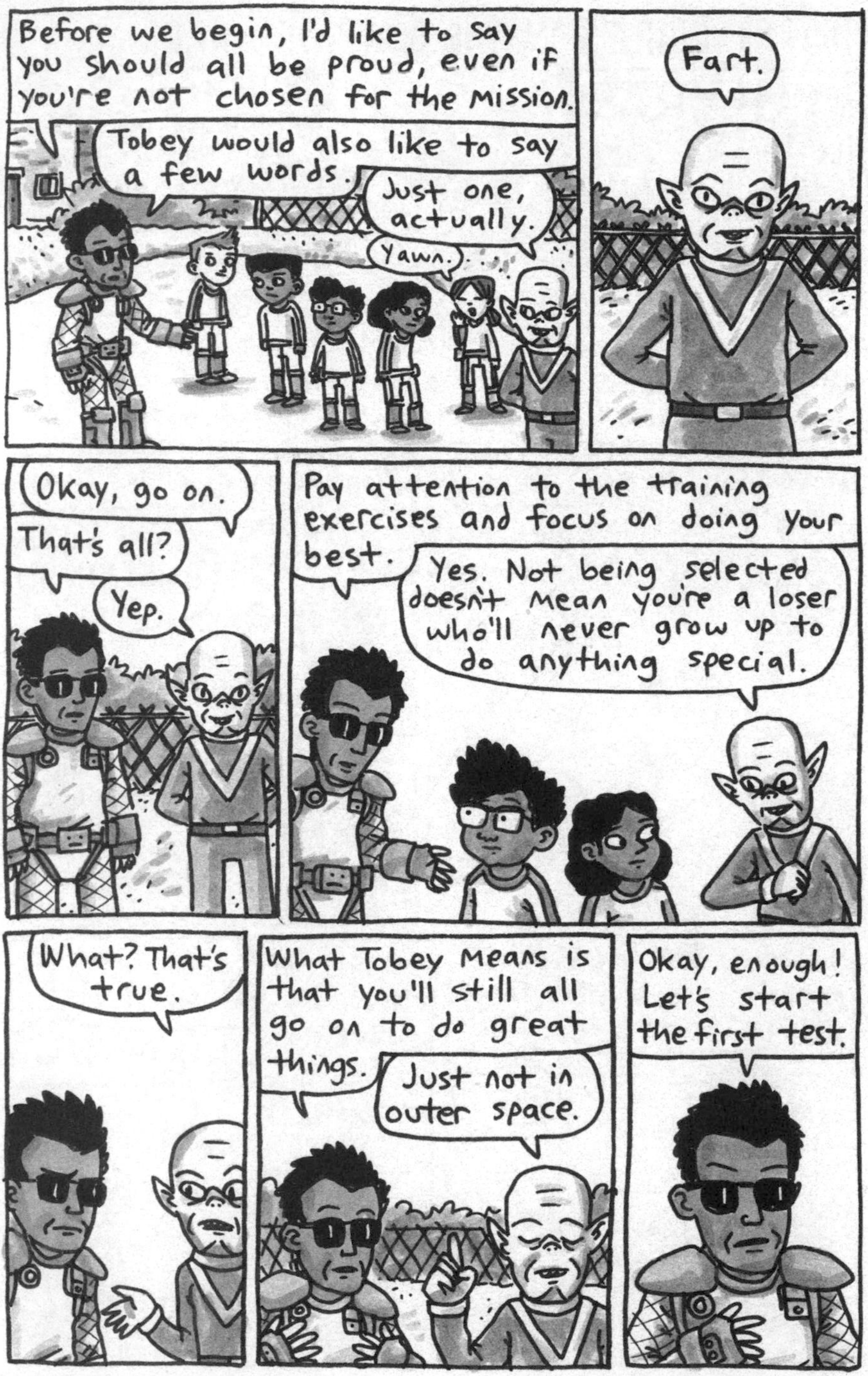
Before we begin, I'd like to say you should all be proud, even if you're not chosen for the mission.
Tobey would also like to say a few words.
Just one, actually.
Yawn.
Fart.
Okay, go on.
That's all?
Yep.
Pay attention to the training exercises and focus on doing your best.
Yes. Not being selected doesn't mean you're a loser who'll never grow up to do anything special.
What? That's true.
What Tobey means is that you'll still all go on to do great things.
Just not in outer space.
Okay, enough! Let's start the first test.

TEST #1: WHAT'S IN THE BOX? YOU ARE!

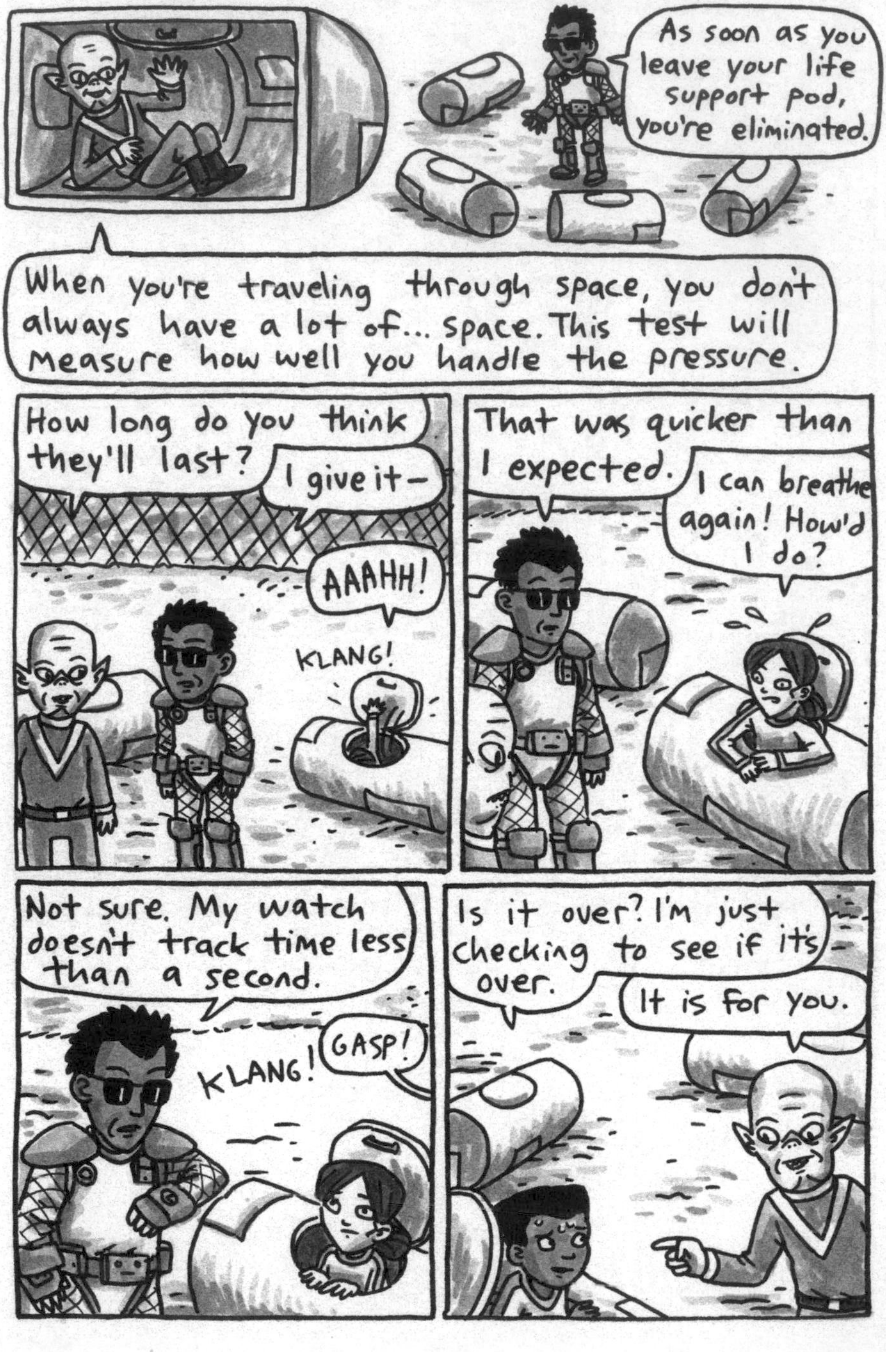

As soon as you leave your life support pod, you're eliminated.
When you're traveling through space, you don't always have a lot of... space. This test will measure how well you handle the pressure.
How long do you think they'll last?
I give it—
AAAHH!
KLANG!
That was quicker than I expected.
I can breathe again! How'd I do?
Not sure. My watch doesn't track time less than a second.
KLANG!
GASP!
Is it over? I'm just checking to see if it's over.
It is for you.

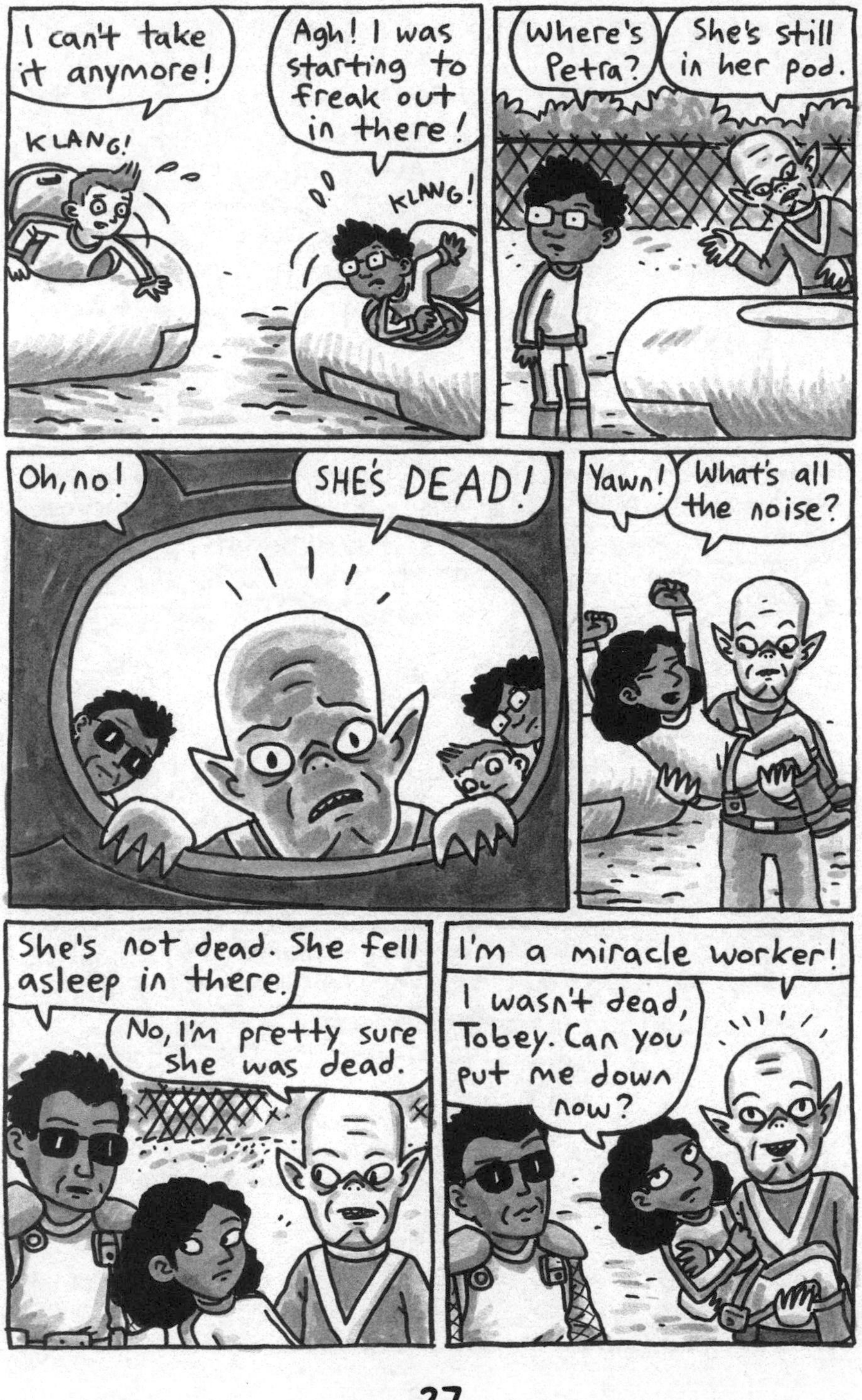
I can't take it anymore!
KLANG!
Agh! I was starting to freak out in there!
KLANG!
Where's Petra?
She's still in her pod.
Oh, no!
SHE'S DEAD!
Yawn!
What's all the noise?
She's not dead. She fell asleep in there.
No, I'm pretty sure she was dead.
I'm a miracle worker!
I wasn't dead, Tobey. Can you put me down now?

TEST #2: EQUIPMENT CHECK

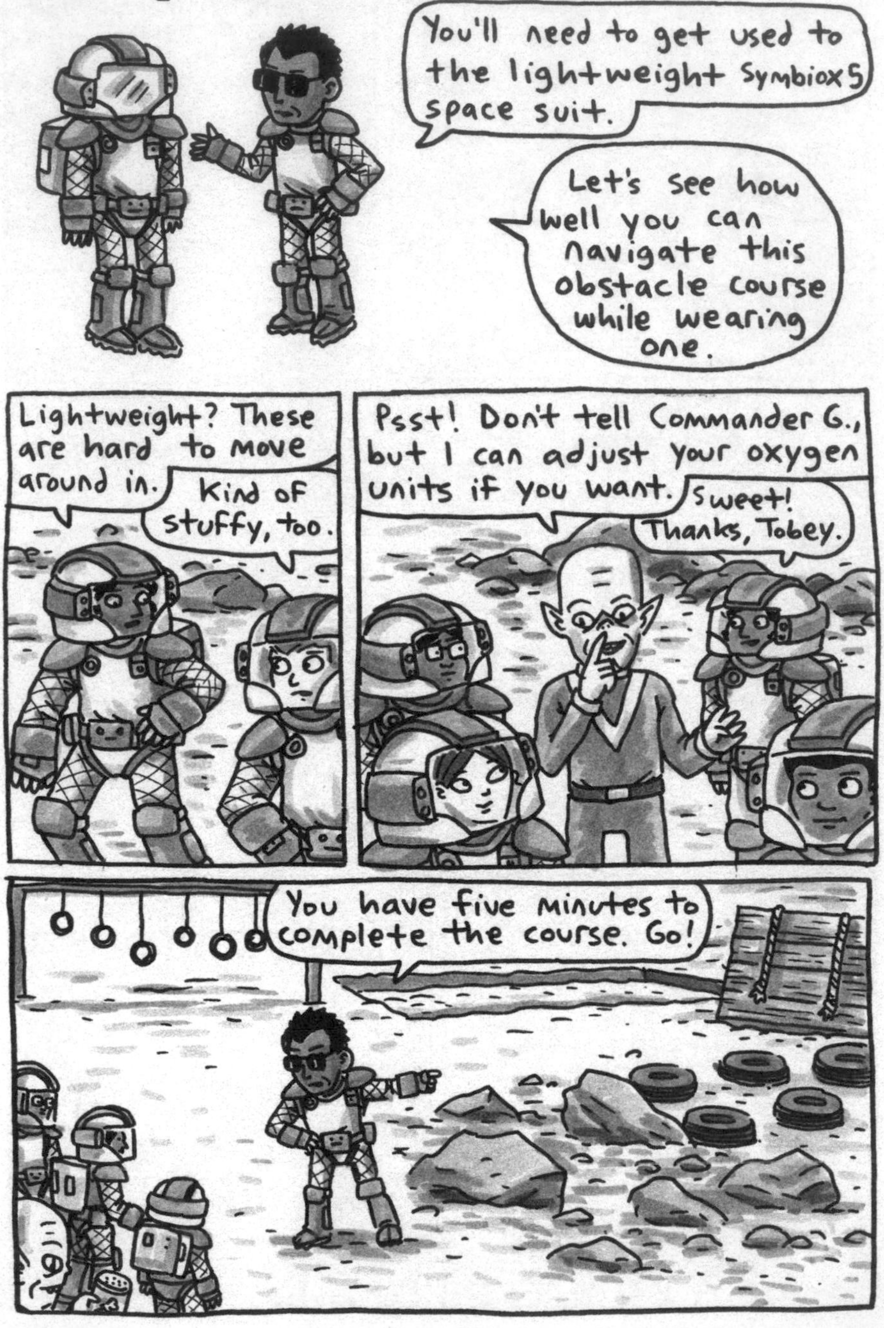

You'll need to get used to the lightweight Symbiox 5 space suit.
Let's see how well you can navigate this obstacle course while wearing one.
Lightweight? These are hard to move around in.
Kind of stuffy, too.
Psst! Don't tell Commander G., but I can adjust your oxygen units if you want.
Sweet! Thanks, Tobey.
You have five minutes to complete the course. Go!

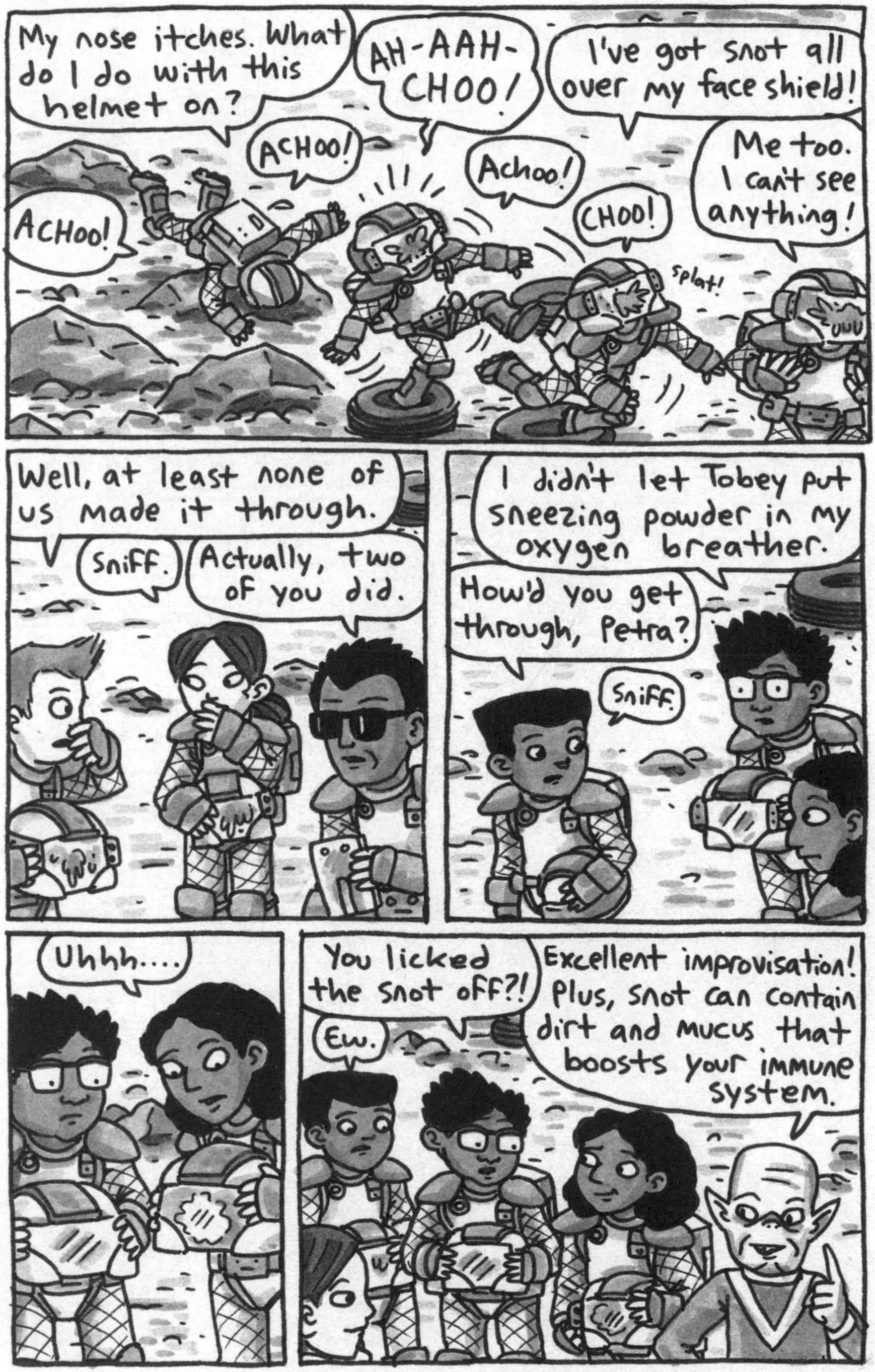
My nose itches. What do I do with this helmet on?
AH-AAH-CHOO!
I've got snot all over my face shield!
ACHOO!
Achoo!
Me too. I can't see anything!
ACHOO!
CHOO!
splat!
Well, at least none of us made it through.
Sniff.
Actually, two of you did.
I didn't let Tobey put sneezing powder in my oxygen breather.
How'd you get through, Petra?
Sniff.
Uhhh....
You licked the snot off?!
Ew.
Excellent improvisation! Plus, snot can contain dirt and mucus that boosts your immune system.

TEST #3: UNDER WHERE? UNDER WATER!

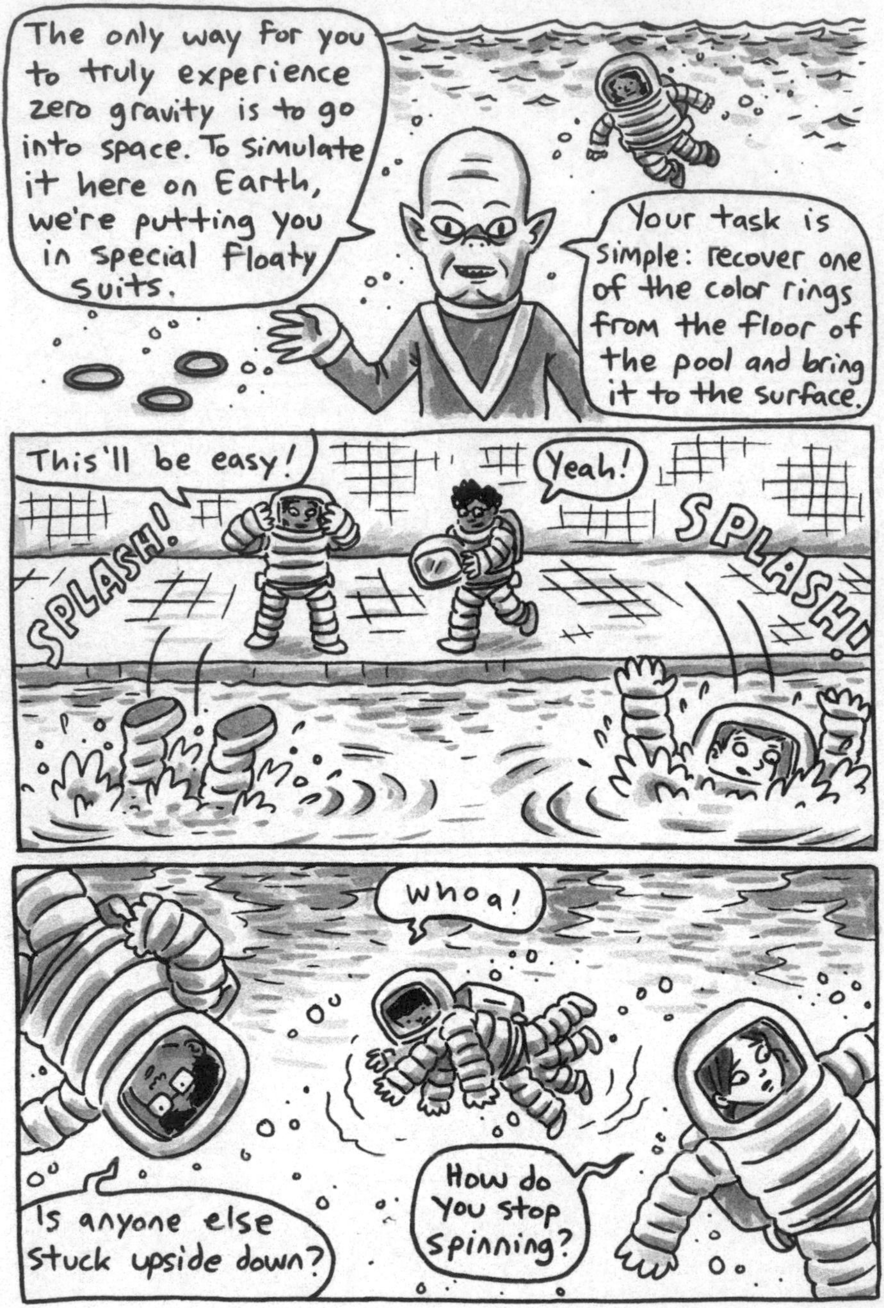

The only way for you to truly experience zero gravity is to go into space. To simulate it here on Earth, we're putting you in special floaty suits.
Your task is simple: recover one of the color rings from the floor of the pool and bring it to the surface.
This'll be easy!
Yeah!
SPLASH!
SPLASH!
Whoa!
Is anyone else stuck upside down?
How do you stop spinning?

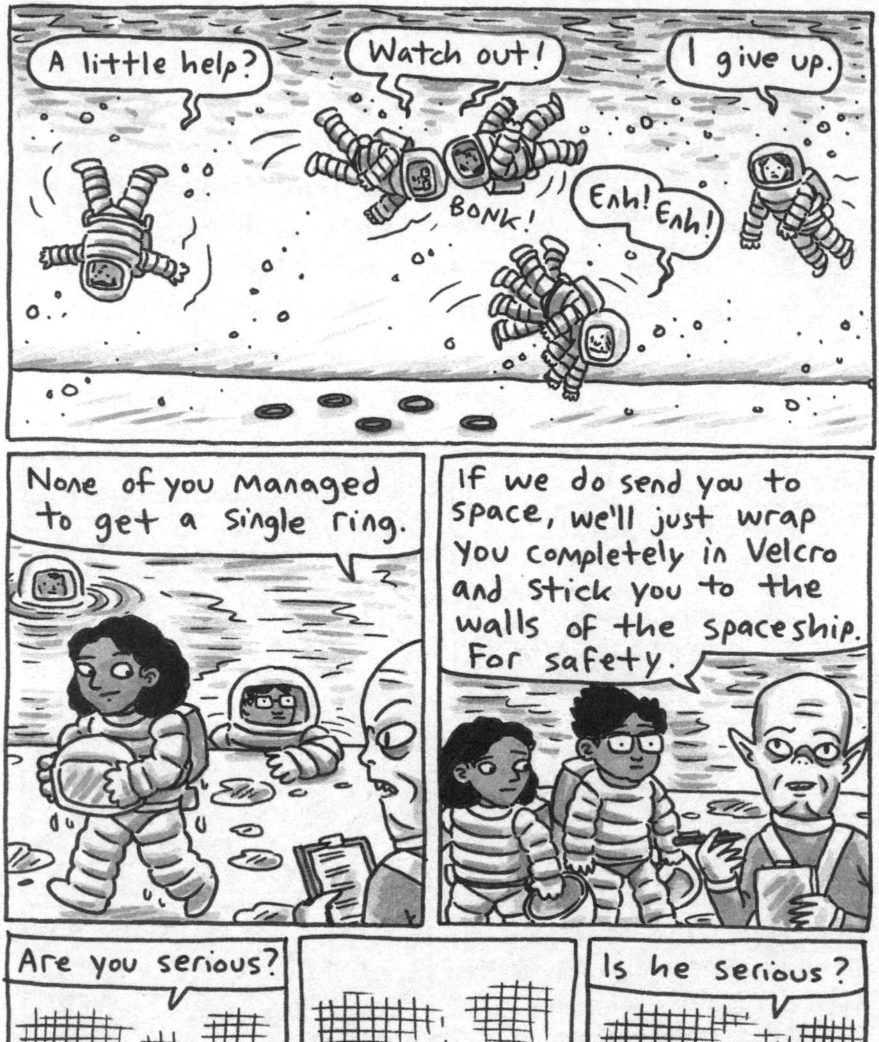
A little help?
Watch out!
I give up.
BONK!
Enh! Enh!
None of you managed to get a single ring.
If we do send you to space, we'll just wrap you completely in Velcro and stick you to the walls of the spaceship. For safety.
Are you serious?
Is he serious?

TEST #4: TEAMWORK!

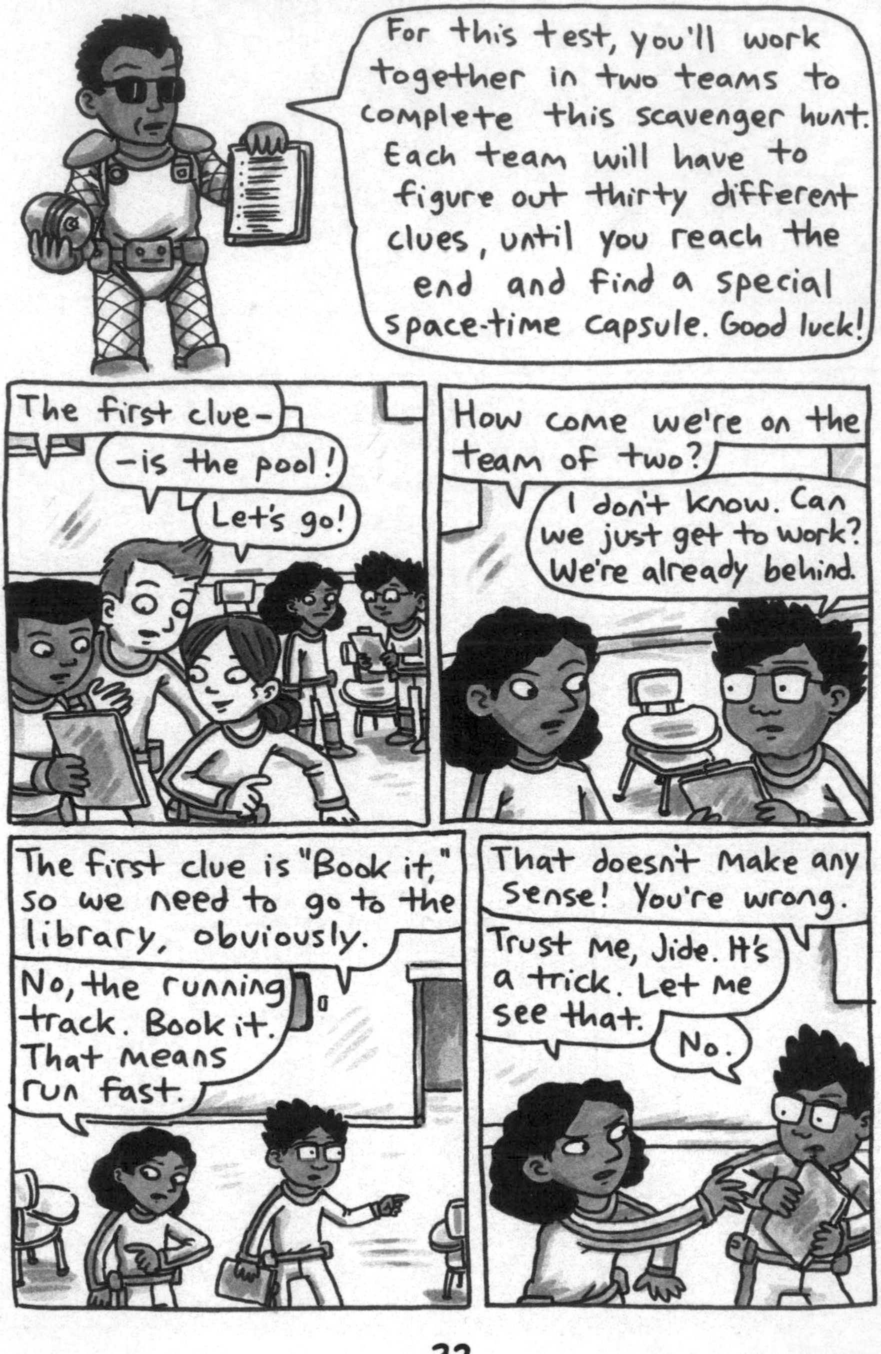
For this test, you'll work together in two teams to complete this scavenger hunt. Each team will have to figure out thirty different clues, until you reach the end and find a special space-time capsule. Good luck!
The first clue-
-is the pool!
Let's go!
How come we're on the team of two?
I don't know. Can we just get to work? We're already behind.
The first clue is "Book it," so we need to go to the library, obviously.
No, the running track. Book it. That means run fast.
That doesn't make any sense! You're wrong.
Trust me, Jide. It's a trick. Let me see that.
No.

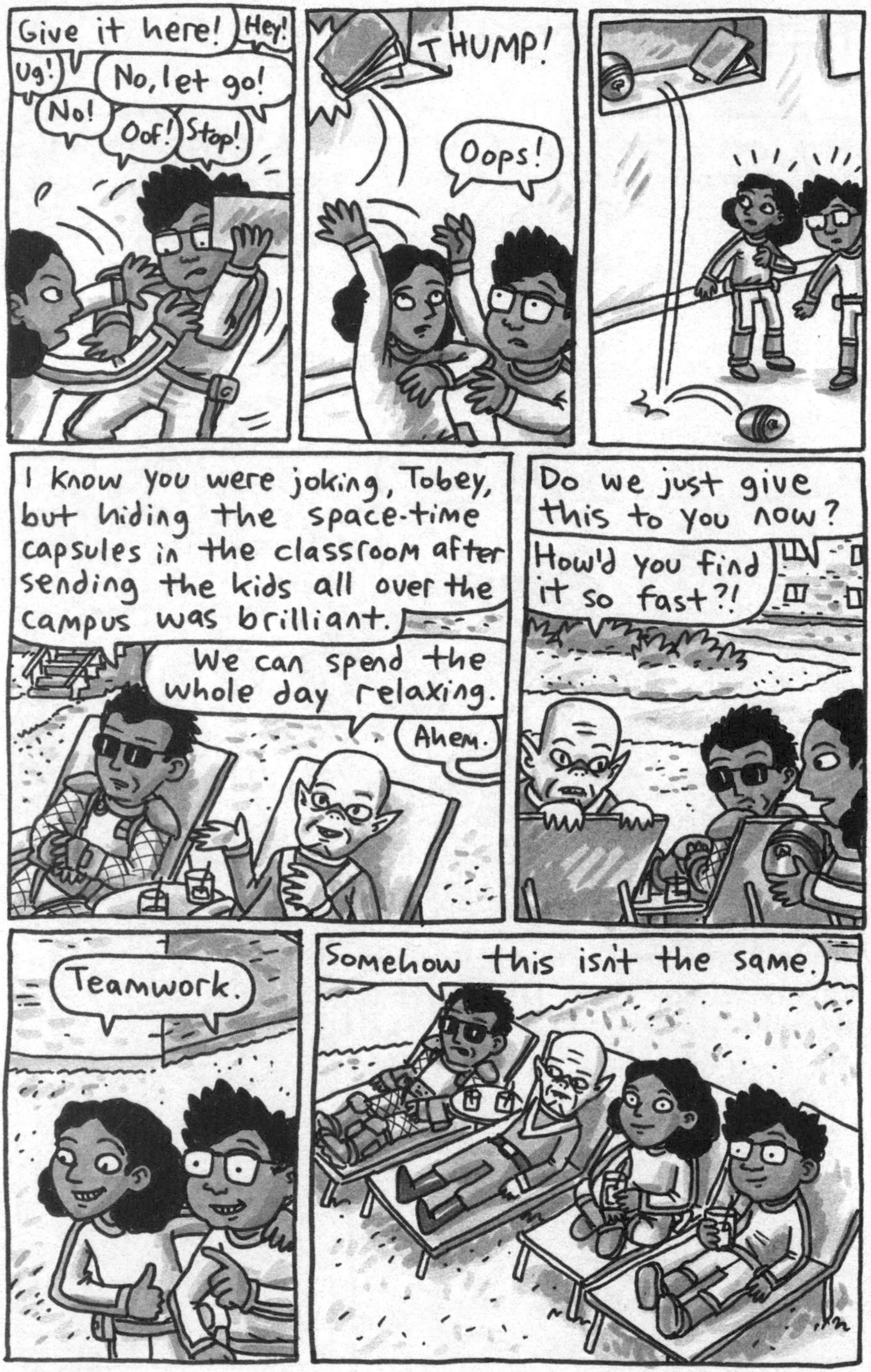
Give it here!
Hey!
Ug!
No, let go!
No!
Oof!
Stop!
THUMP!
Oops!
I know you were joking, Tobey, but hiding the space-time capsules in the classroom after sending the kids all over the campus was brilliant.
We can spend the whole day relaxing.
Ahem.
Do we just give this to you now?
How'd you find it so fast?!
Teamwork.
Somehow this isn't the same.

TEST #5: ASTROPHYSICS!

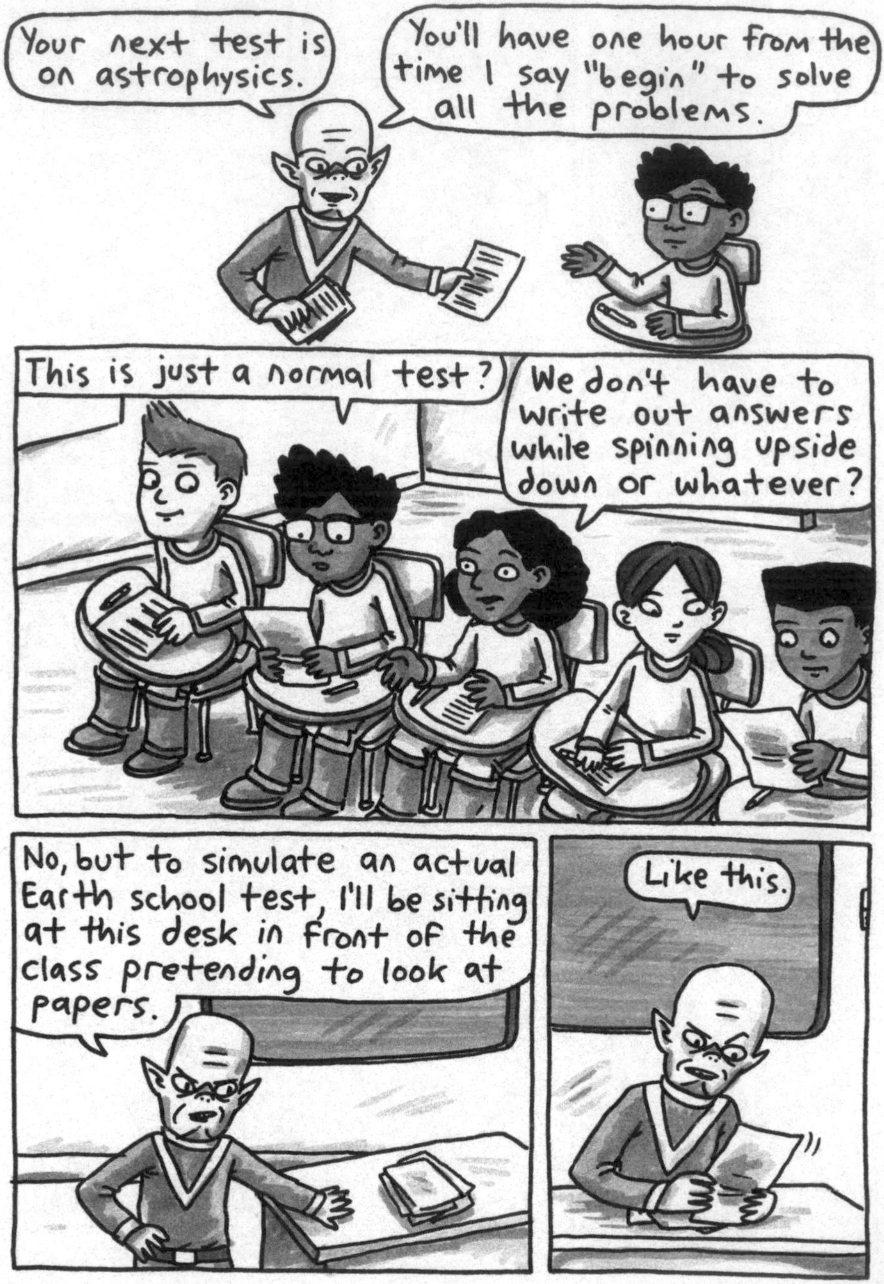
Your next test is on astrophysics.
You'll have one hour from the time I say "begin" to solve all the problems.
This is just a normal test?
We don't have to write out answers while spinning upside down or whatever?
No, but to simulate an actual Earth school test, I'll be sitting at this desk in front of the class pretending to look at papers.
Like this.

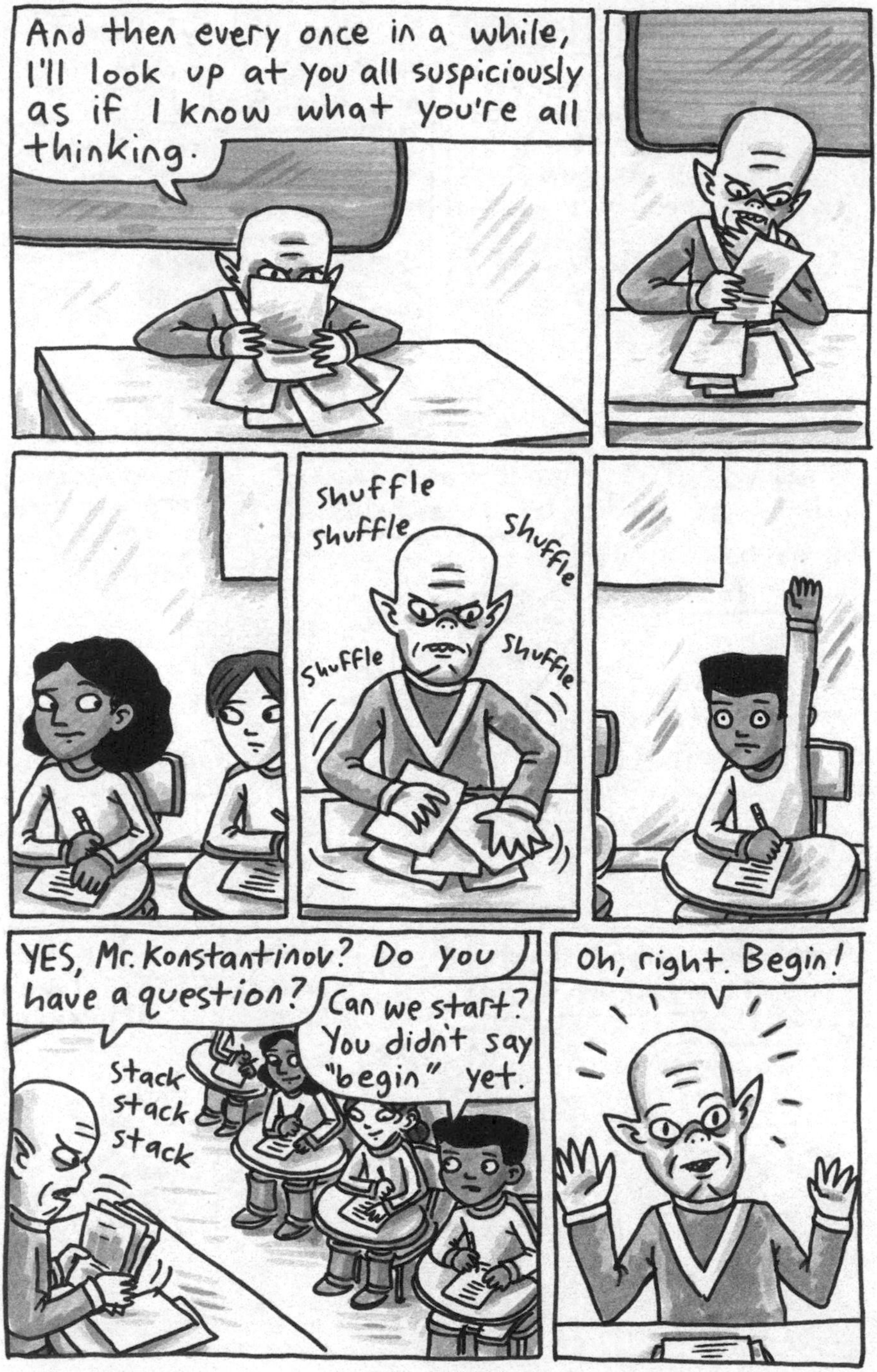
And then every once in a while, I'll look up at you all suspiciously as if I know what you're all thinking.
shuffle
shuffle
Shuffle
Shuffle
Shuffle
YES, Mr. Konstantinov? Do you have a question?
Can we start? You didn't say "begin" yet.
Stack
stack
stack
Oh, right. Begin!

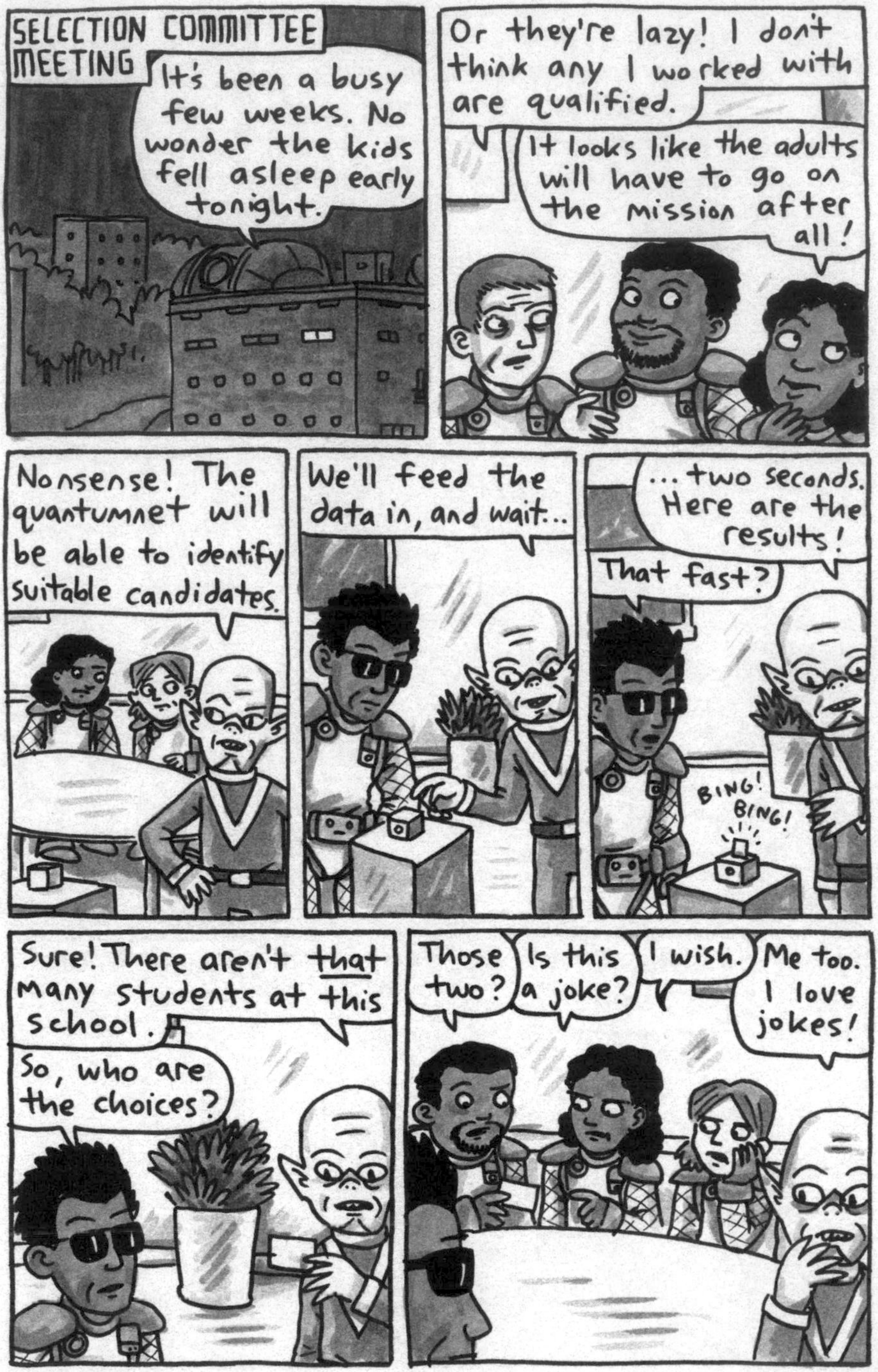
SELECTION COMMITTEE MEETING
It's been a busy few weeks. No wonder the kids fell asleep early tonight.
Or they're lazy! I don't think any I worked with are qualified.
It looks like the adults will have to go on the mission after all!
Nonsense! The quantumnet will be able to identify suitable candidates.
We'll feed the data in, and wait...
... two seconds. Here are the results!
That fast?
BING!
BING!
Sure! There aren't that many students at this school.
So, who are the choices?
Those two?
Is this a joke?
I wish.
Me too. I love jokes!

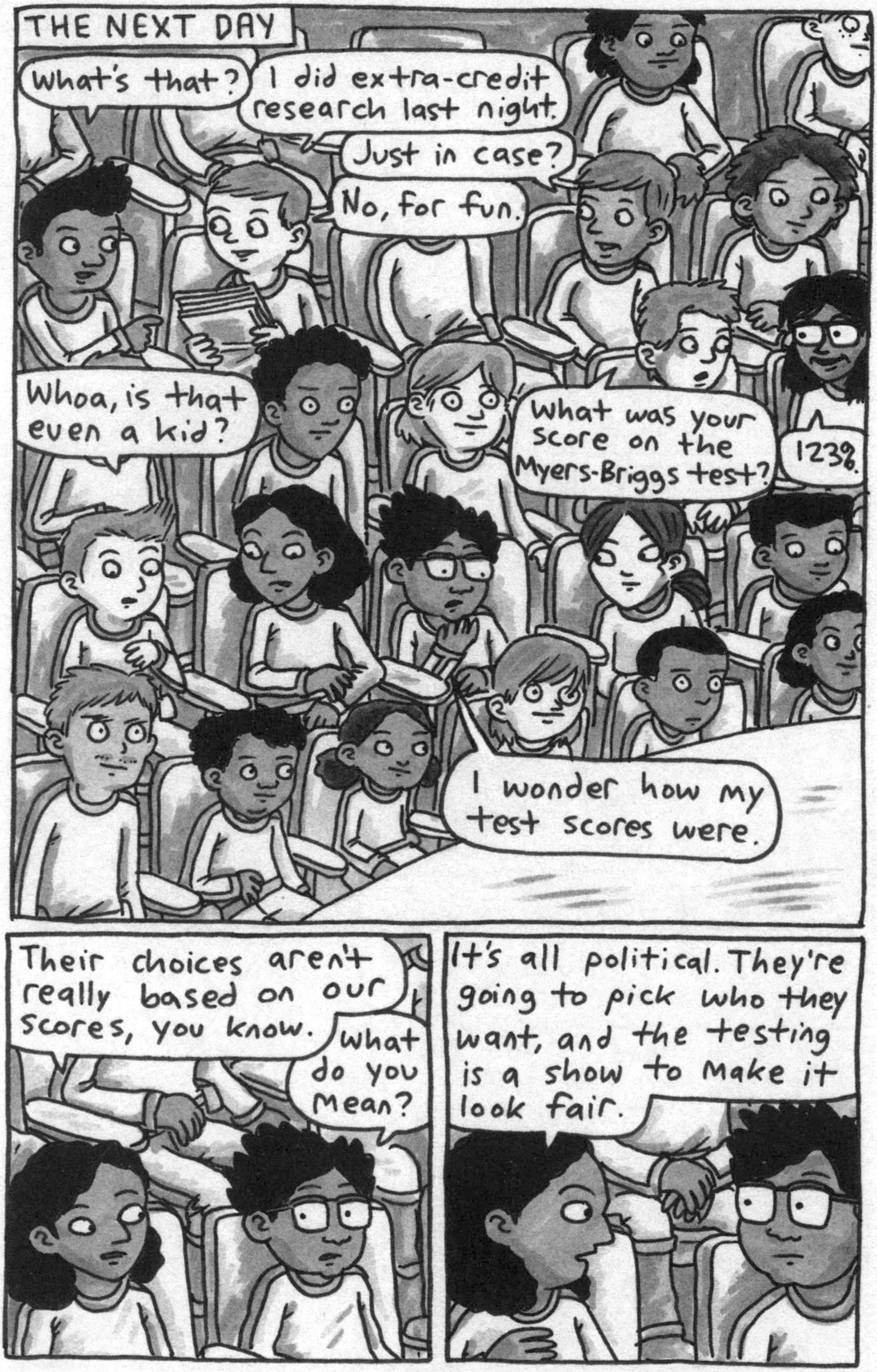
THE NEXT DAY
What's that?
I did extra-credit research last night.
Just in case?
No, for fun.
Whoa, is that even a kid?
What was your score on the Myers-Briggs test?
123%.
I wonder how my test scores were.
Their choices aren't really based on our scores, you know.
What do you mean?
It's all political. They're going to pick who they want, and the testing is a show to make it look fair.

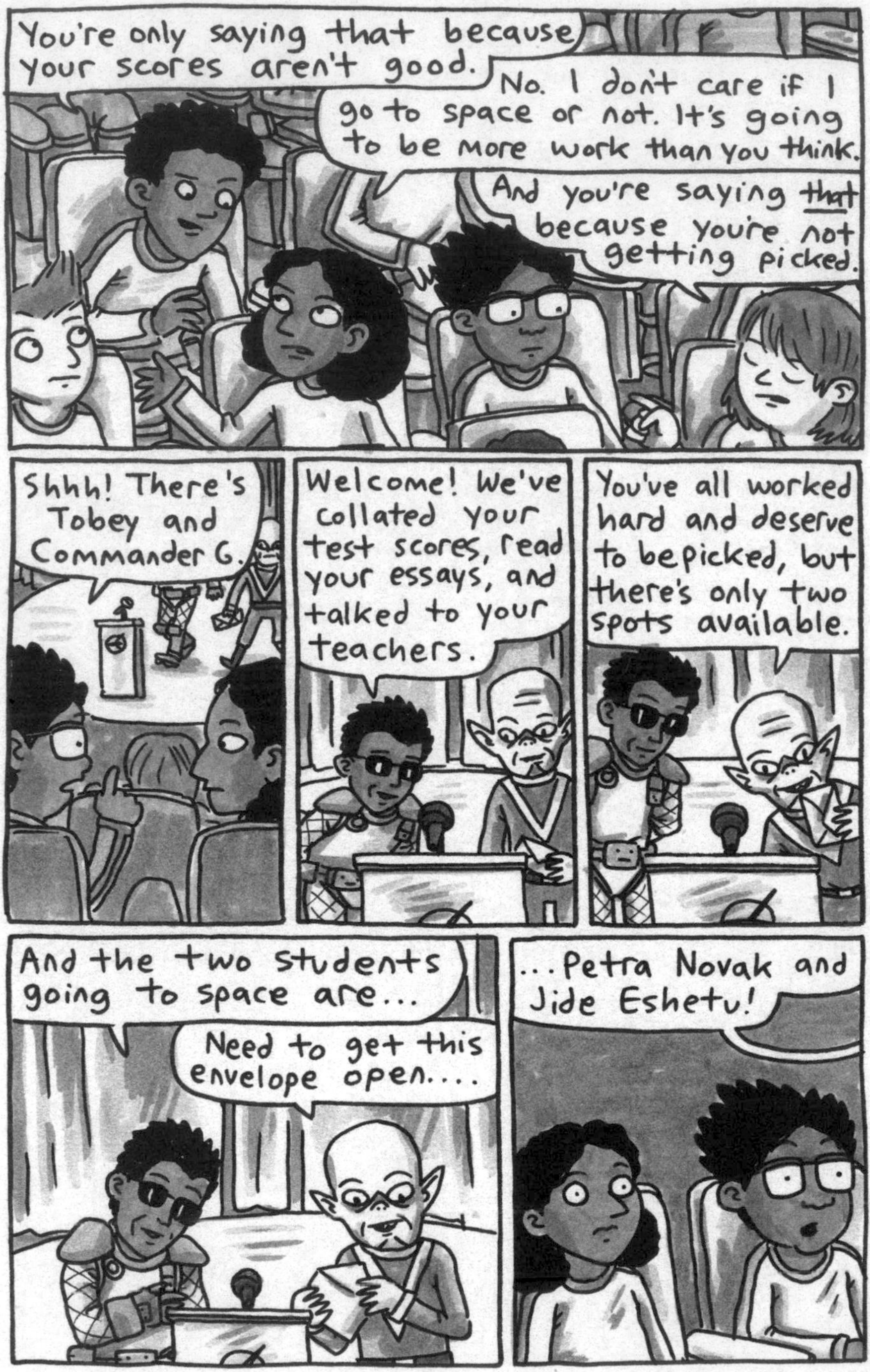
You're only saying that because your scores aren't good.
No. I don't care if I go to space or not. It's going to be more work than you think.
And you're saying that because you're not getting picked.
Shhh! There's Tobey and Commander G.
Welcome! We've collated your test scores, read your essays, and talked to your teachers.
You've all worked hard and deserve to be picked, but there's only two spots available.
And the two students going to space are...
Need to get this envelope open....
...Petra Novak and Jide Eshetu!

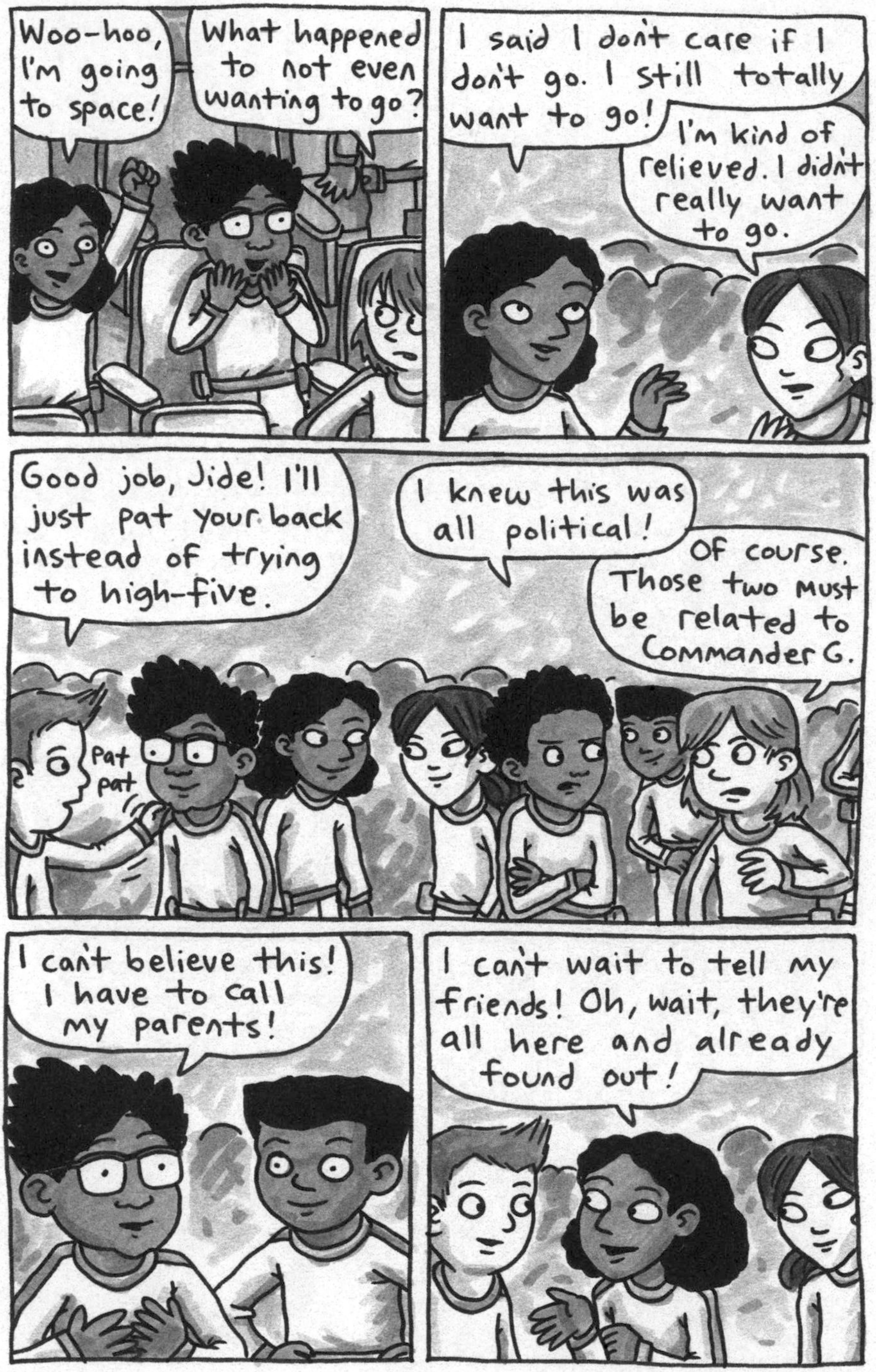
Woo-hoo, I'm going to space!
What happened to not even wanting to go?
I said I don't care if I don't go. I still totally want to go!
I'm kind of relieved. I didn't really want to go.
Good job, Jide! I'll just pat your back instead of trying to high-five.
Pat pat
I knew this was all political!
Of course. Those two must be related to Commander G.
I can't believe this! I have to call my parents!
I can't wait to tell my friends! Oh, wait, they're all here and already found out!

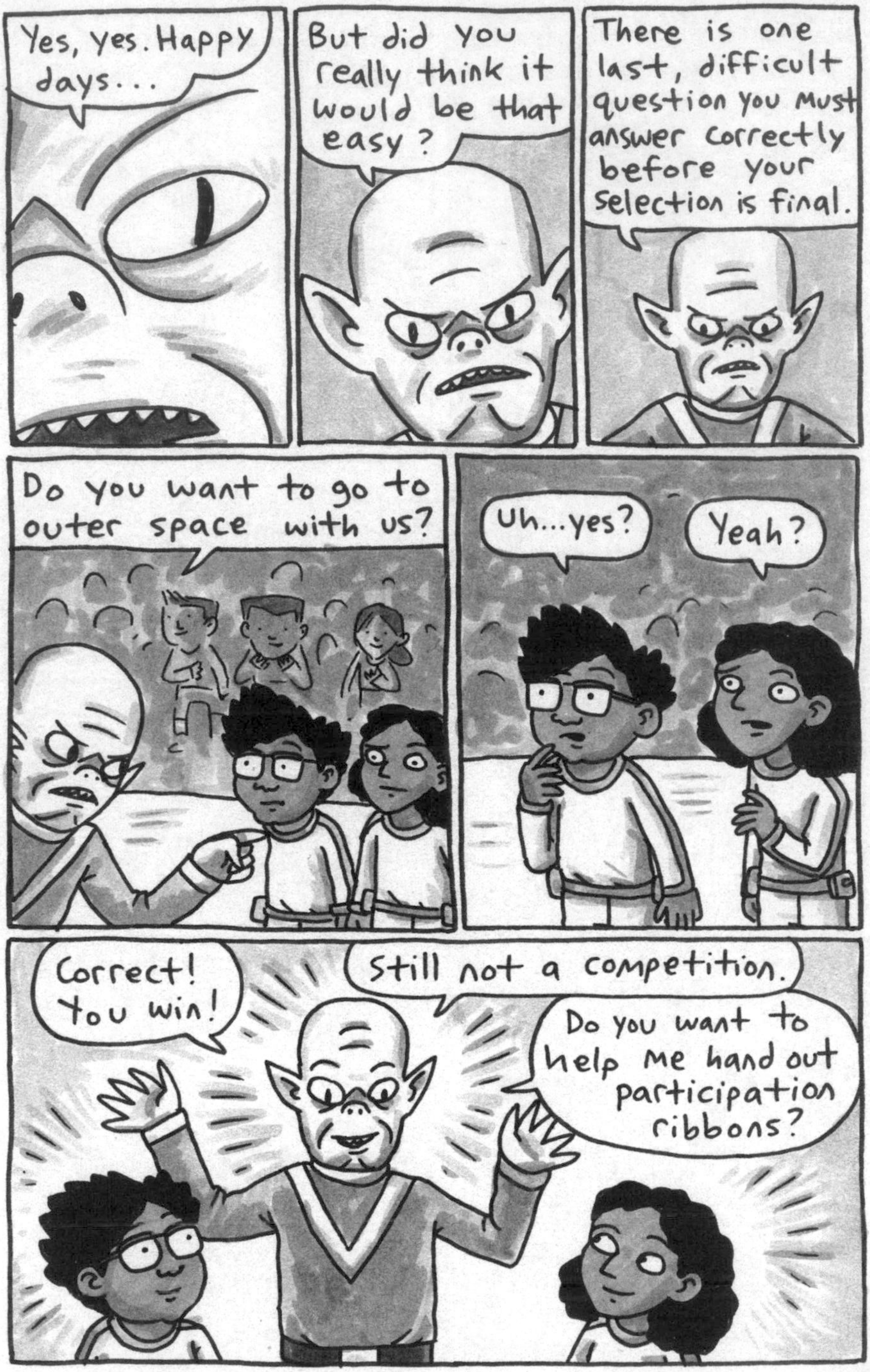
Yes, yes. Happy days...
But did you really think it would be that easy?
There is one last, difficult question you must answer correctly before your selection is final.
Do you want to go to outer space with us?
Uh...yes?
Yeah?
Correct! You win!
Still not a competition.
Do you want to help me hand out participation ribbons?

MARS, OUR DESTINATION!

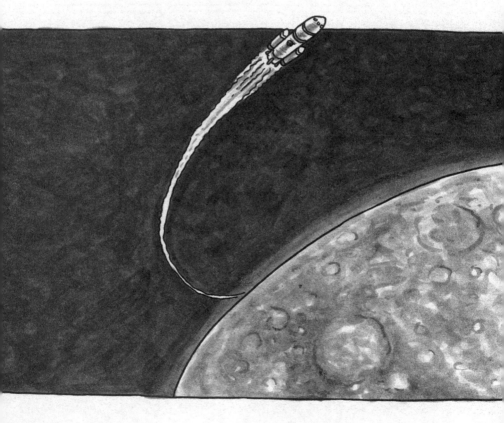

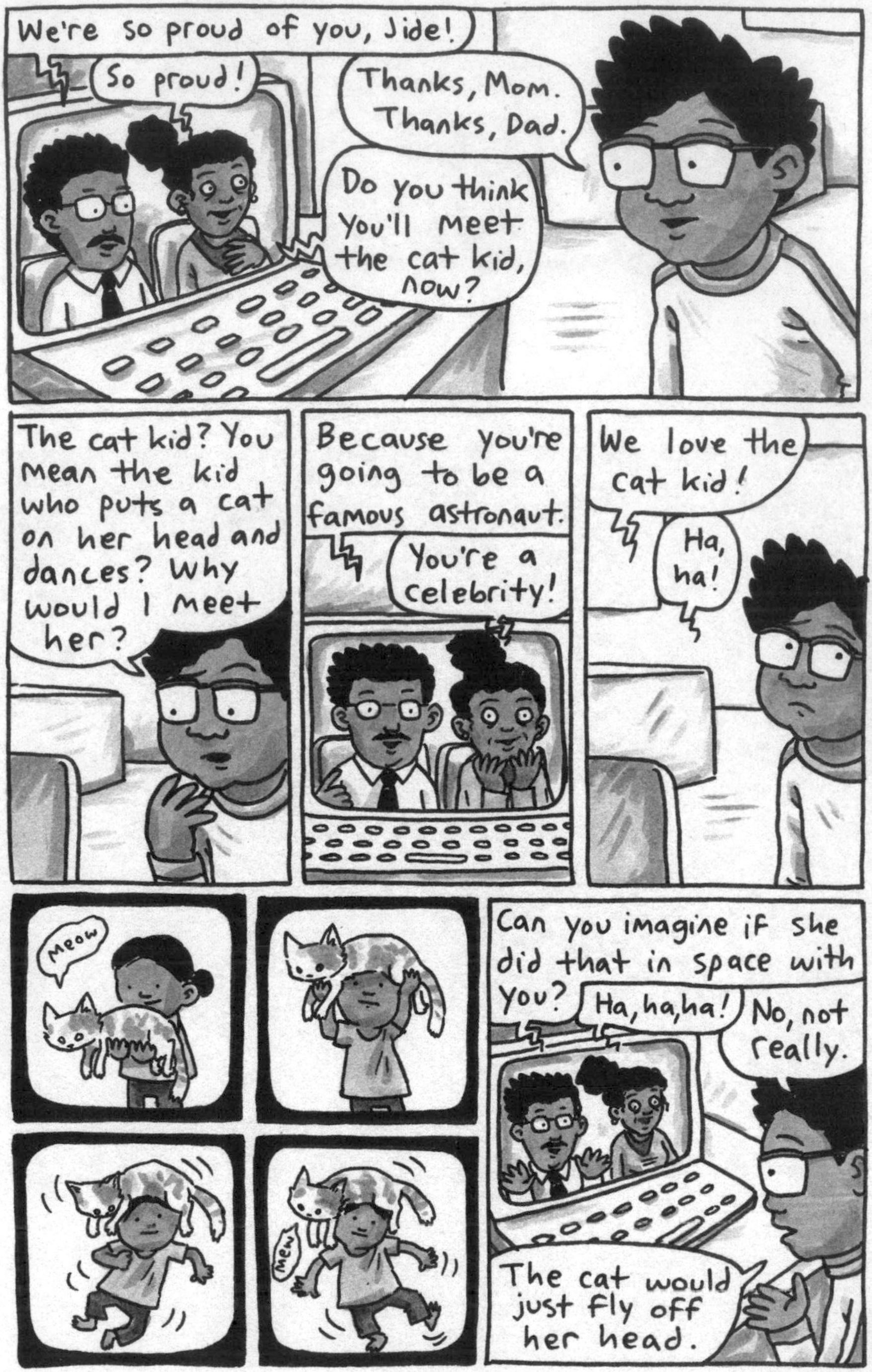
We're so proud of you, Jide!
So proud!
Thanks, Mom. Thanks, Dad.
Do you think you'll meet the cat kid, now?
The cat kid? You mean the kid who puts a cat on her head and dances? Why would I meet her?
Because you're going to be a famous astronaut.
You're a celebrity!
We love the cat kid!
Ha, ha!
MEOW
MEW
Can you imagine if she did that in space with you?
Ha, ha, ha!
No, not really.
The cat would just fly off her head.

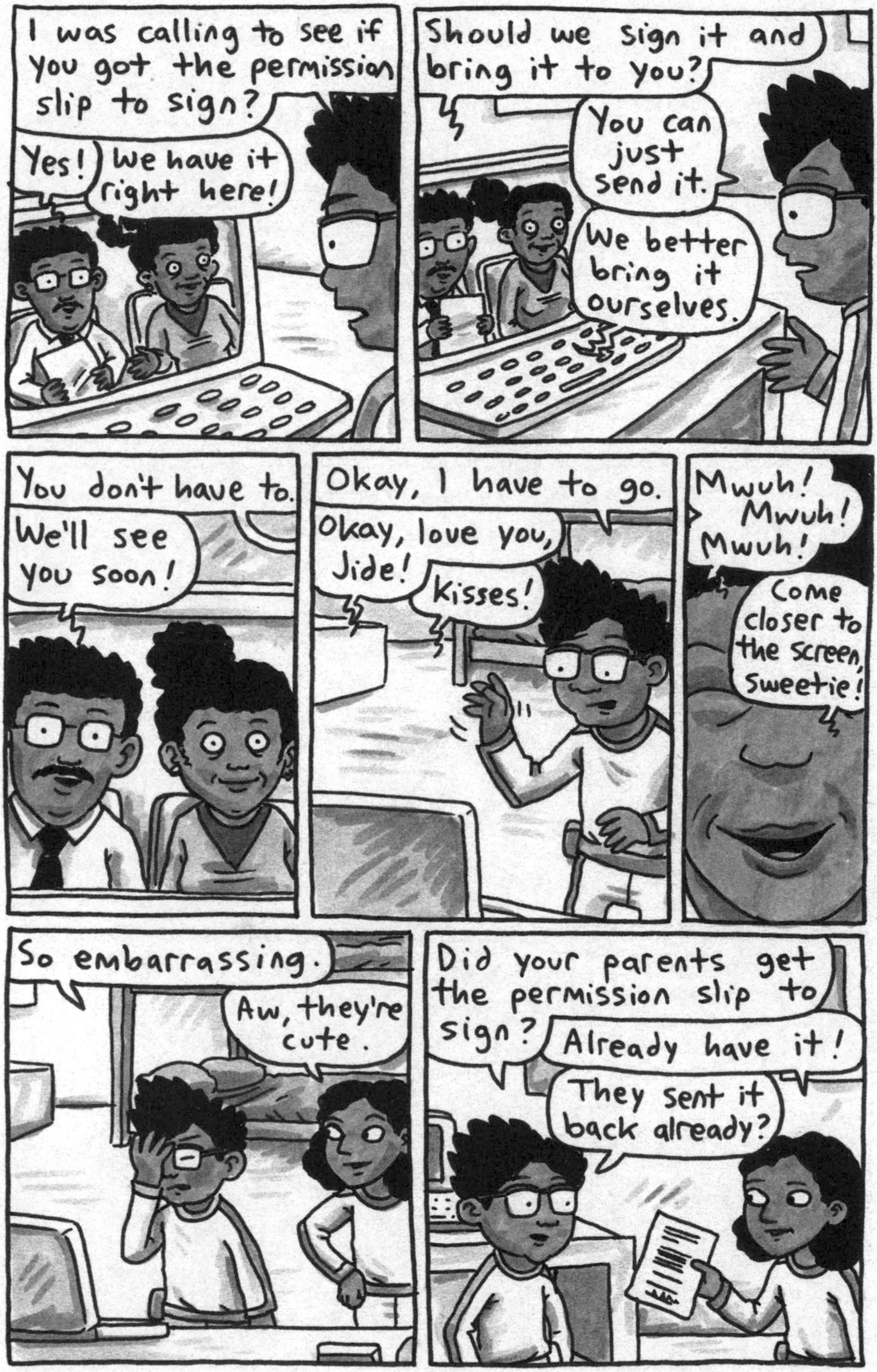
I was calling to see if you got the permission slip to sign?
Yes!
We have it right here!
Should we sign it and bring it to you?
You can just send it.
We better bring it ourselves.
You don't have to.
We'll see you soon!
Okay, I have to go.
Okay, love you, Jide!
Kisses!
Mwuh! Mwuh! Mwuh!
Come closer to the screen, sweetie!
So embarrassing.
Aw, they're cute.
Did your parents get the permission slip to sign?
Already have it!
They sent it back already?

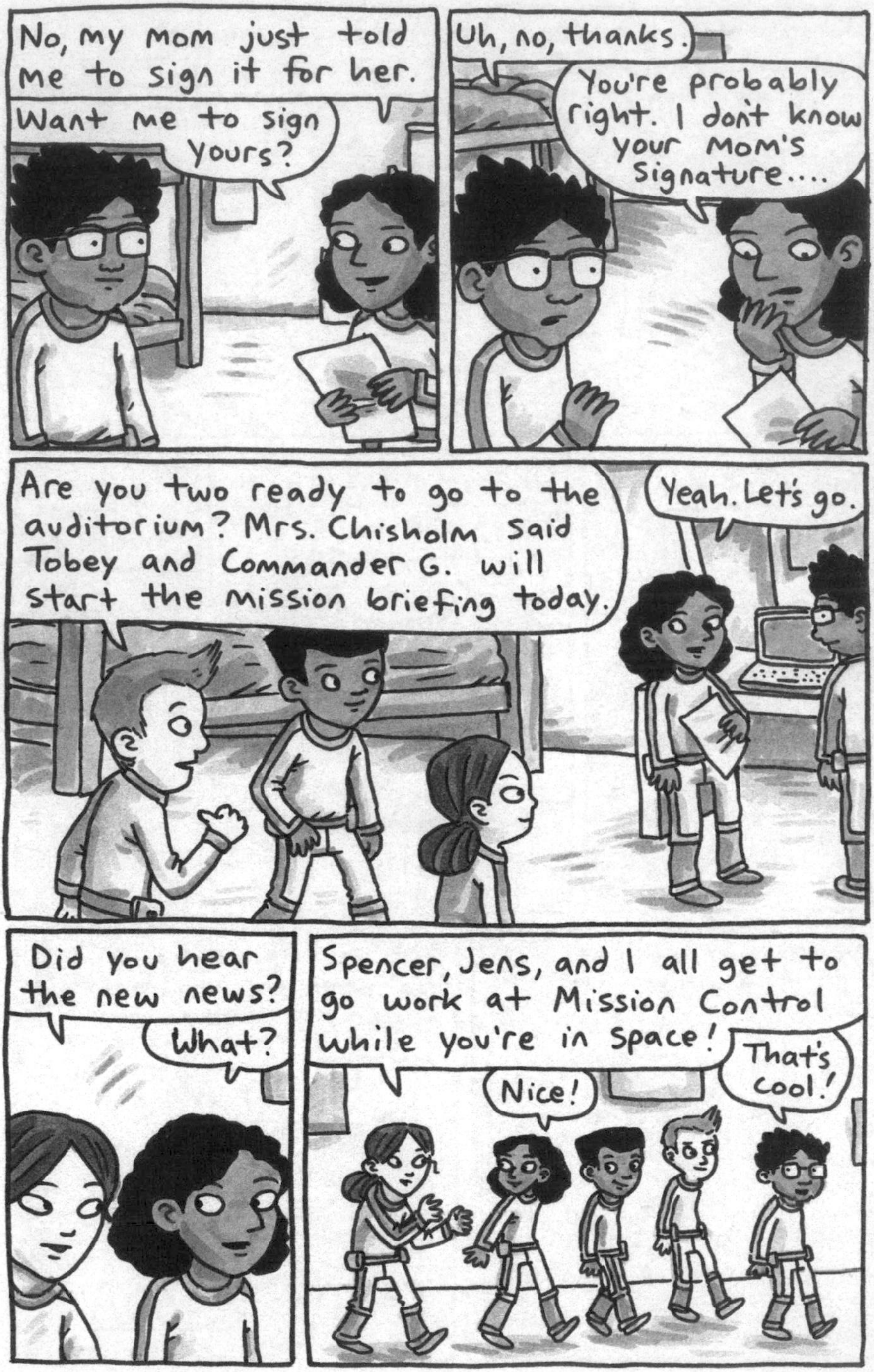
No, my mom just told me to sign it for her.
Want me to sign yours?
Uh, no, thanks.
You're probably right. I don't know your mom's signature....
Are you two ready to go to the auditorium? Mrs. Chisholm said Tobey and Commander G. will start the mission briefing today.
Yeah. Let's go.
Did you hear the new news?
What?
Spencer, Jens, and I all get to go work at Mission Control while you're in space!
Nice!
That's cool!

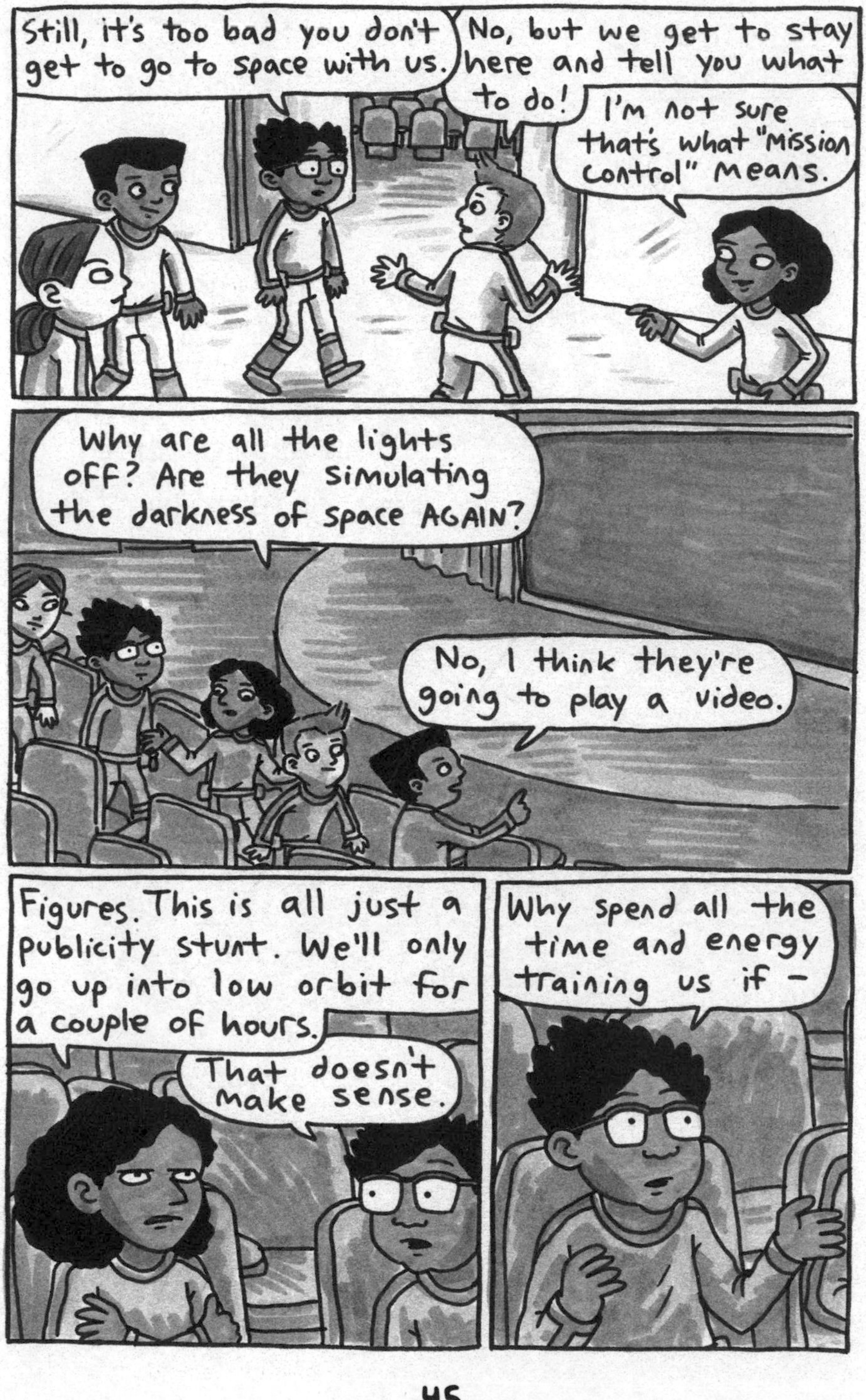
Still, it's too bad you don't get to go to space with us.
No, but we get to stay here and tell you what to do!
I'm not sure that's what "Mission control" means.
Why are all the lights off? Are they simulating the darkness of space AGAIN?
No, I think they're going to play a video.
Figures. This is all just a publicity stunt. We'll only go up into low orbit for a couple of hours.
That doesn't make sense.
Why spend all the time and energy training us if -

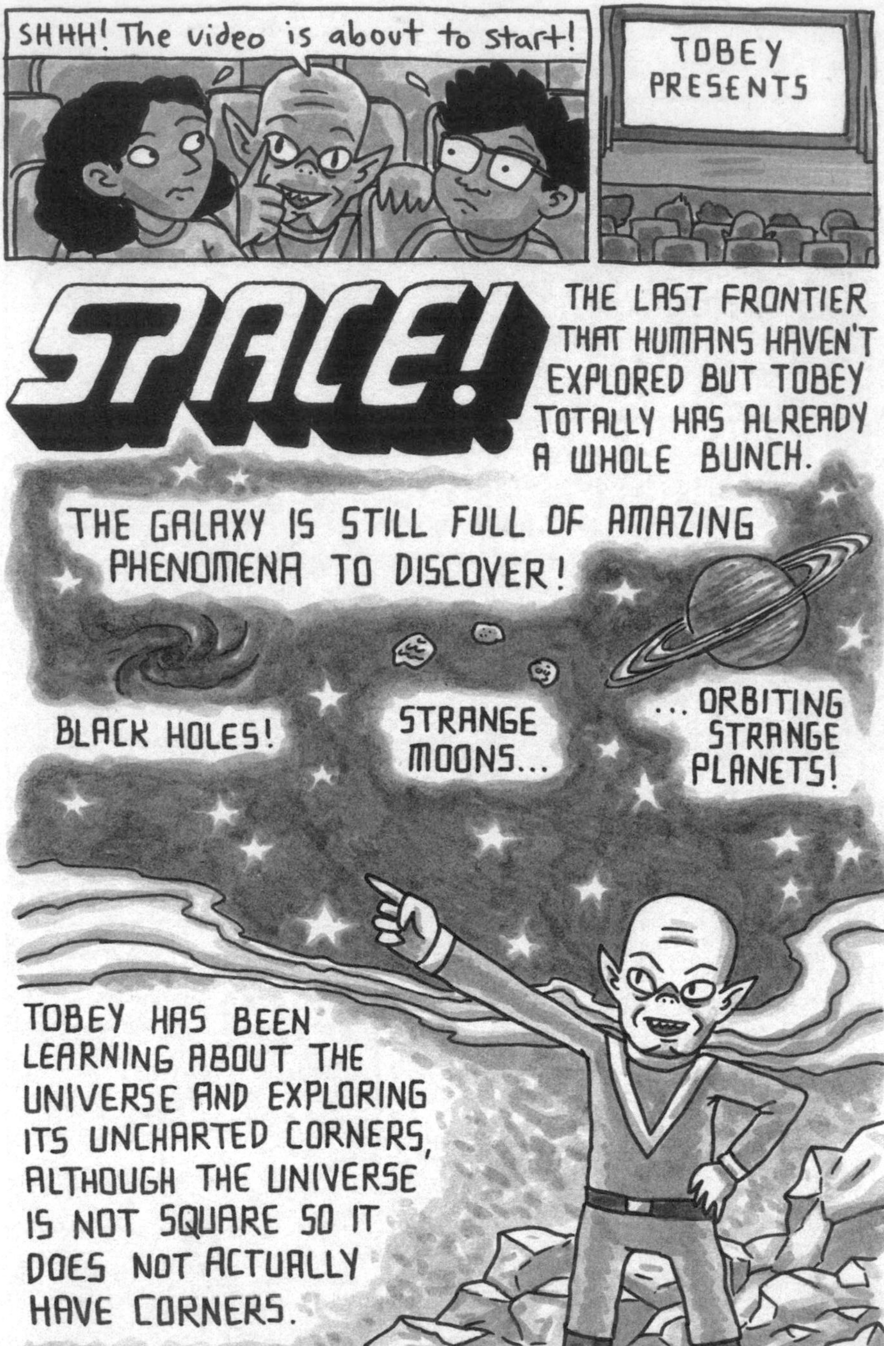
SHHH! The video is about to start!
TOBEY PRESENTS
SPACE!
THE LAST FRONTIER THAT HUMANS HAVEN'T EXPLORED BUT TOBEY TOTALLY HAS ALREADY A WHOLE BUNCH.
THE GALAXY IS STILL FULL OF AMAZING PHENOMENA TO DISCOVER!
BLACK HOLES!
STRANGE MOONS...
...ORBITING STRANGE PLANETS!
TOBEY HAS BEEN LEARNING ABOUT THE UNIVERSE AND EXPLORING ITS UNCHARTED CORNERS, ALTHOUGH THE UNIVERSE IS NOT SQUARE SO IT DOES NOT ACTUALLY HAVE CORNERS.

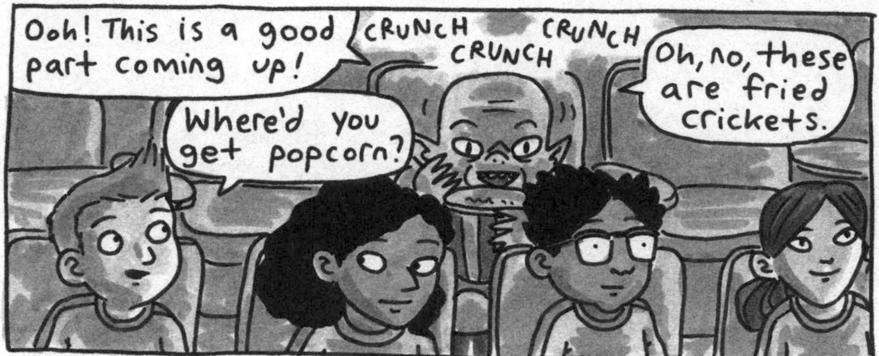
Ooh! This is a good part coming up!
CRUNCH CRUNCH CRUNCH
Where'd you get popcorn?
Oh, no, these are fried crickets.

ALONG THE WAY, HE HAS MET MANY OTHER CULTURES AND LIFE-FORMS, AND HAS MADE IT HIS GOAL TO SHARE HIS LOVE OF ADVENTURE!

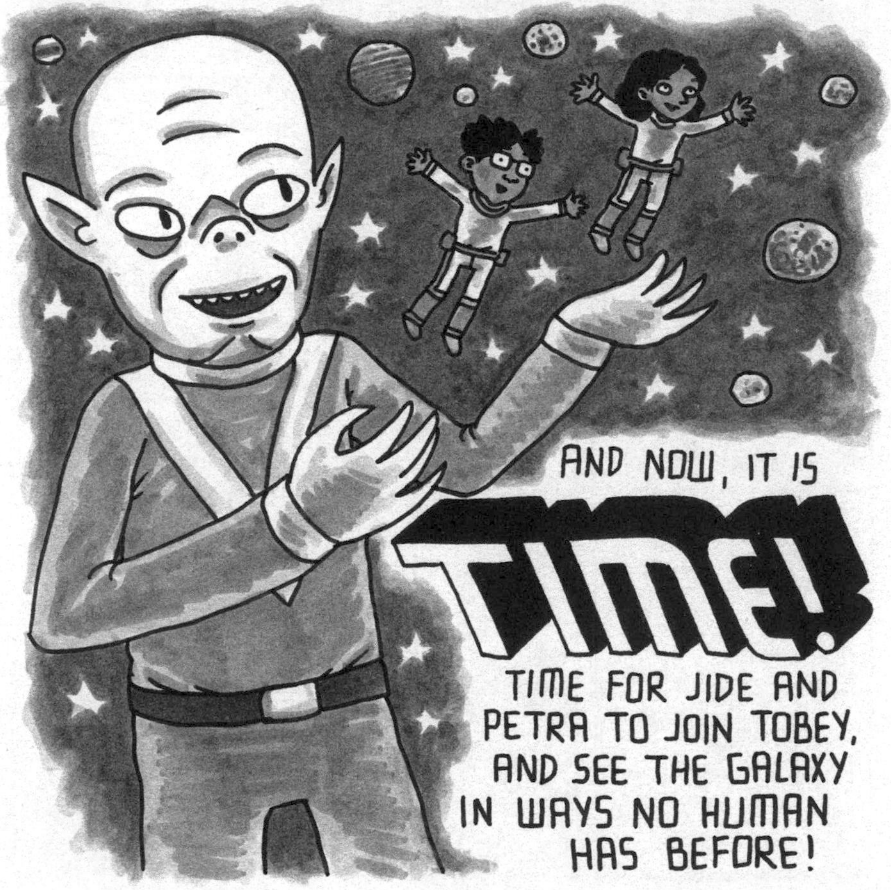
AND NOW, IT IS
TIME!
TIME FOR JIDE AND PETRA TO JOIN TOBEY, AND SEE THE GALAXY IN WAYS NO HUMAN HAS BEFORE!

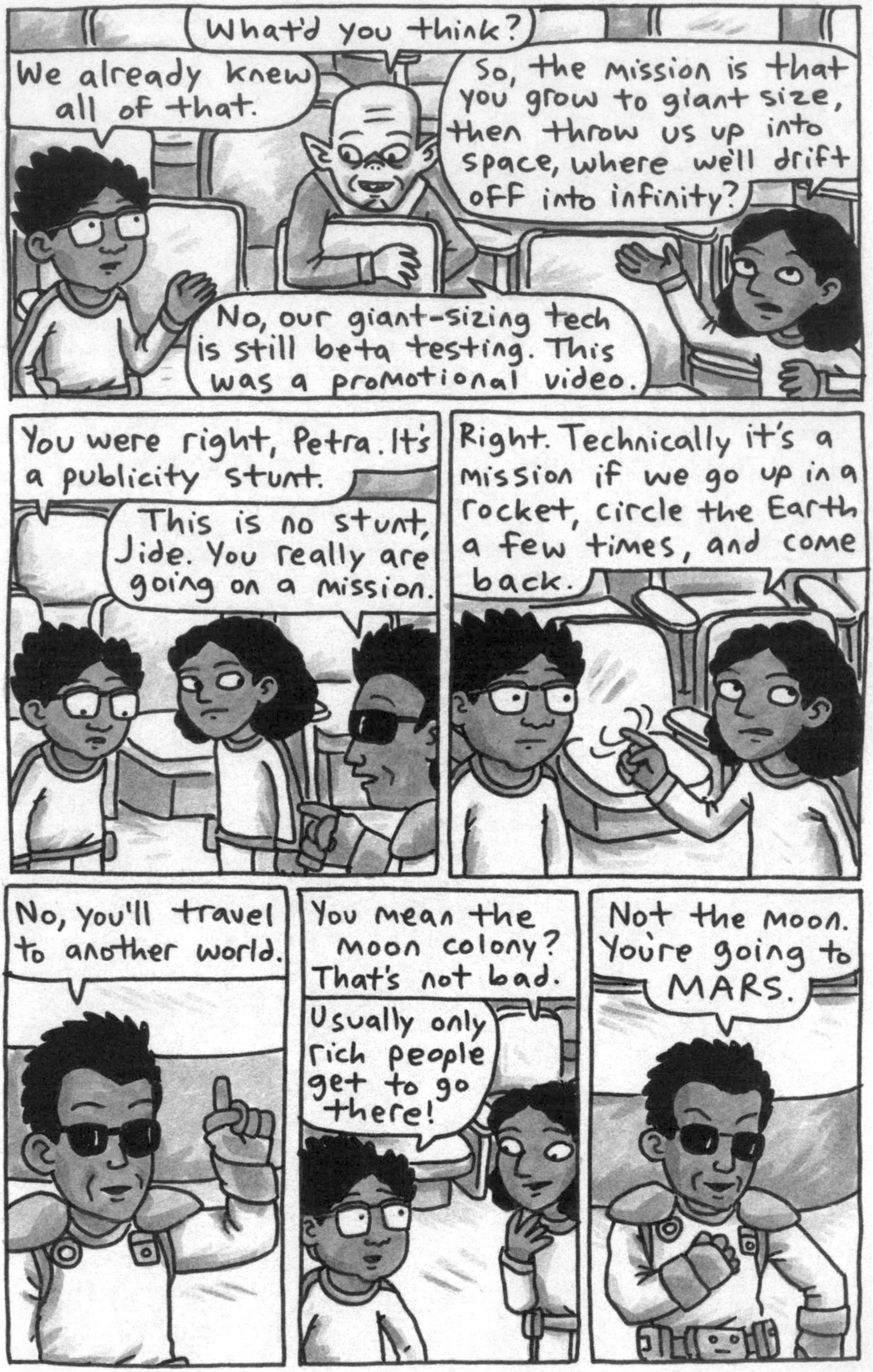
What'd you think?
We already knew all of that.
So, the mission is that you grow to giant size, then throw us up into space, where we'll drift off into infinity?
No, our giant-sizing tech is still beta testing. This was a promotional video.
You were right, Petra. It's a publicity stunt.
This is no stunt, Jide. You really are going on a mission.
Right. Technically it's a mission if we go up in a rocket, circle the Earth a few times, and come back.
No, you'll travel to another world.
You mean the moon colony? That's not bad.
Usually only rich people get to go there!
Not the moon. You're going to MARS.

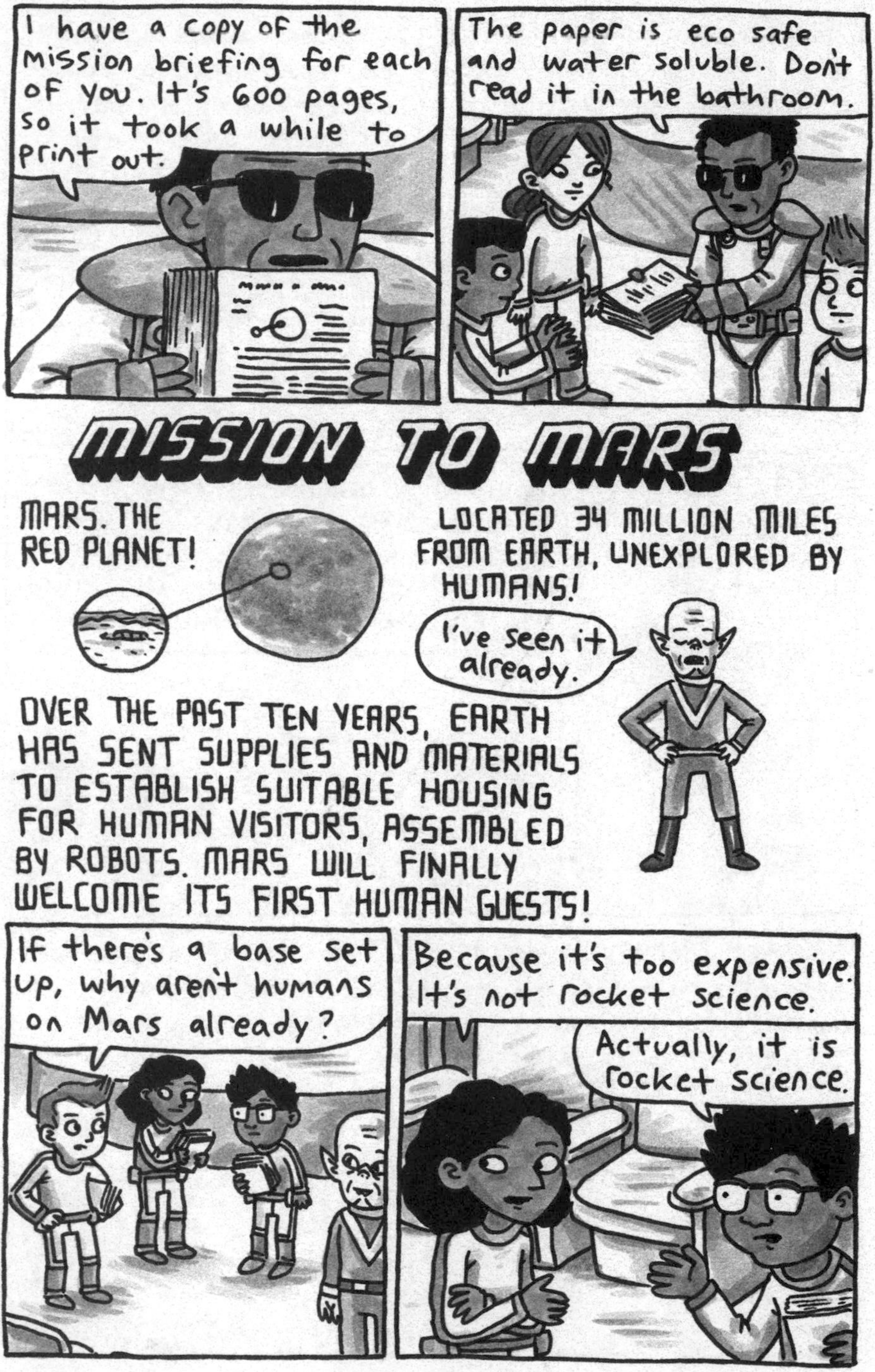
I have a copy of the mission briefing for each of you. It's 600 pages, so it took a while to print out.
The paper is eco safe and water soluble. Don't read it in the bathroom.
MISSION TO MARS
MARS. THE RED PLANET!
LOCATED 34 MILLION MILES FROM EARTH, UNEXPLORED BY HUMANS!
I've seen it already.
OVER THE PAST TEN YEARS, EARTH HAS SENT SUPPLIES AND MATERIALS TO ESTABLISH SUITABLE HOUSING FOR HUMAN VISITORS, ASSEMBLED BY ROBOTS. MARS WILL FINALLY WELCOME ITS FIRST HUMAN GUESTS!
If there's a base set up, why aren't humans on Mars already?
Because it's too expensive. It's not rocket science.
Actually, it is rocket science.

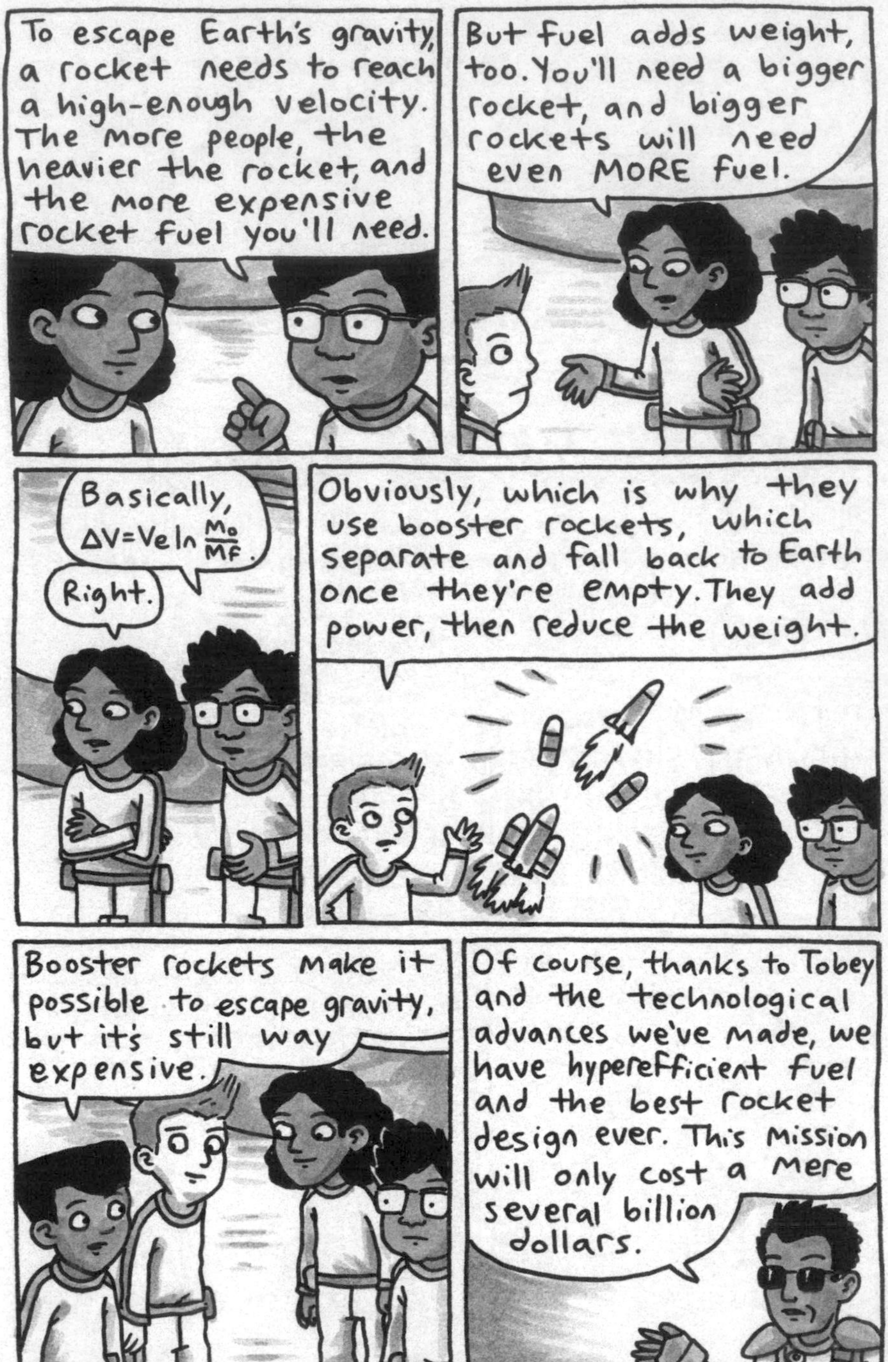
To escape Earth's gravity, a rocket needs to reach a high-enough velocity. The more people, the heavier the rocket, and the more expensive rocket fuel you'll need.
But fuel adds weight, too. You'll need a bigger rocket, and bigger rockets will need even MORE fuel.
Basically, ΔV=Veln Mo/MF.
Right.
Obviously, which is why they use booster rockets, which separate and fall back to Earth once they're empty. They add power, then reduce the weight.
Booster rockets make it possible to escape gravity, but it's still way expensive.
Of course, thanks to Tobey and the technological advances we've made, we have hyperefficient fuel and the best rocket design ever. This mission will only cost a mere several billion dollars.

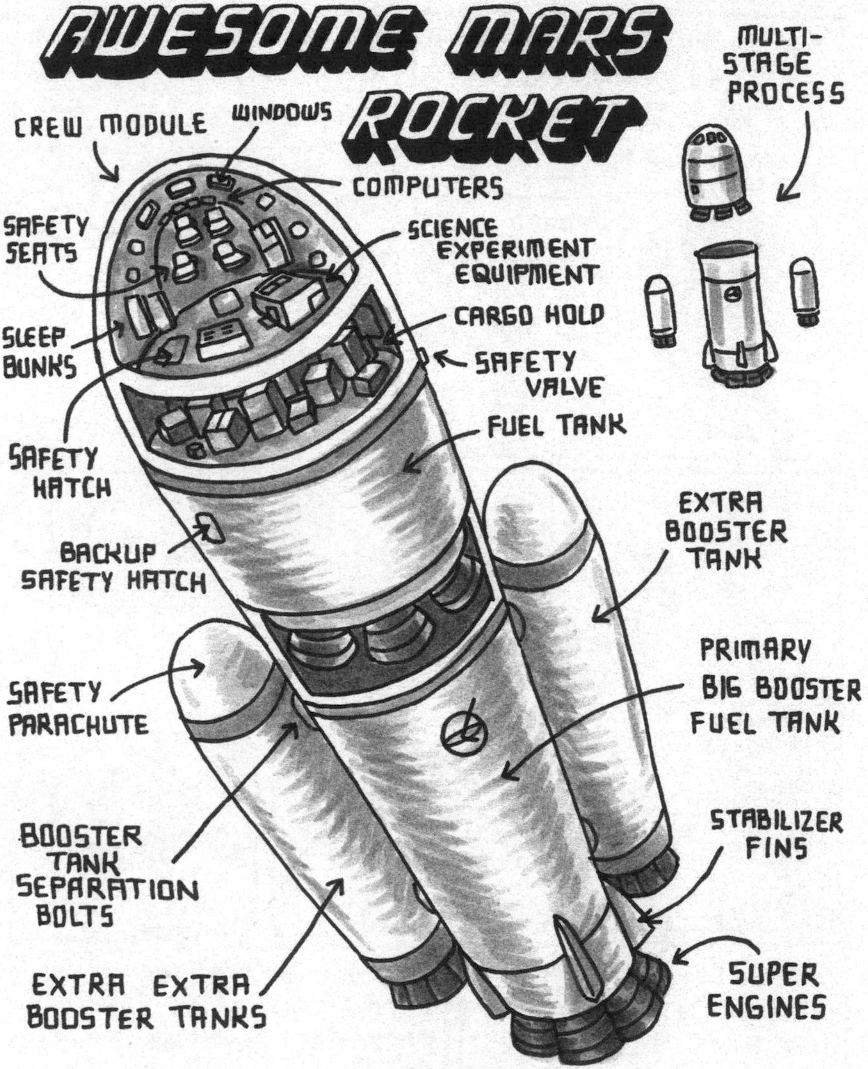
AWESOME MARS ROCKET
MULTI-STAGE PROCESS
CREW MODULE
WINDOWS
COMPUTERS
SAFETY SEATS
SCIENCE EXPERIMENT EQUIPMENT
CARGO HOLD
SLEEP BUNKS
SAFETY VALVE
FUEL TANK
SAFETY HATCH
EXTRA BOOSTER TANK
BACKUP SAFETY HATCH
PRIMARY BIG BOOSTER FUEL TANK
SAFETY PARACHUTE
STABILIZER FINS
BOOSTER TANK SEPARATION BOLTS
SUPER ENGINES
EXTRA EXTRA BOOSTER TANKS

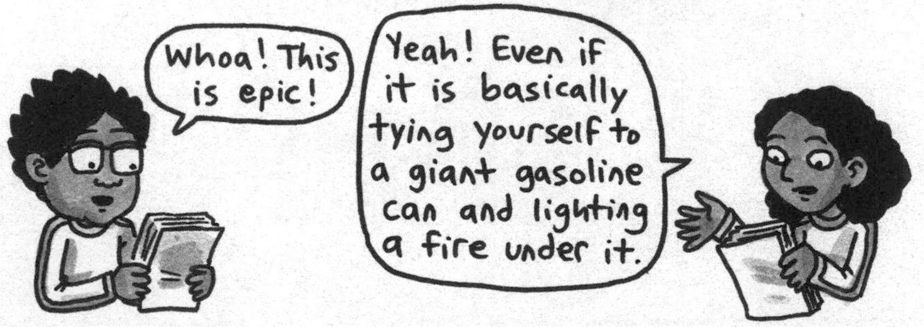
Whoa! This is epic!
Yeah! Even if it is basically tying yourself to a giant gasoline can and lighting a fire under it.

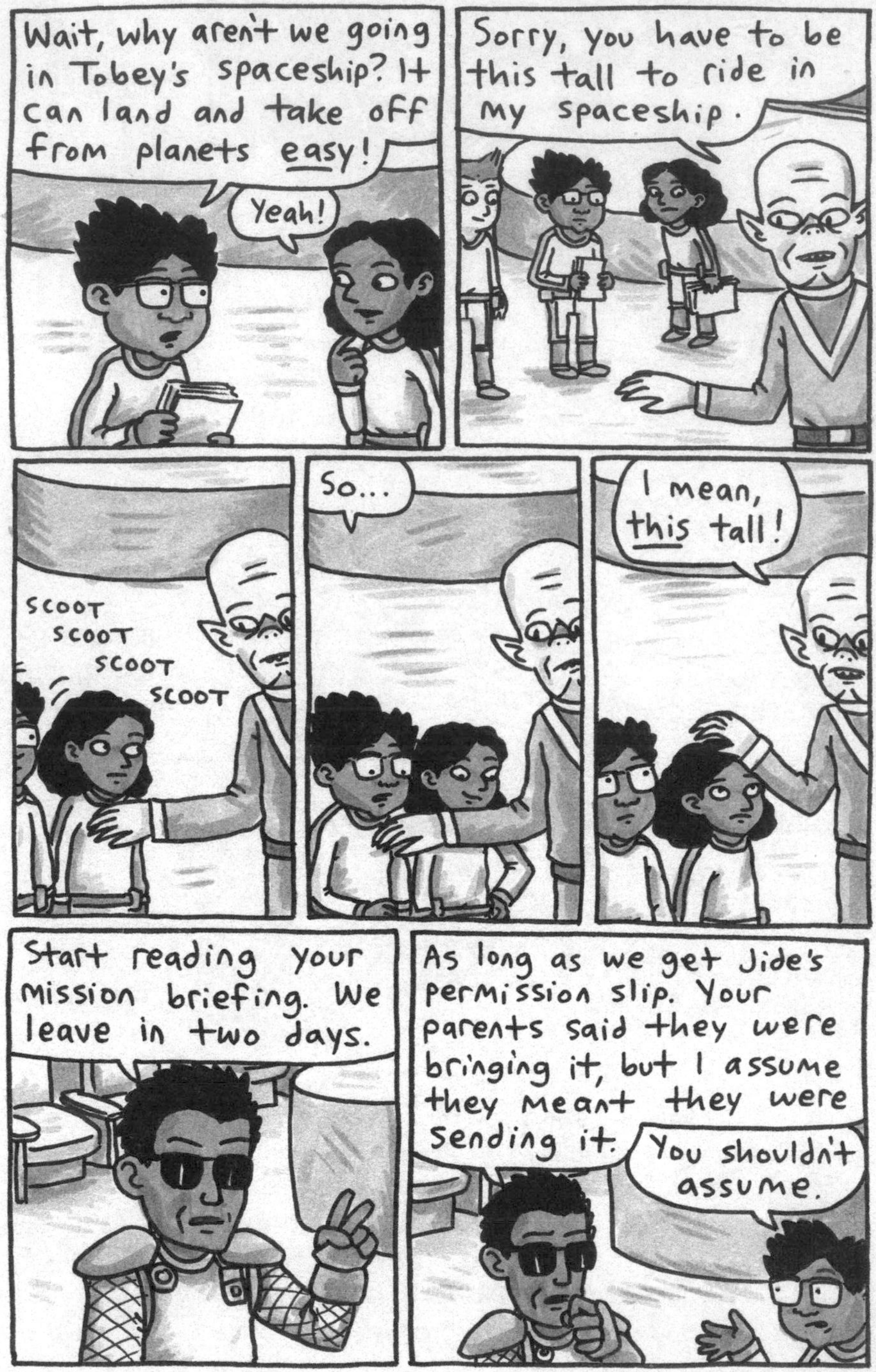
Wait, why aren't we going in Tobey's spaceship? It can land and take off from planets easy!
Yeah!
Sorry, you have to be this tall to ride in my spaceship.
SCOOT
SCOOT
SCOOT
SCOOT
So...
I mean, this tall!
Start reading your mission briefing. We leave in two days.
As long as we get Jide's permission slip. Your parents said they were bringing it, but I assume they meant they were sending it.
You shouldn't assume.

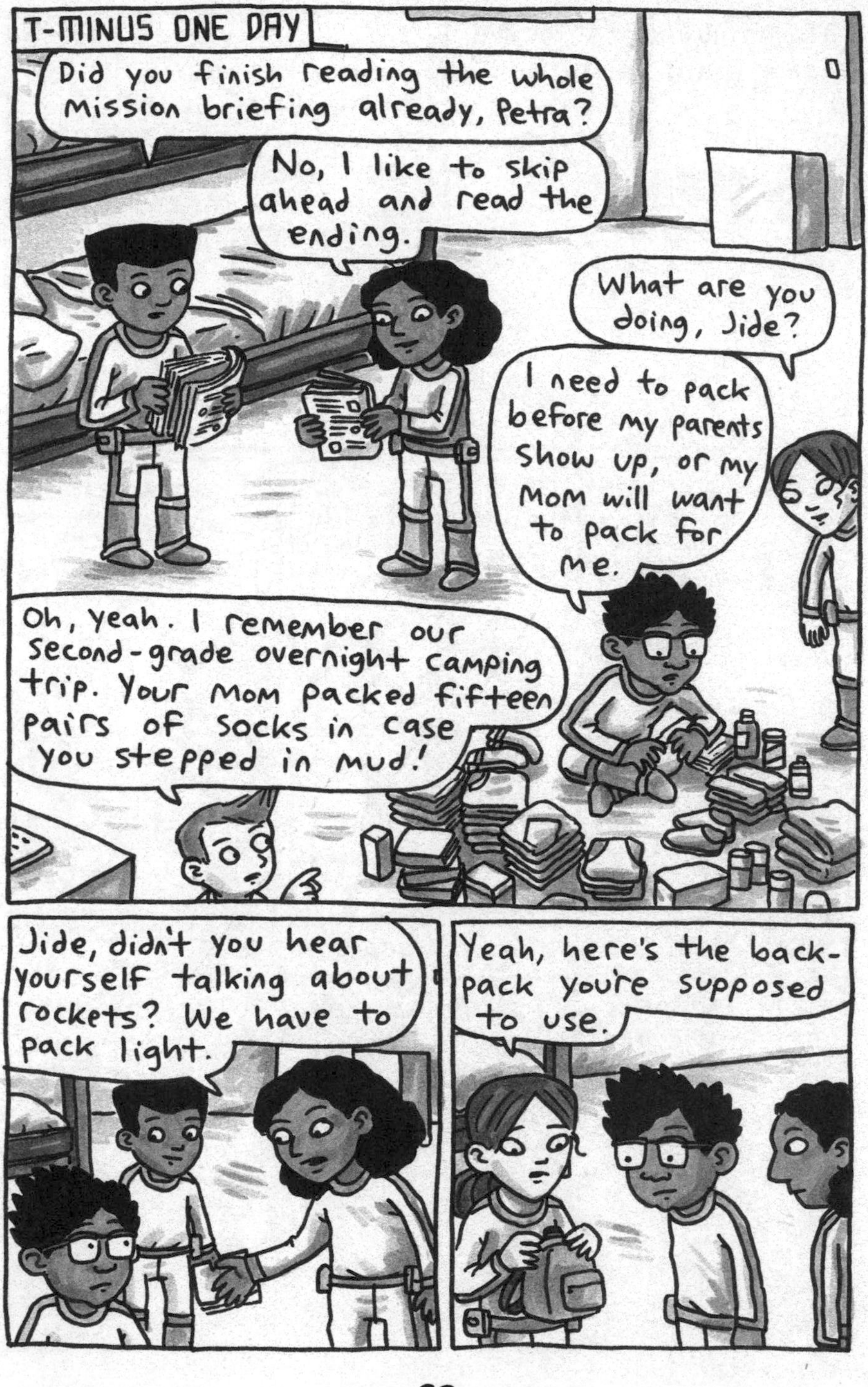
T-MINUS ONE DAY
Did you finish reading the whole mission briefing already, Petra?
No, I like to skip ahead and read the ending.
What are you doing, Jide?
I need to pack before my parents show up, or my Mom will want to pack for me.
Oh, yeah. I remember our second-grade overnight camping trip. Your Mom packed fifteen pairs of socks in case you stepped in mud!
Jide, didn't you hear yourself talking about rockets? We have to pack light.
Yeah, here's the back-pack you're supposed to use.

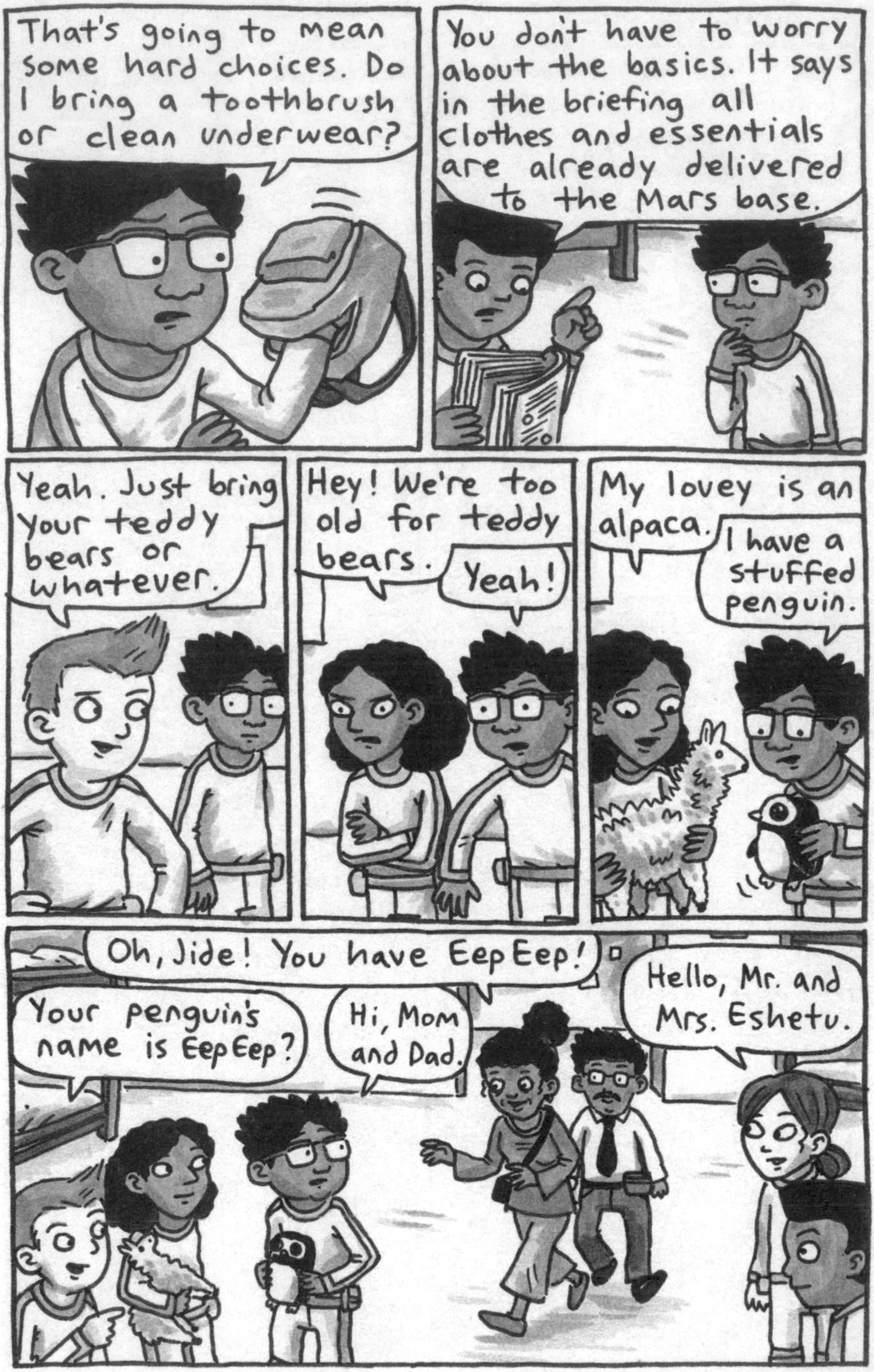
That's going to mean some hard choices. Do I bring a toothbrush or clean underwear?
You don't have to worry about the basics. It says in the briefing all clothes and essentials are already delivered to the Mars base.
Yeah. Just bring your teddy bears or whatever.
Hey! We're too old for teddy bears.
Yeah!
My lovey is an alpaca.
I have a stuffed penguin.
Oh, Jide! You have Eep Eep!
Your penguin's name is Eep Eep?
Hi, Mom and Dad.
Hello, Mr. and Mrs. Eshetu.

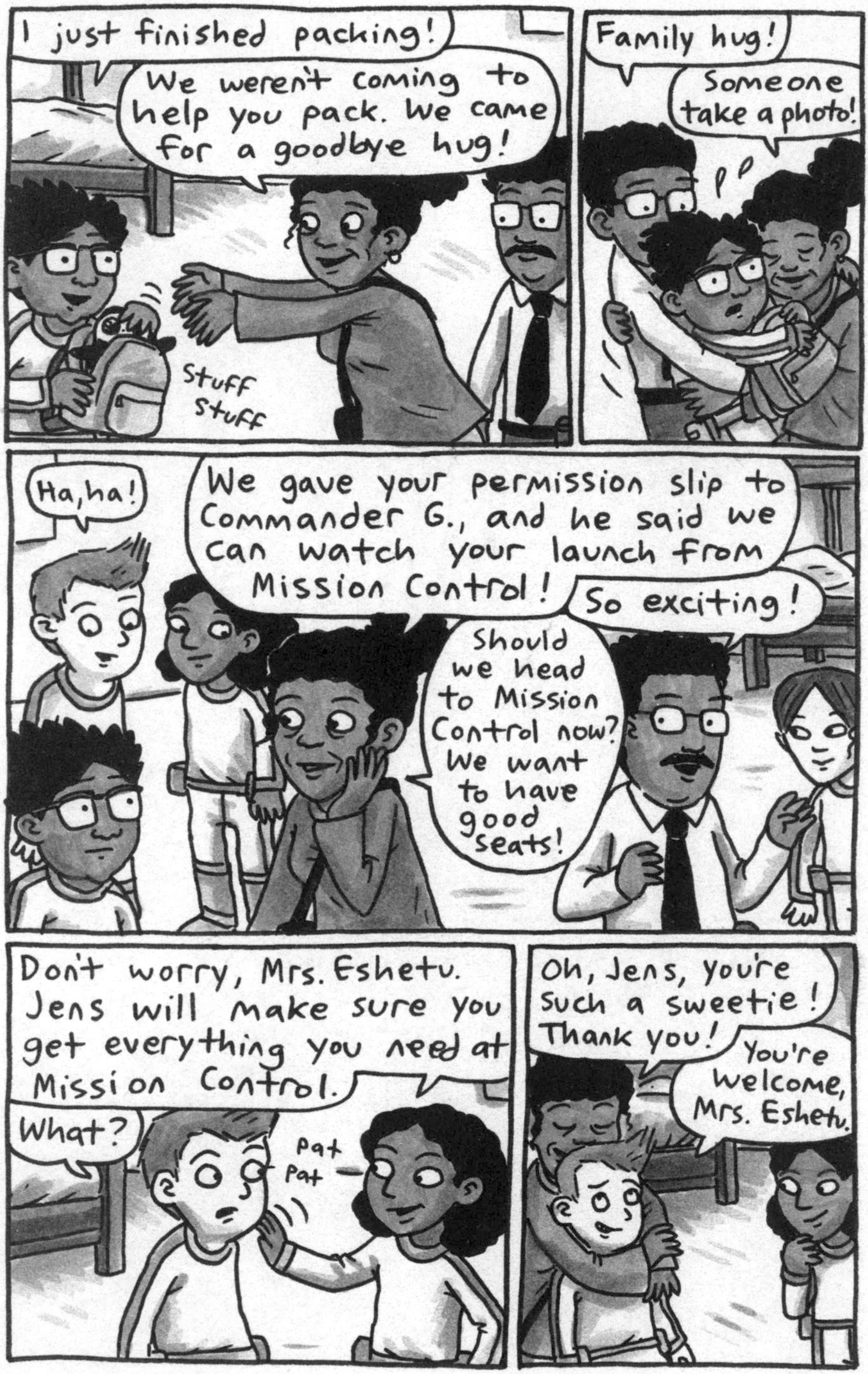

I just finished packing!
We weren't coming to help you pack. We came for a goodbye hug!
Stuff stuff
Family hug!
Someone take a photo!
Ha, ha!
We gave your permission slip to Commander G., and he said we can watch your launch from Mission Control!
So exciting!
Should we head to Mission Control now? We want to have good seats!
Don't worry, Mrs. Eshetu. Jens will make sure you get everything you need at Mission Control.
What?
Pat Pat
Oh, Jens, you're such a sweetie! Thank you!
You're welcome, Mrs. Eshetu.

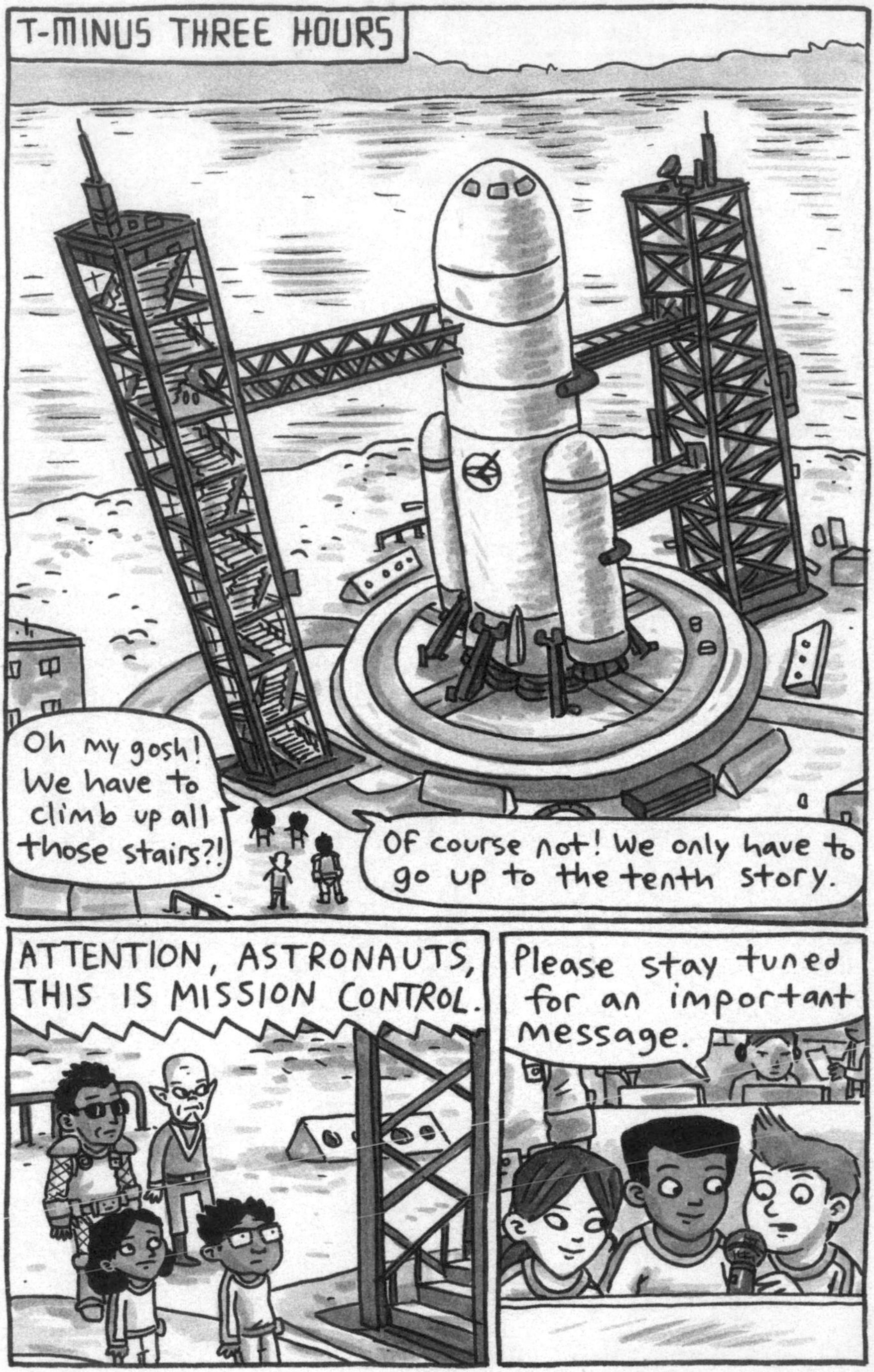
T-MINUS THREE HOURS
Oh my gosh! We have to climb up all those stairs?!
Of course not! We only have to go up to the tenth story.
ATTENTION, ASTRONAUTS, THIS IS MISSION CONTROL.
Please stay tuned for an important message.

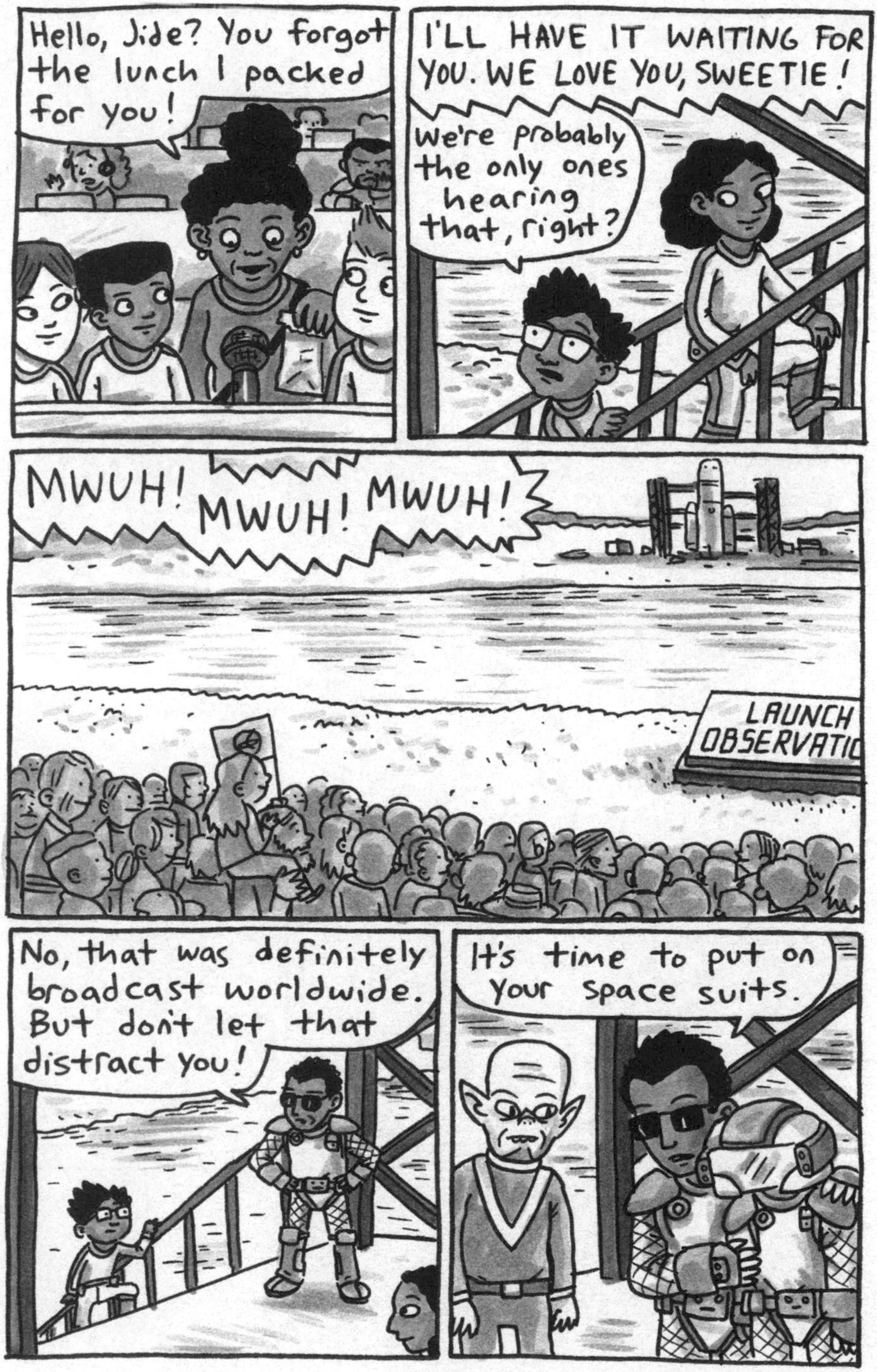
Hello, Jide? You forgot the lunch I packed for you!
I'LL HAVE IT WAITING FOR YOU. WE LOVE YOU, SWEETIE!
We're probably the only ones hearing that, right?
MWUH! MWUH! MWUH!
LAUNCH OBSERVATIO
No, that was definitely broadcast worldwide. But don't let that distract you!
It's time to put on your space suits.

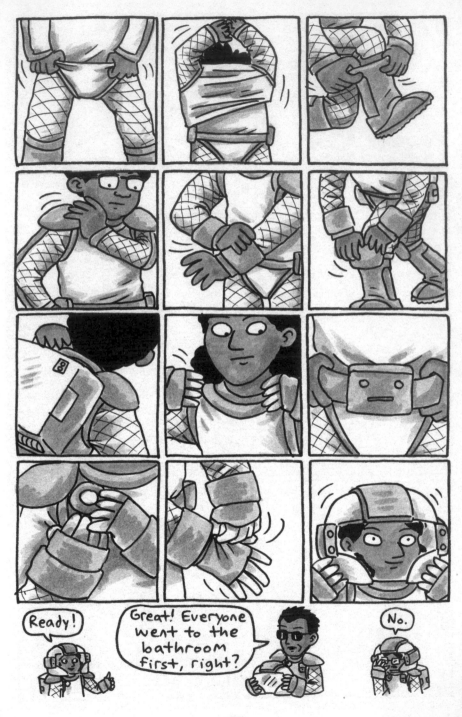

Ready!

Great! Everyone went to the bathroom first, right?

No.

58

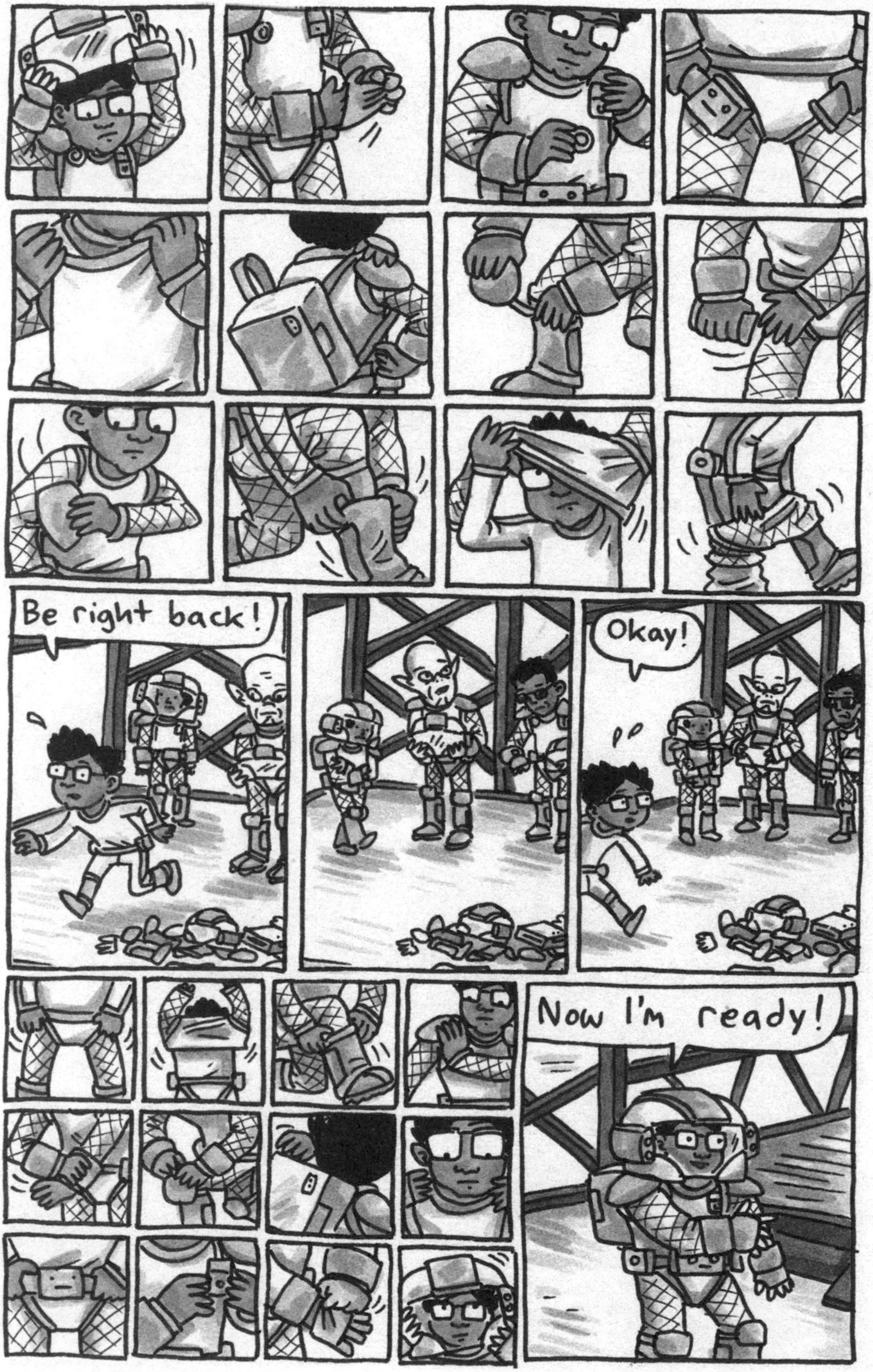
Be right back!
Okay!
Now I'm ready!

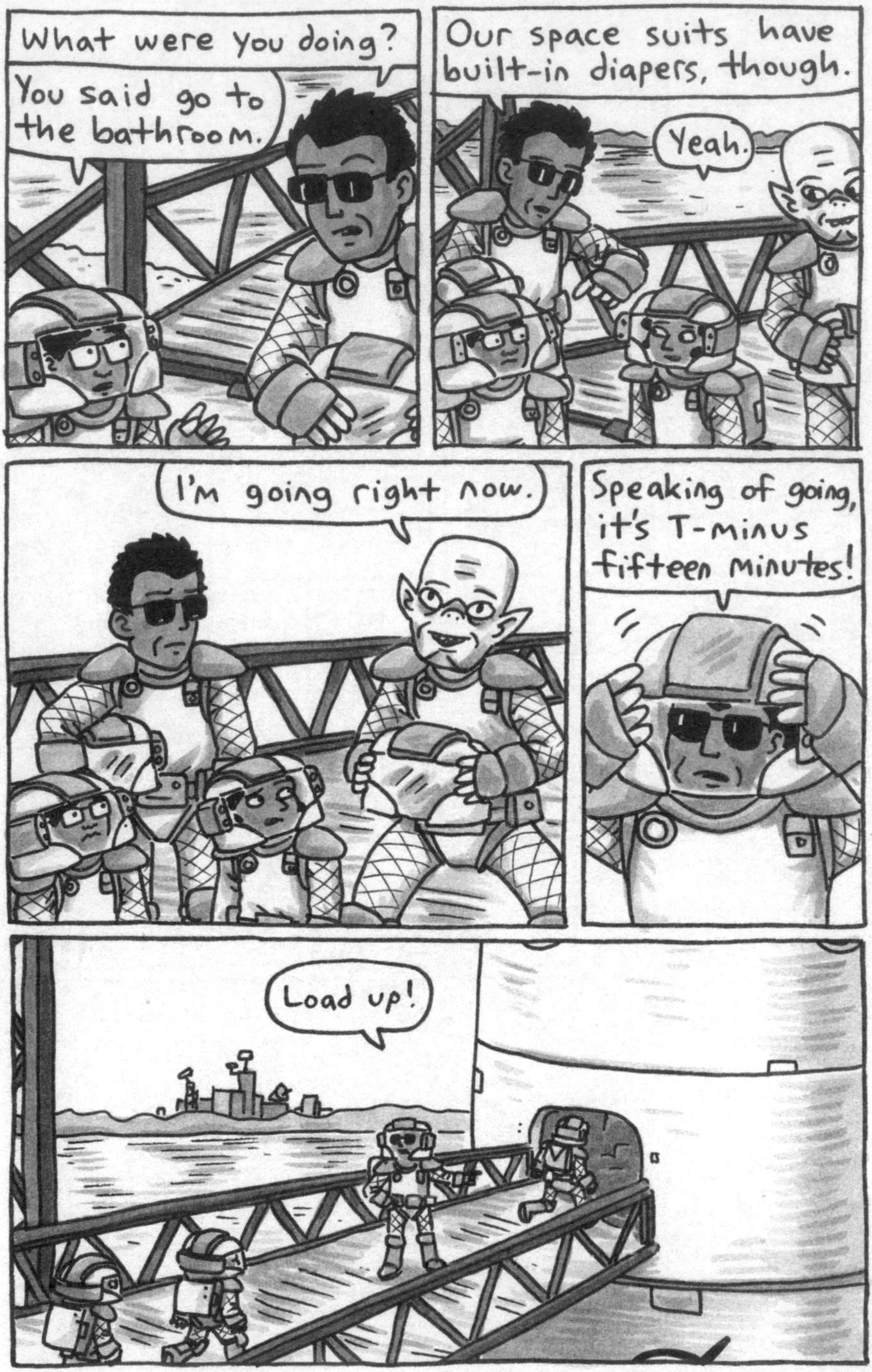
What were you doing?
You said go to the bathroom.
Our space suits have built-in diapers, though.
Yeah.
I'm going right now.
Speaking of going, it's T-minus fifteen minutes!
Load up!

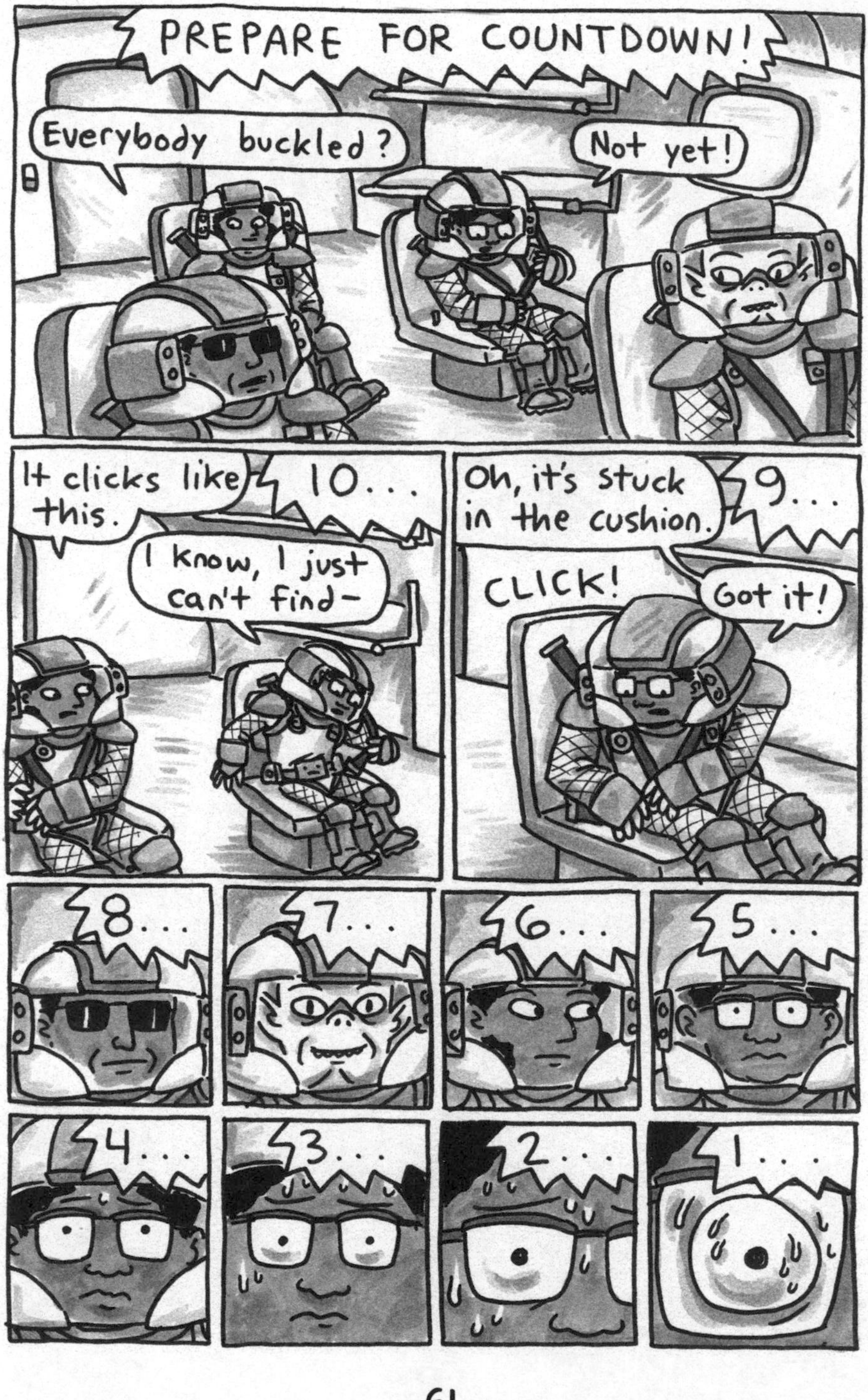
PREPARE FOR COUNTDOWN!
Everybody buckled?
Not yet!
It clicks like this.
10...
I know, I just can't find-
Oh, it's stuck in the cushion.
9...
CLICK!
Got it!
8...
7...
6...
5...
4...
3...
2...
1...

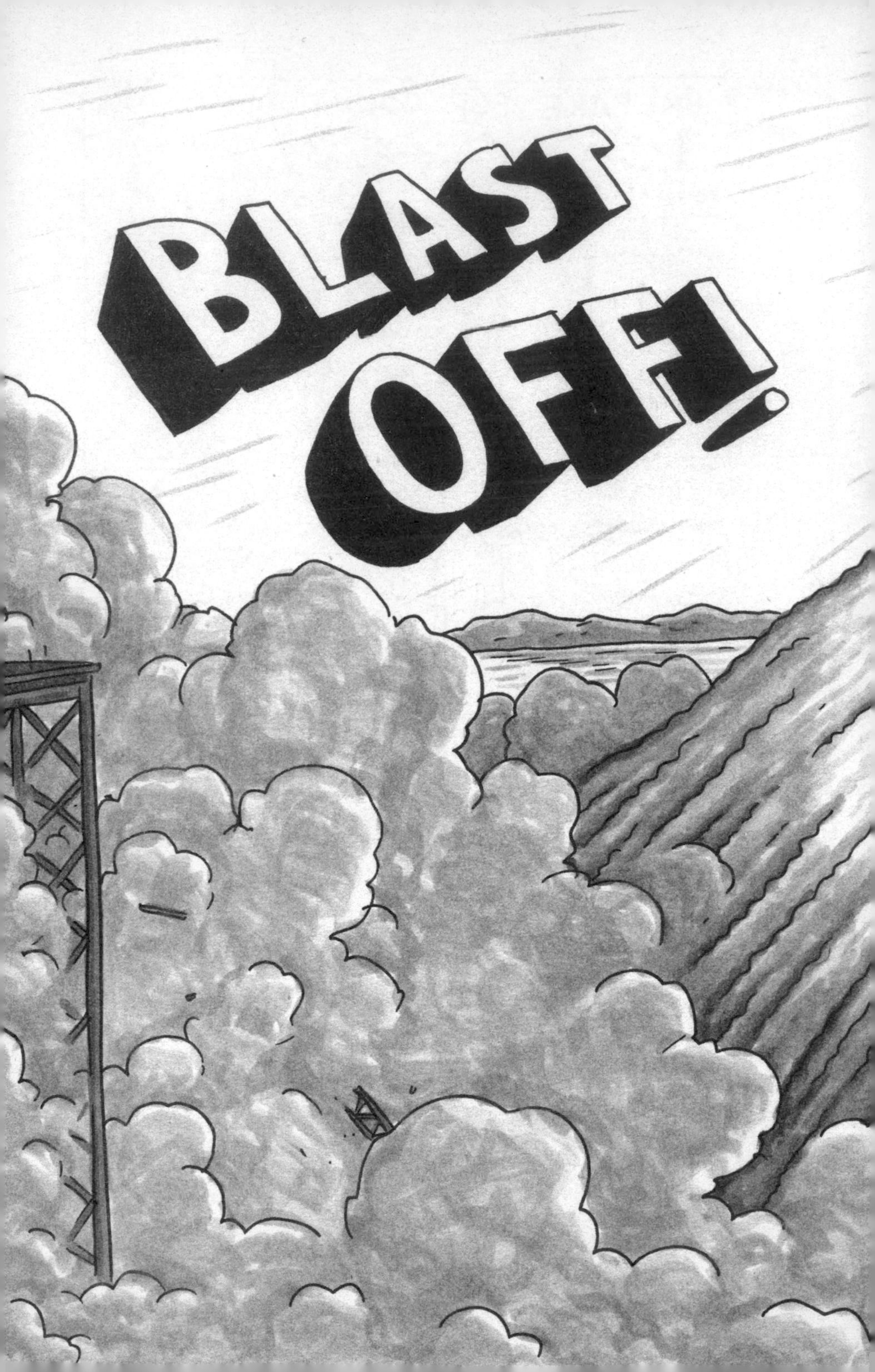
BLAST OFF!

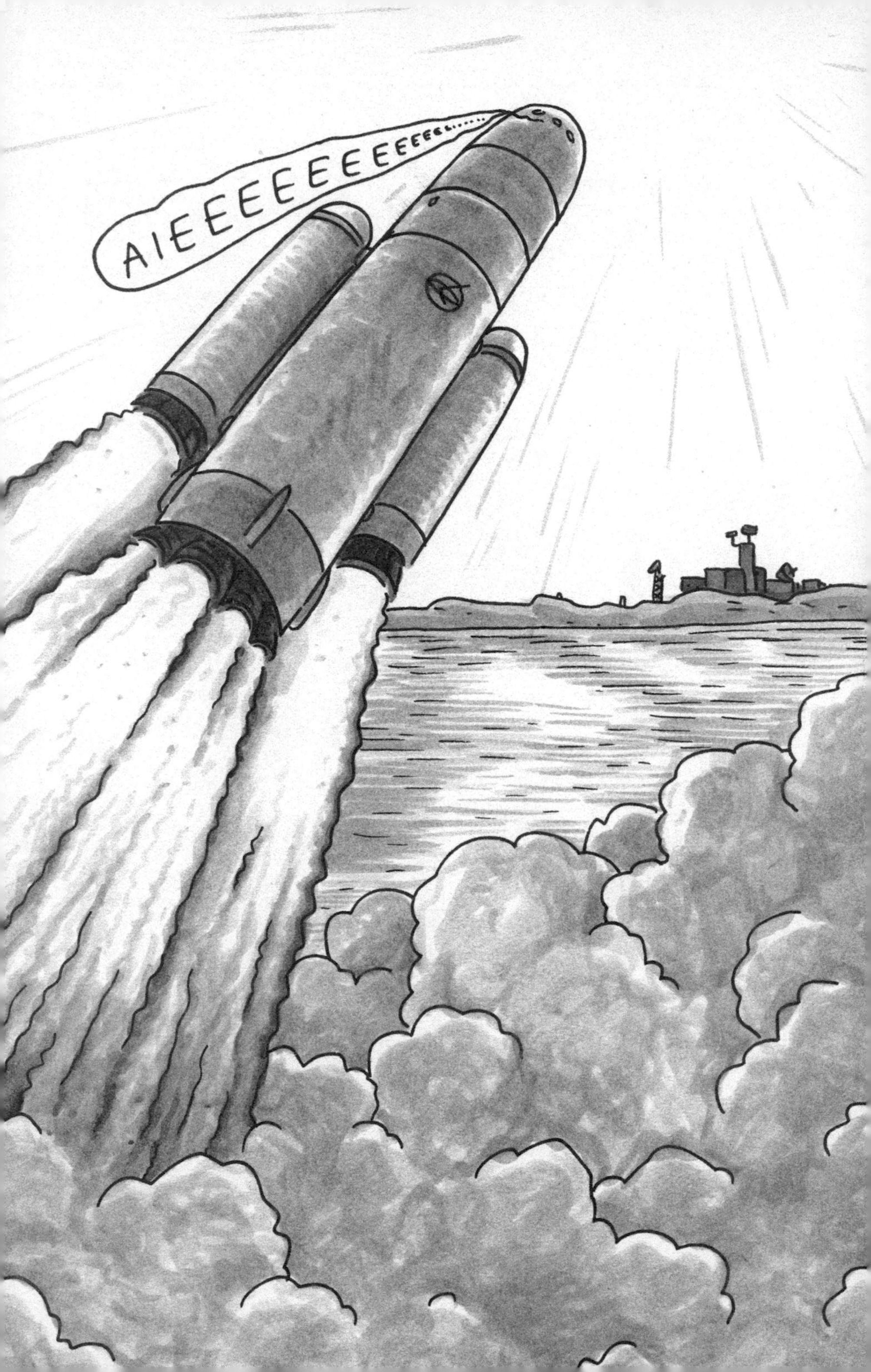
AIEEEEEEEEEEEEEE......

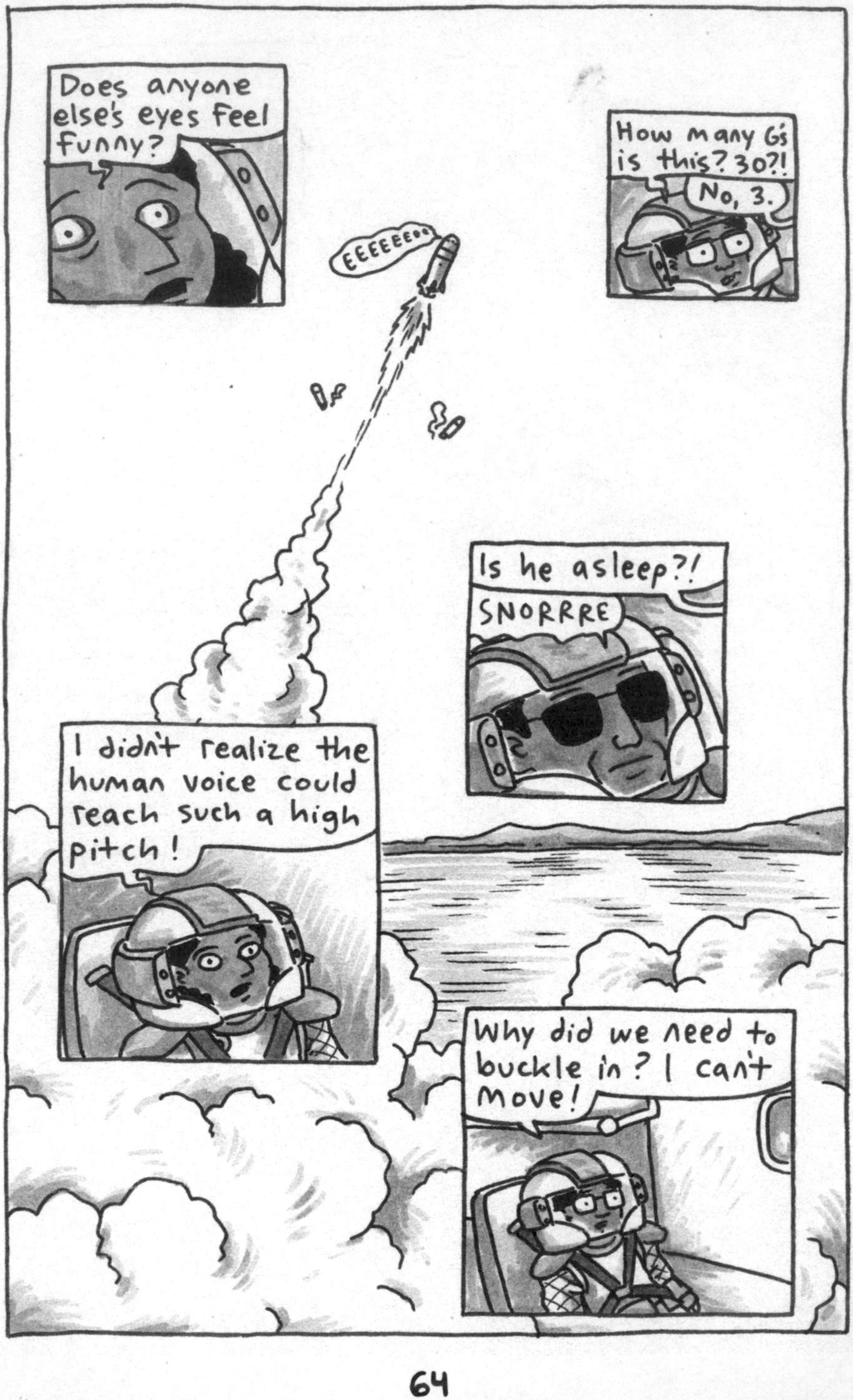
Does anyone else's eyes feel funny?
How many G's is this? 30?!
No, 3.
EEEEEEee
Is he asleep?!
SNORRRE
I didn't realize the human voice could reach such a high pitch!
Why did we need to buckle in? I can't move!

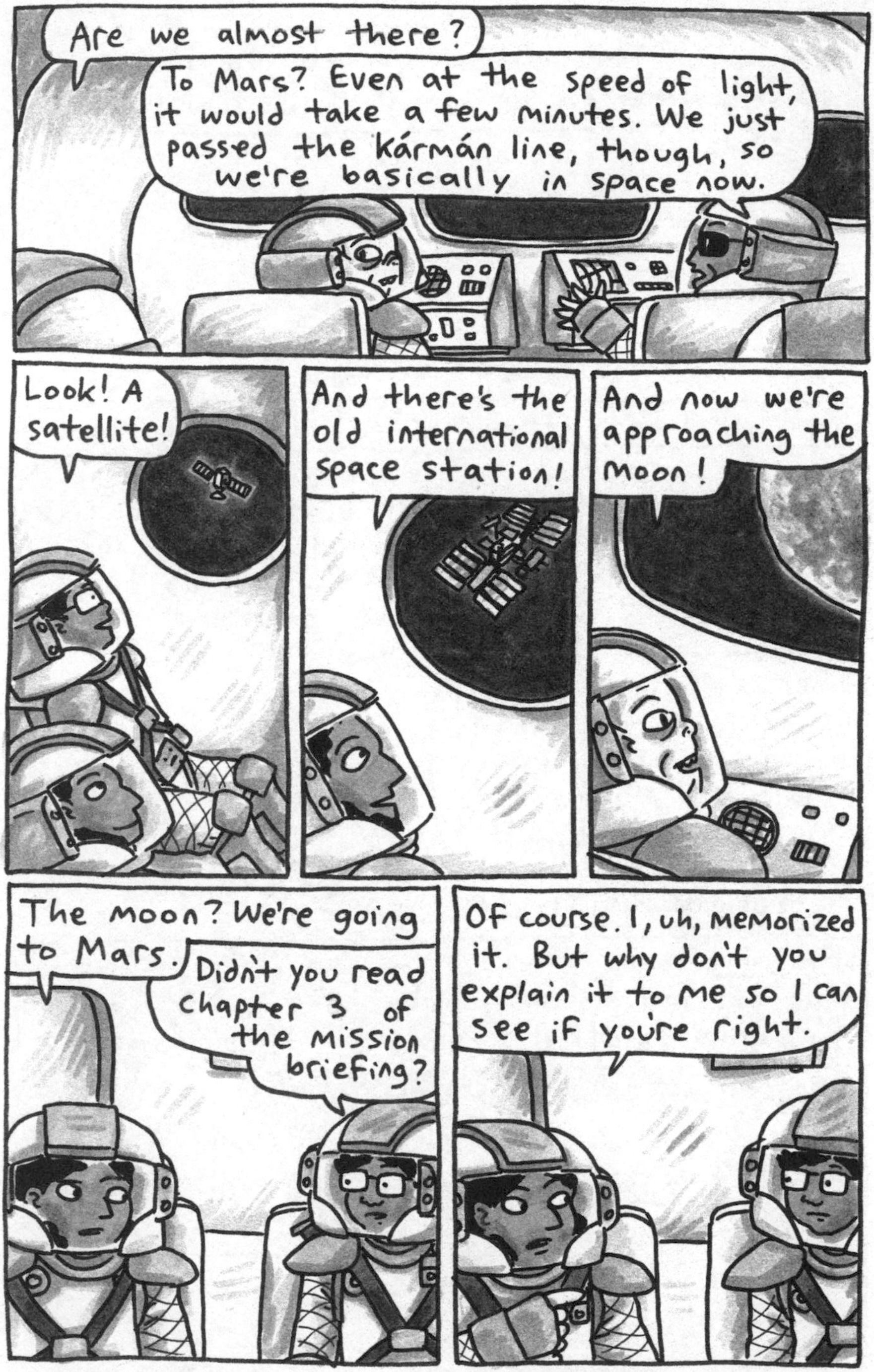

Are we almost there?
To Mars? Even at the speed of light, it would take a few minutes. We just passed the kármán line, though, so we're basically in space now.
Look! A satellite!
And there's the old international space station!
And now we're approaching the moon!
The moon? We're going to Mars.
Didn't you read chapter 3 of the mission briefing?
Of course. I, uh, memorized it. But why don't you explain it to me so I can see if you're right.

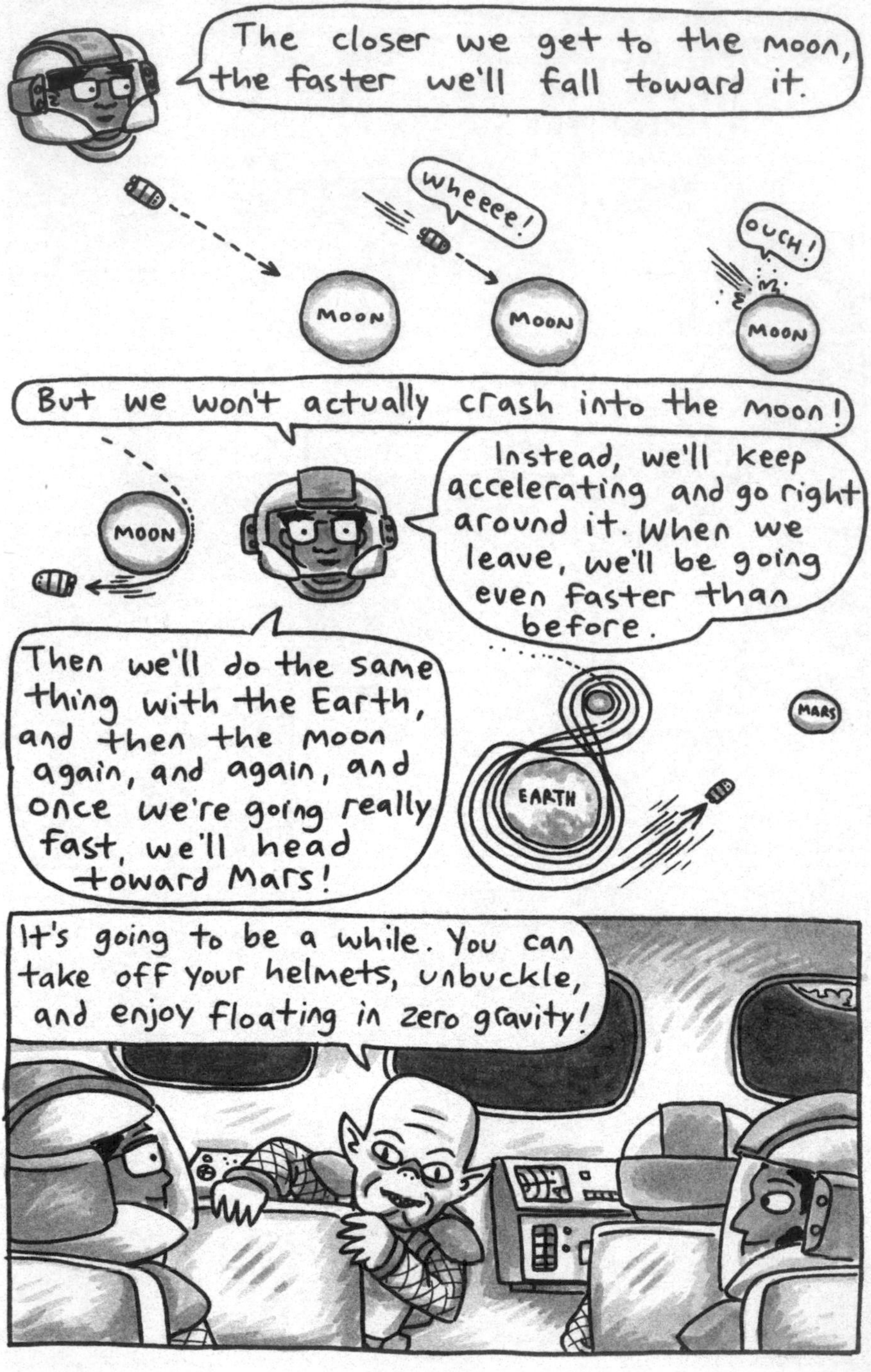
The closer we get to the moon, the faster we'll fall toward it.
wheeee!
OUCH!
MOON
MOON
MOON
But we won't actually crash into the moon!
Instead, we'll keep accelerating and go right around it. When we leave, we'll be going even faster than before.
MOON
Then we'll do the same thing with the Earth, and then the moon again, and again, and once we're going really fast, we'll head toward Mars!
EARTH
MARS
It's going to be a while. You can take off your helmets, unbuckle, and enjoy floating in zero gravity!

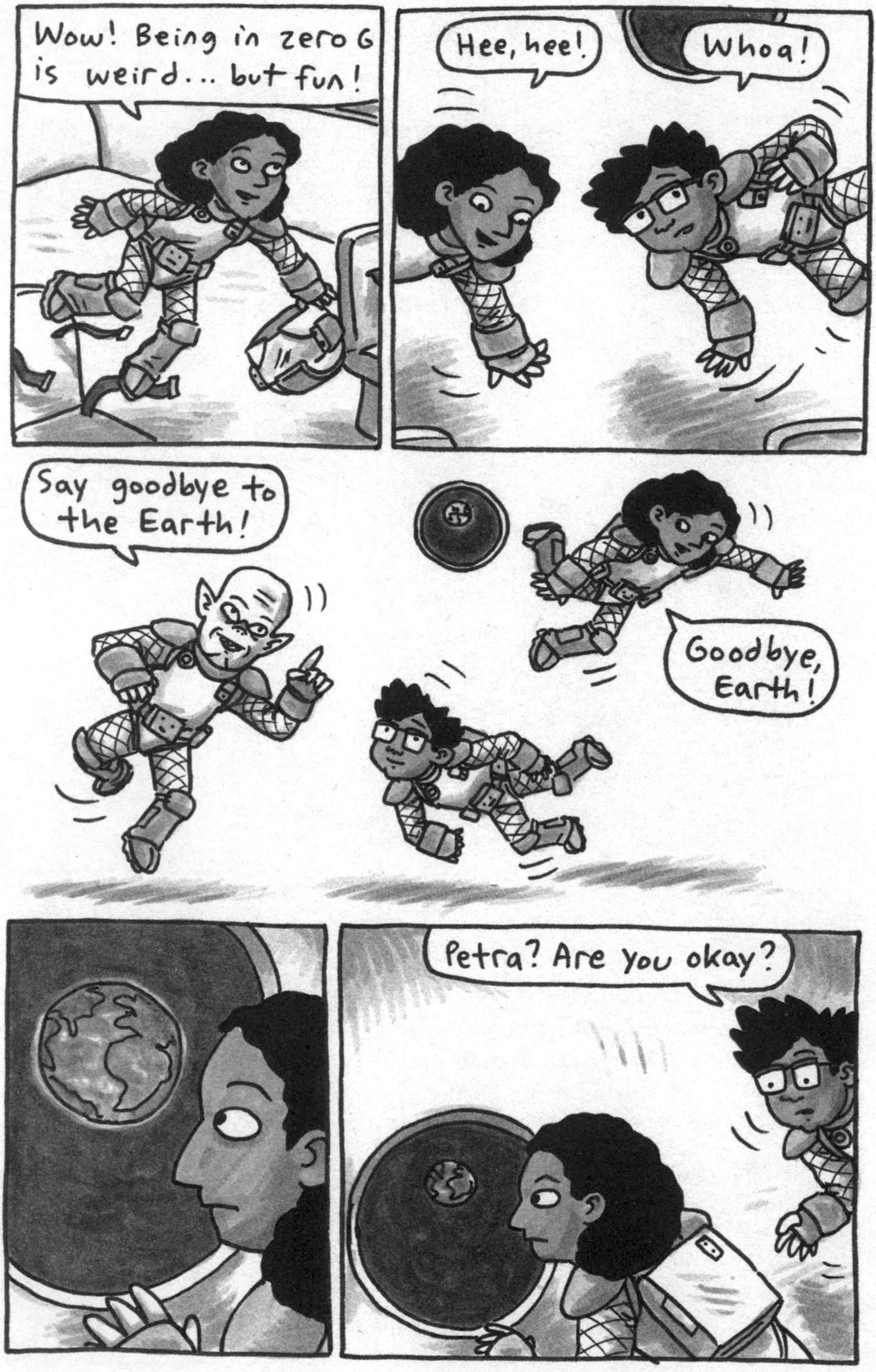

Wow! Being in zero G is weird... but fun!
Hee, hee!
Whoa!
Say goodbye to the Earth!
Goodbye, Earth!
Petra? Are you okay?

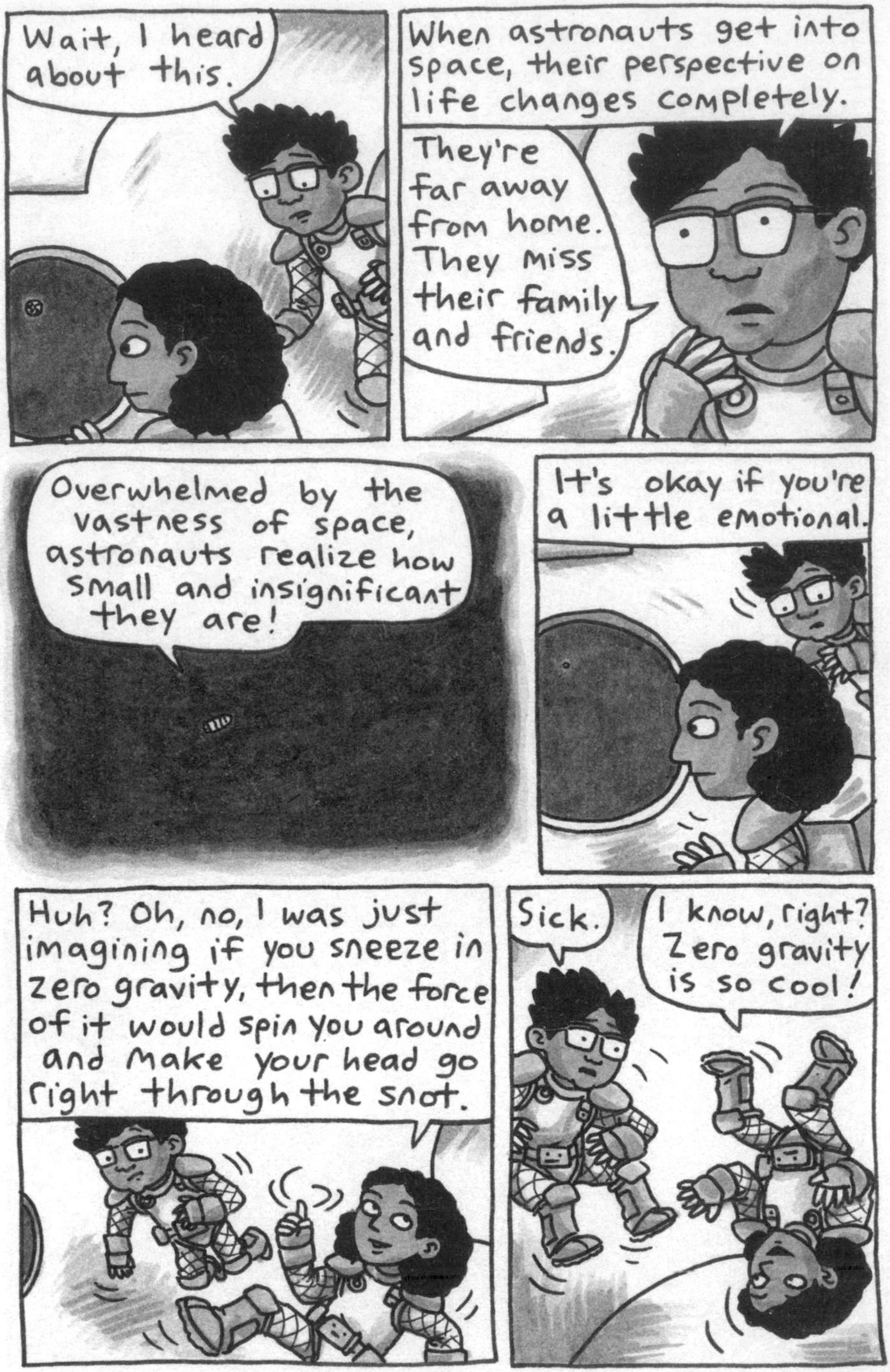
Wait, I heard about this.
When astronauts get into space, their perspective on life changes completely.
They're far away from home. They miss their family and friends.
Overwhelmed by the vastness of space, astronauts realize how small and insignificant they are!
It's okay if you're a little emotional.
Huh? Oh, no, I was just imagining if you sneeze in zero gravity, then the force of it would spin you around and make your head go right through the snot.
Sick.
I know, right? Zero gravity is so cool!

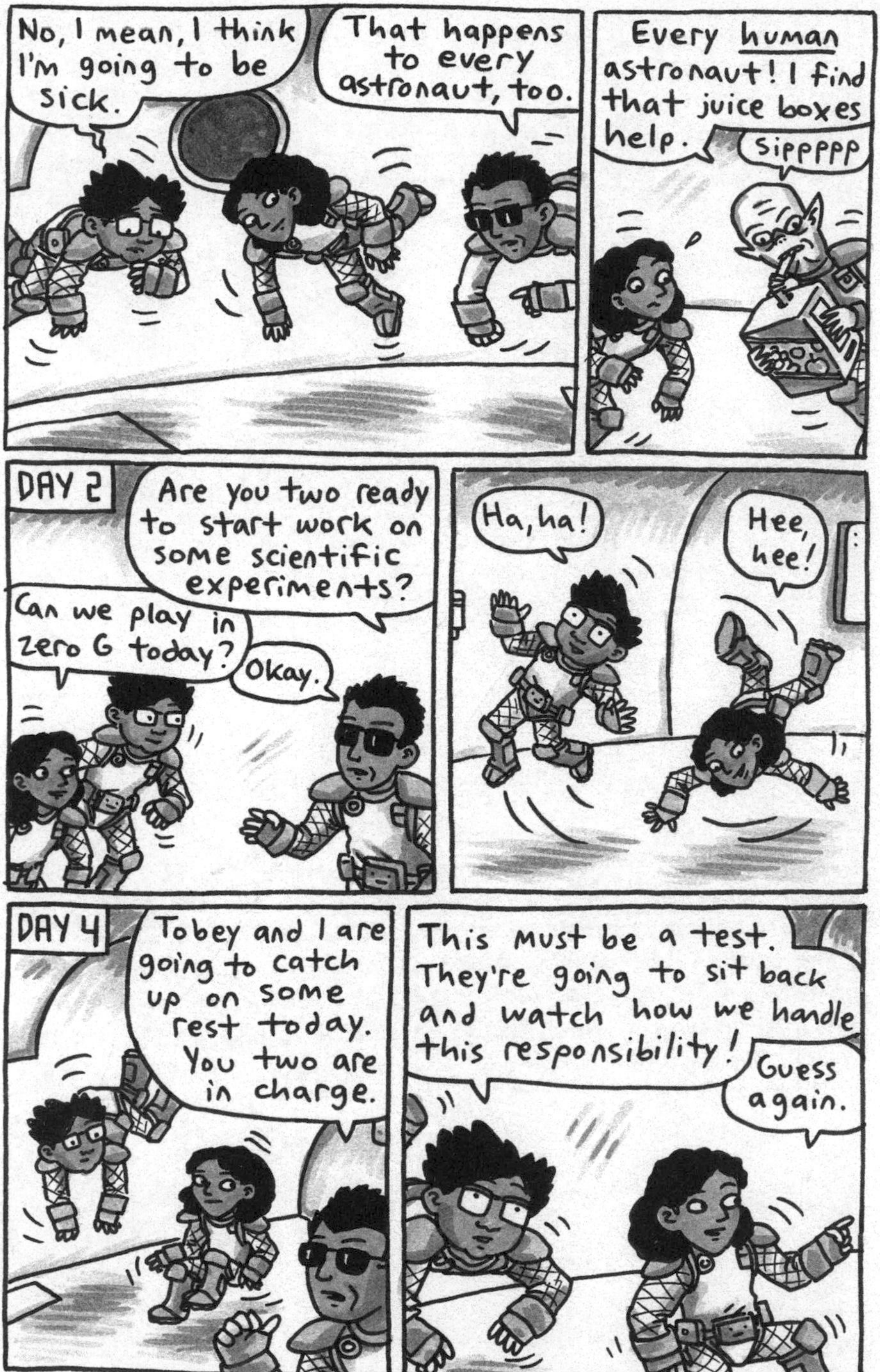
No, I mean, I think I'm going to be sick.
That happens to every astronaut, too.
Every human astronaut! I find that juice boxes help.
Sipppppp
DAY 2
Are you two ready to start work on some scientific experiments?
Can we play in zero G today?
Okay.
Ha, ha!
Hee, hee!
DAY 4
Tobey and I are going to catch up on some rest today. You two are in charge.
This must be a test. They're going to sit back and watch how we handle this responsibility!
Guess again.

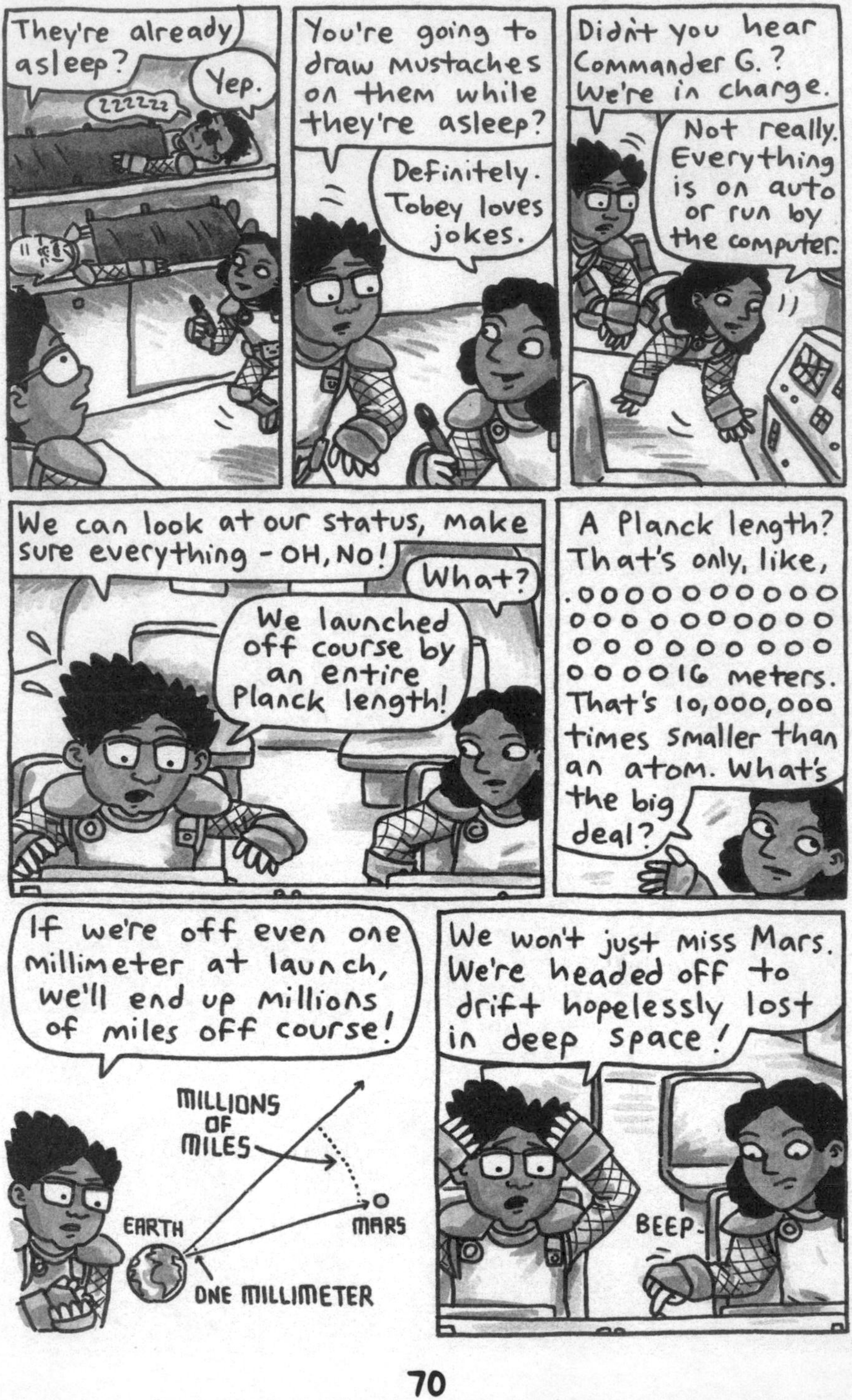
They're already asleep?
Yep.
ZZZZZZ
You're going to draw mustaches on them while they're asleep?
Definitely. Tobey loves jokes.
Didn't you hear Commander G.? We're in charge.
Not really. Everything is on auto or run by the computer.
We can look at our status, make sure everything - OH, NO!
What?
We launched off course by an entire Planck length!
A Planck length? That's only, like, .00000000000000000000000000000000016 meters. That's 10,000,000 times smaller than an atom. What's the big deal?
If we're off even one millimeter at launch, we'll end up millions of miles off course!
MILLIONS OF MILES
EARTH
MARS
ONE MILLIMETER
We won't just miss Mars. We're headed off to drift hopelessly lost in deep space!
BEEP-

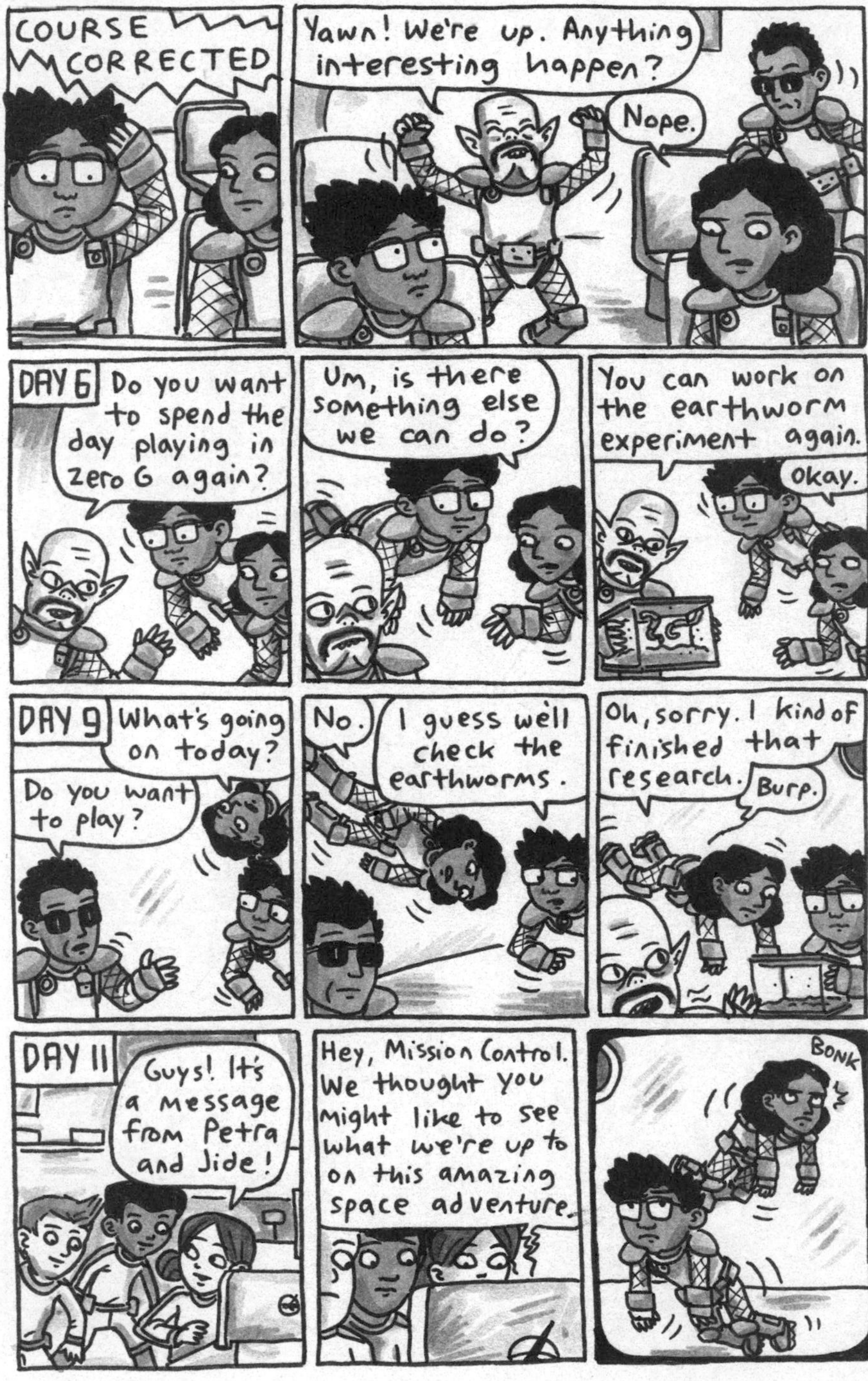
COURSE CORRECTED
Yawn! We're up. Anything interesting happen?
Nope.
DAY 6
Do you want to spend the day playing in zero G again?
Um, is there something else we can do?
You can work on the earthworm experiment again.
Okay.
DAY 9
What's going on today?
Do you want to play?
No.
I guess we'll check the earthworms.
Oh, sorry. I kind of finished that research.
Burp.
DAY 11
Guys! It's a message from Petra and Jide!
Hey, Mission Control. We thought you might like to see what we're up to on this amazing space adventure.
BONK

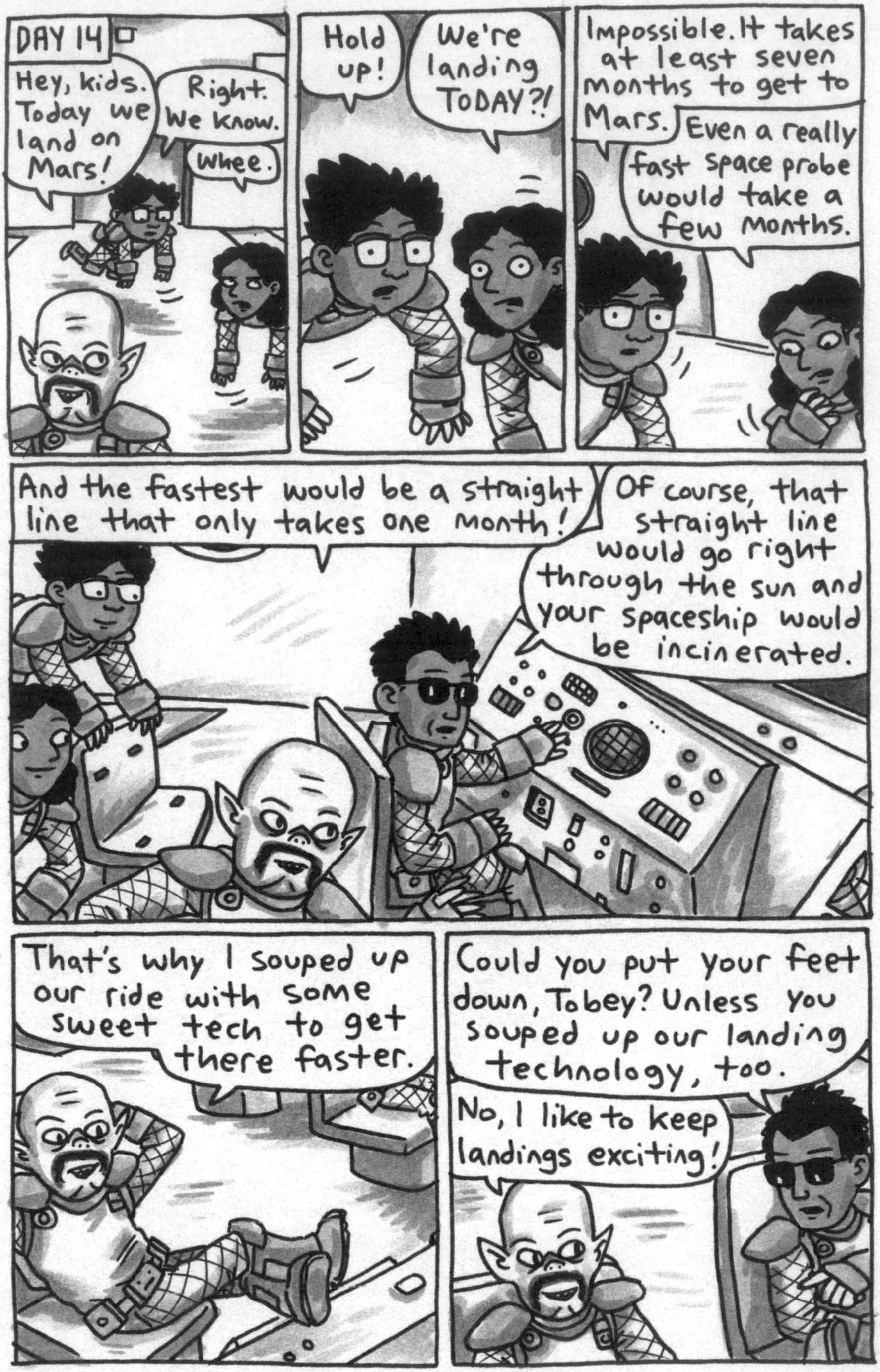
DAY 14
Hey, kids. Today we land on Mars!
Right. We know.
Whee.
Hold up!
We're landing TODAY?!
Impossible. It takes at least seven months to get to Mars.
Even a really fast space probe would take a few months.
And the fastest would be a straight line that only takes one month!
Of course, that straight line would go right through the sun and your spaceship would be incinerated.
That's why I souped up our ride with some sweet tech to get there faster.
Could you put your feet down, Tobey? Unless you souped up our landing technology, too.
No, I like to keep landings exciting!

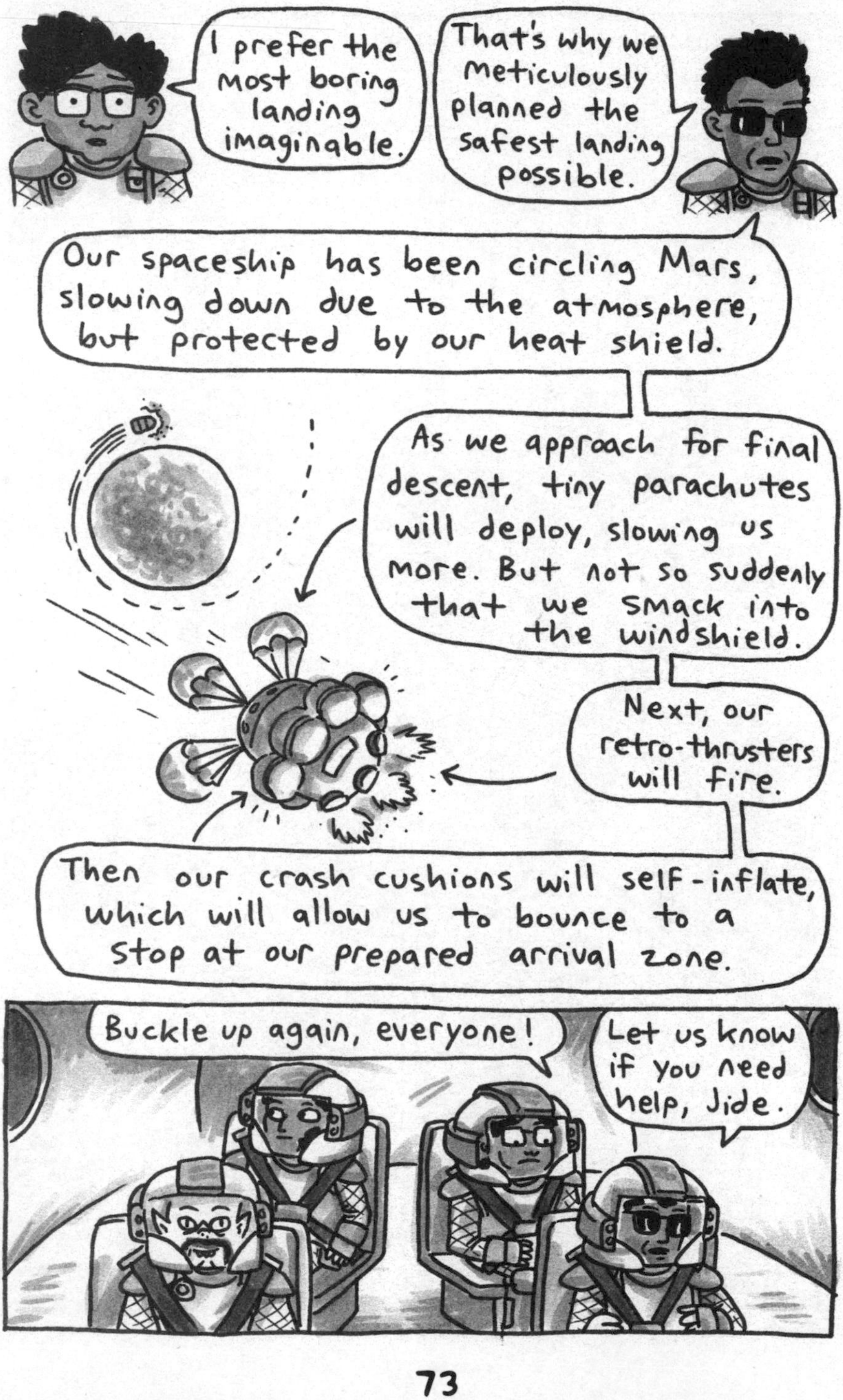

I prefer the most boring landing imaginable.
That's why we meticulously planned the safest landing possible.
Our spaceship has been circling Mars, slowing down due to the atmosphere, but protected by our heat shield.
As we approach for final descent, tiny parachutes will deploy, slowing us more. But not so suddenly that we smack into the windshield.
Next, our retro-thrusters will fire.
Then our crash cushions will self-inflate, which will allow us to bounce to a stop at our prepared arrival zone.
Buckle up again, everyone!
Let us know if you need help, Jide.

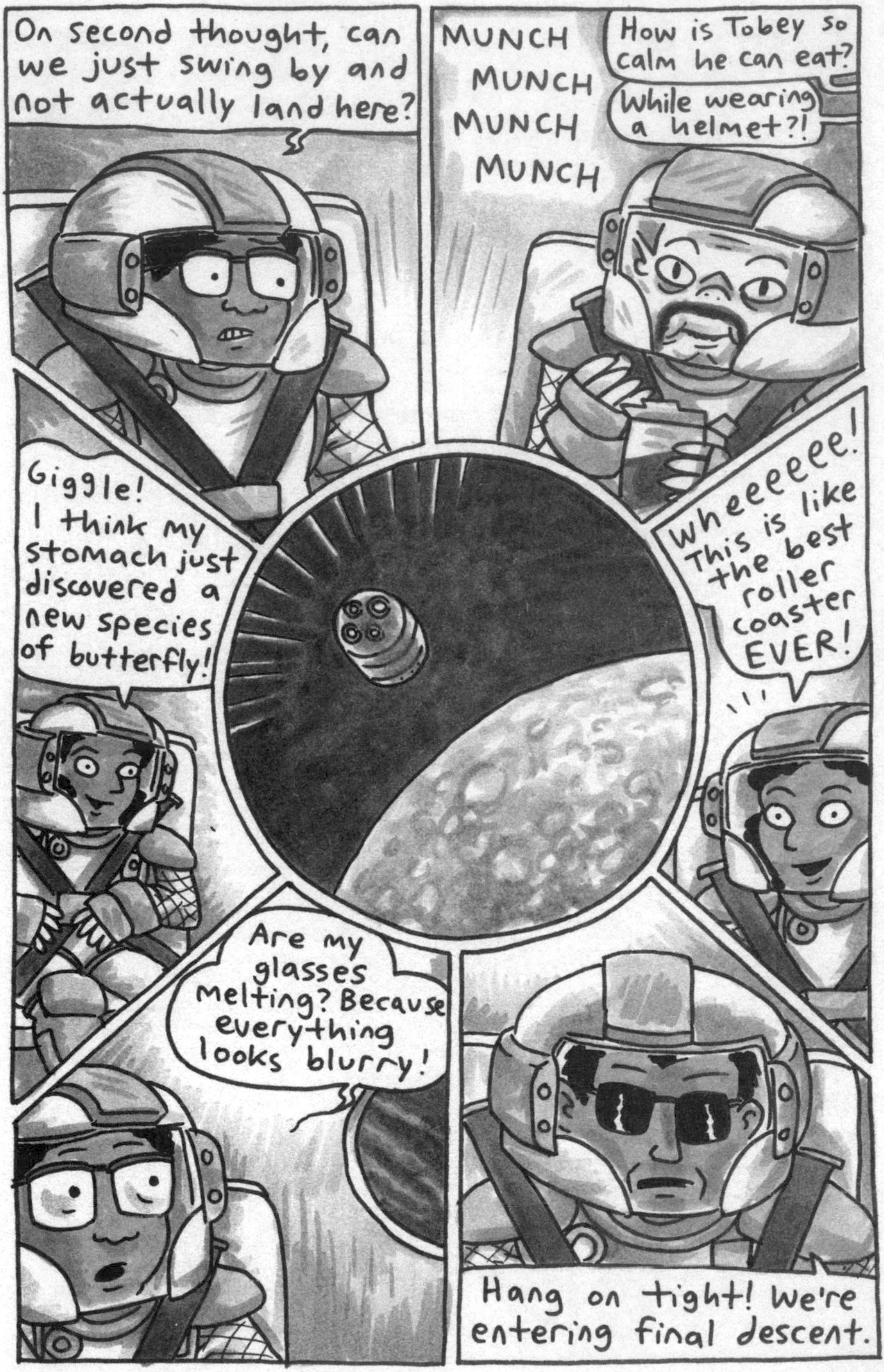
On second thought, can we just swing by and not actually land here?
MUNCH MUNCH MUNCH MUNCH
How is Tobey so calm he can eat?
While wearing a helmet?!
Giggle! I think my stomach just discovered a new species of butterfly!
wheeeeee! This is like the best roller coaster EVER!
Are my glasses melting? Because everything looks blurry!
Hang on tight! We're entering final descent.

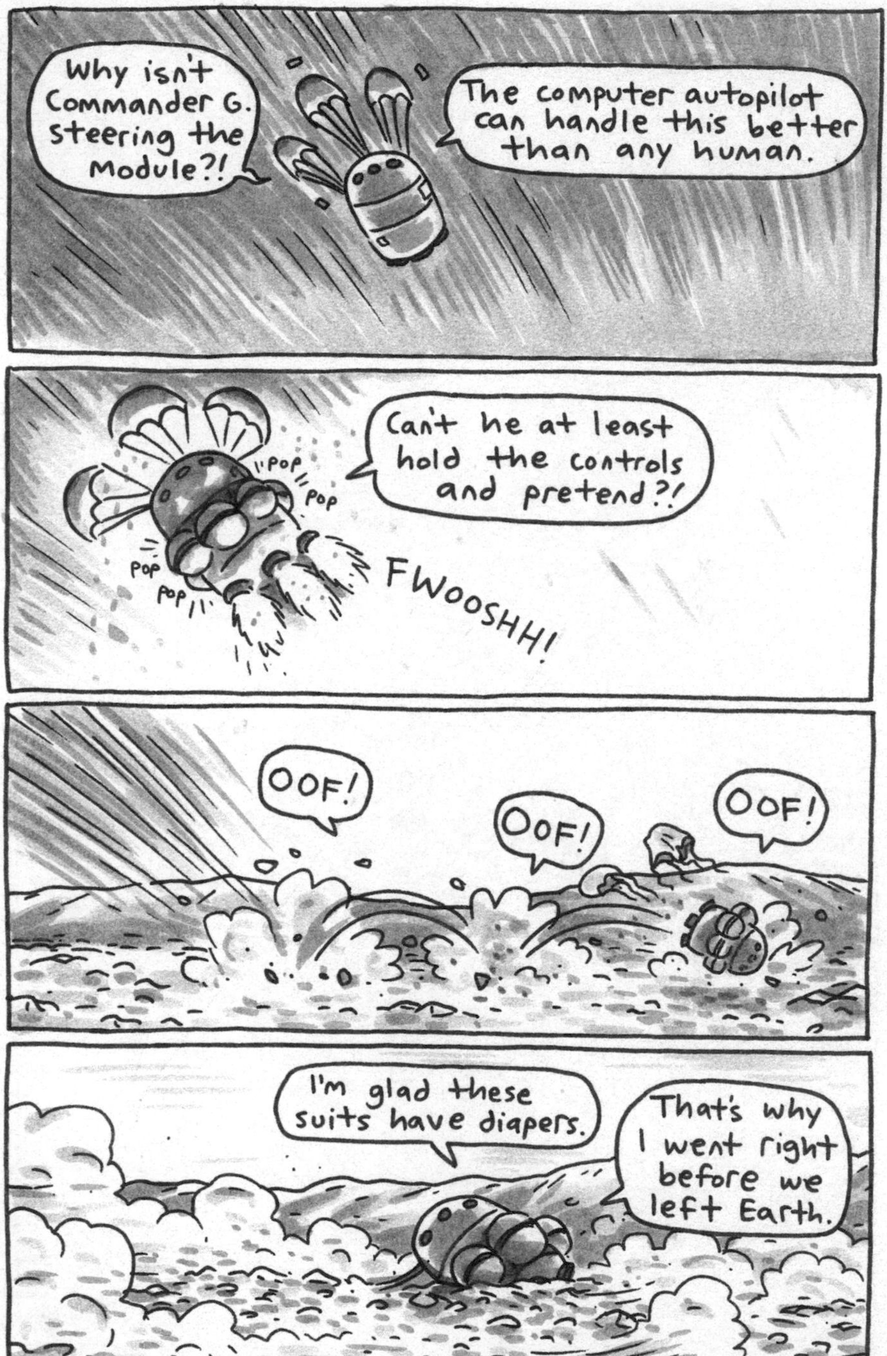

Why isn't Commander G. steering the Module?!
The computer autopilot can handle this better than any human.
Can't he at least hold the controls and pretend?!
POP
POP
POP
POP
FWOOSHH!
OOF!
OOF!
OOF!
I'm glad these suits have diapers.
That's why I went right before we left Earth.

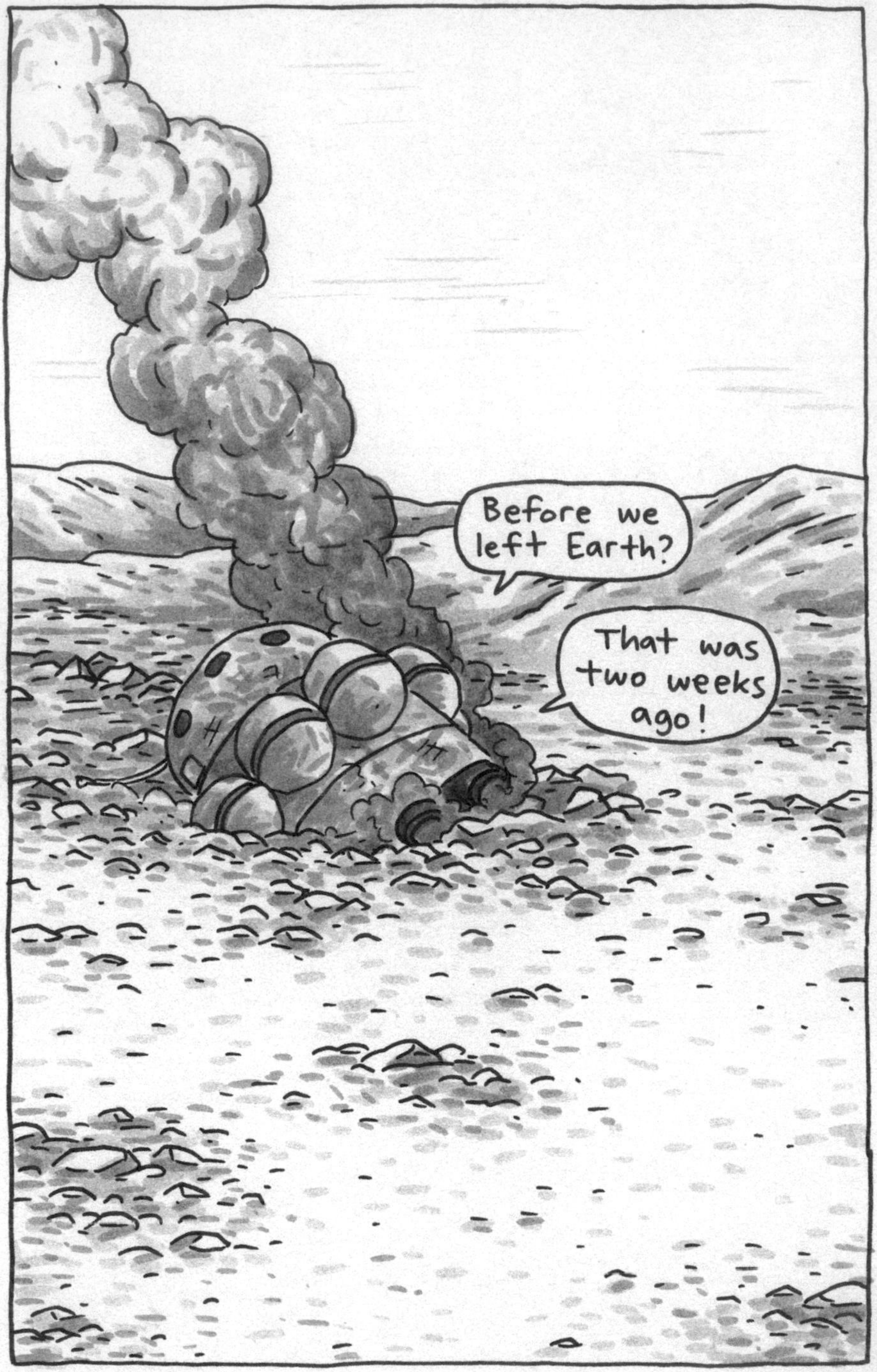
Before we left Earth?
That was two weeks ago!

RED CARPET ON THE RED PLANET

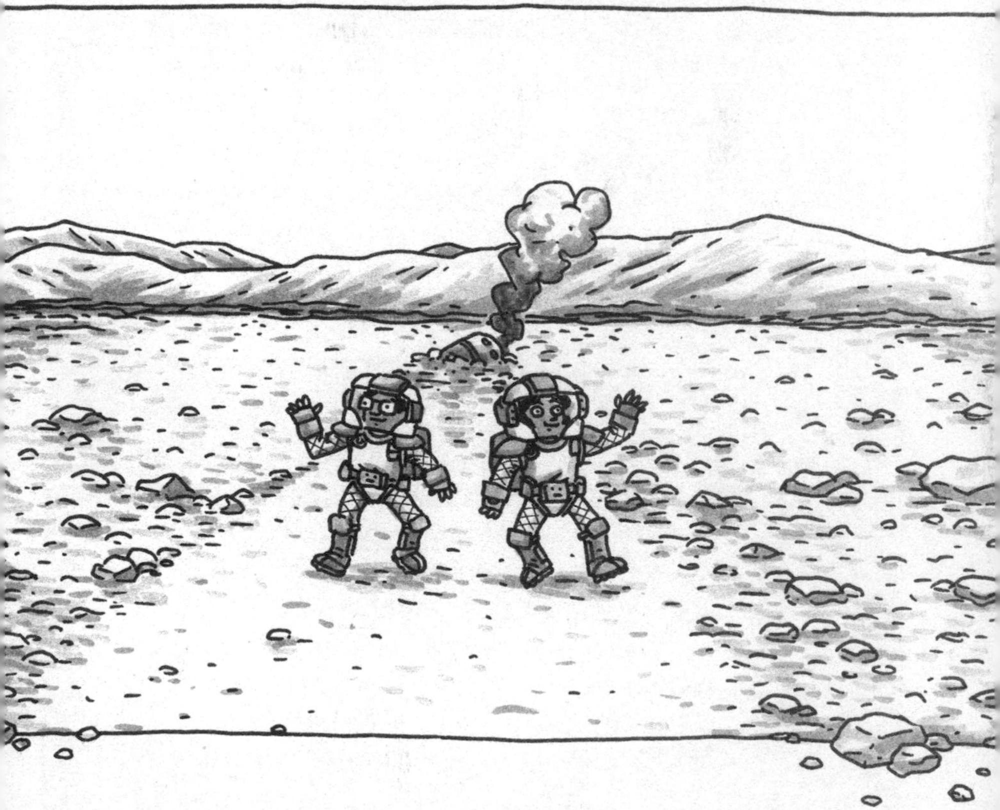

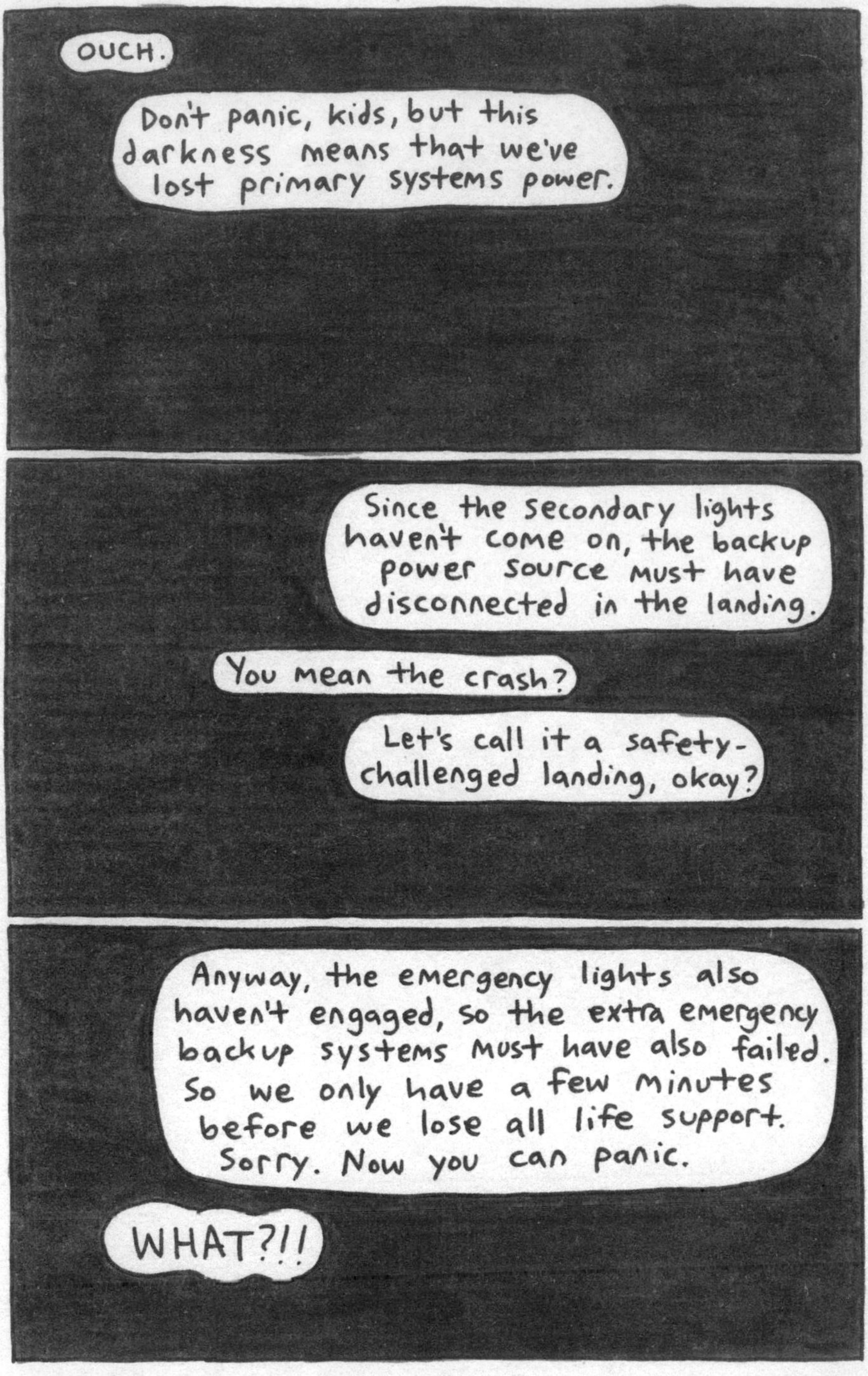
OUCH.
Don't panic, kids, but this darkness means that we've lost primary systems power.
Since the secondary lights haven't come on, the backup power source must have disconnected in the landing.
You mean the crash?
Let's call it a safety-challenged landing, okay?
Anyway, the emergency lights also haven't engaged, so the extra emergency backup systems must have also failed. So we only have a few minutes before we lose all life support. Sorry. Now you can panic.
WHAT?!!

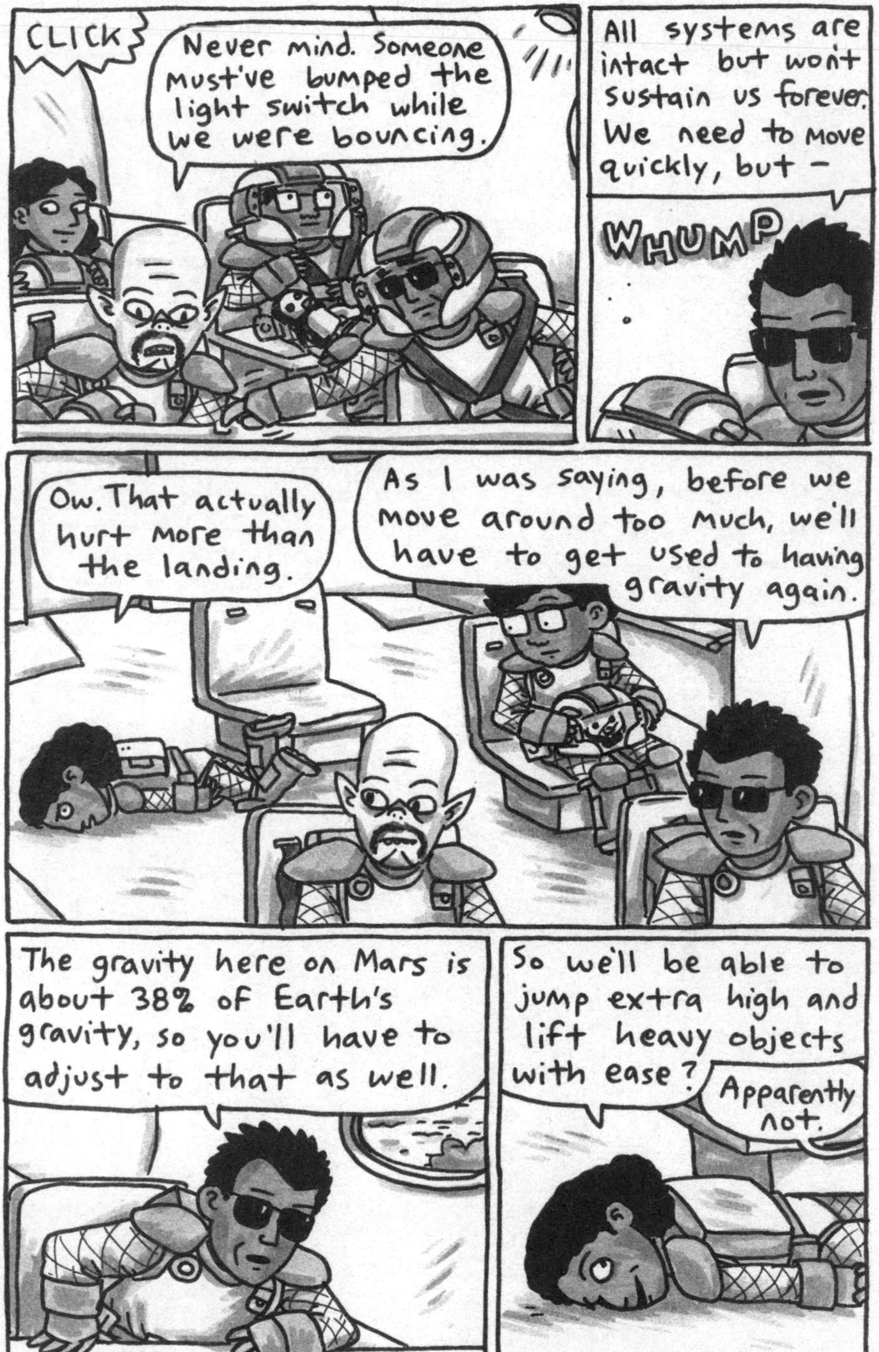
CLICK
Never mind. Someone must've bumped the light switch while we were bouncing.
All systems are intact but won't sustain us forever. We need to move quickly, but -
WHUMP
Ow. That actually hurt more than the landing.
As I was saying, before we move around too much, we'll have to get used to having gravity again.
The gravity here on Mars is about 38% of Earth's gravity, so you'll have to adjust to that as well.
So we'll be able to jump extra high and lift heavy objects with ease?
Apparently not.

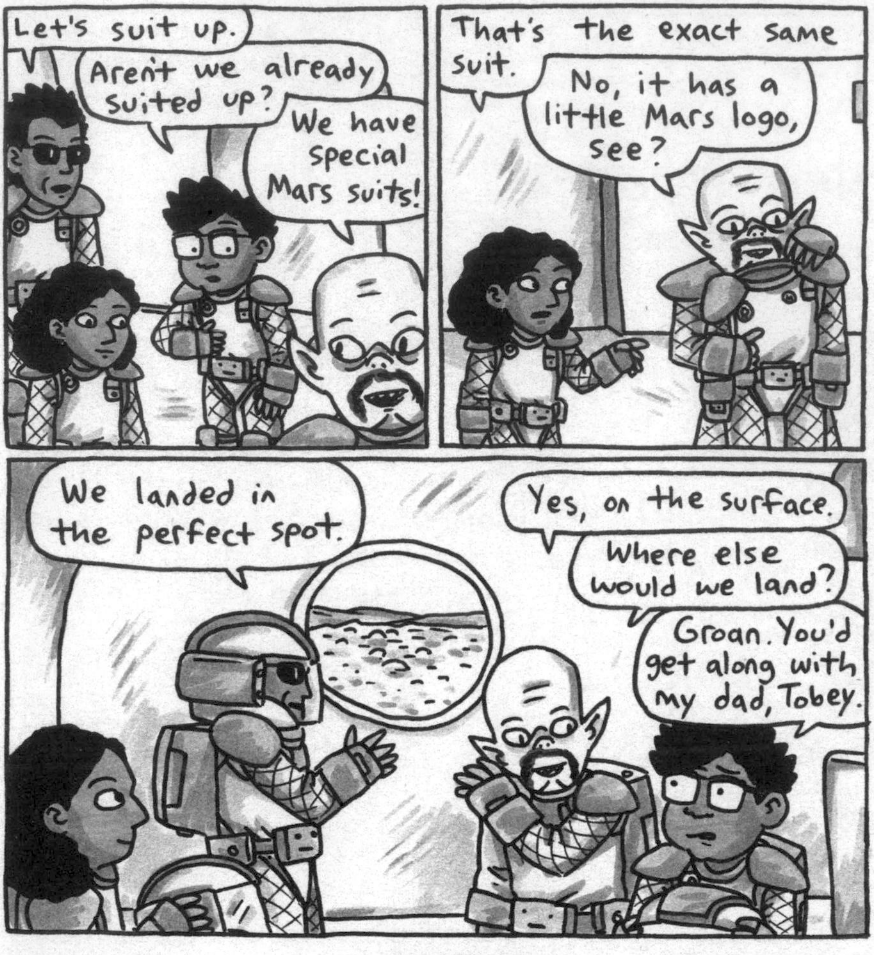
Let's suit up.
Aren't we already suited up?
We have special Mars suits!
That's the exact same suit.
No, it has a little Mars logo, see?
We landed in the perfect spot.
Yes, on the surface.
Where else would we land?
Groan. You'd get along with my dad, Tobey.

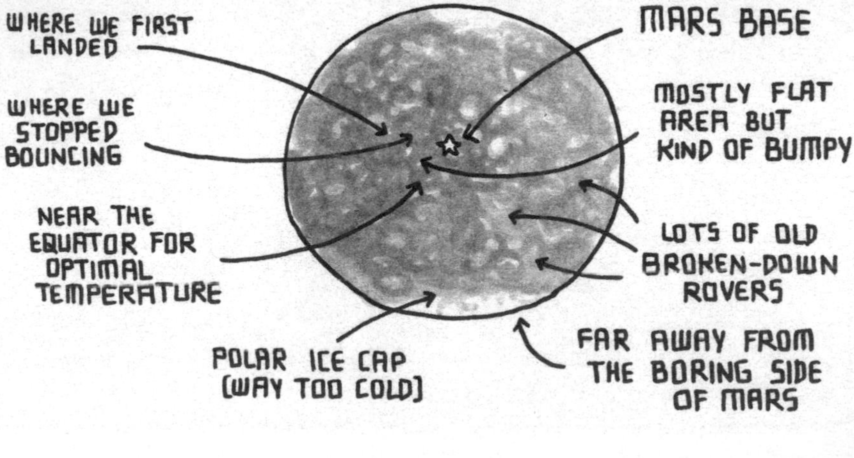
WHERE WE FIRST LANDED
WHERE WE STOPPED BOUNCING
NEAR THE EQUATOR FOR OPTIMAL TEMPERATURE
POLAR ICE CAP (WAY TOO COLD)
MARS BASE
MOSTLY FLAT AREA BUT KIND OF BUMPY
LOTS OF OLD BROKEN-DOWN ROVERS
FAR AWAY FROM THE BORING SIDE OF MARS

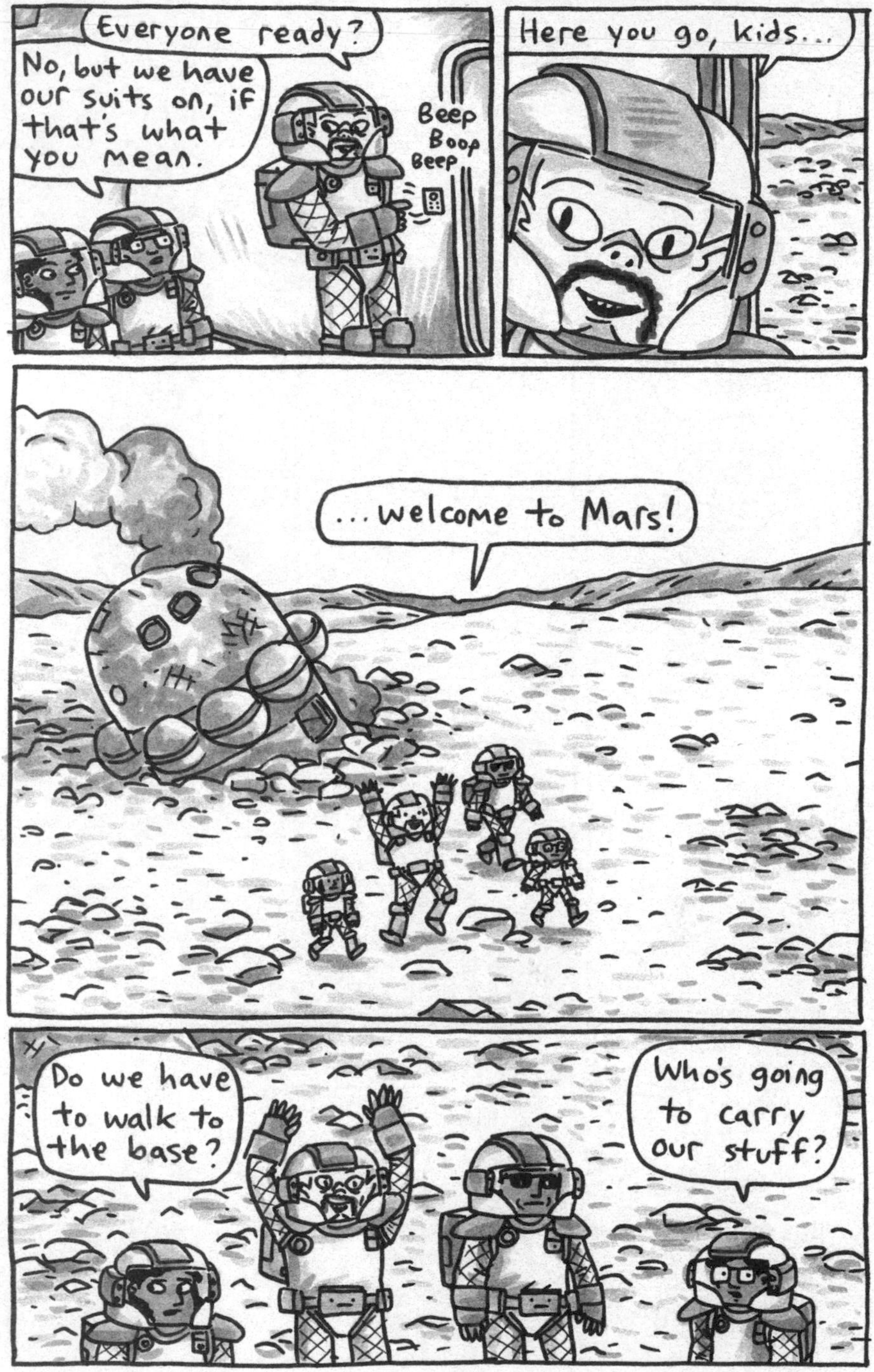
Everyone ready?
No, but we have our suits on, if that's what you mean.
Beep Boop Beep
Here you go, kids...
...welcome to Mars!
Do we have to walk to the base?
Who's going to carry our stuff?

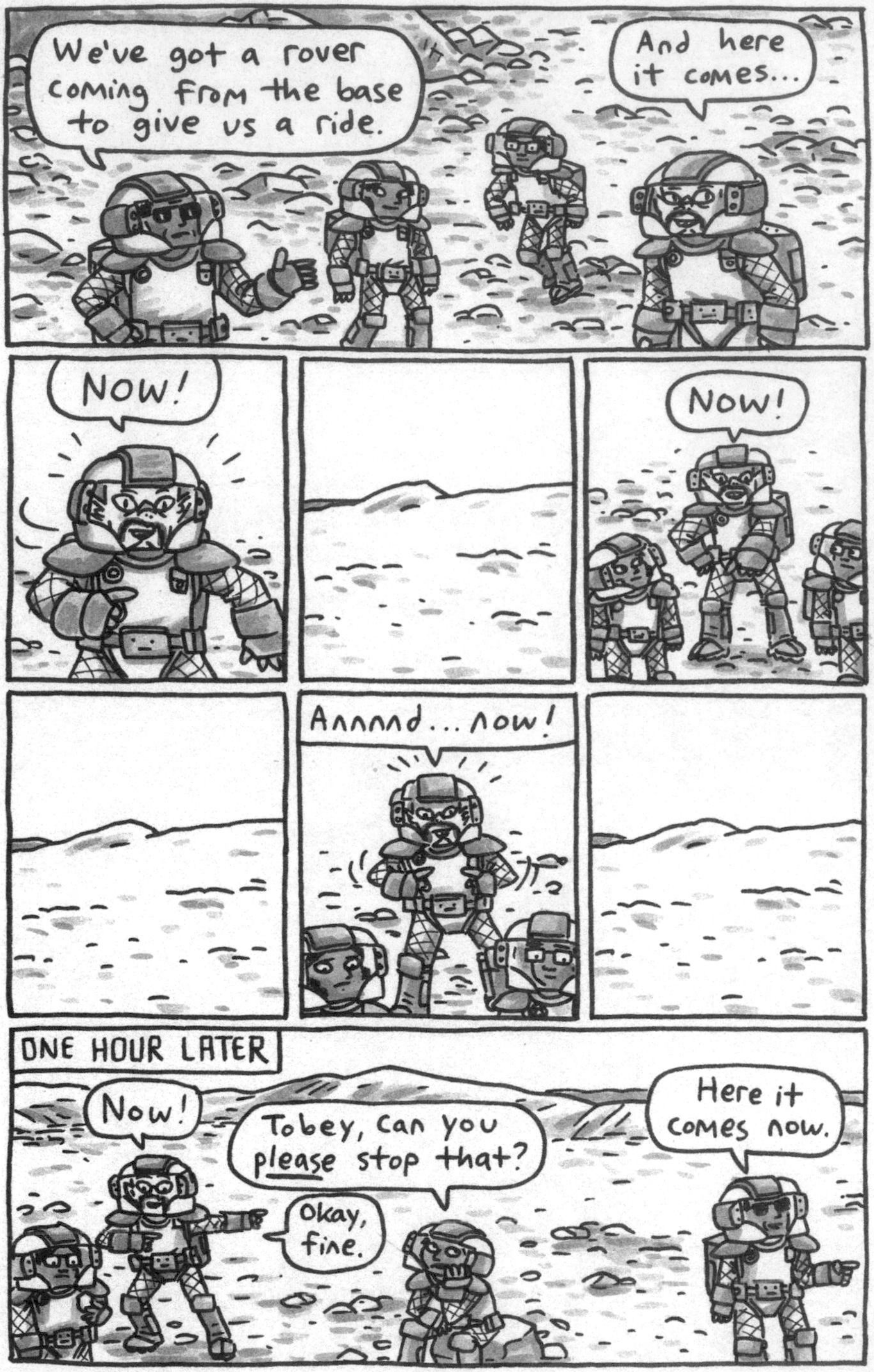
We've got a rover coming from the base to give us a ride.
And here it comes...
NOW!
NOW!
Annnnd... now!
ONE HOUR LATER
Now!
Tobey, can you please stop that?
Okay, fine.
Here it comes now.

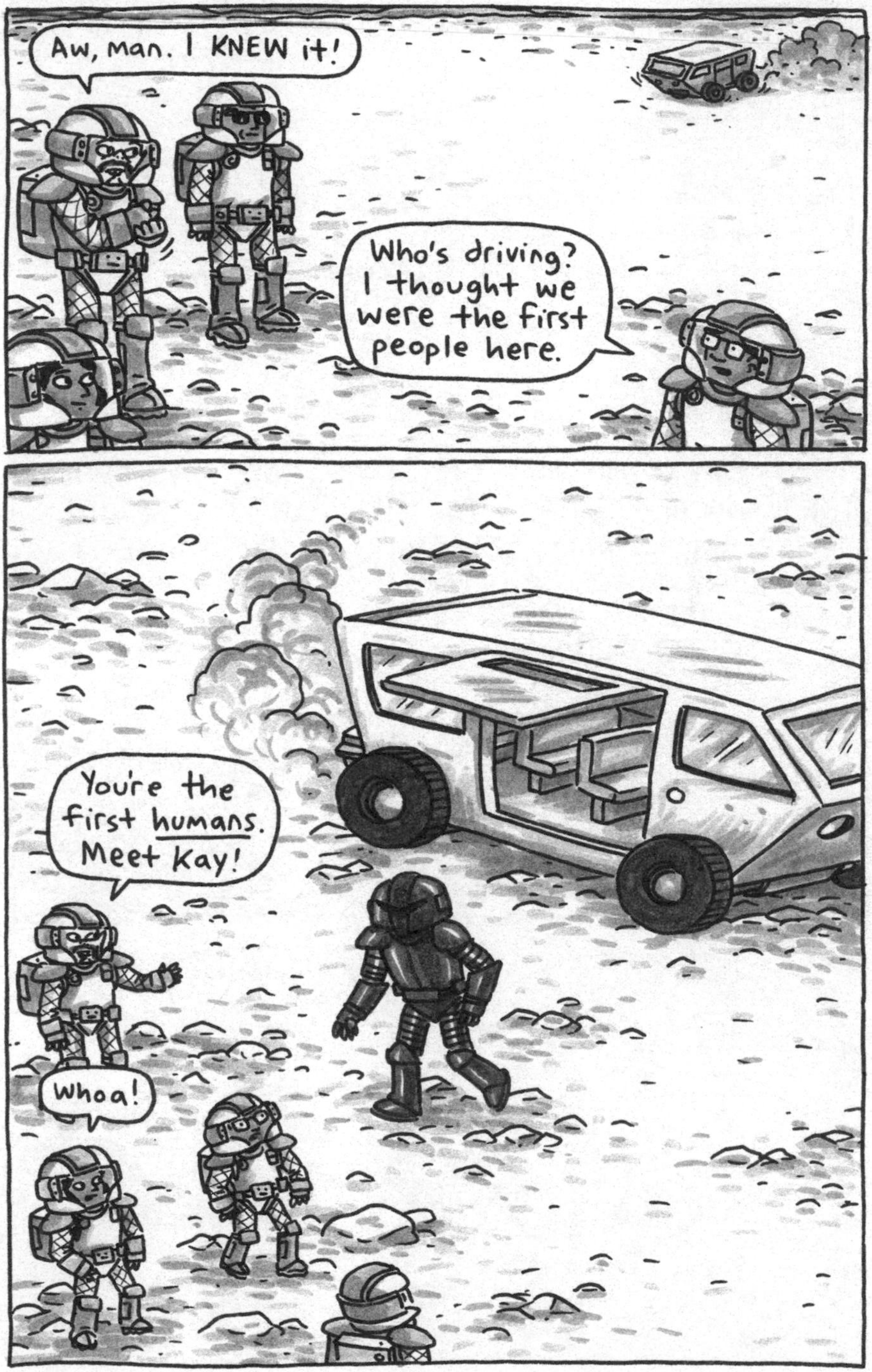
Aw, man. I KNEW it!
Who's driving? I thought we were the first people here.
You're the first humans. Meet Kay!
Whoa!

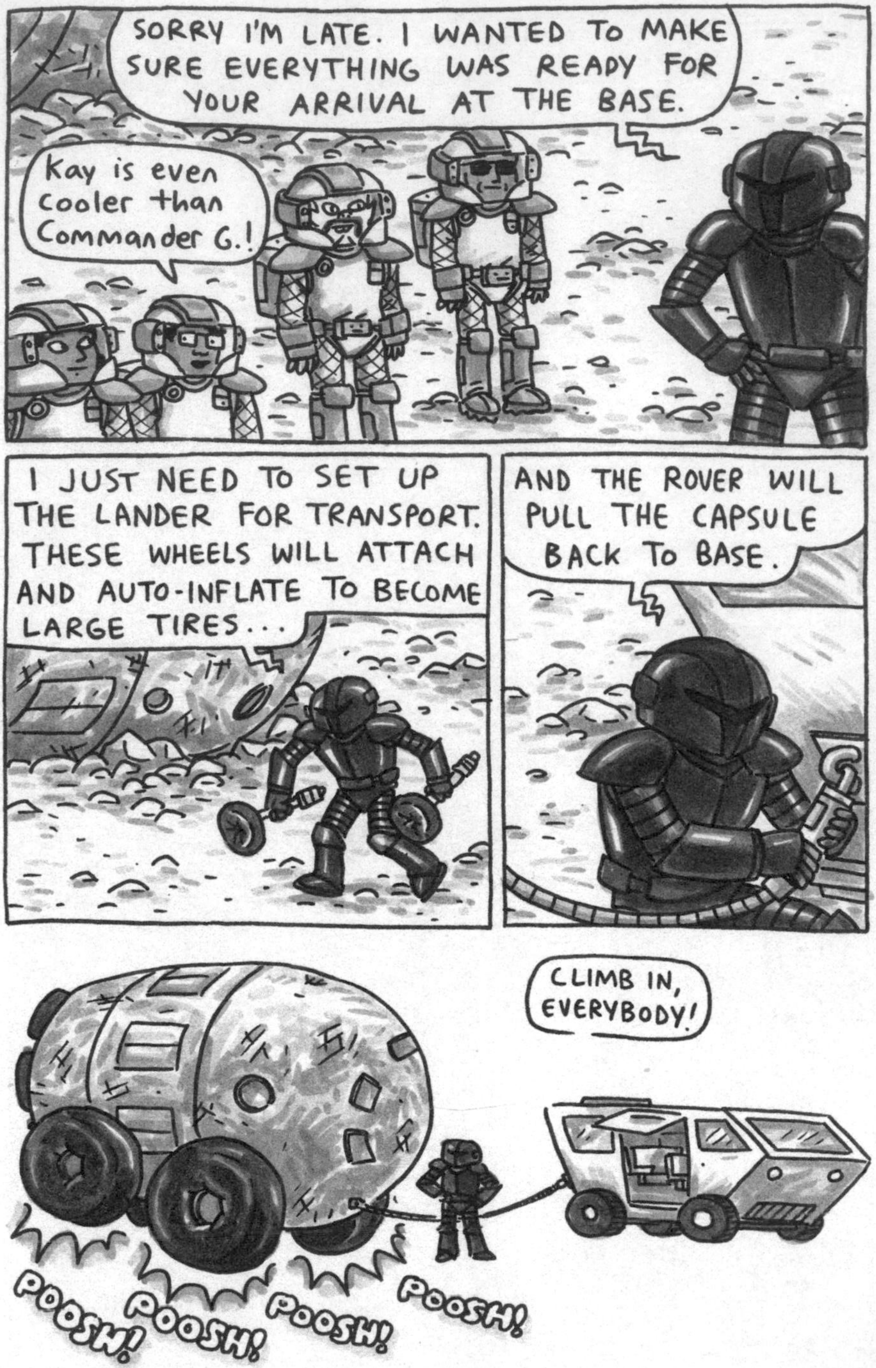
SORRY I'M LATE. I WANTED TO MAKE SURE EVERYTHING WAS READY FOR YOUR ARRIVAL AT THE BASE.
Kay is even cooler than Commander G.!
I JUST NEED TO SET UP THE LANDER FOR TRANSPORT. THESE WHEELS WILL ATTACH AND AUTO-INFLATE TO BECOME LARGE TIRES...
AND THE ROVER WILL PULL THE CAPSULE BACK TO BASE.
CLIMB IN, EVERYBODY!
POOSH!
POOSH!
POOSH!
POOSH!

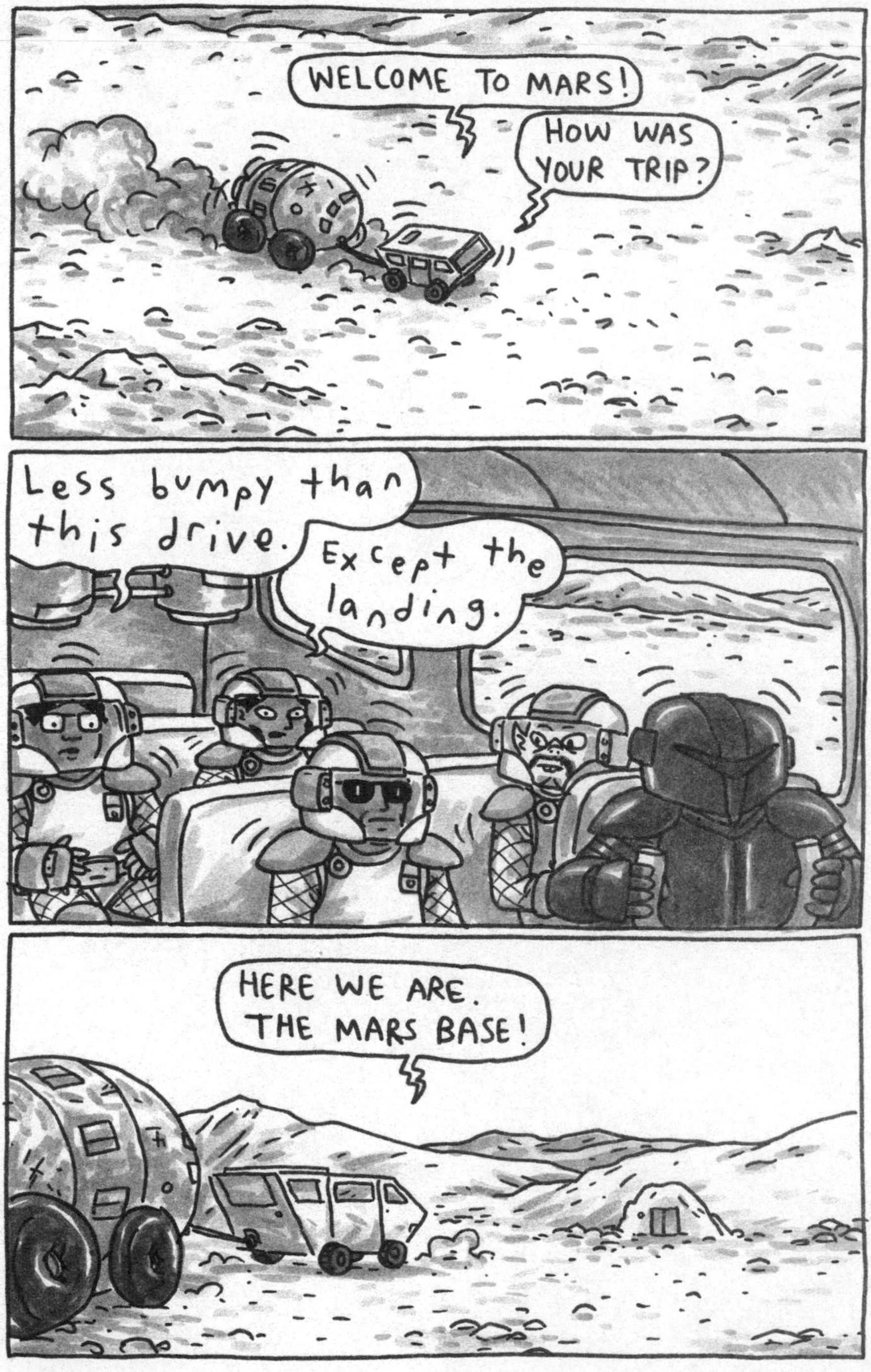
WELCOME TO MARS!
HOW WAS YOUR TRIP?
Less bumpy than this drive.
Except the landing.
HERE WE ARE. THE MARS BASE!

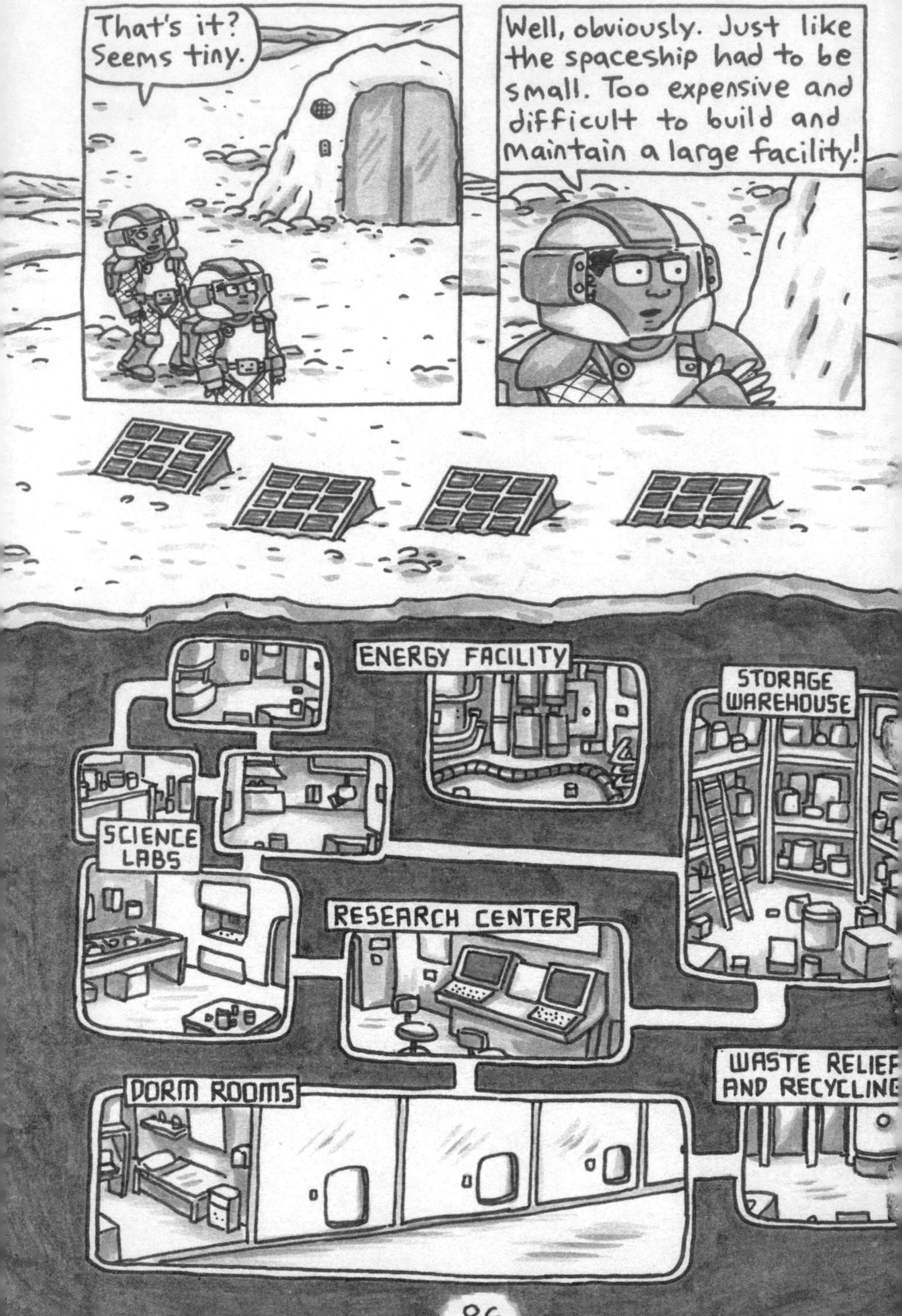
That's it? Seems tiny.
Well, obviously. Just like the spaceship had to be small. Too expensive and difficult to build and maintain a large facility!
ENERGY FACILITY
STORAGE WAREHOUSE
SCIENCE LABS
RESEARCH CENTER
DORM ROOMS
WASTE RELIEF AND RECYCLING

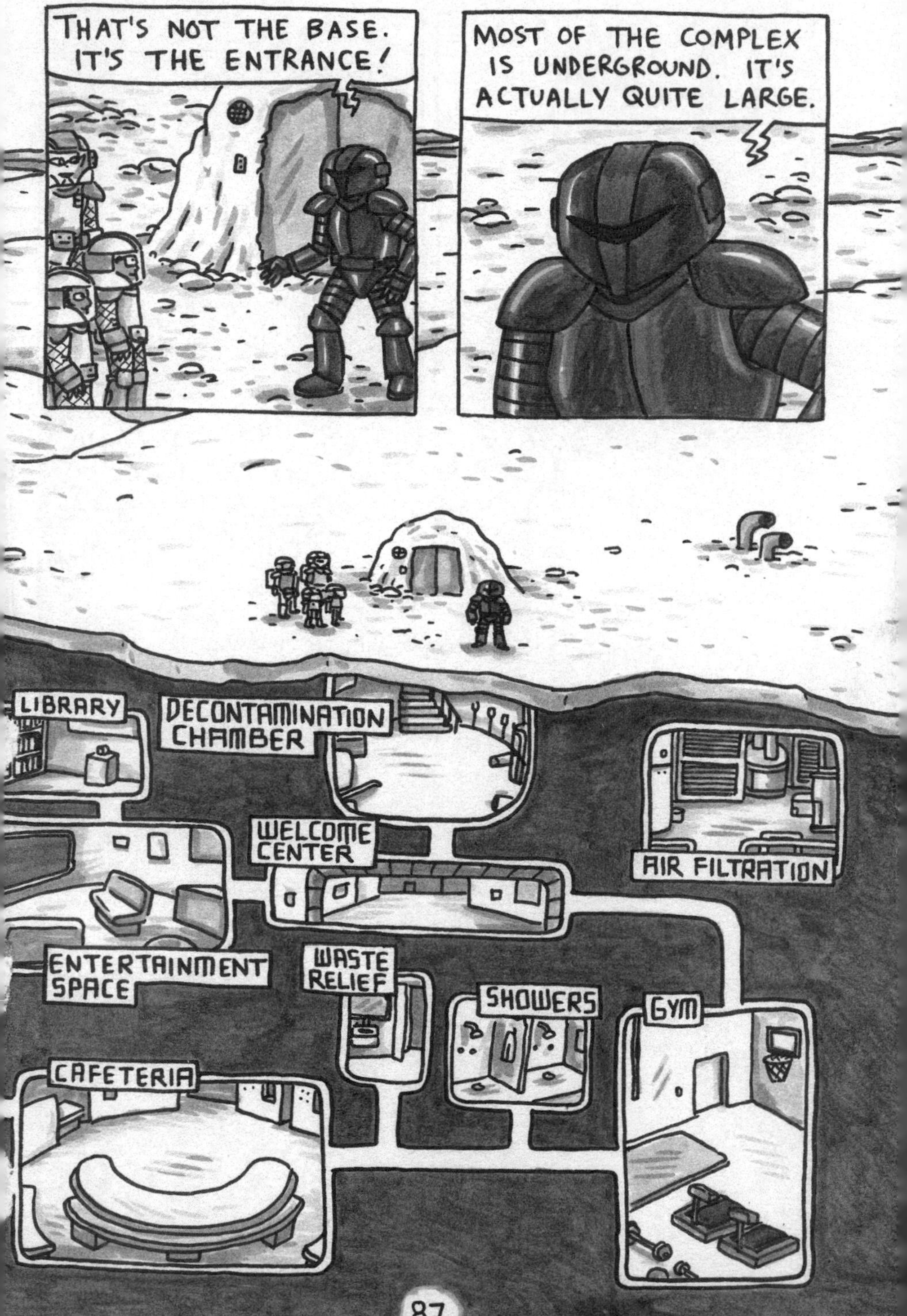
THAT'S NOT THE BASE. IT'S THE ENTRANCE!
MOST OF THE COMPLEX IS UNDERGROUND. IT'S ACTUALLY QUITE LARGE.
LIBRARY
DECONTAMINATION CHAMBER
WELCOME CENTER
AIR FILTRATION
ENTERTAINMENT SPACE
WASTE RELIEF
SHOWERS
GYM
CAFETERIA

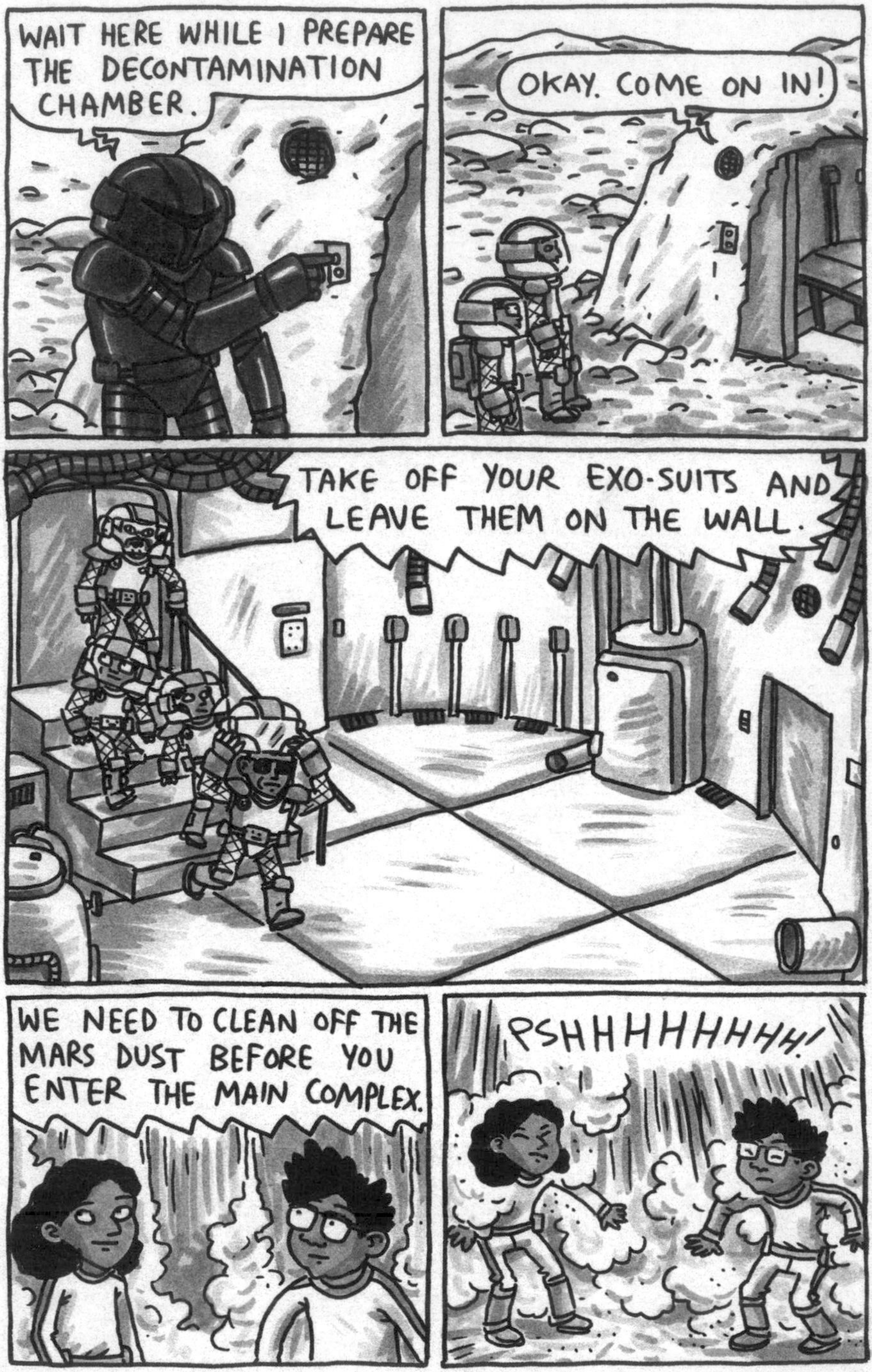
WAIT HERE WHILE I PREPARE THE DECONTAMINATION CHAMBER.
OKAY. COME ON IN!
TAKE OFF YOUR EXO-SUITS AND LEAVE THEM ON THE WALL.
WE NEED TO CLEAN OFF THE MARS DUST BEFORE YOU ENTER THE MAIN COMPLEX.
PSHHHHHHHH!

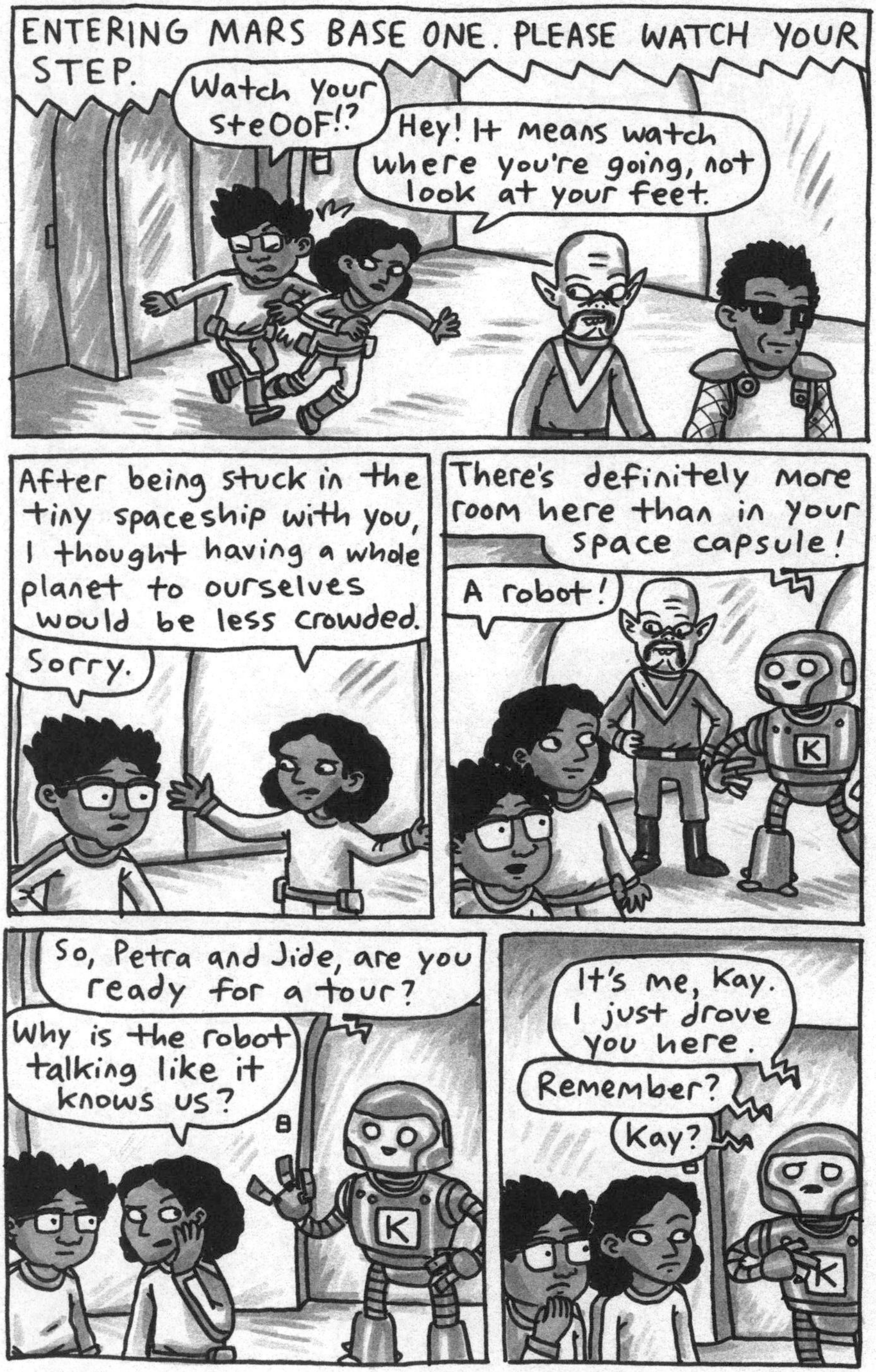
ENTERING MARS BASE ONE. PLEASE WATCH YOUR STEP.
Watch your steOOF!?
Hey! It means watch where you're going, not look at your feet.
After being stuck in the tiny spaceship with you, I thought having a whole planet to ourselves would be less crowded.
Sorry.
There's definitely more room here than in your space capsule!
A robot!
K
So, Petra and Jide, are you ready for a tour?
Why is the robot talking like it knows us?
K
It's me, Kay. I just drove you here.
Remember?
Kay?
K

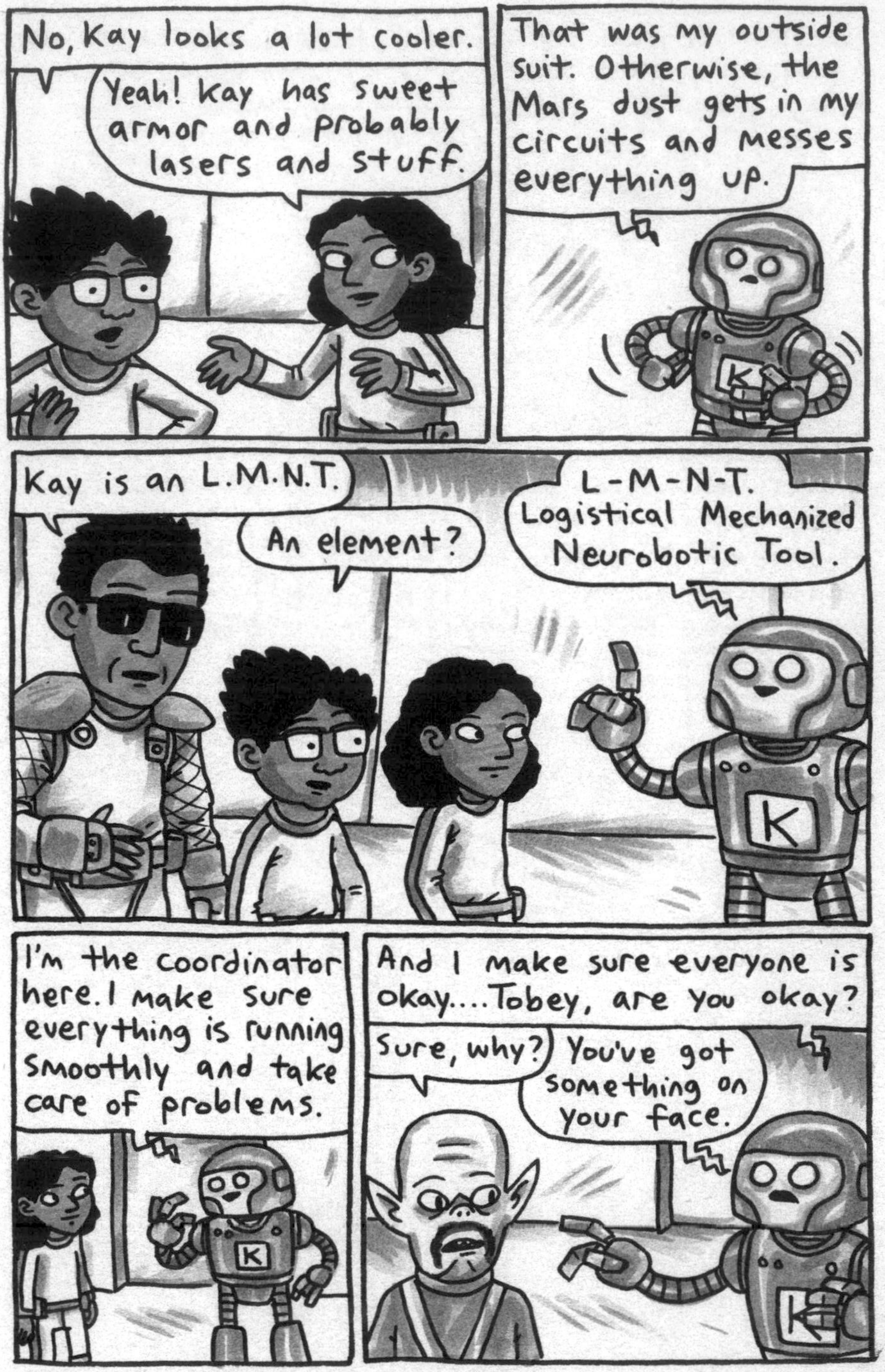

No, Kay looks a lot cooler.
Yeah! Kay has sweet armor and probably lasers and stuff.
That was my outside suit. Otherwise, the Mars dust gets in my circuits and messes everything up.
Kay is an L.M.N.T.
An element?
L-M-N-T. Logistical Mechanized Neurobotic Tool.
I'm the coordinator here. I make sure everything is running smoothly and take care of problems.
And I make sure everyone is okay.... Tobey, are you okay?
Sure, why?
You've got something on your face.

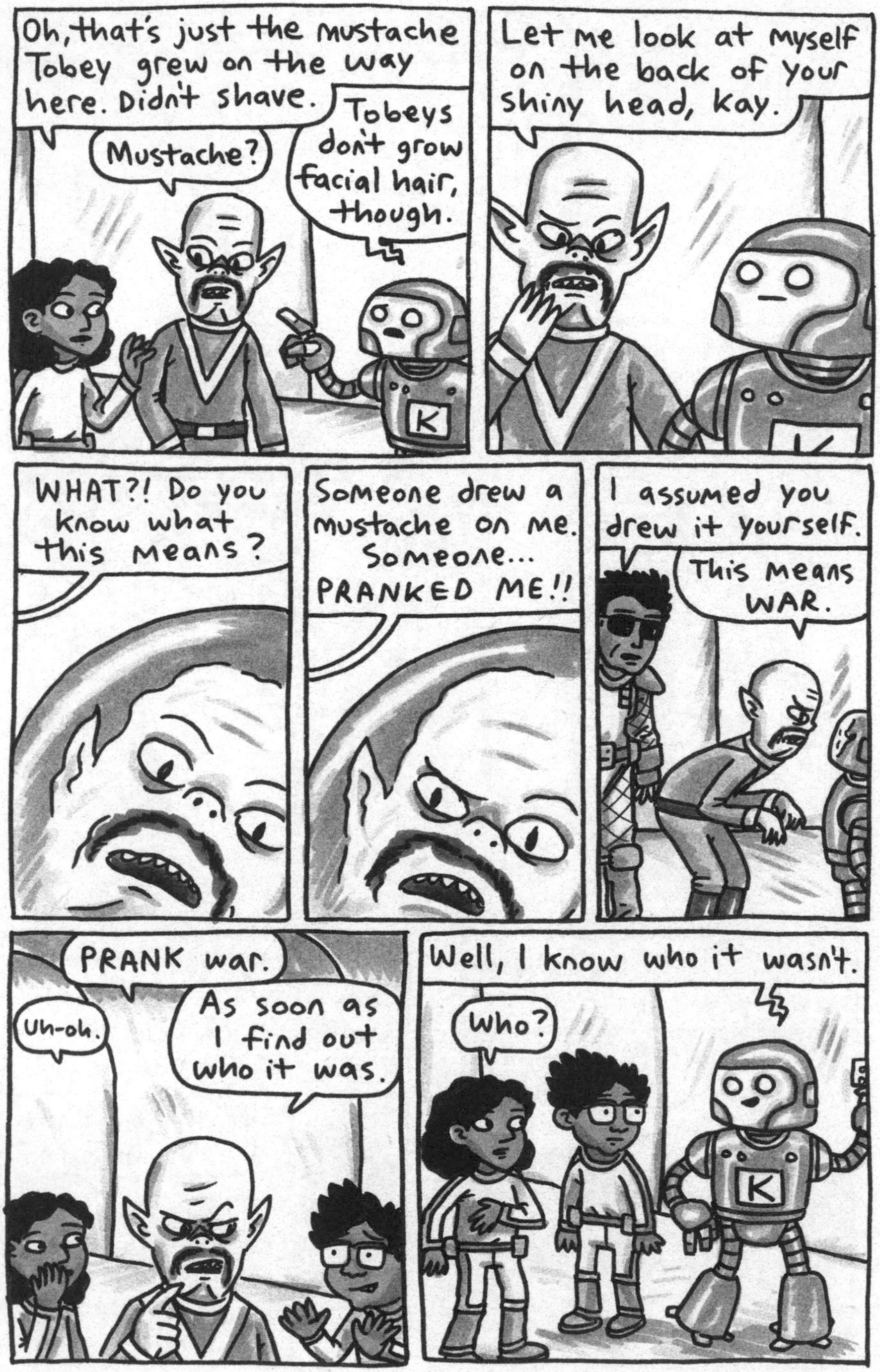

Oh, that's just the mustache Tobey grew on the way here. Didn't shave.
Mustache?
Tobeys don't grow facial hair, though.
Let me look at myself on the back of your shiny head, kay.
K
WHAT?! Do you know what this means?
Someone drew a mustache on me. Someone... PRANKED ME!!
I assumed you drew it yourself.
This means WAR.
PRANK war.
Uh-oh.
As soon as I find out who it was.
Well, I know who it wasn't.
Who?
K

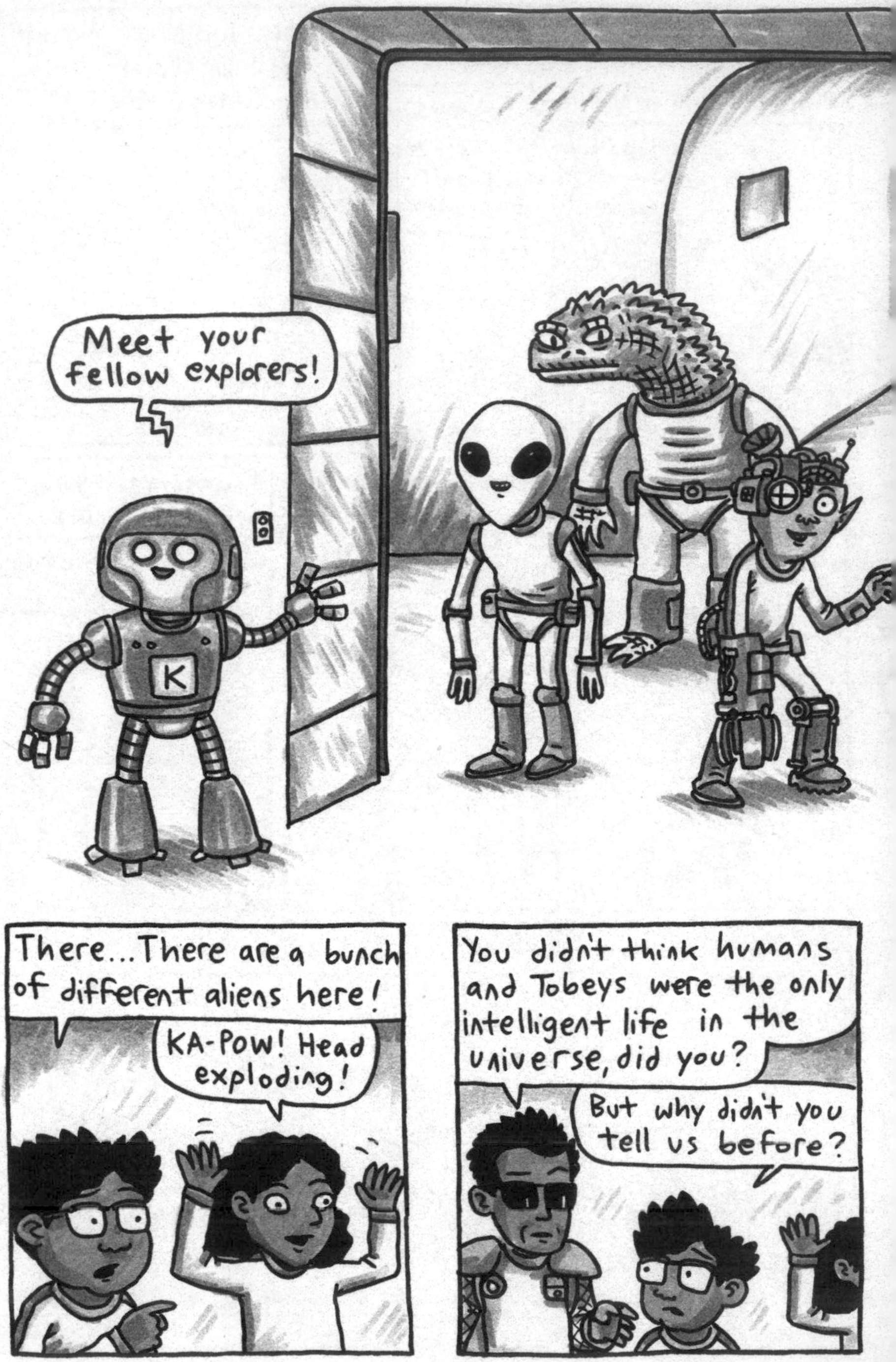
Meet your fellow explorers!
There... There are a bunch of different aliens here!
KA-POW! Head exploding!
You didn't think humans and Tobeys were the only intelligent life in the universe, did you?
But why didn't you tell us before?

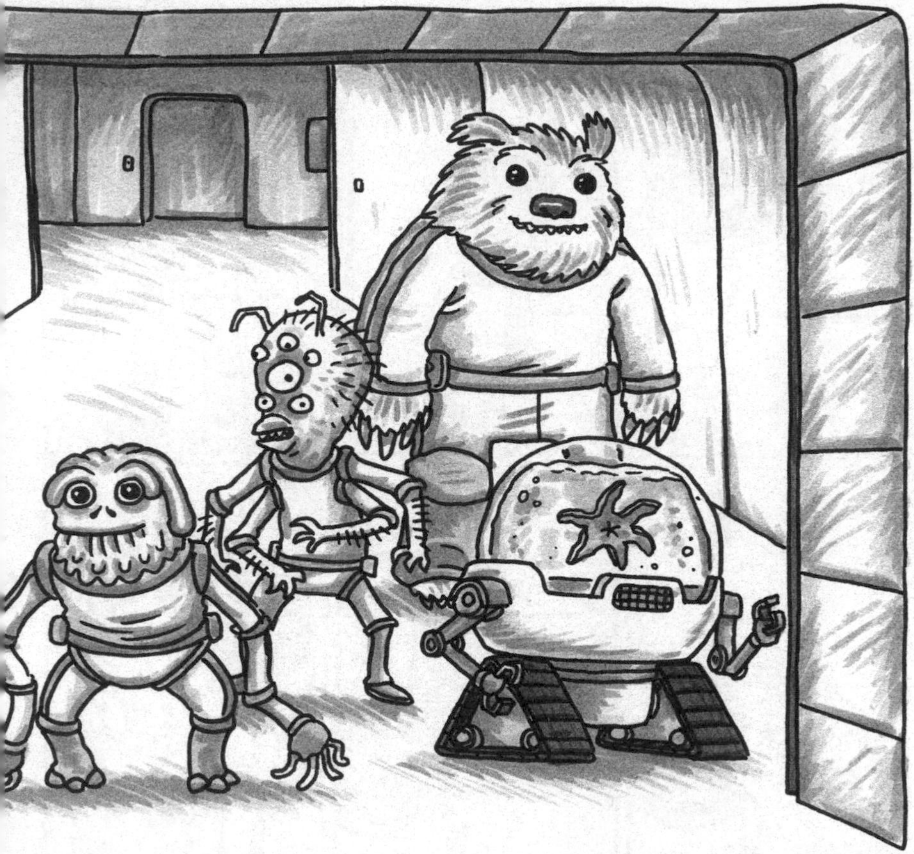

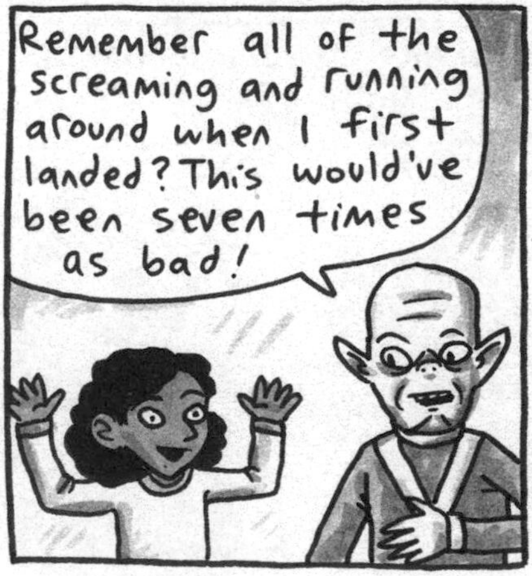
Remember all of the screaming and running around when I first landed? This would've been seven times as bad!

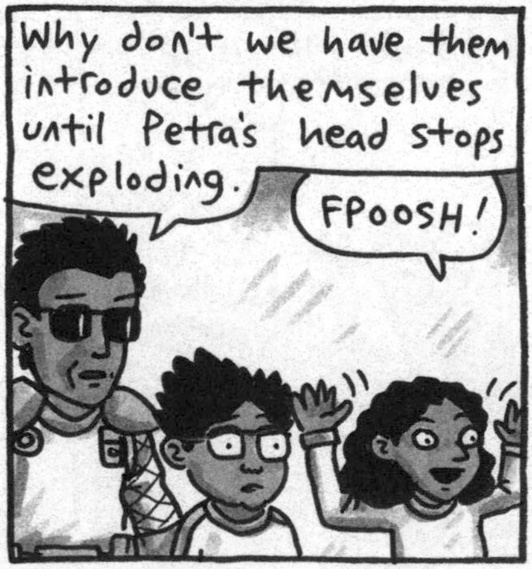
Why don't we have them introduce themselves until Petra's head stops exploding.
FPOOSH!

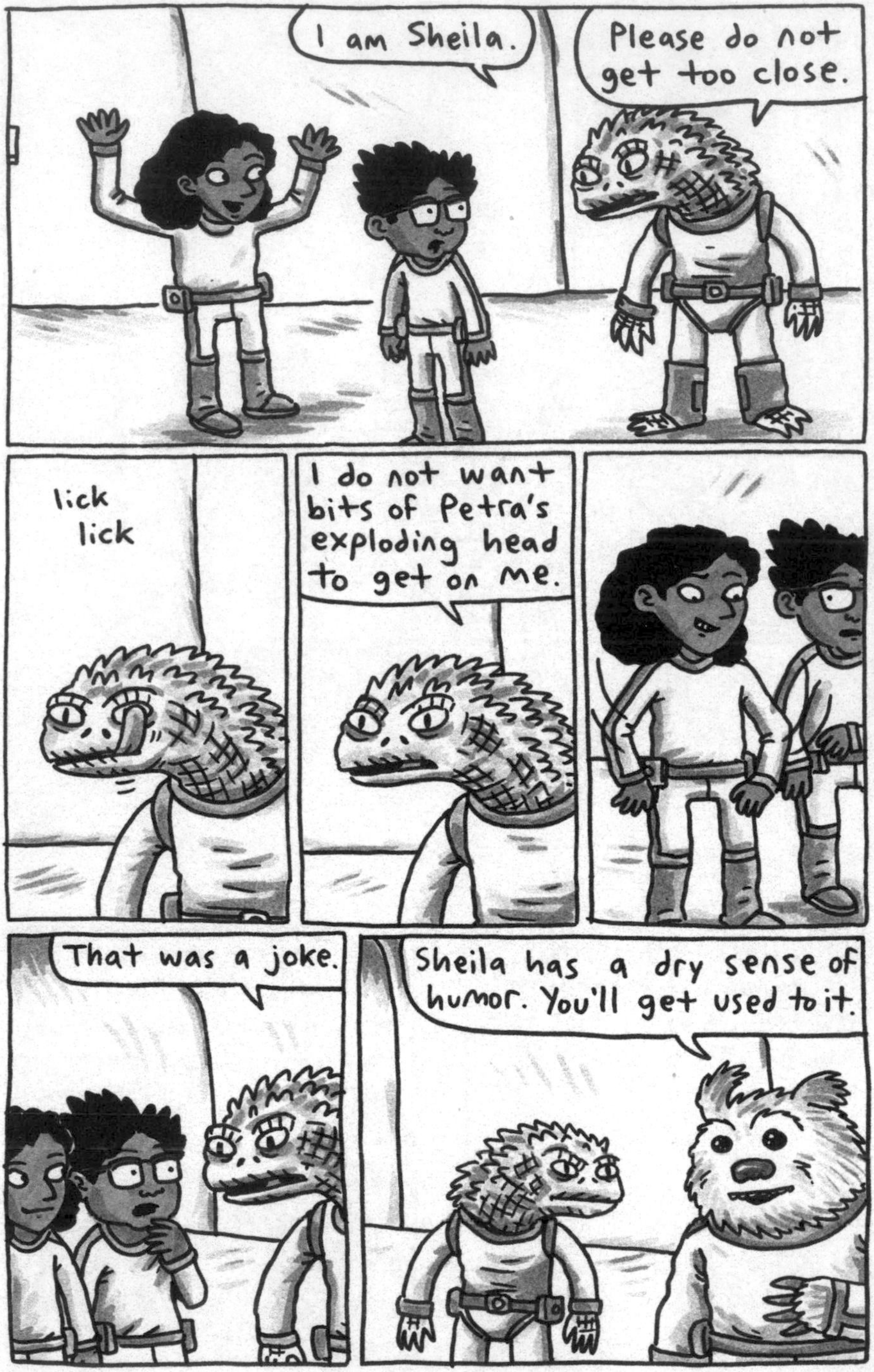
I am Sheila.
Please do not get too close.
lick lick
I do not want bits of Petra's exploding head to get on me.
That was a joke.
Sheila has a dry sense of humor. You'll get used to it.

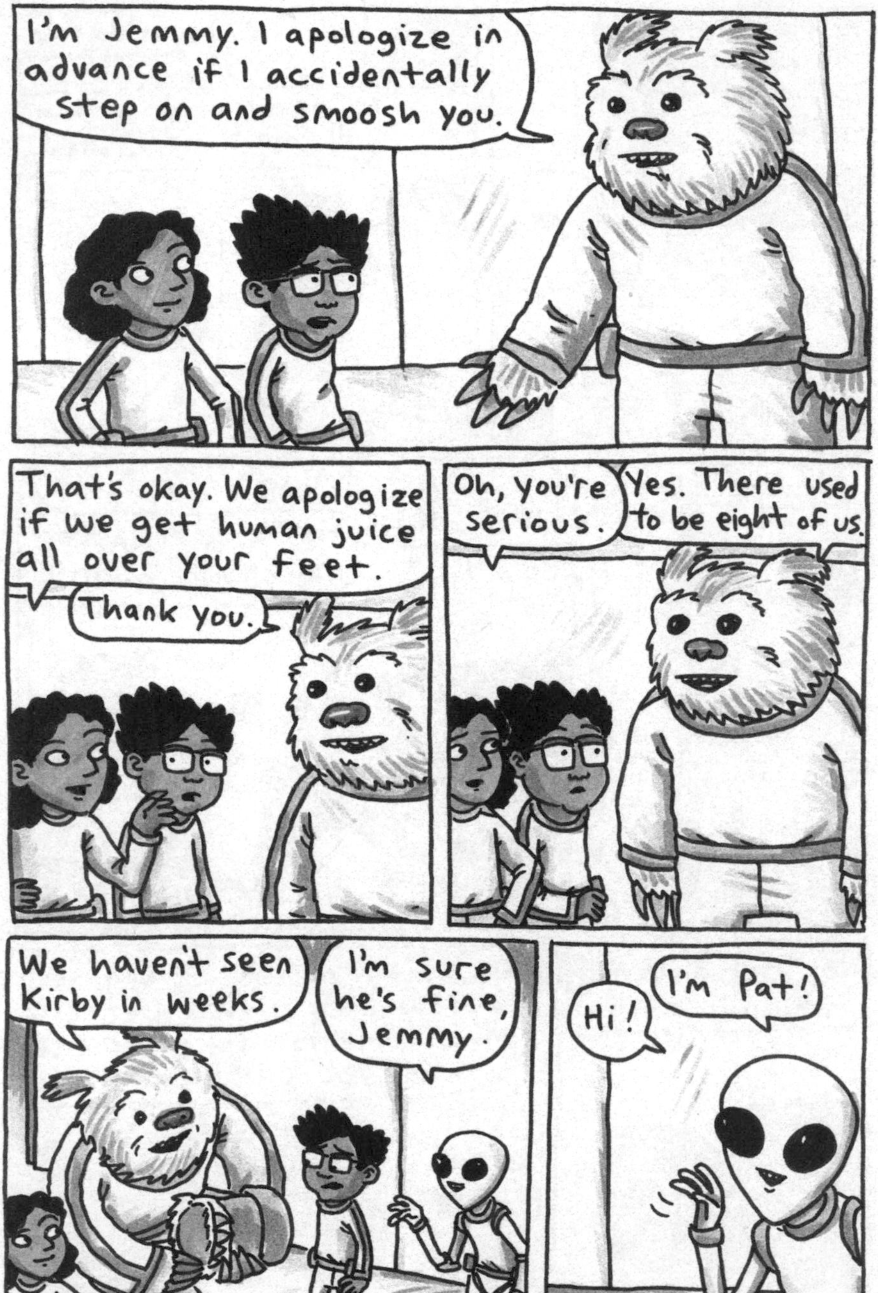
I'm Jemmy. I apologize in advance if I accidentally step on and smoosh you.
That's okay. We apologize if we get human juice all over your feet.
Thank you.
Oh, you're serious.
Yes. There used to be eight of us.
We haven't seen Kirby in weeks.
I'm sure he's fine, Jemmy.
Hi!
I'm Pat!

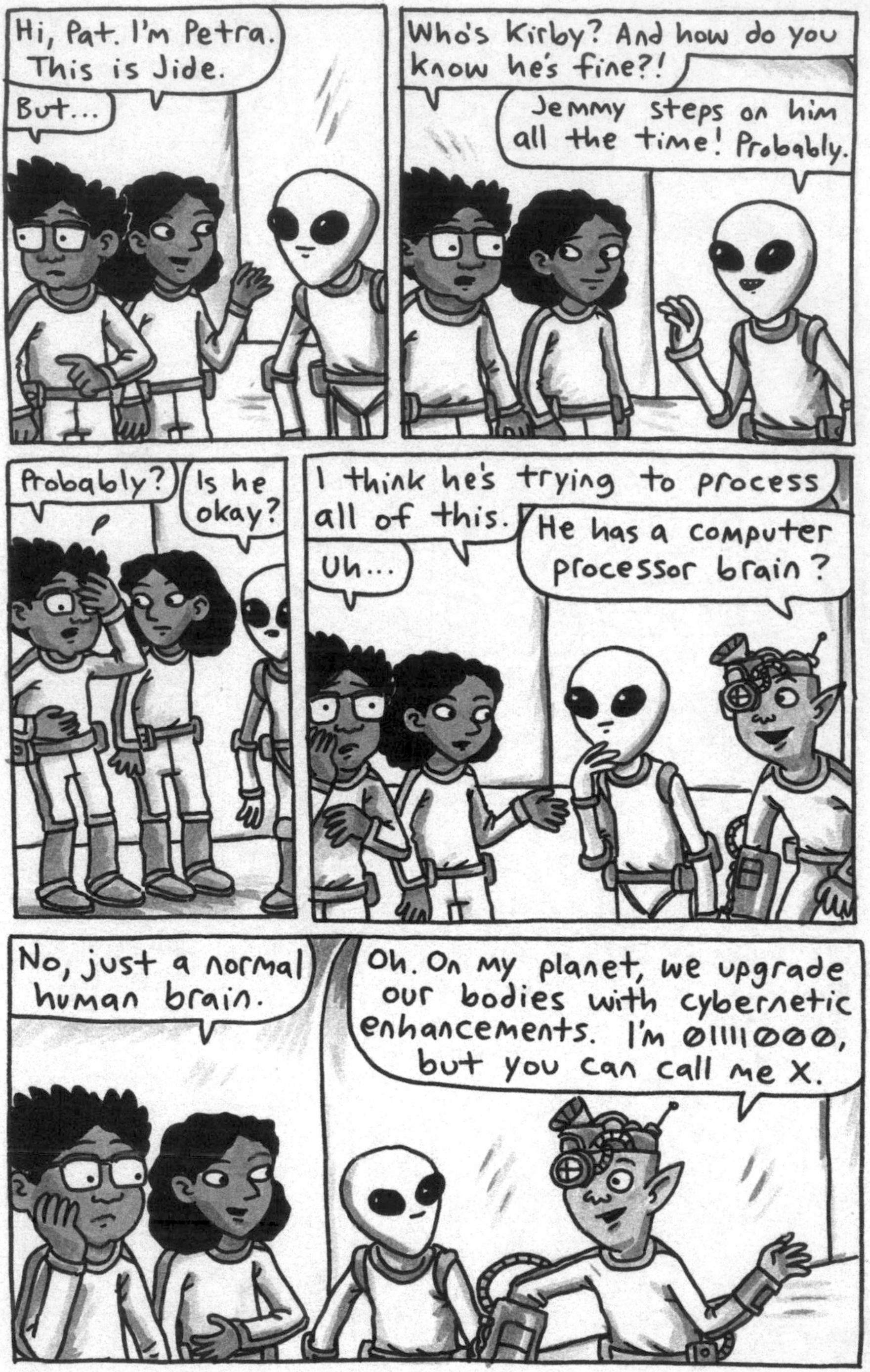
Hi, Pat. I'm Petra. This is Jide.
But...
Who's Kirby? And how do you know he's fine?!
Jemmy steps on him all the time! Probably.
Probably?
Is he okay?
I think he's trying to process all of this.
Uh...
He has a computer processor brain?
No, just a normal human brain.
Oh. On my planet, we upgrade our bodies with cybernetic enhancements. I'm 01111000, but you can call me X.

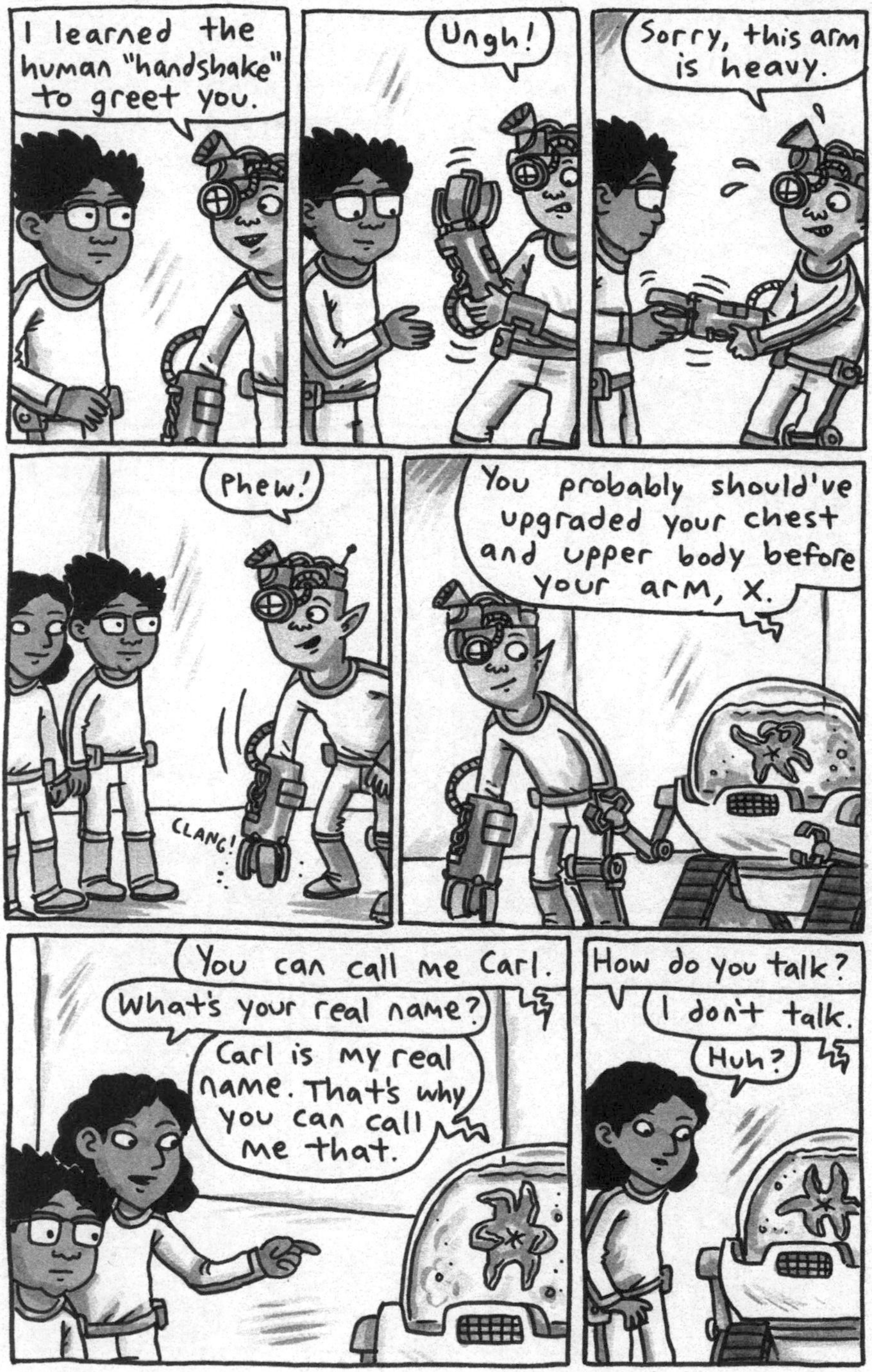

I learned the human "handshake" to greet you.
Ungh!
Sorry, this arm is heavy.
Phew!
CLANG!
You probably should've upgraded your chest and upper body before your arm, X.
You can call me Carl.
What's your real name?
Carl is my real name. That's why you can call me that.
How do you talk?
I don't talk.
Huh?

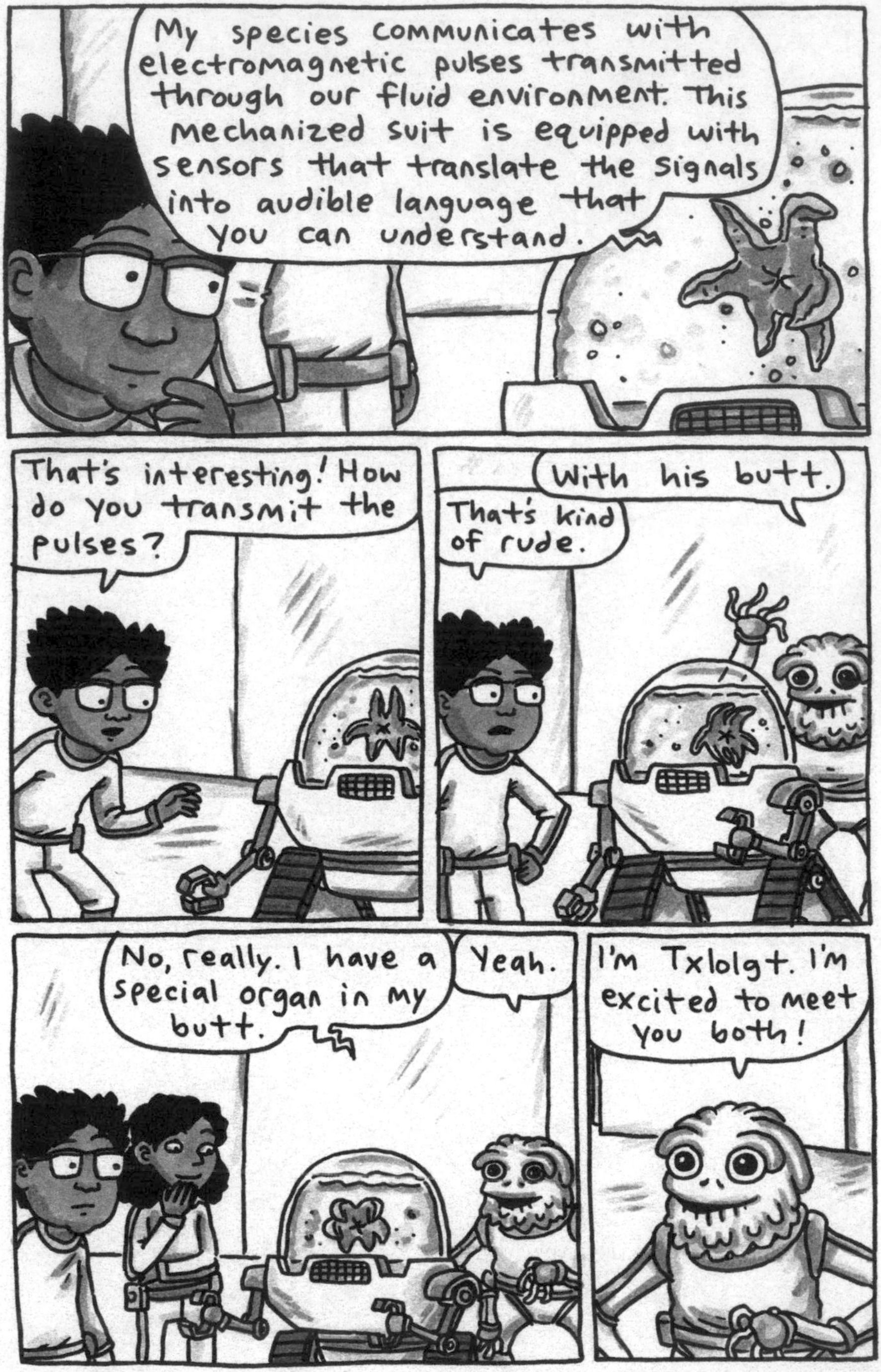

My species communicates with electromagnetic pulses transmitted through our fluid environment. This mechanized suit is equipped with sensors that translate the signals into audible language that you can understand.
That's interesting! How do you transmit the pulses?
With his butt.
That's kind of rude.
No, really. I have a special organ in my butt.
Yeah.
I'm Txlolgt. I'm excited to meet you both!

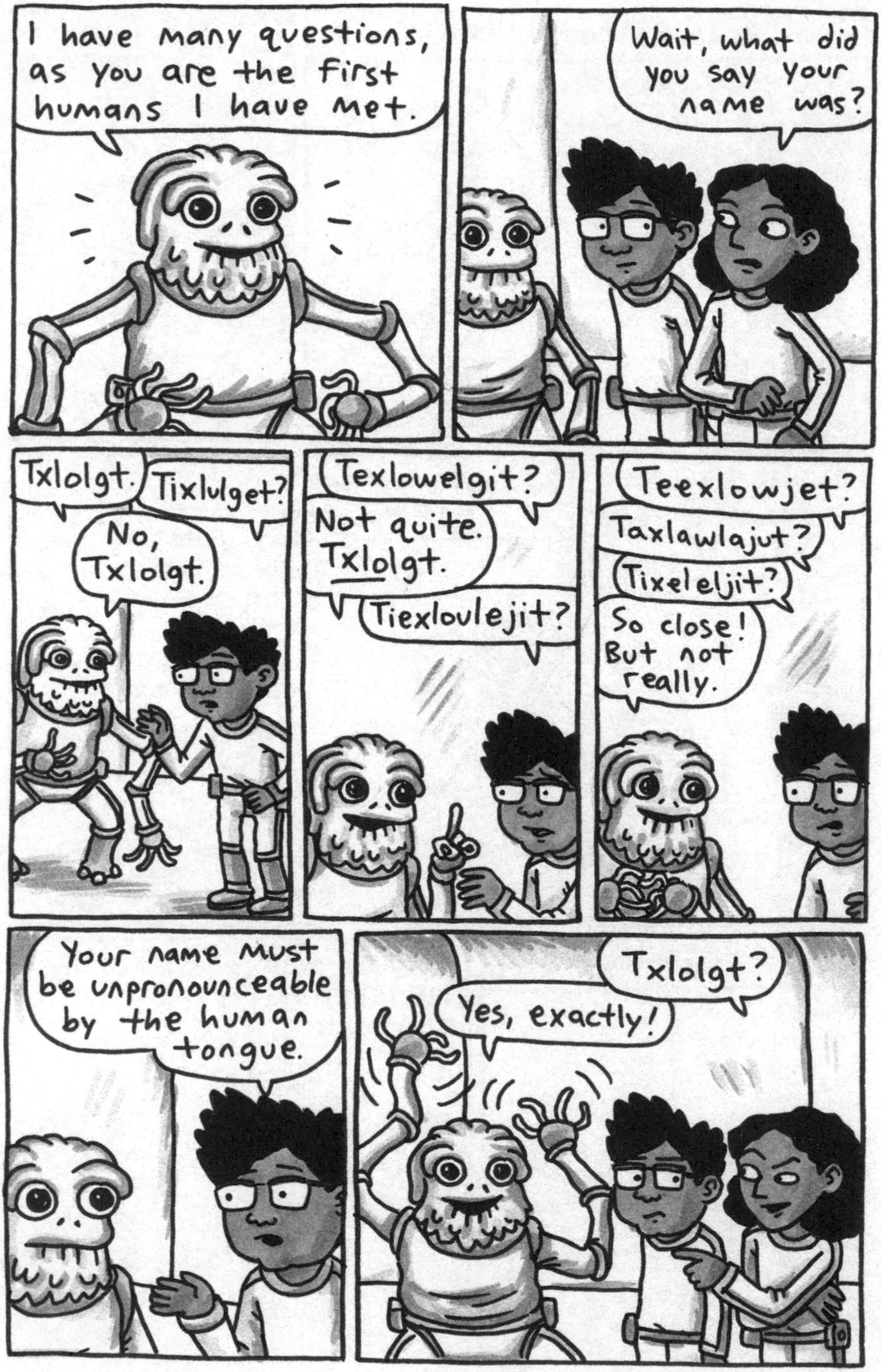
I have many questions, as you are the first humans I have met.
Wait, what did you say your name was?
Txlolgt.
Tixlulget?
No, Txlolgt.
Texlowelgit?
Not quite. Txlolgt.
Tiexloulejit?
Teexlowjet?
Taxlawlajut?
Tixeleljit?
So close! But not really.
Your name must be unpronounceable by the human tongue.
Txlolgt?
Yes, exactly!

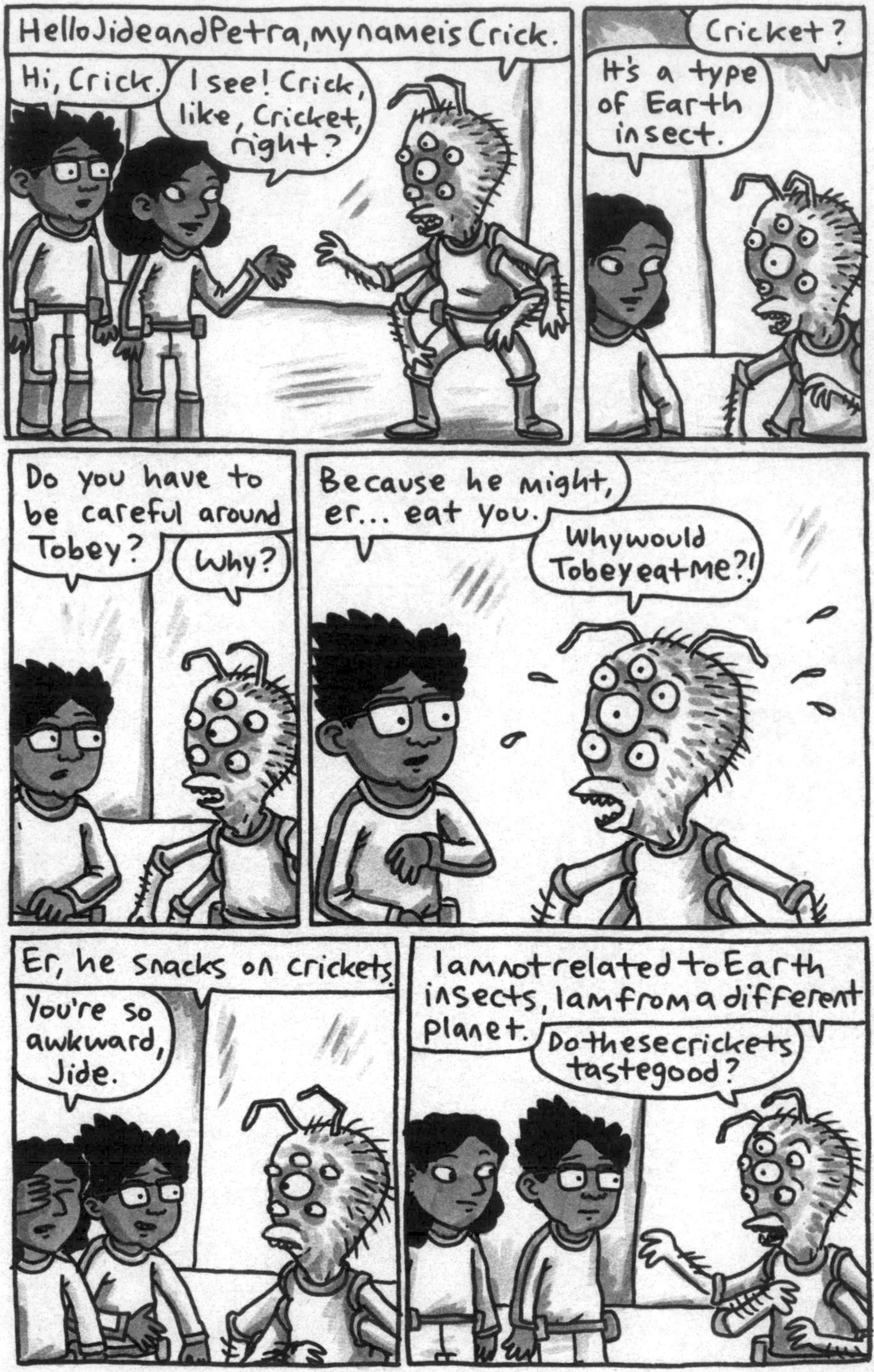
HelloJideandPetra,mynameisCrick.
Hi, Crick.
I see! Crick, like, Cricket, right?
Cricket?
It's a type of Earth insect.
Do you have to be careful around Tobey?
Why?
Because he might, er... eat you.
WhywouldTobeyeatMe?!
Er, he snacks on crickets.
You're so awkward, Jide.
IamnotrelatedtoEarth insects, Iamfromadifferent planet.
Dothesecrickets tastegood?

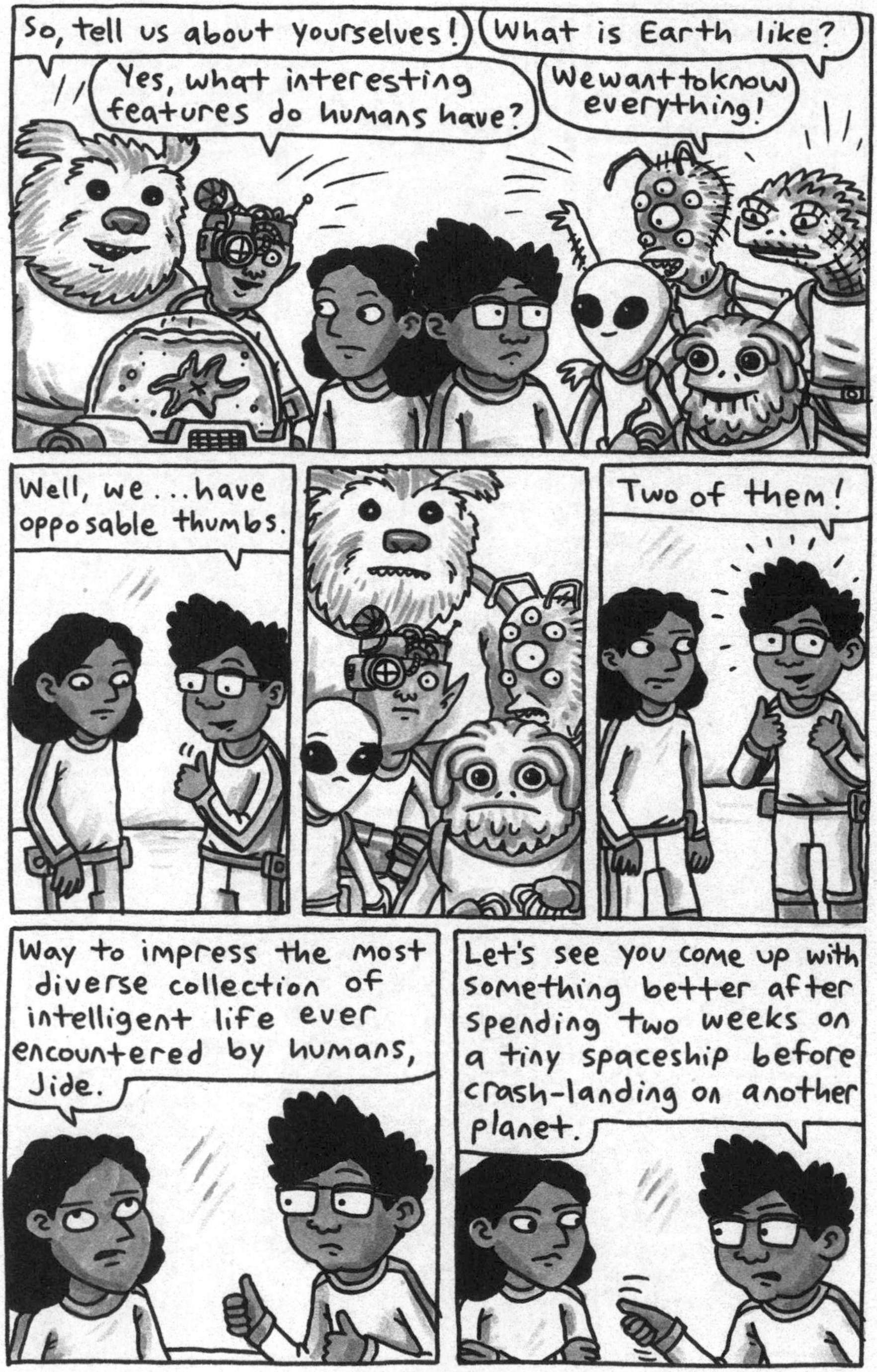
So, tell us about yourselves!
What is Earth like?
Yes, what interesting features do humans have?
We want to know everything!
Well, we...have opposable thumbs.
Two of them!
Way to impress the most diverse collection of intelligent life ever encountered by humans, Jide.
Let's see you come up with something better after spending two weeks on a tiny spaceship before crash-landing on another planet.

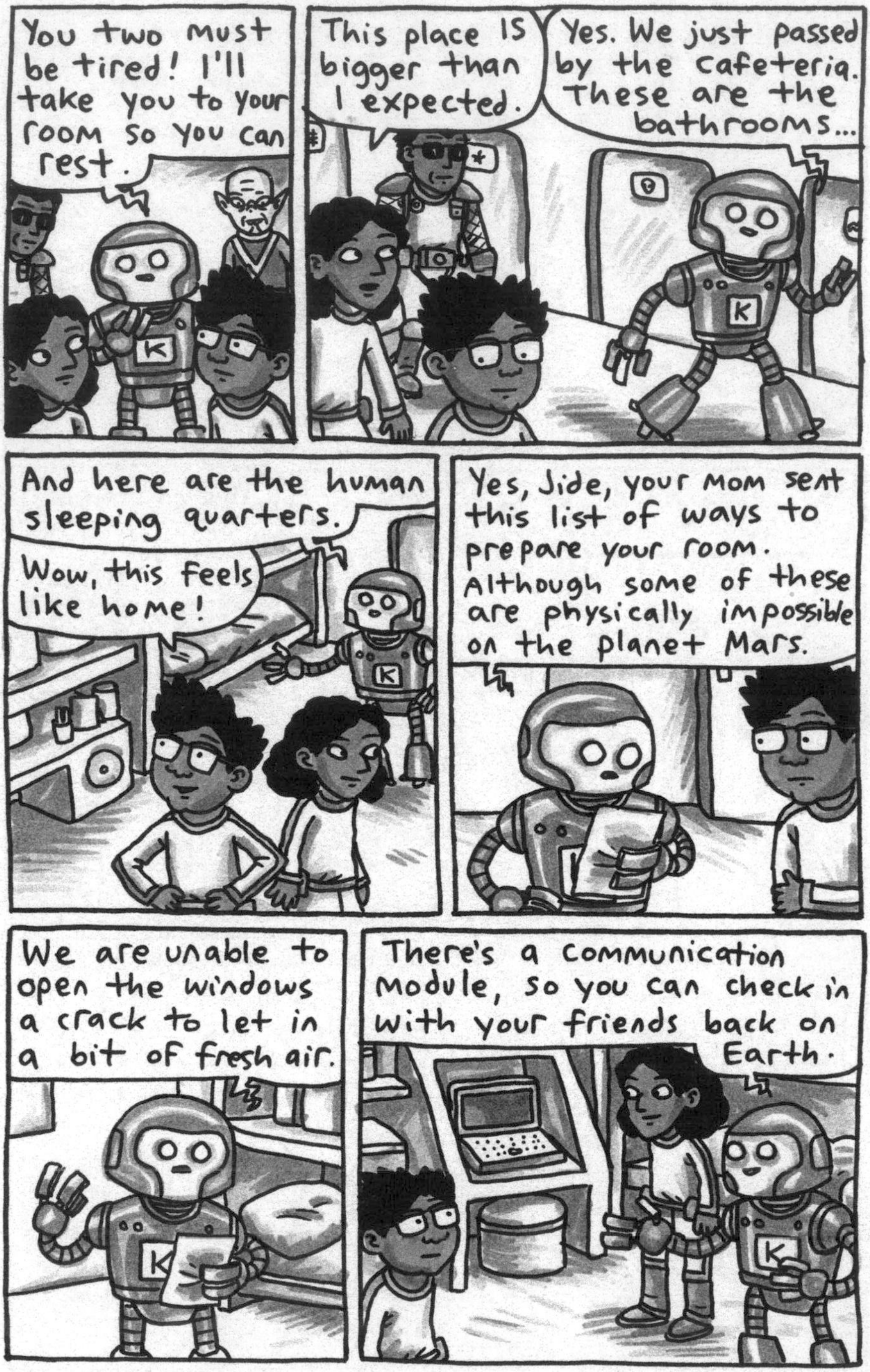
You two must be tired! I'll take you to your room so you can rest.
This place IS bigger than I expected.
Yes. We just passed by the cafeteria. These are the bathrooms...
And here are the human sleeping quarters.
Wow, this feels like home!
Yes, Jide, your mom sent this list of ways to prepare your room. Although some of these are physically impossible on the planet Mars.
We are unable to open the windows a crack to let in a bit of fresh air.
There's a communication module, so you can check in with your friends back on Earth.

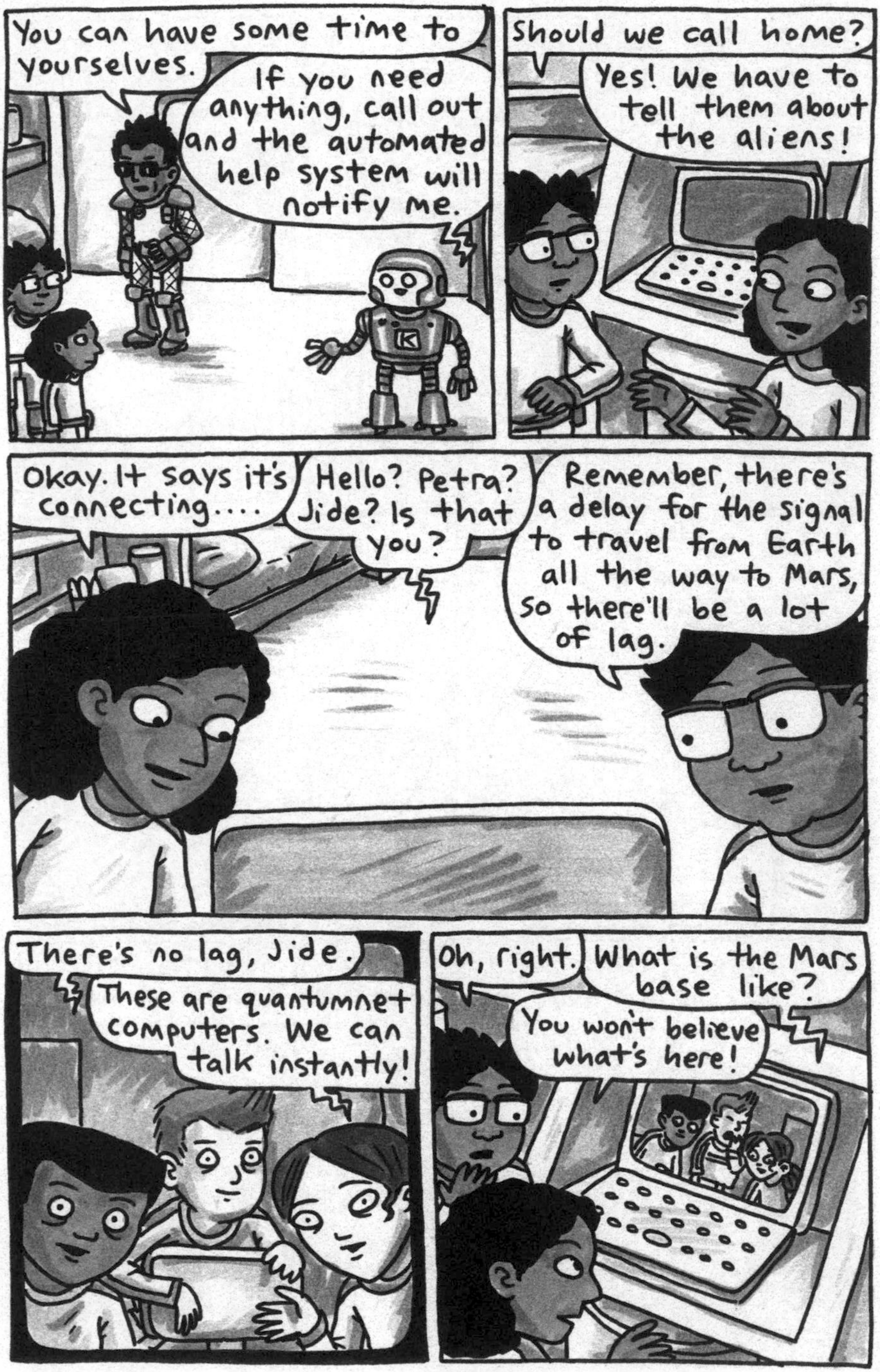
You can have some time to yourselves.
If you need anything, call out and the automated help system will notify me.
Should we call home?
Yes! We have to tell them about the aliens!
Okay. It says it's connecting....
Hello? Petra? Jide? Is that you?
Remember, there's a delay for the signal to travel from Earth all the way to Mars, so there'll be a lot of lag.
There's no lag, Jide.
These are quantumnet computers. We can talk instantly!
Oh, right.
What is the Mars base like?
You won't believe what's here!

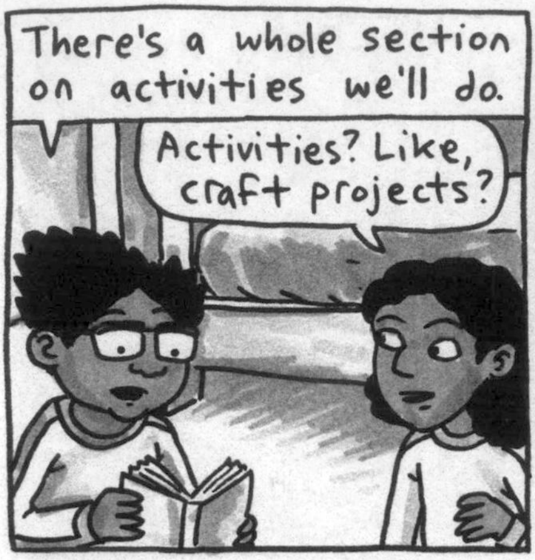
There's a whole section on activities we'll do.
Activities? Like, craft projects?

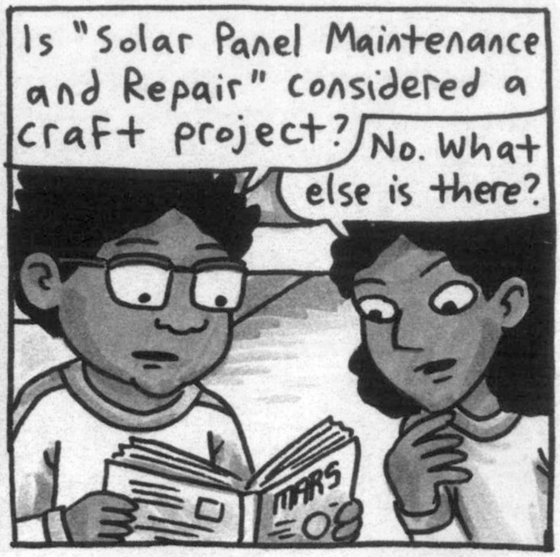
Is "Solar Panel Maintenance and Repair" considered a craft project?
No. What else is there?
MARS

MARTIAN GARDENING

TRY TO GROW A VARIETY OF EDIBLE PLANTS IN MARTIAN SOIL AND MAKE DELICIOUS* MEALS WITH THEM.

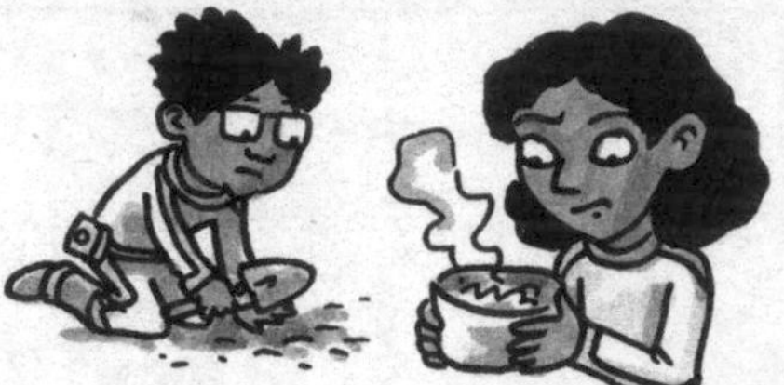

* ADULT AND KID OPINIONS OF DELICIOUS MAY DIFFER.

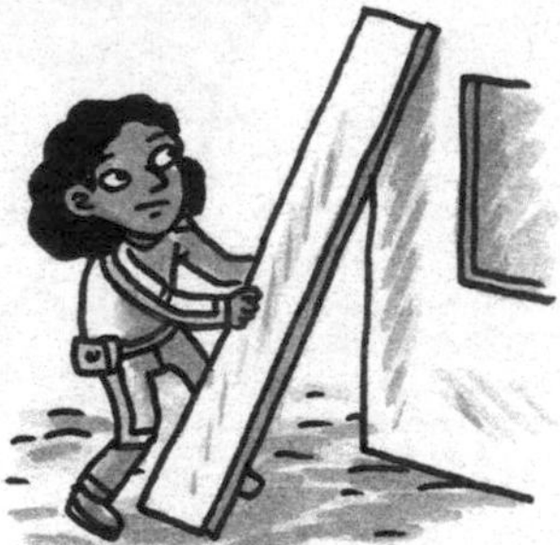

MOBILE HABITAT CONSTRUCTION

DESIGN AND BUILD PORTABLE SHELTERS THAT CAN ENDURE THE EXTREME CONDITIONS OF BARREN PLANETS.

SYSTEMS RESOURCE ANALYSIS

OPERATE STATISTICAL SOFTWARE TO MANAGE RESOURCE ALLOCATION UTILIZING DATA RELAY METHODS WITHIN THE SCOPE OF DISTRIBUTION THEORY MECHANICS AND RELATED EFFICIENCY TOOLS FOR THE PURPOSE OF INCREASED MISSION SUCCESS PROBABILITY.

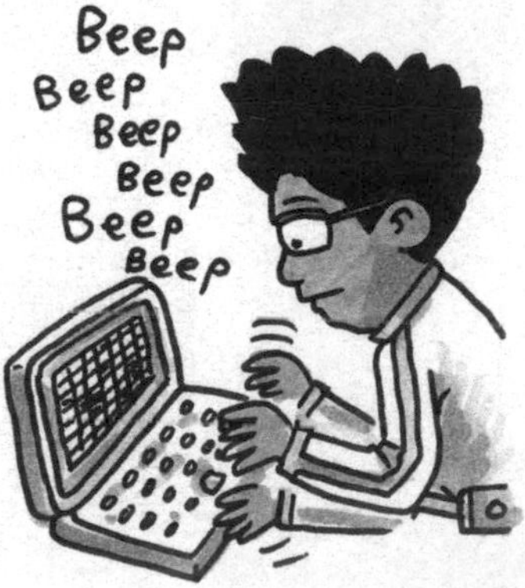
Beep
Beep
Beep
Beep
Beep
Beep

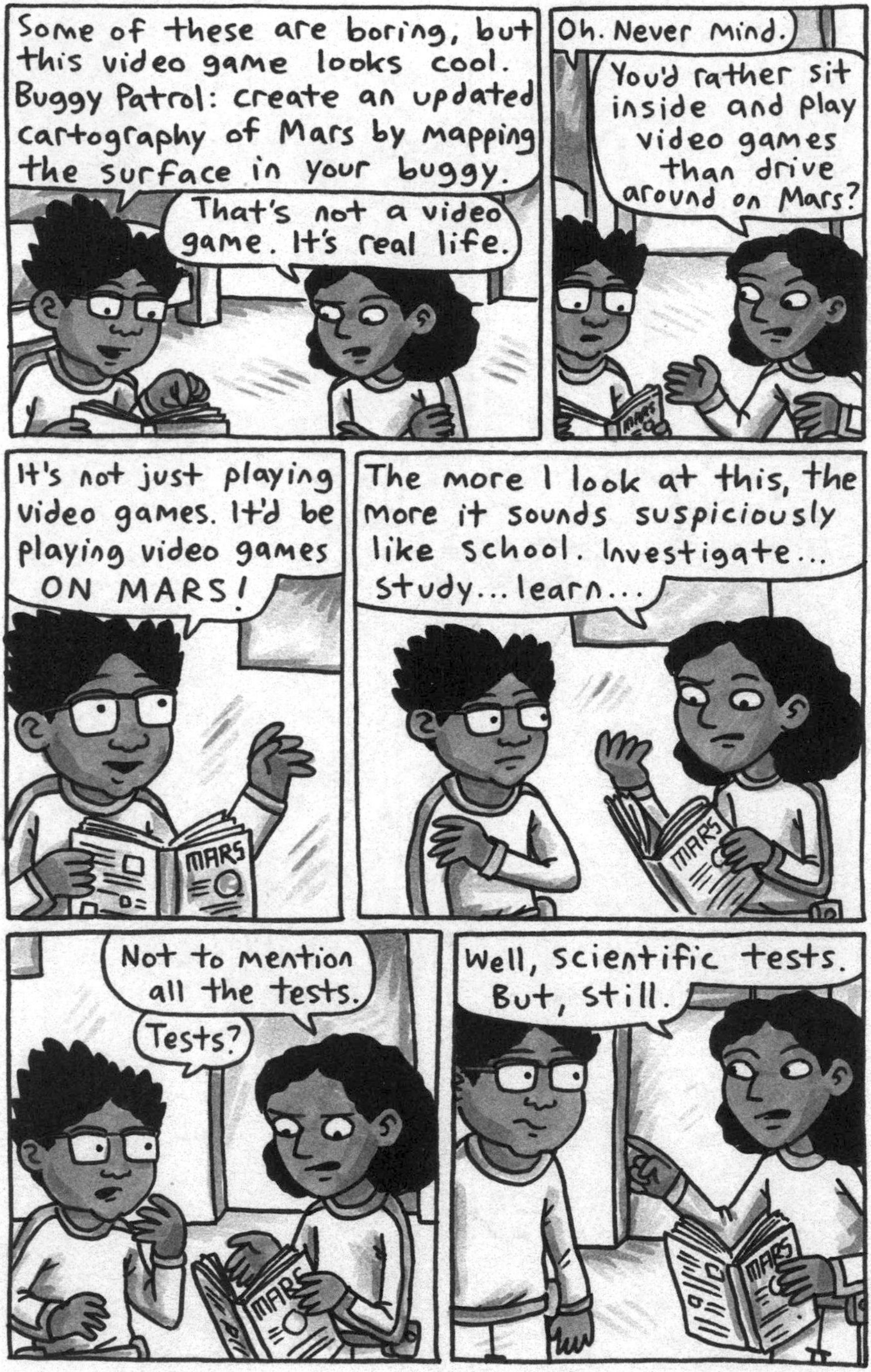
Some of these are boring, but this video game looks cool. Buggy Patrol: create an updated cartography of Mars by mapping the surface in your buggy.
That's not a video game. It's real life.
Oh. Never mind.
You'd rather sit inside and play video games than drive around on Mars?
MARS
It's not just playing video games. It'd be playing video games ON MARS!
MARS
The more I look at this, the more it sounds suspiciously like school. Investigate... study... learn...
MARS
Not to mention all the tests.
Tests?
MARS
Well, scientific tests. But, still.
MARS

108

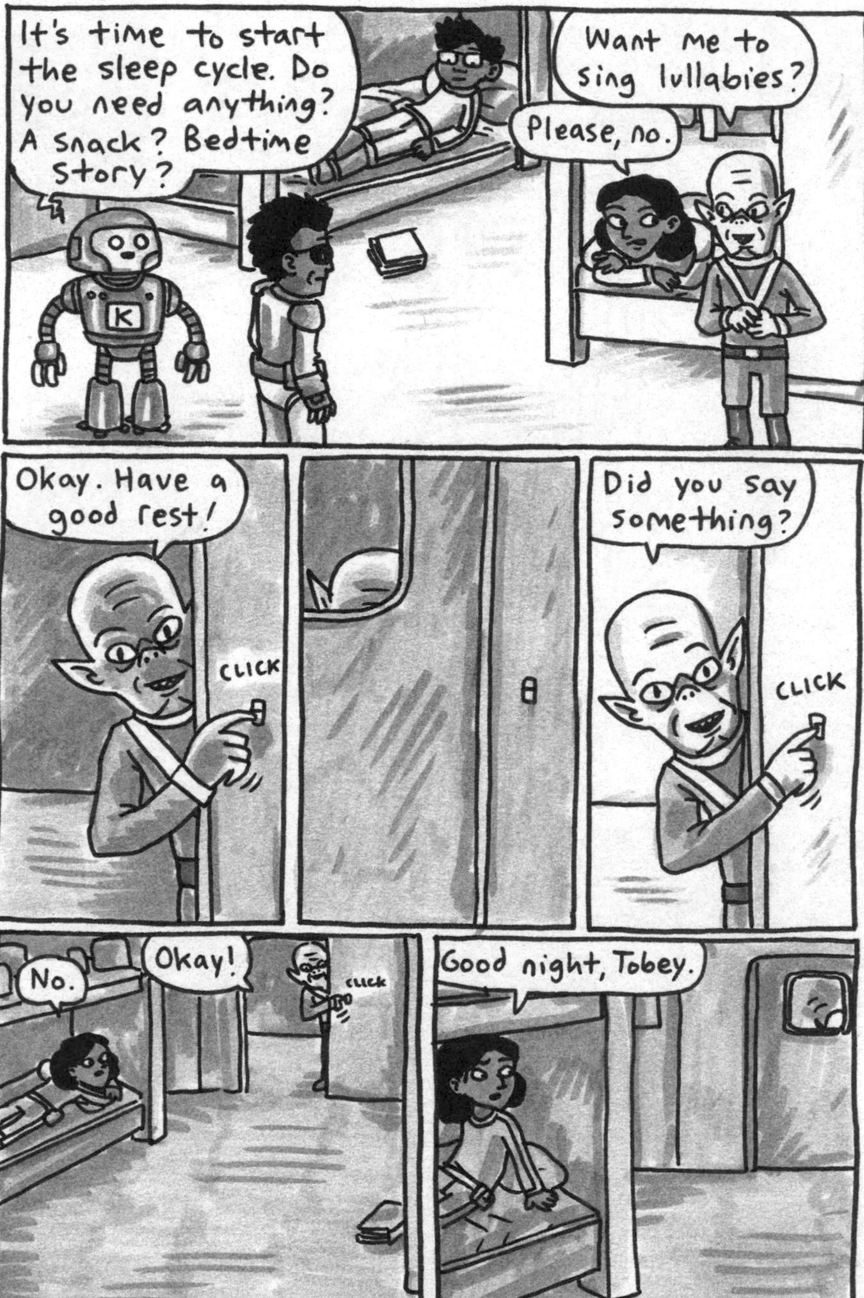
It's time to start the sleep cycle. Do you need anything? A snack? Bedtime story?
Want me to sing lullabies?
Please, no.
Okay. Have a good rest!
CLICK
Did you say something?
CLICK
No.
Okay!
CLICK
Good night, Tobey.

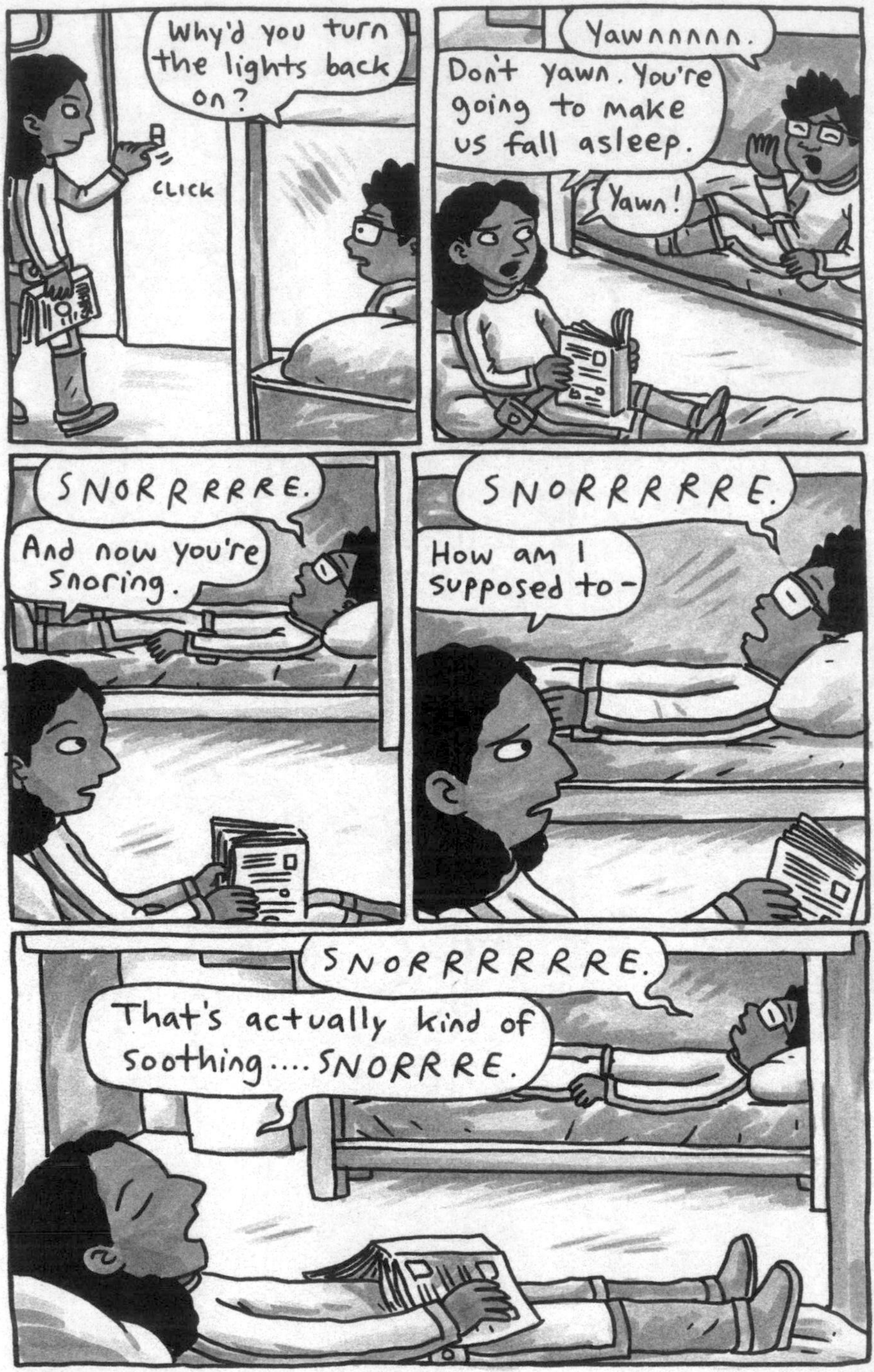
Why'd you turn the lights back on?
CLICK
Yawnnnnn.
Don't yawn. You're going to make us fall asleep.
Yawn!
SNORRRRRE.
And now you're snoring.
SNORRRRRRE.
How am I supposed to-
SNORRRRRRRE.
That's actually kind of soothing.... SNORRRE.

LIFE ON MARS

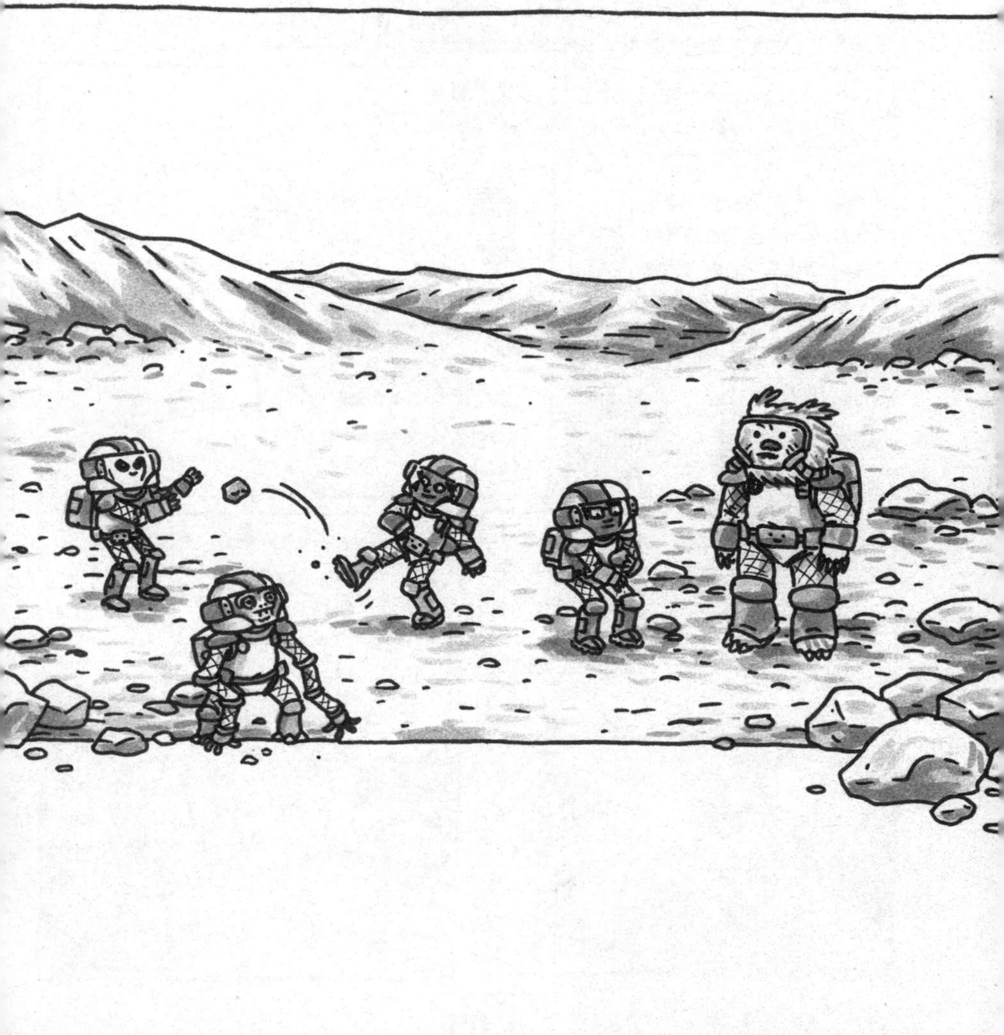

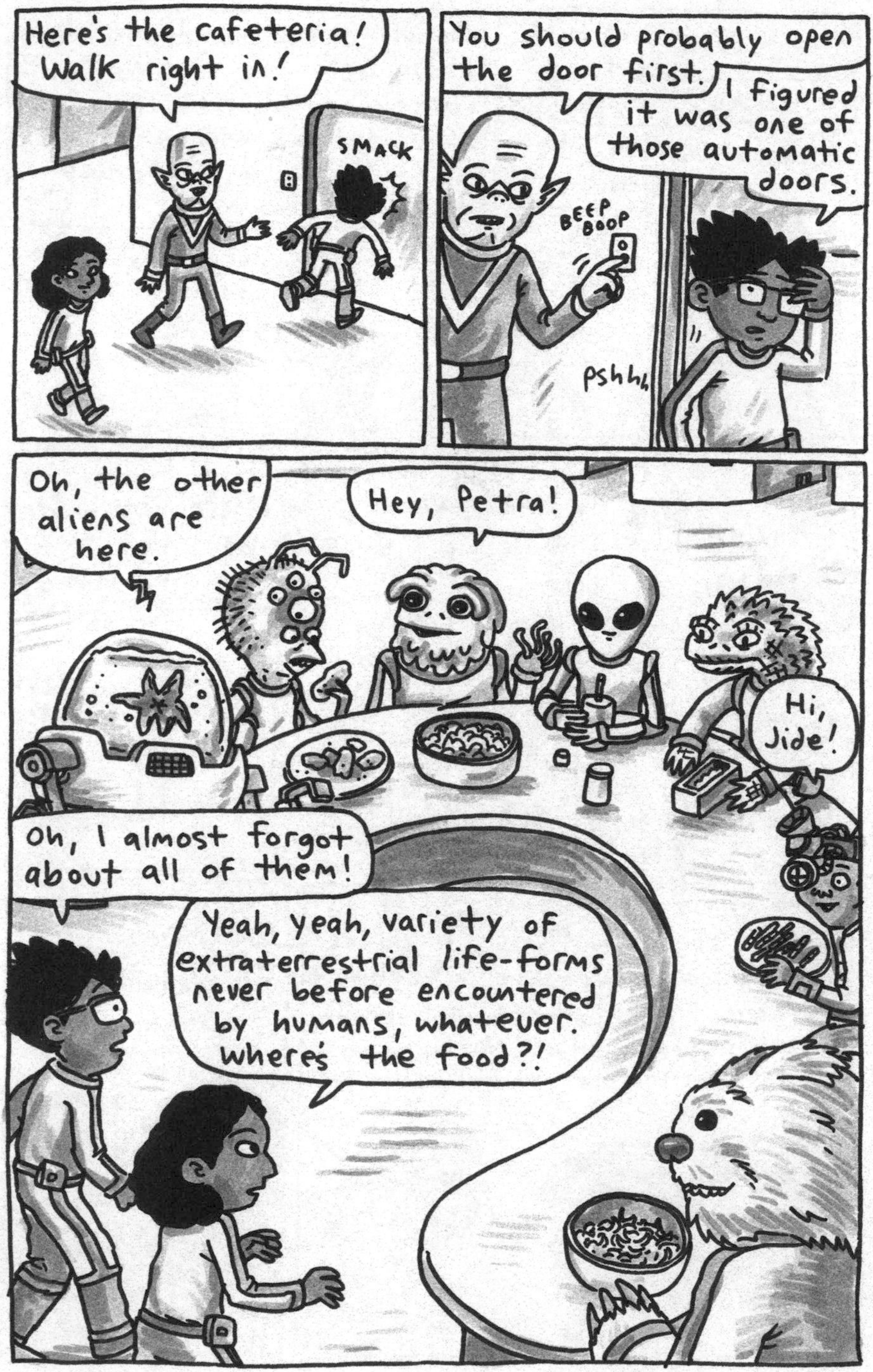
Here's the cafeteria! Walk right in!
SMACK
You should probably open the door first.
I figured it was one of those automatic doors.
BEEP BOOP
pshhh
Oh, the other aliens are here.
Hey, Petra!
Hi, Jide!
Oh, I almost forgot about all of them!
Yeah, yeah, variety of extraterrestrial life-forms never before encountered by humans, whatever. Where's the food?!

117

MARS MISSION DESIGNATION: BIOMECHATRONICS

121

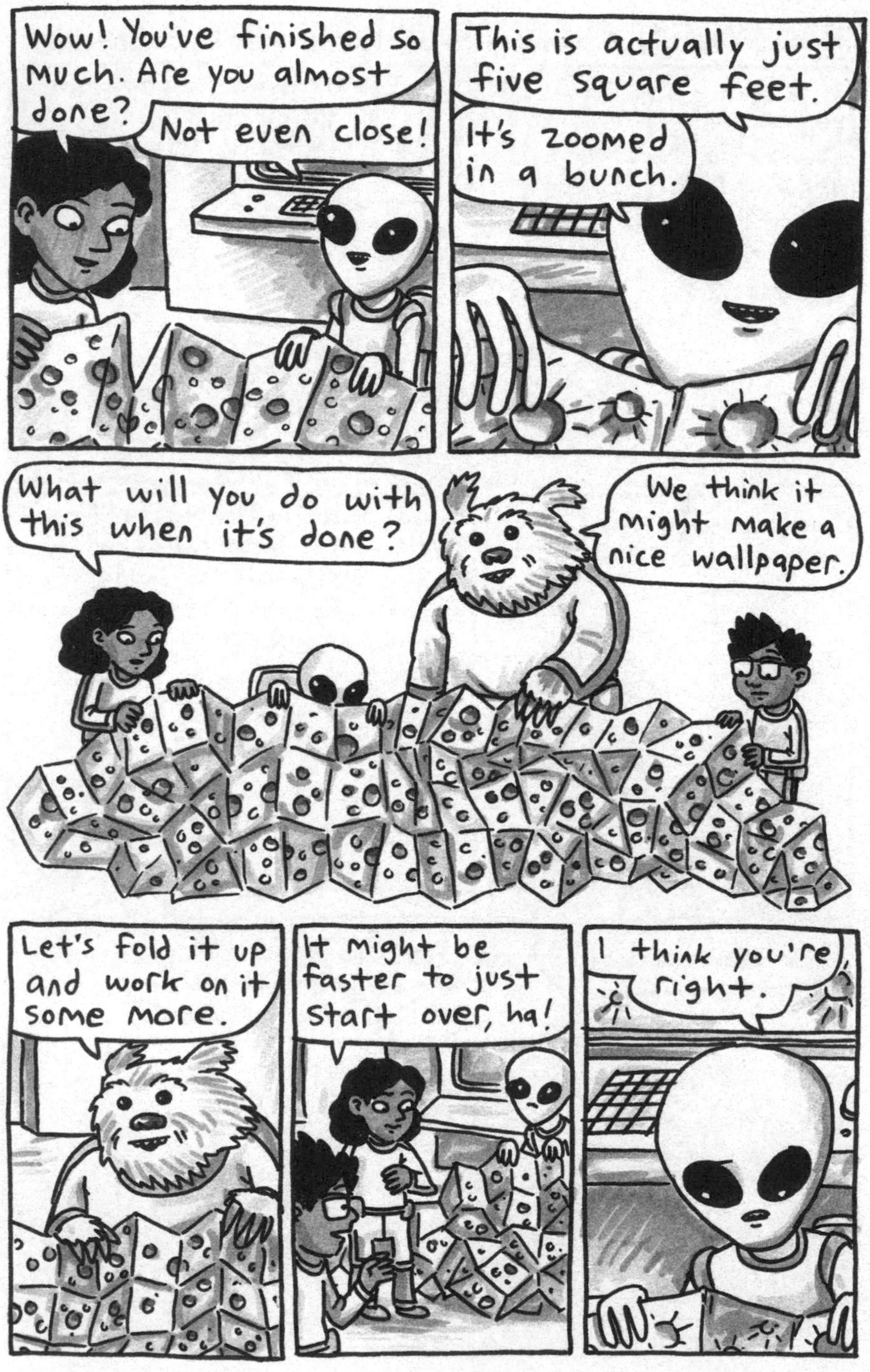

Wow! You've finished so much. Are you almost done?
Not even close!
This is actually just five square feet.
It's zoomed in a bunch.
What will you do with this when it's done?
We think it might make a nice wallpaper.
Let's fold it up and work on it some more.
It might be faster to just start over, ha!
I think you're right.

127

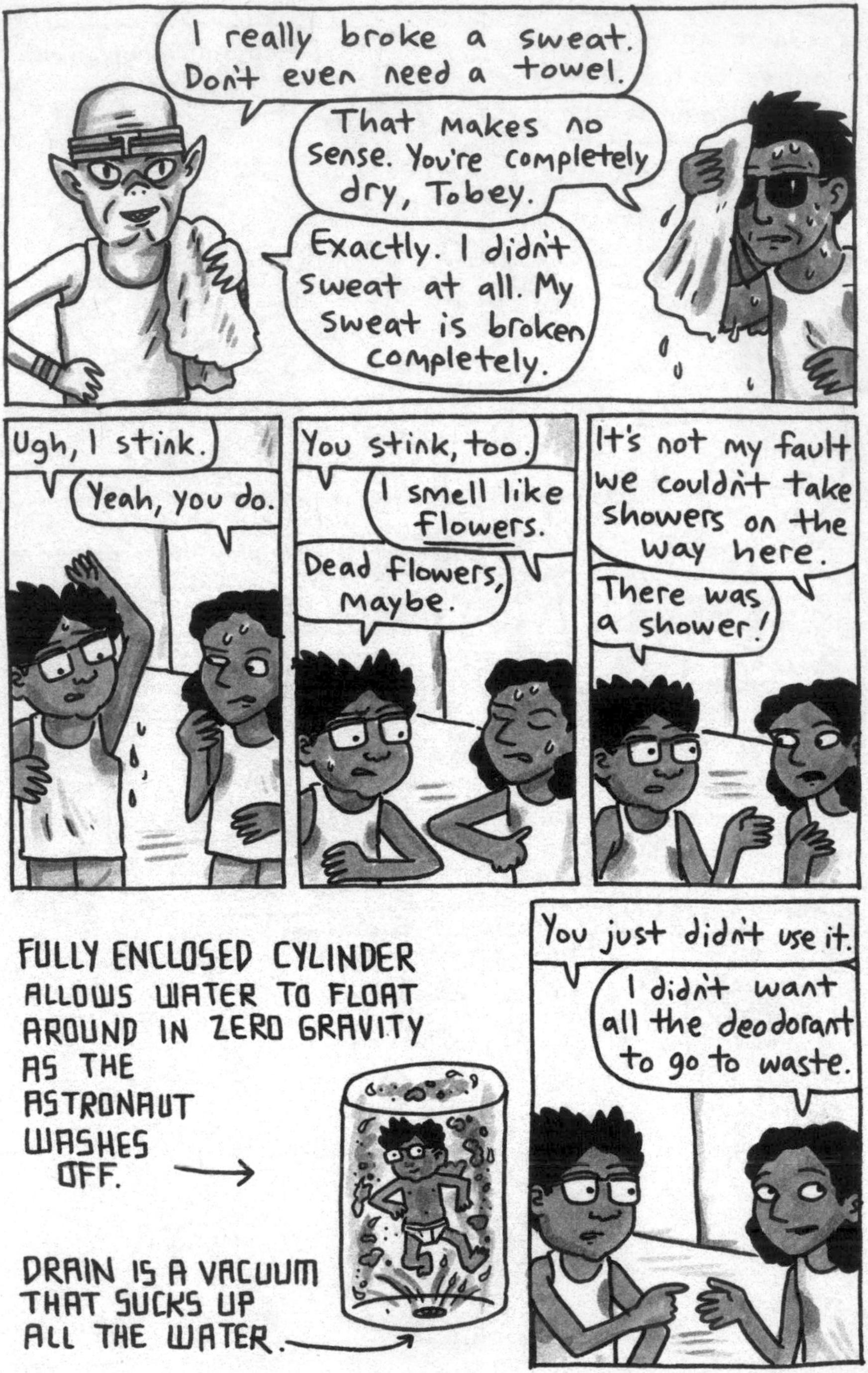
I really broke a sweat. Don't even need a towel.
That makes no sense. You're completely dry, Tobey.
Exactly. I didn't sweat at all. My sweat is broken completely.
Ugh, I stink.
Yeah, you do.
You stink, too.
I smell like flowers.
Dead flowers, maybe.
It's not my fault we couldn't take showers on the way here.
There was a shower!
FULLY ENCLOSED CYLINDER ALLOWS WATER TO FLOAT AROUND IN ZERO GRAVITY AS THE ASTRONAUT WASHES OFF.
DRAIN IS A VACUUM THAT SUCKS UP ALL THE WATER.
You just didn't use it.
I didn't want all the deodorant to go to waste.

131

133

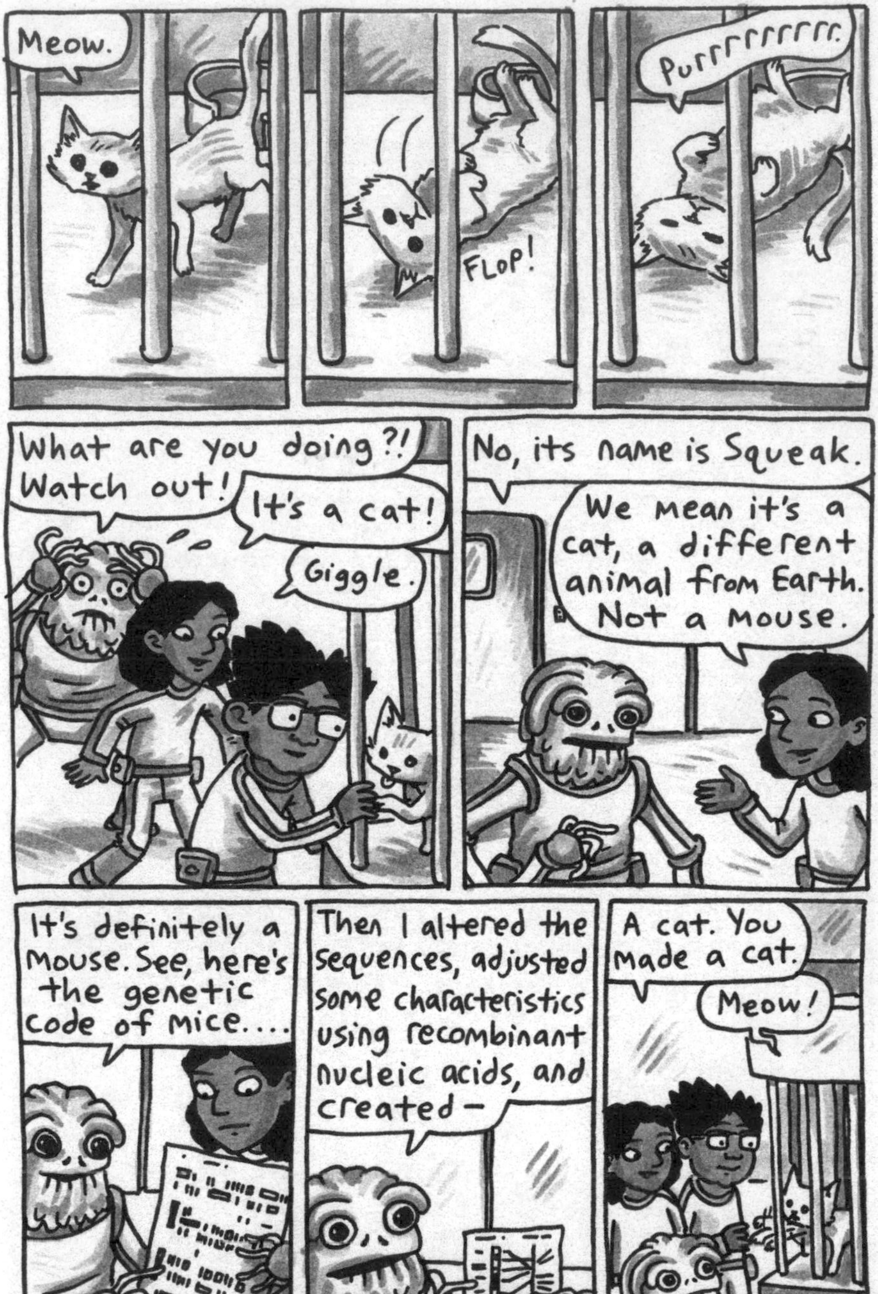
Meow.
FLOP!
Purrrrrrrrr.
What are you doing?! Watch out!
It's a cat!
Giggle.
No, its name is Squeak.
We mean it's a cat, a different animal from Earth. Not a mouse.
It's definitely a mouse. See, here's the genetic code of mice....
Then I altered the sequences, adjusted some characteristics using recombinant nucleic acids, and created–
A cat. You made a cat.
Meow!

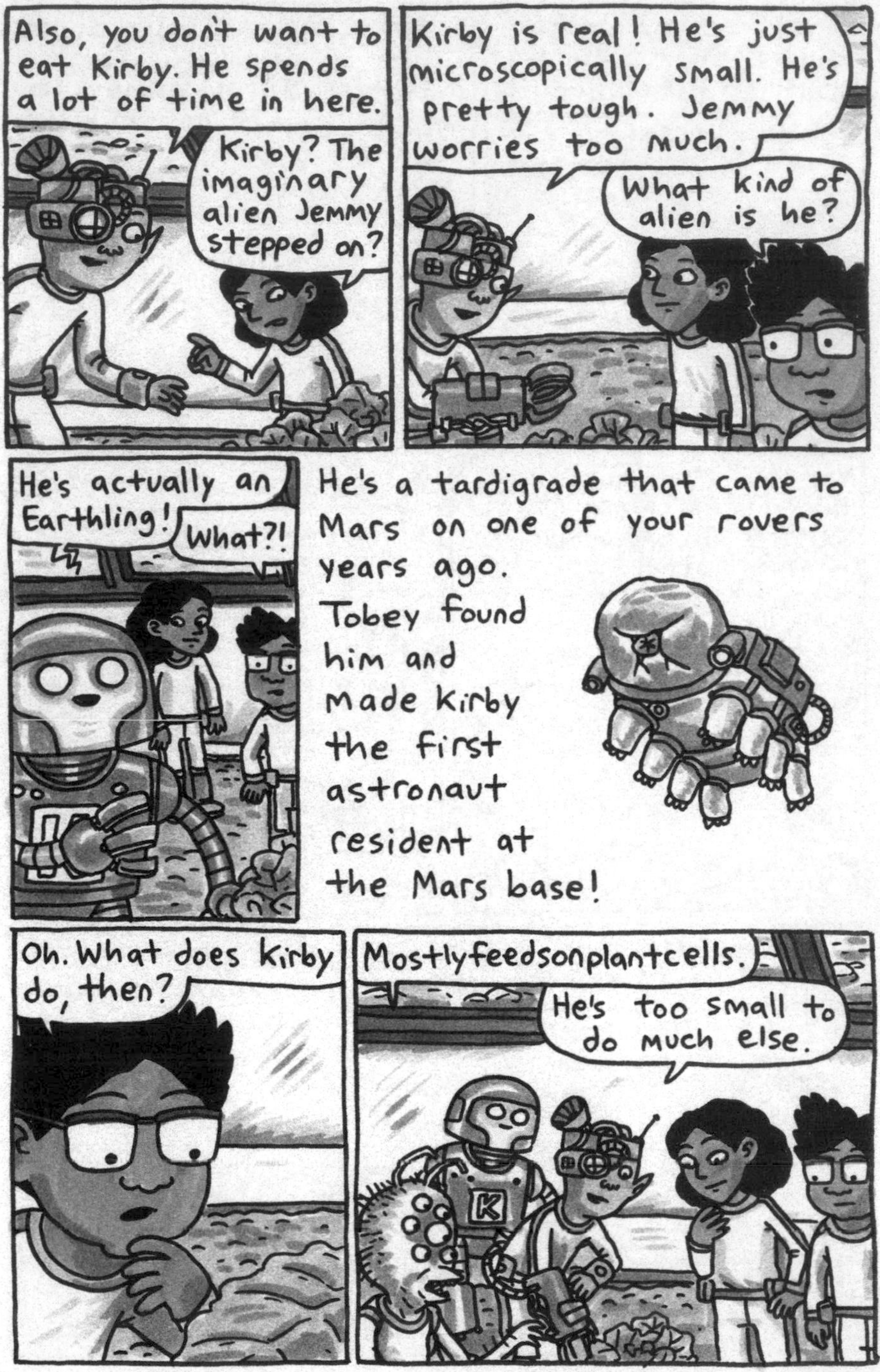
Also, you don't want to eat Kirby. He spends a lot of time in here.
Kirby? The imaginary alien Jemmy stepped on?
Kirby is real! He's just microscopically small. He's pretty tough. Jemmy worries too much.
What kind of alien is he?
He's actually an Earthling!
What?!
He's a tardigrade that came to Mars on one of your rovers years ago.
Tobey found him and made Kirby the first astronaut resident at the Mars base!
Oh. What does Kirby do, then?
Mostlyfeedsonplantcells.
He's too small to do much else.

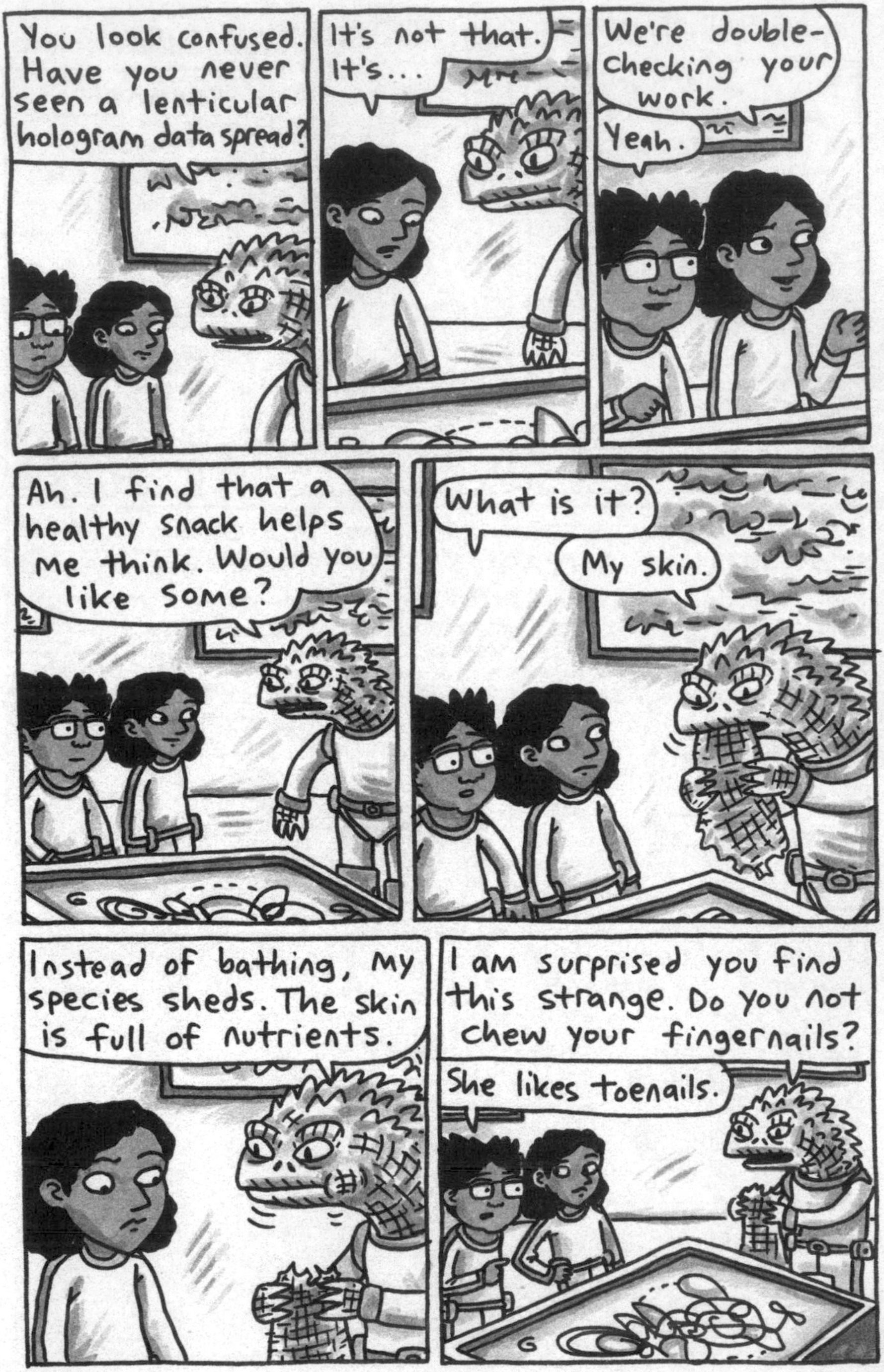

You look confused. Have you never seen a lenticular hologram data spread?
It's not that. It's...
We're double-checking your work.
Yeah.
Ah. I find that a healthy snack helps me think. Would you like some?
What is it?
My skin.
Instead of bathing, my species sheds. The skin is full of nutrients.
I am surprised you find this strange. Do you not chew your fingernails?
She likes toenails.

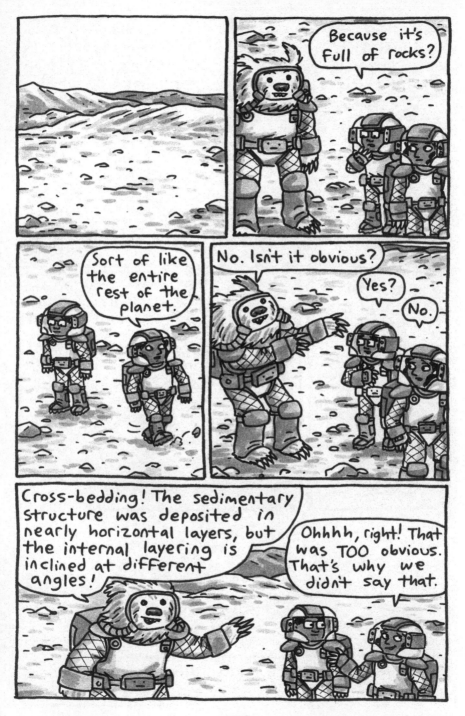

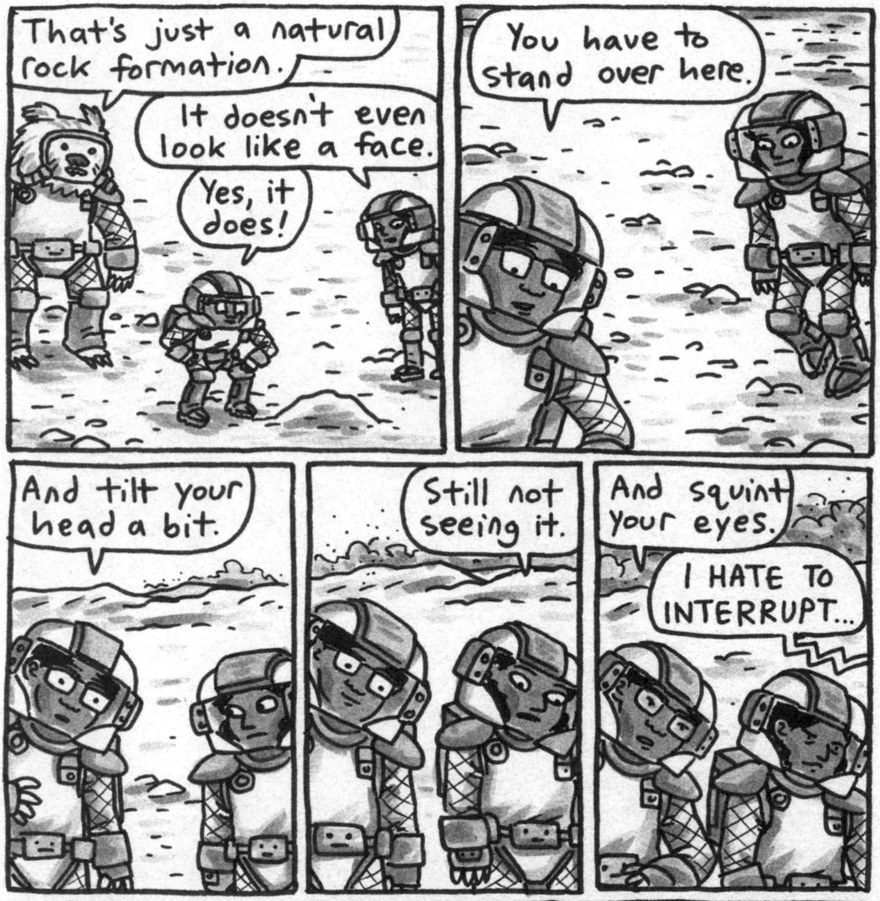
That's just a natural rock formation.
It doesn't even look like a face.
Yes, it does!
You have to stand over here.
And tilt your head a bit.
Still not seeing it.
And squint your eyes.
I HATE TO INTERRUPT...
...BUT THERE'S A DUST STORM COMING! RUN FOR THE BUGGY!
TOO LATE!

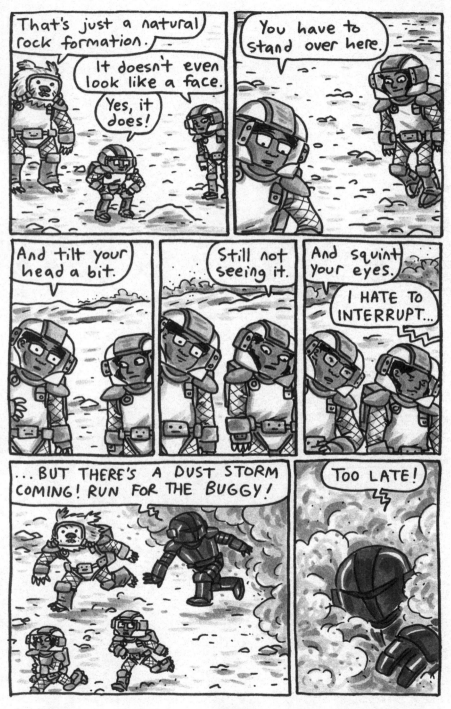

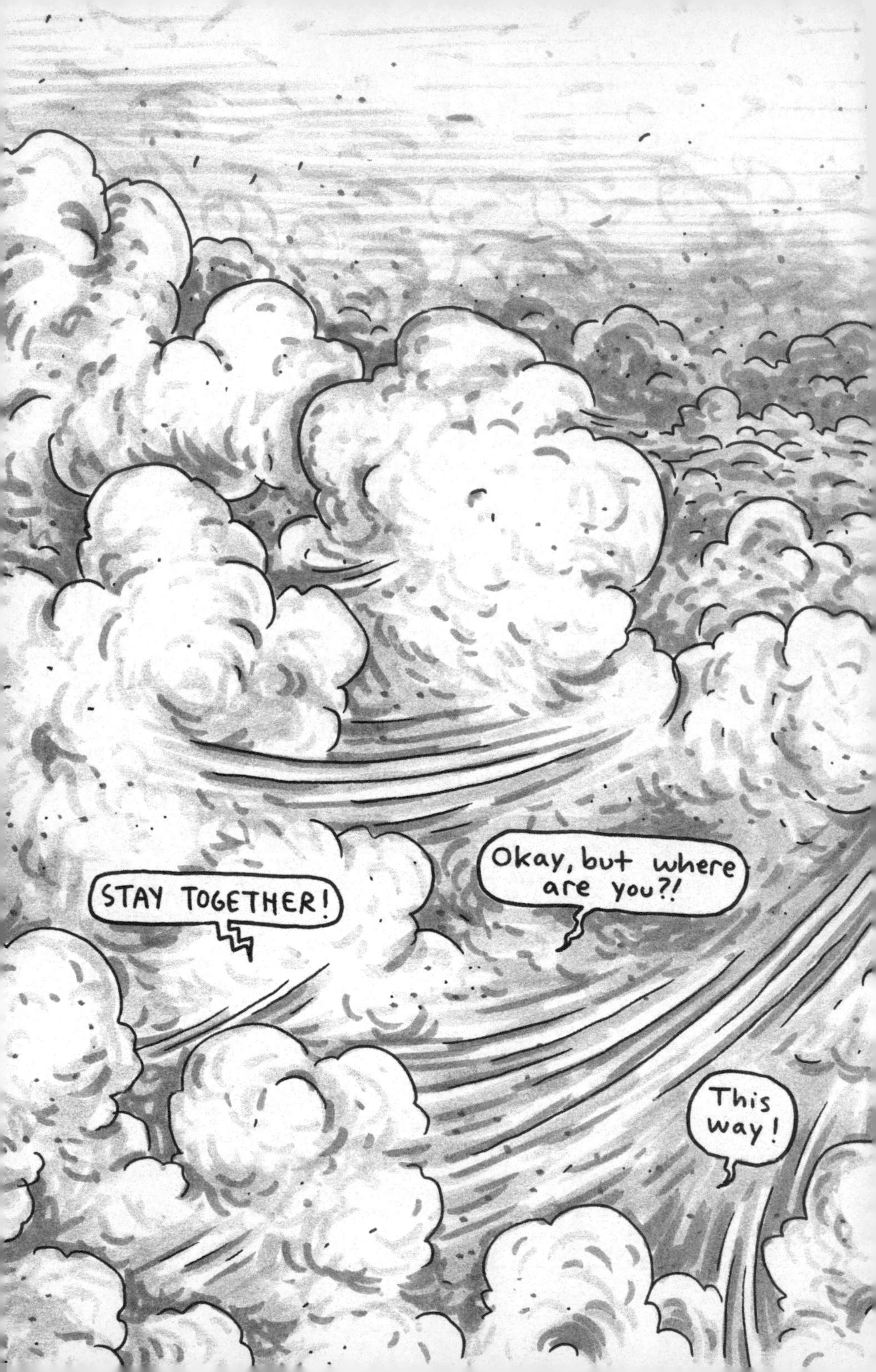
STAY TOGETHER!
Okay, but where are you?!
This way!

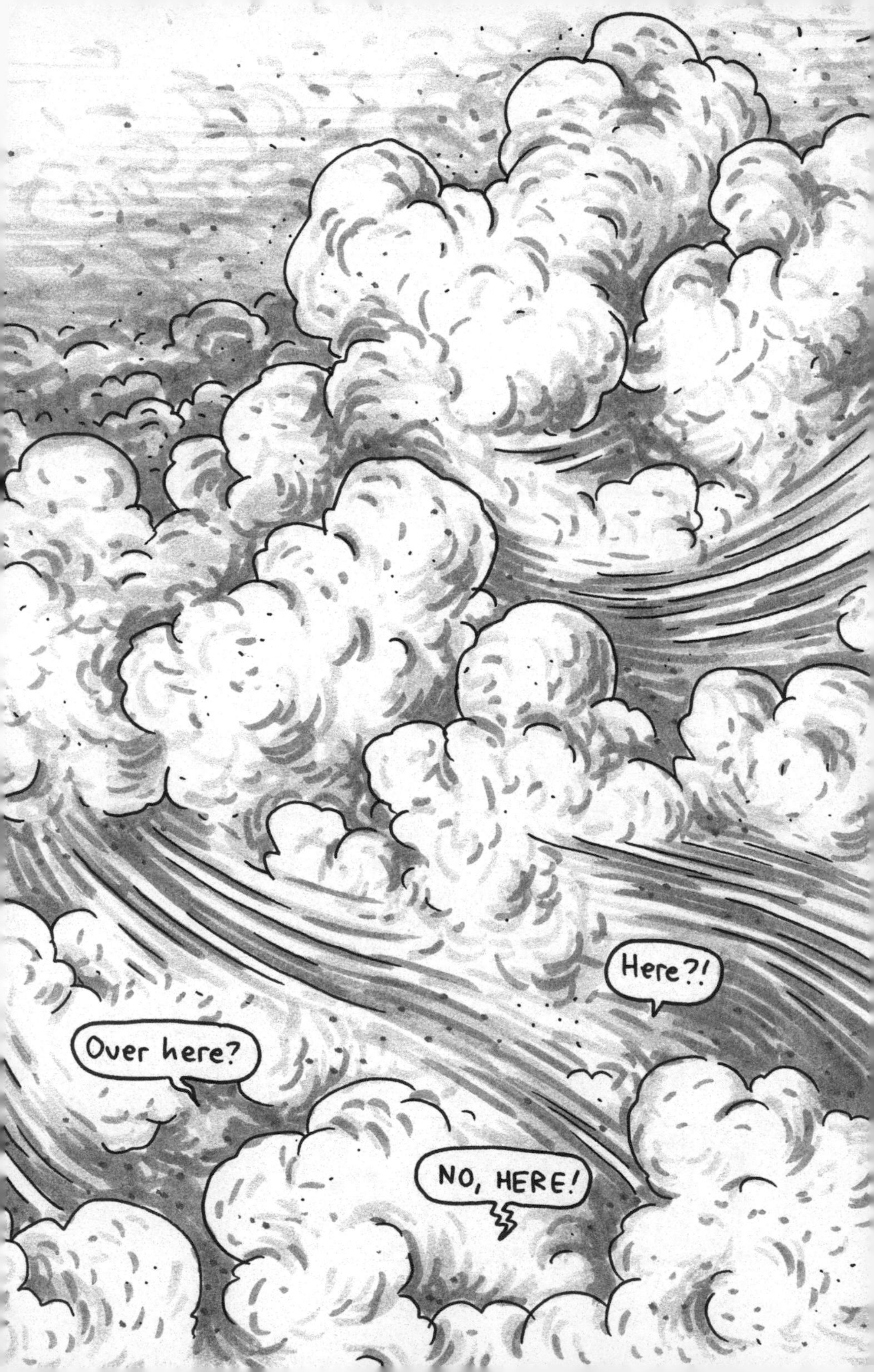
Here?!
Over here?
NO, HERE!

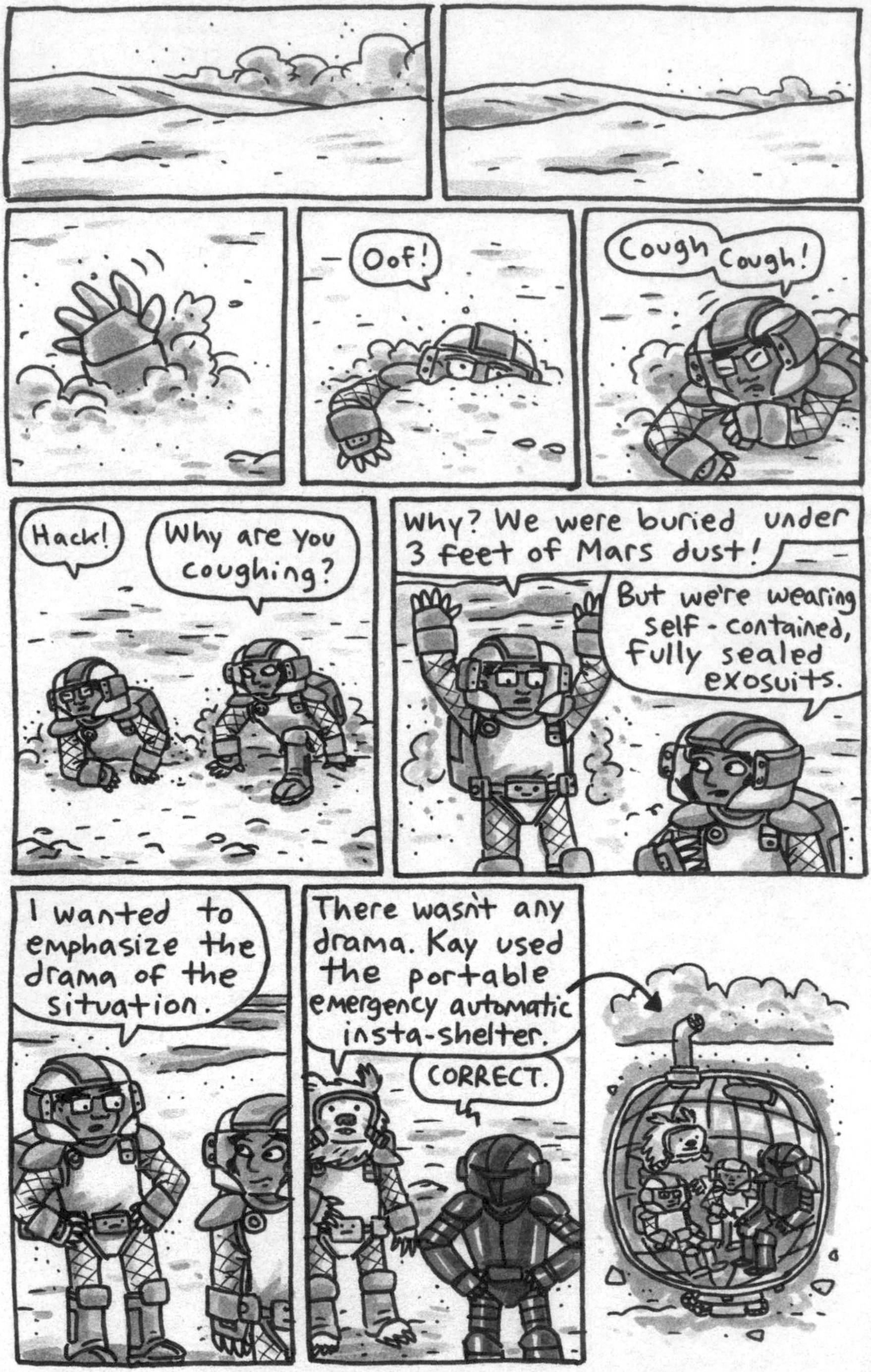
Oof!
Cough
Cough!
Hack!
Why are you coughing?
Why? We were buried under 3 feet of Mars dust!
But we're wearing self-contained, fully sealed exosuits.
I wanted to emphasize the drama of the situation.
There wasn't any drama. Kay used the portable emergency automatic insta-shelter.
CORRECT.

151

152

153

SPUDNIK

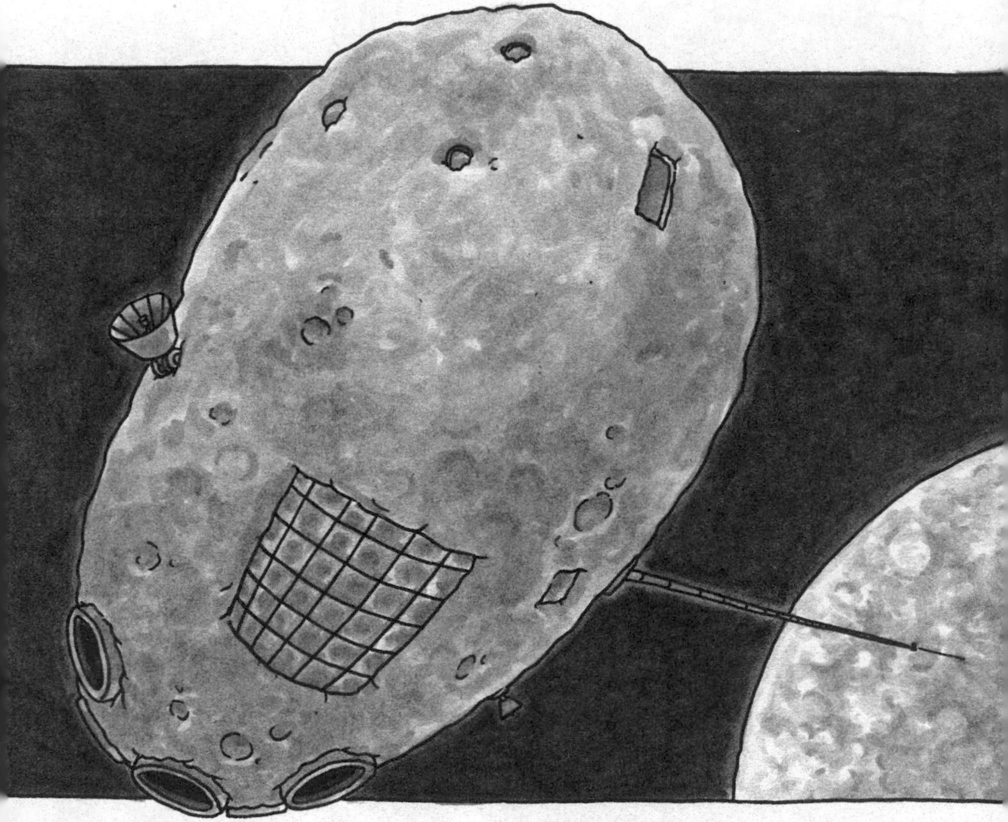

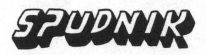

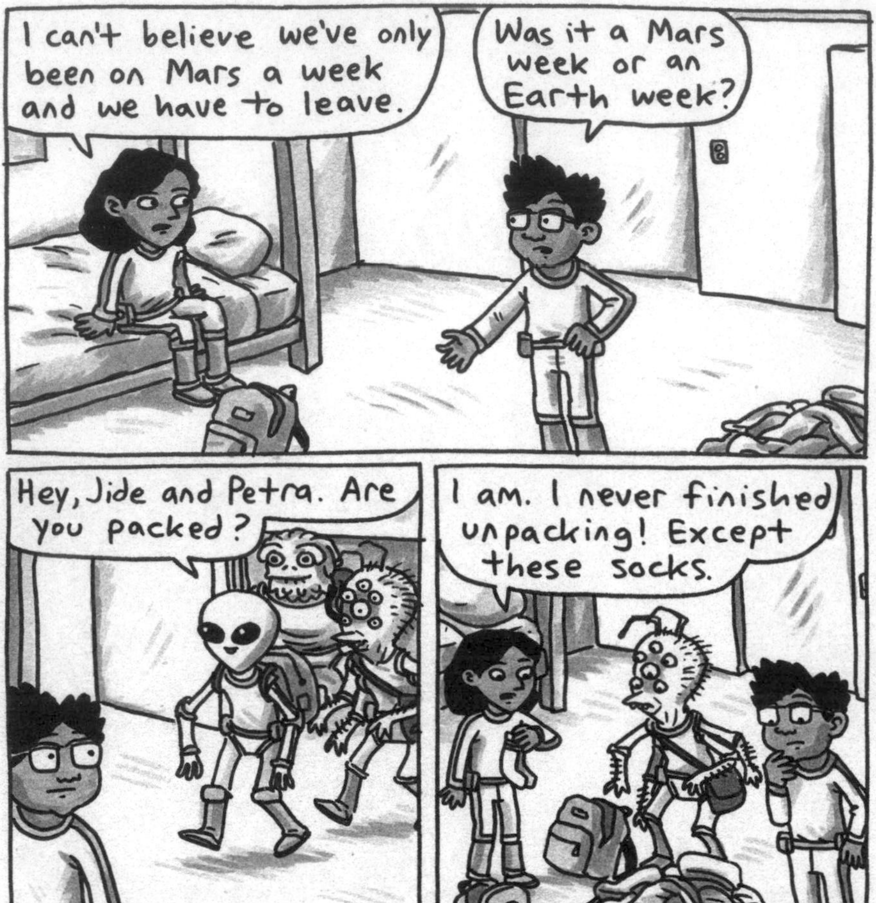
I can't believe we've only been on Mars a week and we have to leave.
Was it a Mars week or an Earth week?
Hey, Jide and Petra. Are you packed?
I am. I never finished unpacking! Except these socks.
I can't say I'll miss the view.
Yeah, the sunsets and sunrises are pretty much the same.
MARS

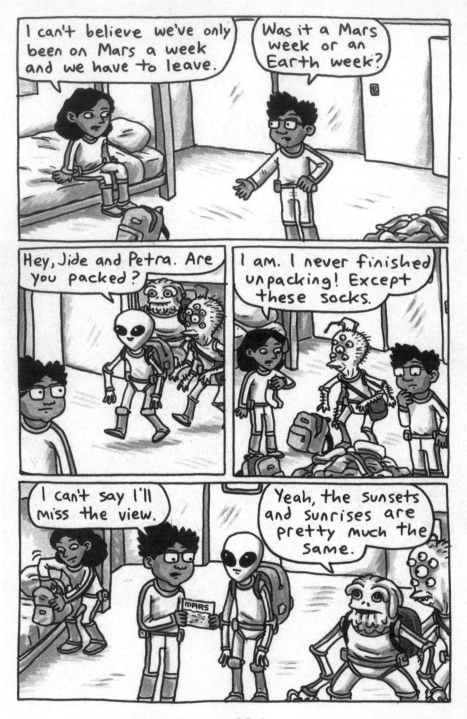

159

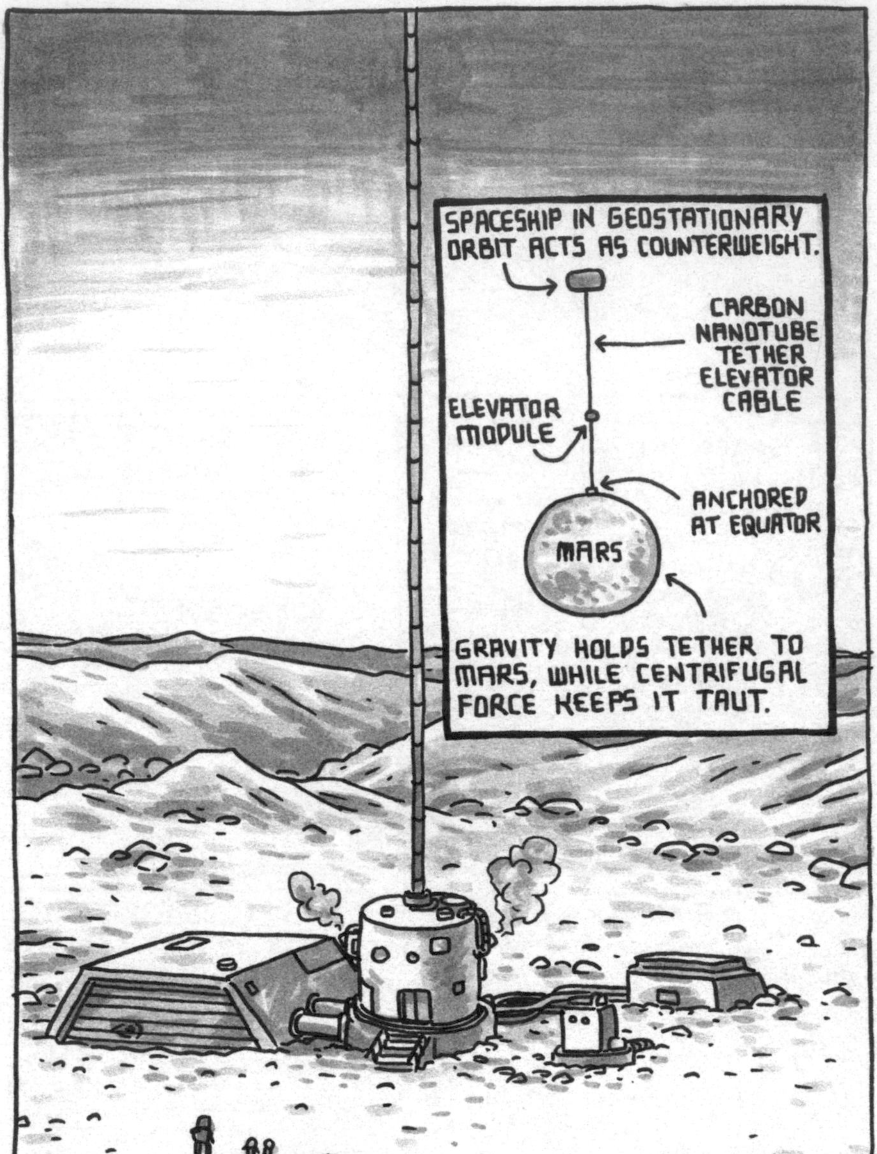
SPACESHIP IN GEOSTATIONARY ORBIT ACTS AS COUNTERWEIGHT.
CARBON NANOTUBE TETHER ELEVATOR CABLE
ELEVATOR MODULE
ANCHORED AT EQUATOR
MARS
GRAVITY HOLDS TETHER TO MARS, WHILE CENTRIFUGAL FORCE KEEPS IT TAUT.
Whoa!

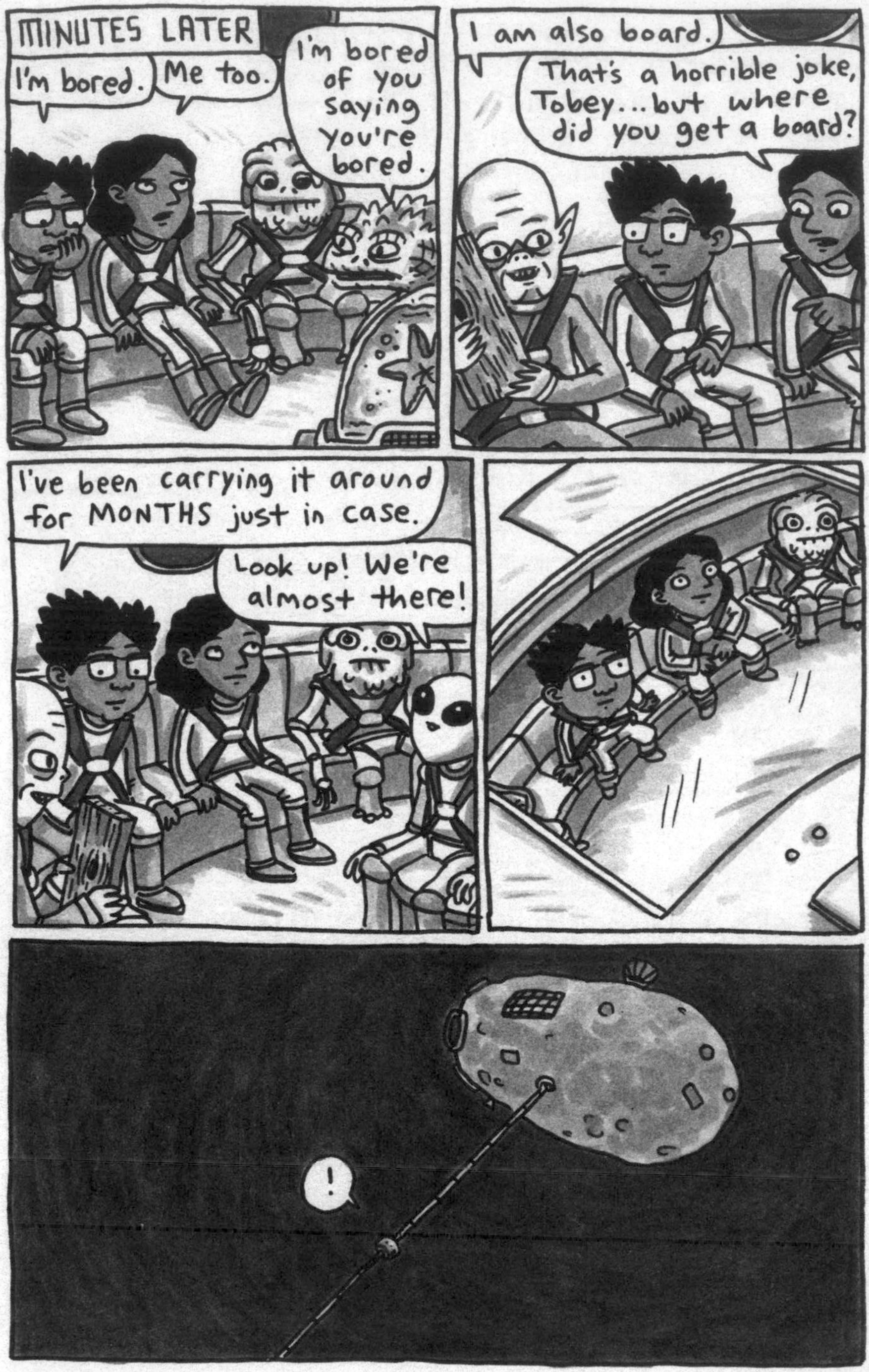
MINUTES LATER
I'm bored.
Me too.
I'm bored of you saying you're bored.
I am also board.
That's a horrible joke, Tobey...but where did you get a board?
I've been carrying it around for MONTHS just in case.
Look up! We're almost there!
!

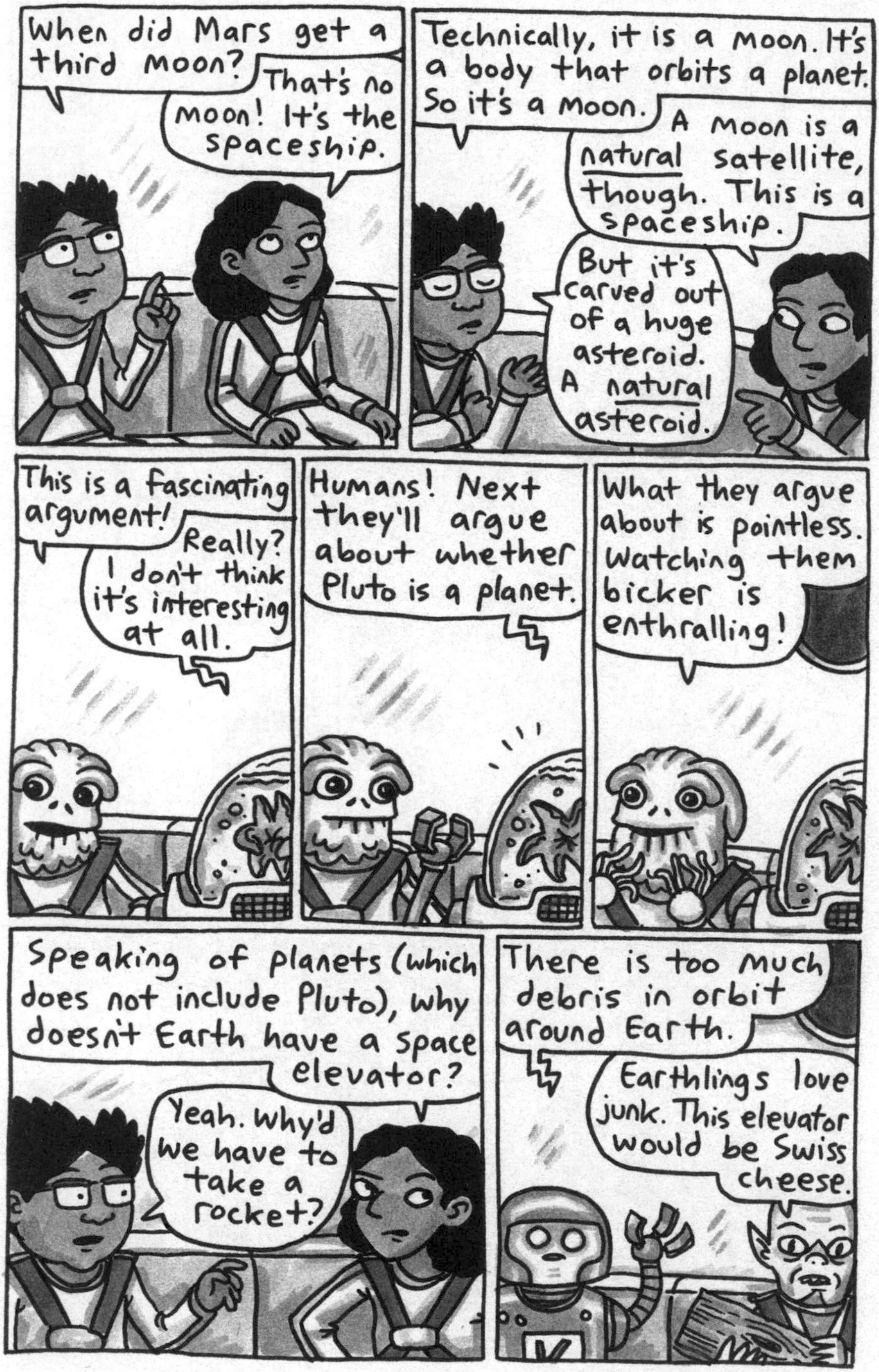
When did Mars get a third moon?
That's no moon! It's the spaceship.
Technically, it is a moon. It's a body that orbits a planet. So it's a moon.
A moon is a natural satellite, though. This is a spaceship.
But it's carved out of a huge asteroid. A natural asteroid.
This is a fascinating argument!
Really? I don't think it's interesting at all.
Humans! Next they'll argue about whether Pluto is a planet.
What they argue about is pointless. Watching them bicker is enthralling!
Speaking of planets (which does not include Pluto), why doesn't Earth have a space elevator?
Yeah. Why'd we have to take a rocket?
There is too much debris in orbit around Earth.
Earthlings love junk. This elevator would be Swiss cheese.

168

173

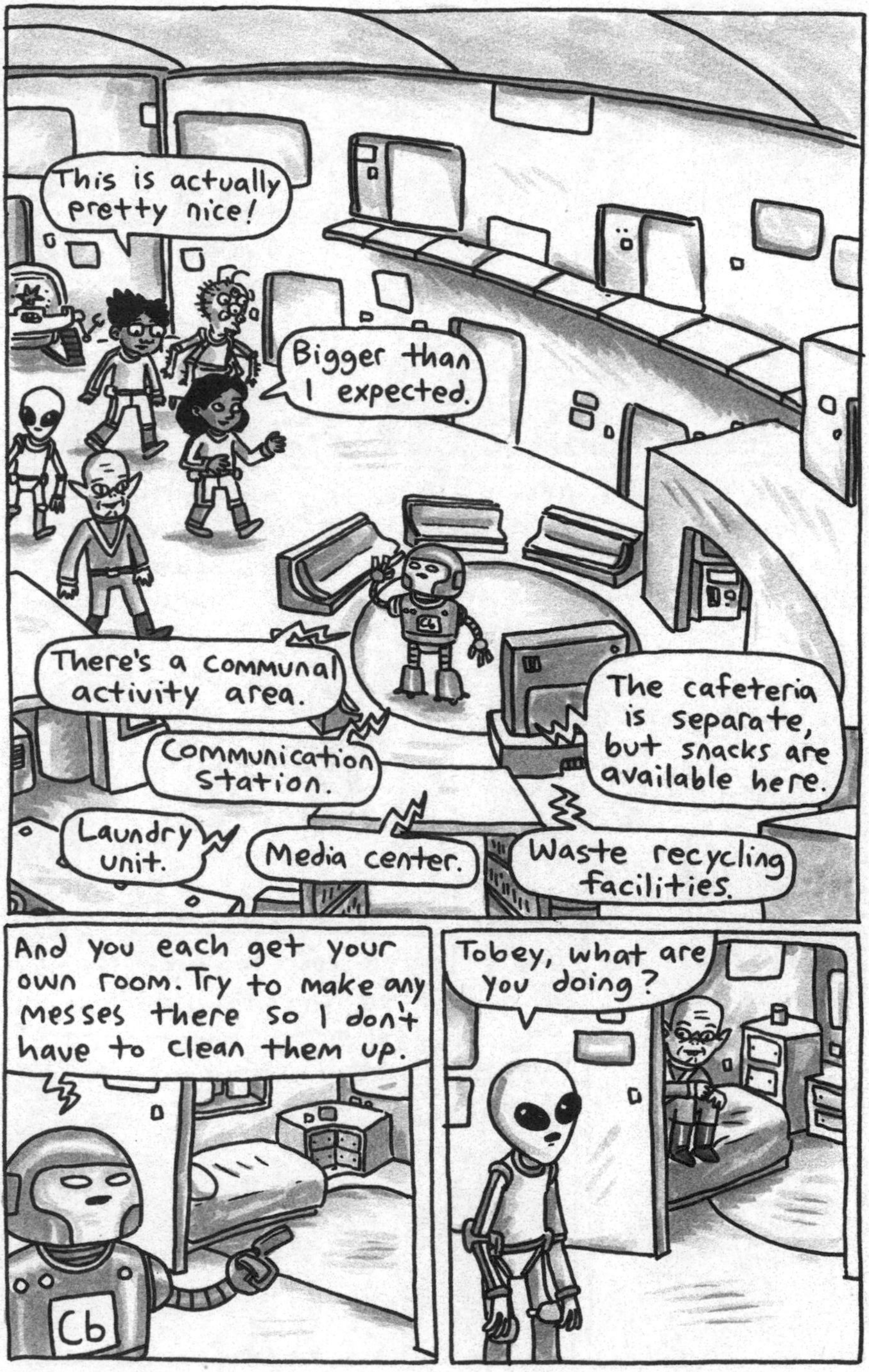
This is actually pretty nice!
Bigger than I expected.
There's a communal activity area.
Communication station.
The cafeteria is separate, but snacks are available here.
Laundry unit.
Media center.
Waste recycling facilities.
And you each get your own room. Try to make any messes there so I don't have to clean them up.
Cb
Tobey, what are you doing?

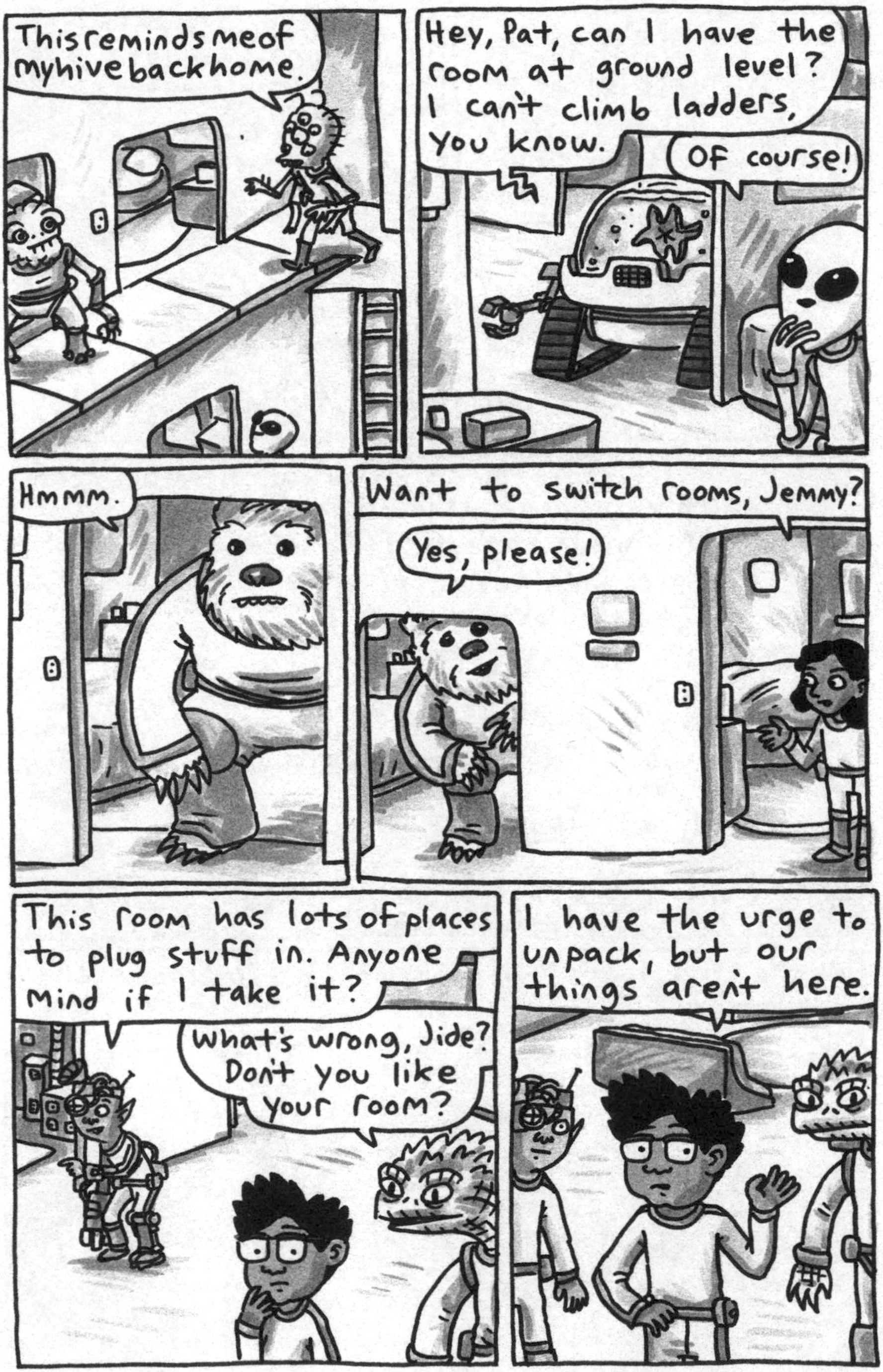
This reminds me of my hive back home.
Hey, Pat, can I have the room at ground level? I can't climb ladders, you know.
Of course!
Hmmm.
Want to switch rooms, Jemmy?
Yes, please!
This room has lots of places to plug stuff in. Anyone mind if I take it?
What's wrong, Jide? Don't you like your room?
I have the urge to unpack, but our things aren't here.

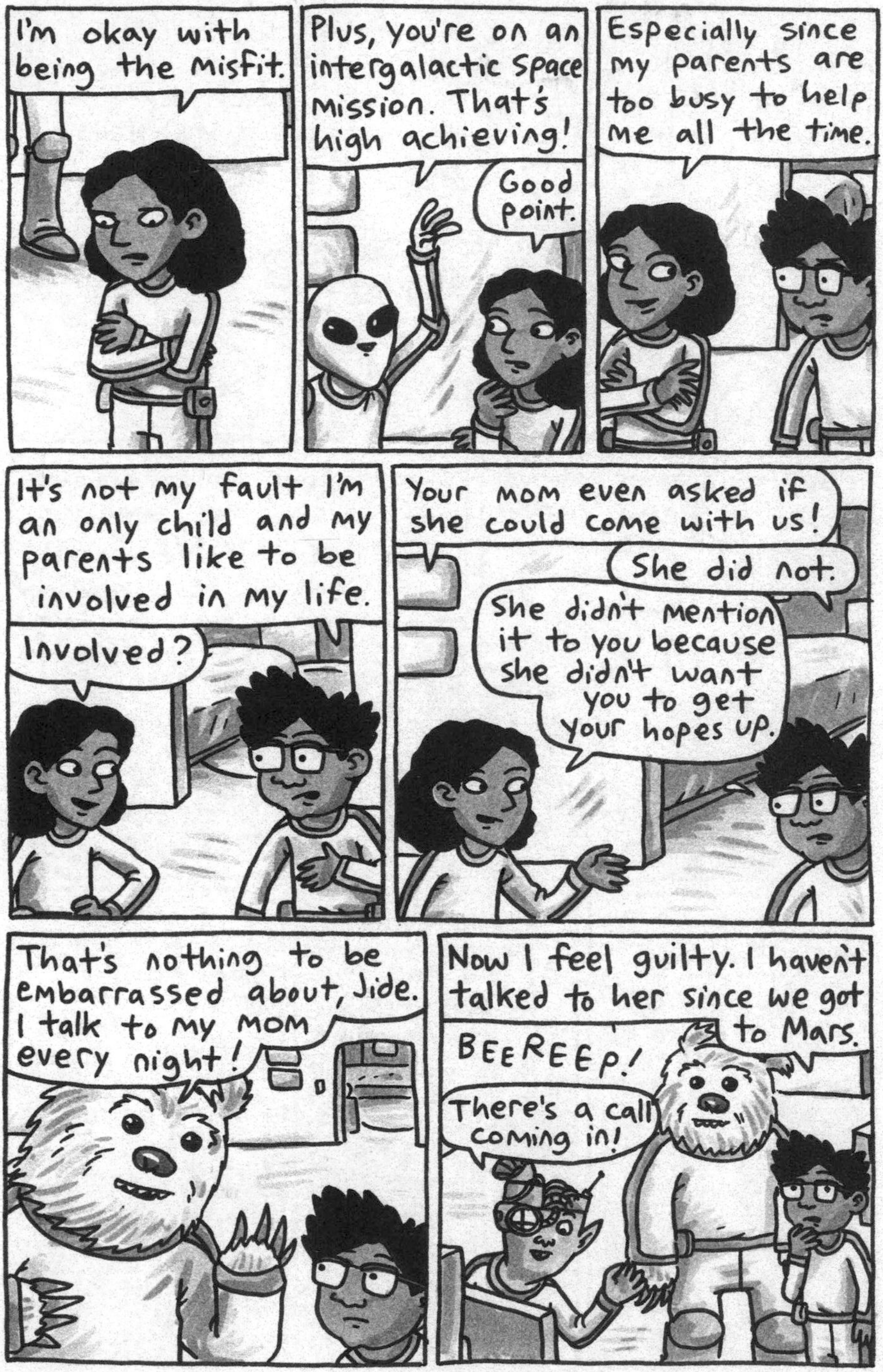

I'm okay with being the misfit.
Plus, you're on an intergalactic space mission. That's high achieving!
Good point.
Especially since my parents are too busy to help me all the time.
It's not my fault I'm an only child and my parents like to be involved in my life.
Involved?
Your mom even asked if she could come with us!
She did not.
She didn't mention it to you because she didn't want you to get your hopes up.
That's nothing to be embarrassed about, Jide. I talk to my MOM every night!
Now I feel guilty. I haven't talked to her since we got to Mars.
BEEREEP!
There's a call coming in!

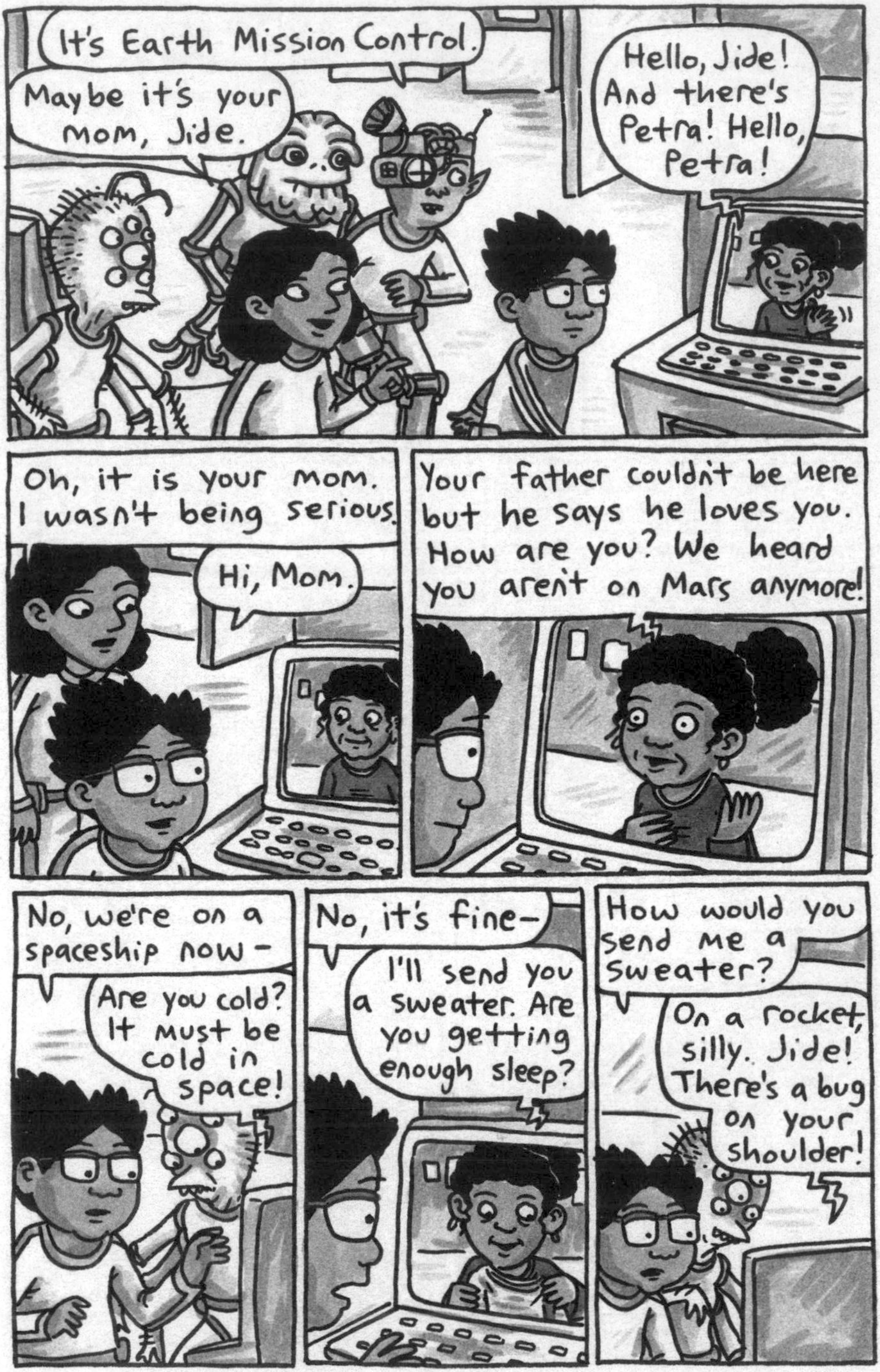
It's Earth Mission Control.
Maybe it's your mom, Jide.
Hello, Jide! And there's Petra! Hello, Petra!
Oh, it is your mom. I wasn't being serious.
Hi, Mom.
Your father couldn't be here but he says he loves you. How are you? We heard you aren't on Mars anymore!
No, we're on a spaceship now-
Are you cold? It must be cold in space!
No, it's fine-
I'll send you a sweater. Are you getting enough sleep?
How would you send me a sweater?
On a rocket, silly, Jide! There's a bug on your shoulder!

184

185

HIGH ORBIT, HIGH ALERT

Cb

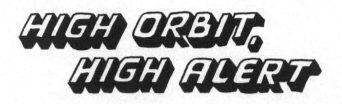

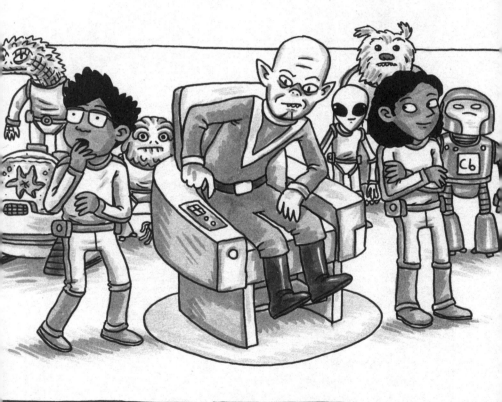

189

192

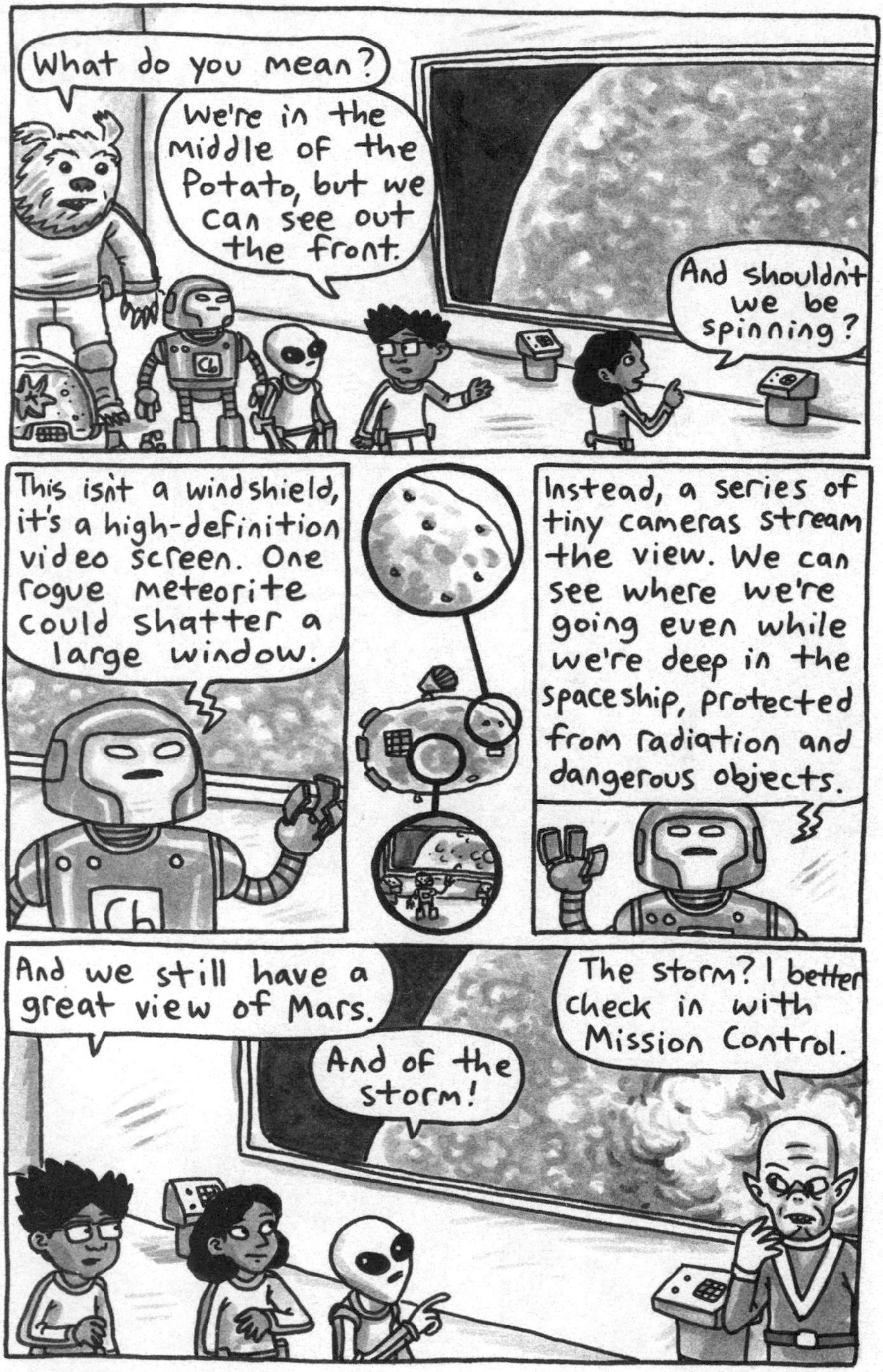
What do you mean?
We're in the middle of the Potato, but we can see out the front.
And shouldn't we be spinning?
This isn't a windshield, it's a high-definition video screen. One rogue meteorite could shatter a large window.
Instead, a series of tiny cameras stream the view. We can see where we're going even while we're deep in the spaceship, protected from radiation and dangerous objects.
And we still have a great view of Mars.
And of the storm!
The storm? I better check in with Mission Control.

196

197

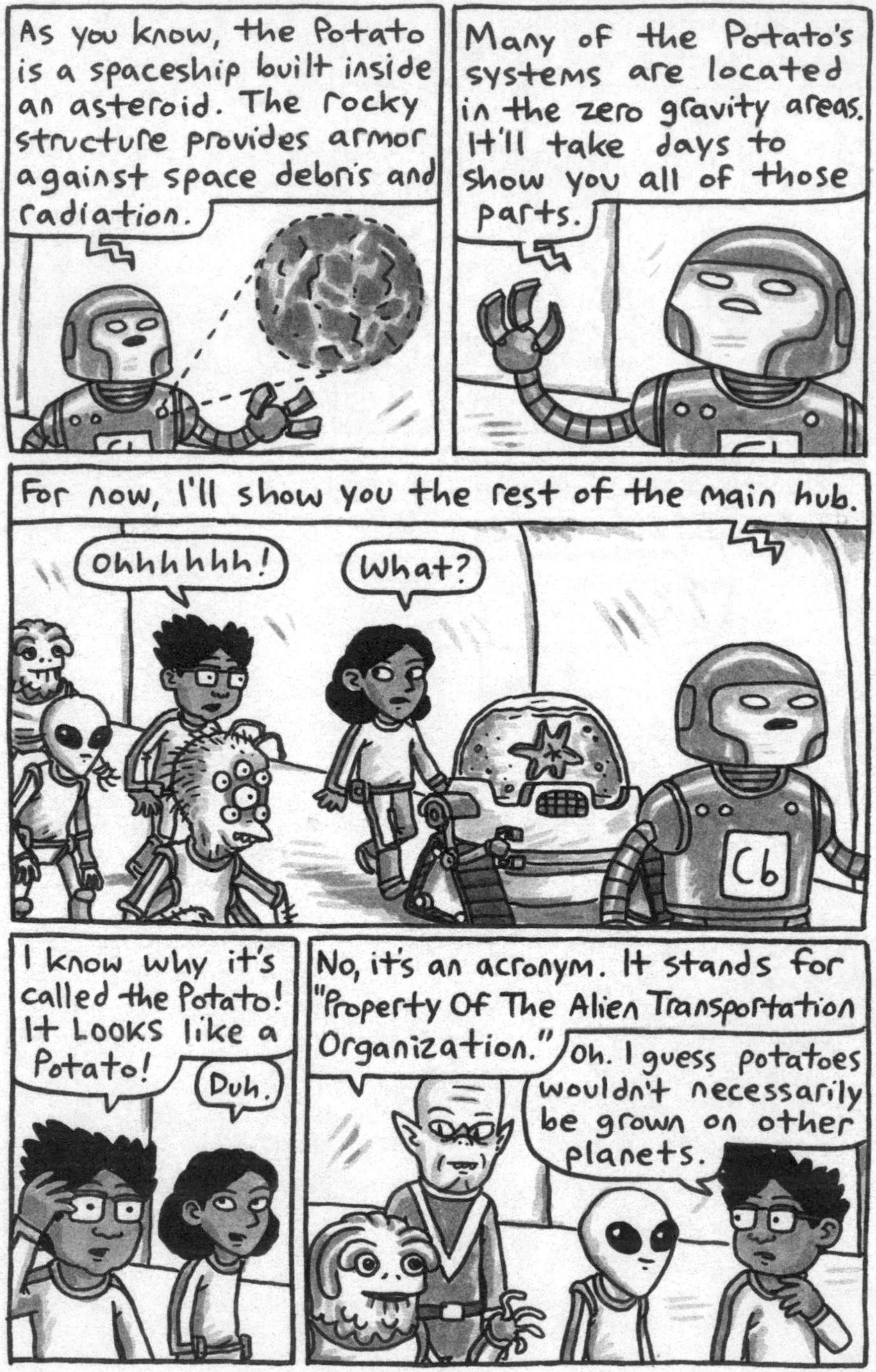
As you know, the Potato is a spaceship built inside an asteroid. The rocky structure provides armor against space debris and radiation.
Many of the Potato's systems are located in the zero gravity areas. It'll take days to show you all of those parts.
For now, I'll show you the rest of the main hub.
Ohhhhhh!
What?
Cb
I know why it's called the Potato! It LOOKS like a Potato!
Duh.
No, it's an acronym. It stands for "Property Of The Alien Transportation Organization."
Oh. I guess potatoes wouldn't necessarily be grown on other planets.

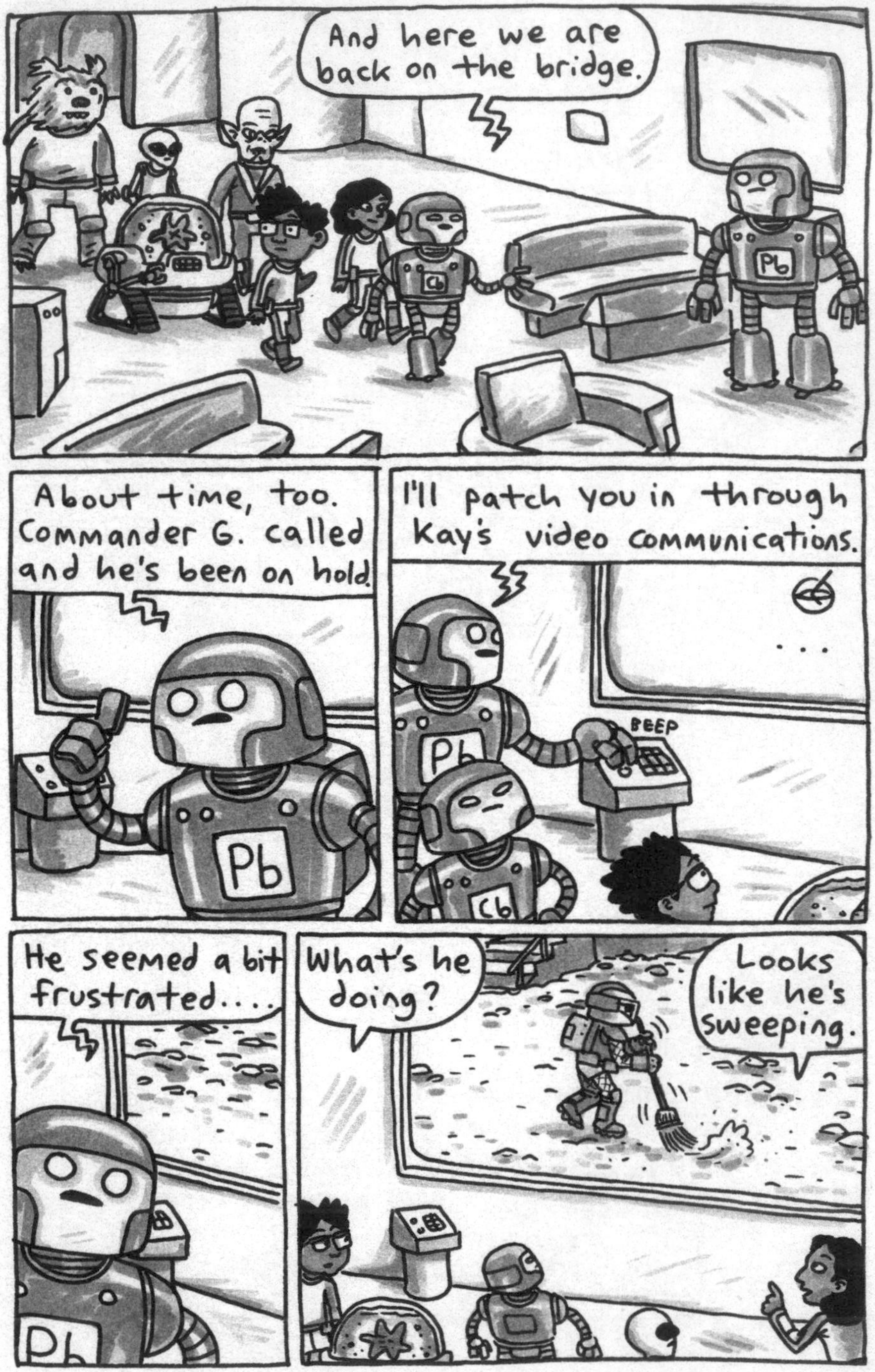
And here we are back on the bridge.
About time, too. Commander G. called and he's been on hold.
I'll patch you in through Kay's video communications.
BEEP
He seemed a bit frustrated....
What's he doing?
Looks like he's sweeping.

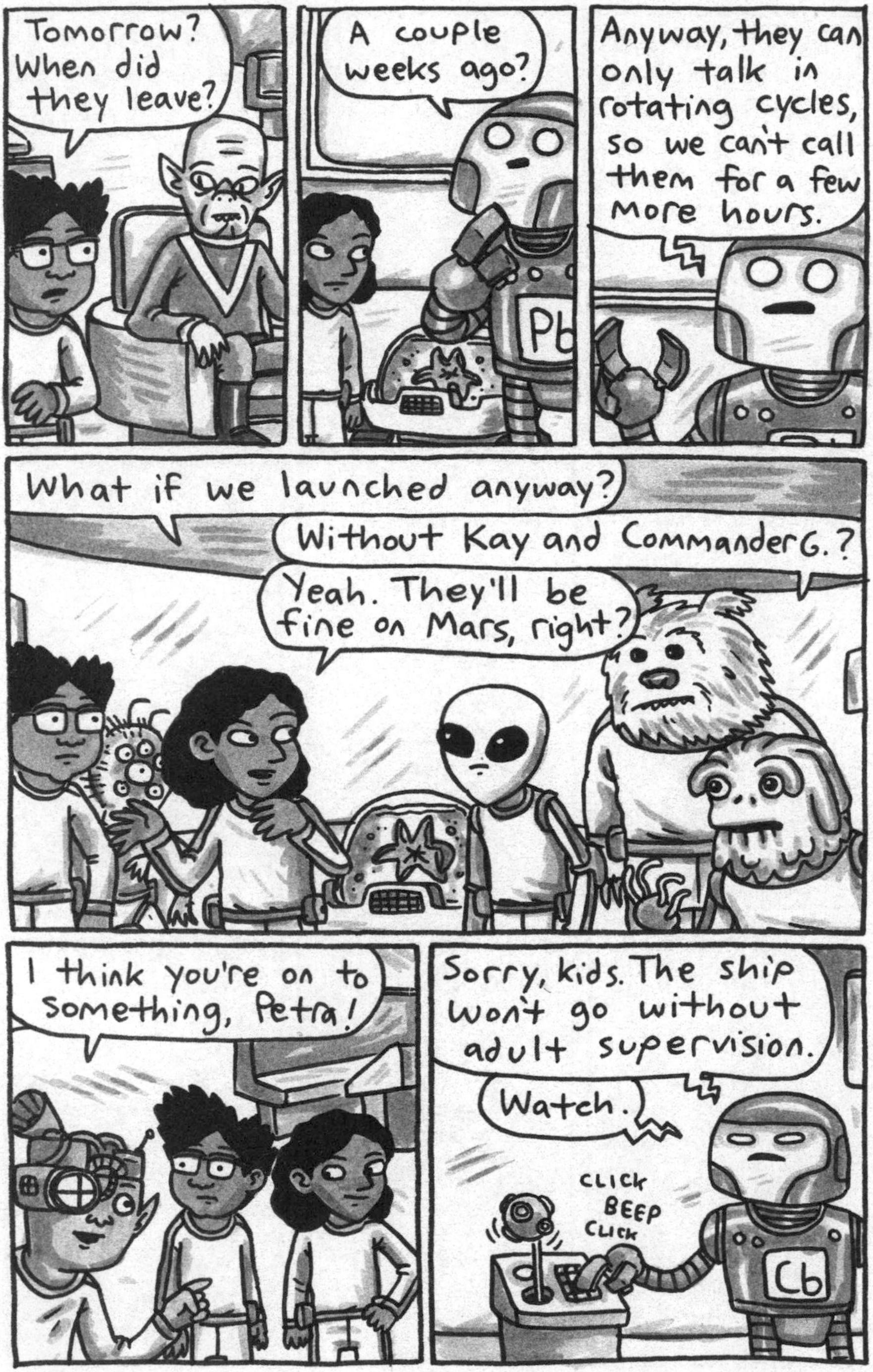
Tomorrow? When did they leave?
A couple weeks ago?
Pb
Anyway, they can only talk in rotating cycles, so we can't call them for a few more hours.
What if we launched anyway?
Without Kay and Commander G.?
Yeah. They'll be fine on Mars, right?
I think you're on to something, Petra!
Sorry, kids. The ship won't go without adult supervision.
Watch.
CLICK
BEEP
CLICK
Cb

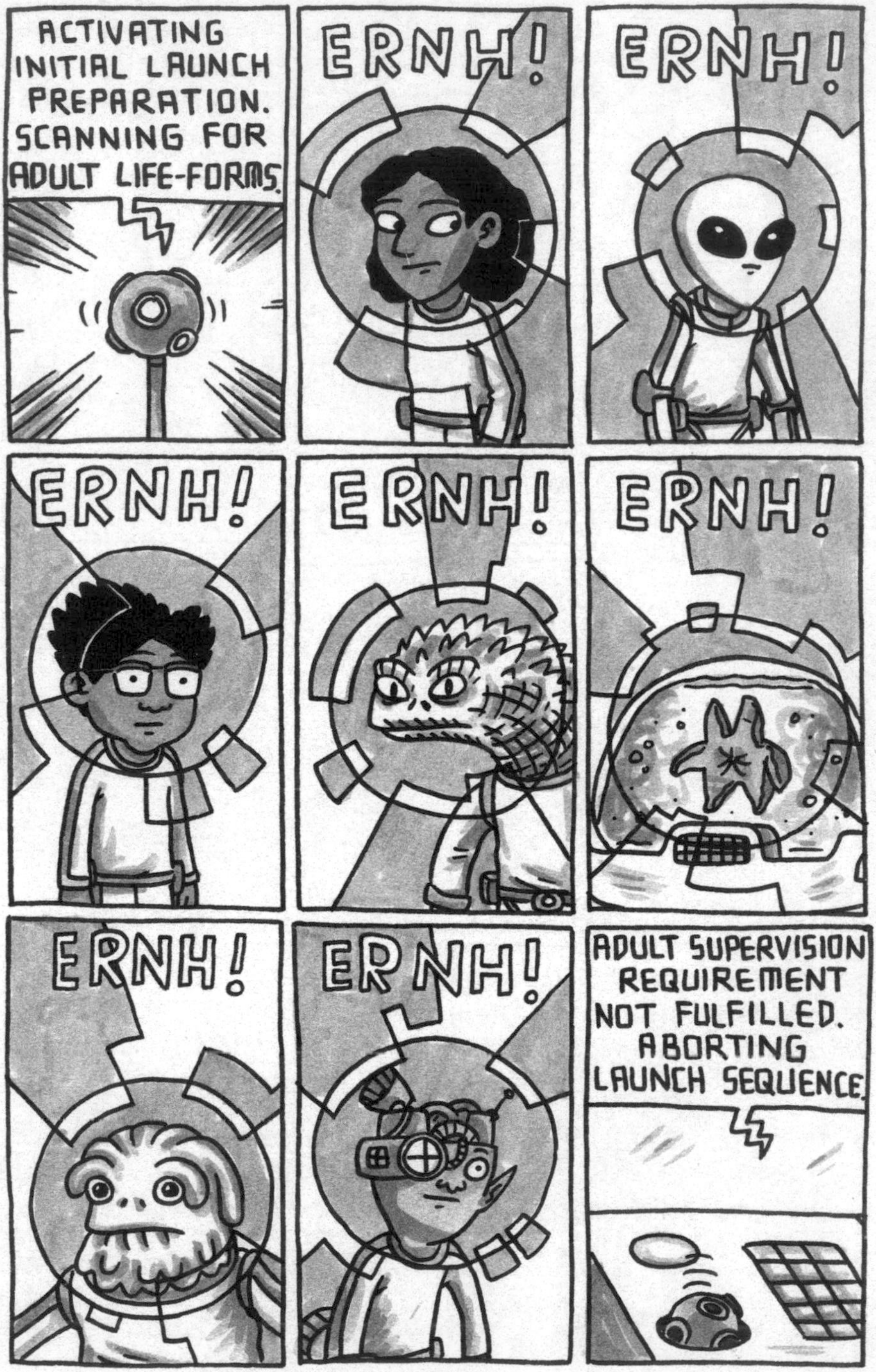
ACTIVATING INITIAL LAUNCH PREPARATION. SCANNING FOR ADULT LIFE-FORMS.
ERNH!
ERNH!
ERNH!
ERNH!
ERNH!
ERNH!
ERNH!
ADULT SUPERVISION REQUIREMENT NOT FULFILLED. ABORTING LAUNCH SEQUENCE.

THE TOBEY DRIVE SHRINKS THE SPACE-TIME AROUND IT, WHILE STAYING THE SAME ITSELF. IT TRAVELS A SHORT DISTANCE OVER COMPRESSED SPACE-TIME, AND WHEN IT DEACTIVATES, THE UNCOMPRESSED SPACE-TIME LEAVES THE SHIP A GREAT DISTANCE AWAY FROM WHERE IT STARTED.

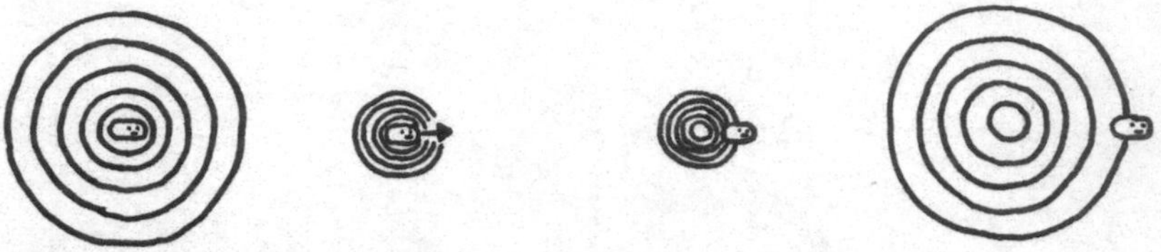

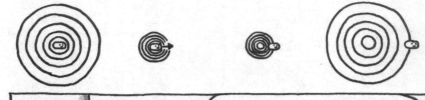

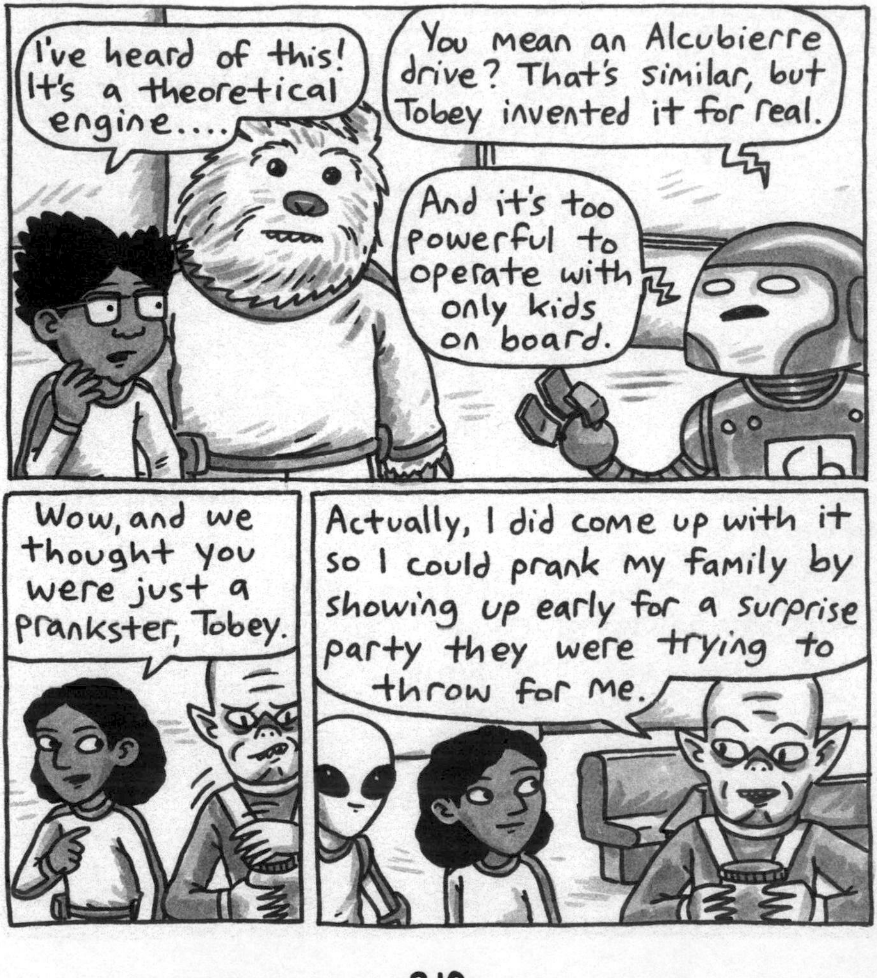
I've heard of this! It's a theoretical engine....
You mean an Alcubierre drive? That's similar, but Tobey invented it for real.
And it's too powerful to operate with only kids on board.
Wow, and we thought you were just a prankster, Tobey.
Actually, I did come up with it so I could prank my family by showing up early for a surprise party they were trying to throw for me.

213

216

217

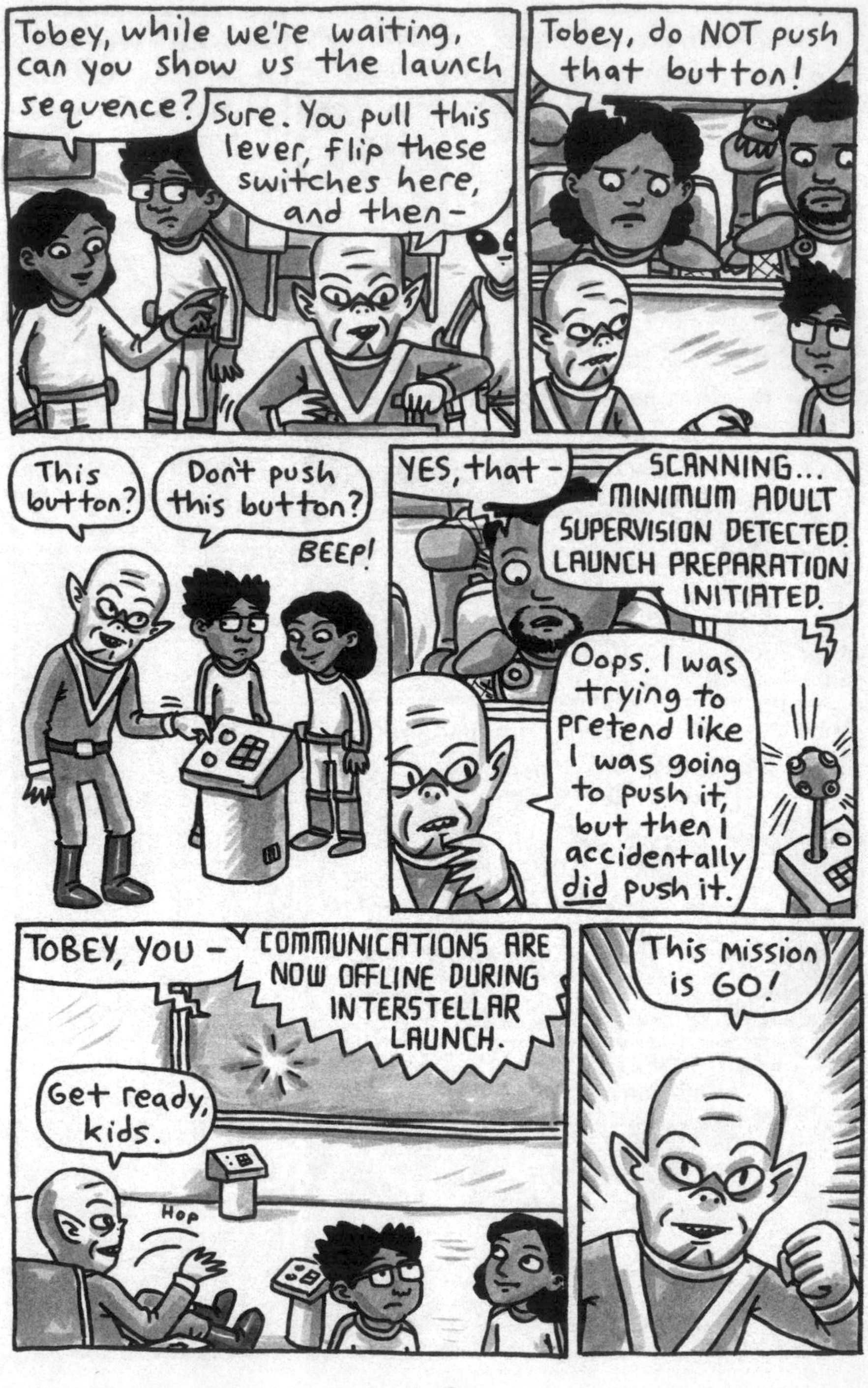
Tobey, while we're waiting, can you show us the launch sequence?
Sure. You pull this lever, flip these switches here, and then-
Tobey, do NOT push that button!
This button?
Don't push this button?
BEEP!
YES, that-
SCANNING... MINIMUM ADULT SUPERVISION DETECTED. LAUNCH PREPARATION INITIATED.
Oops. I was trying to pretend like I was going to push it, but then I accidentally did push it.
TOBEY, YOU-
COMMUNICATIONS ARE NOW OFFLINE DURING INTERSTELLAR LAUNCH.
Get ready, kids.
HOP
This mission is GO!

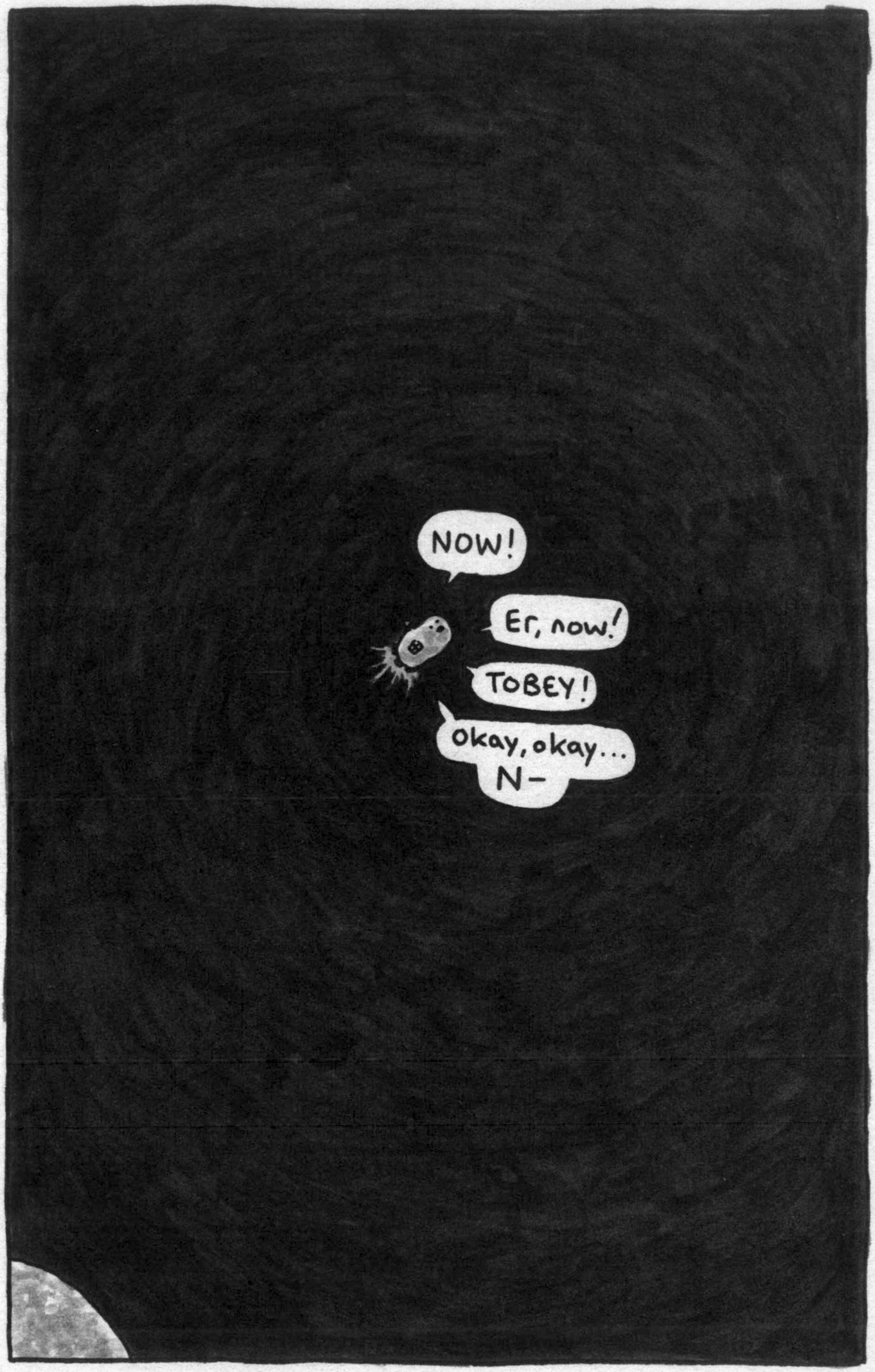
NOW!
Er, now!
TOBEY!
Okay, okay... N-

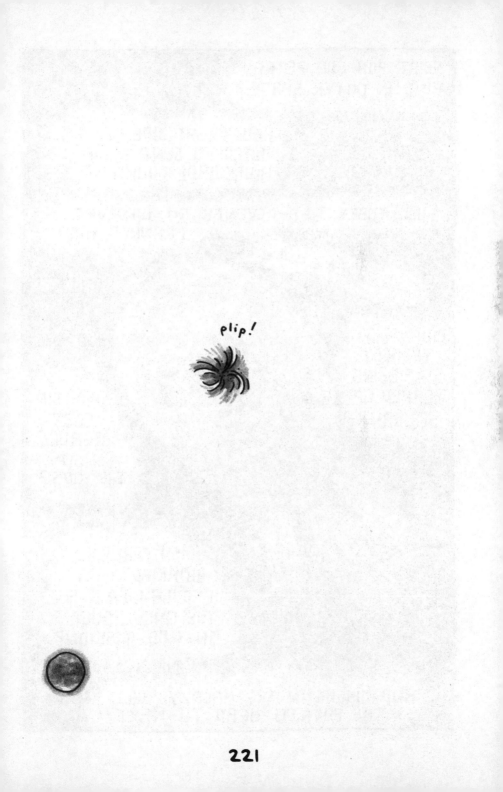

plip!

THE MISADVENTURES CONTINUE IN BOOK 2:

From the author of the
New York Times bestselling Jedi Academy series
A TOTAL WASTE OF
SPACE-TIME!
JEFFREY BROWN

COMING IN 2021!

LUCY & ANDY NEANDERTHAL

ROCK THE BOAT

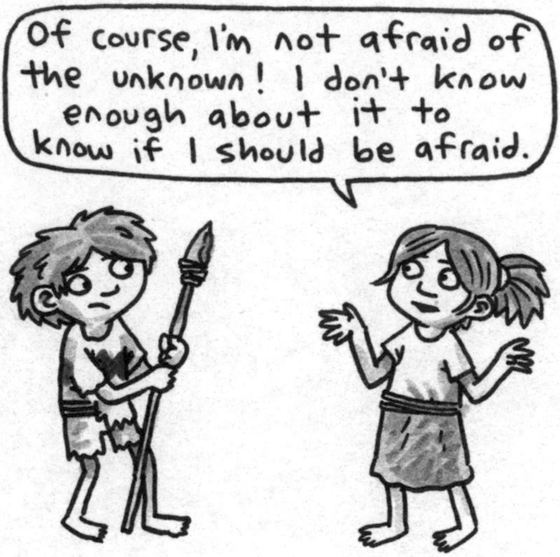
Of course, I'm not afraid of the unknown! I don't know enough about it to know if I should be afraid.

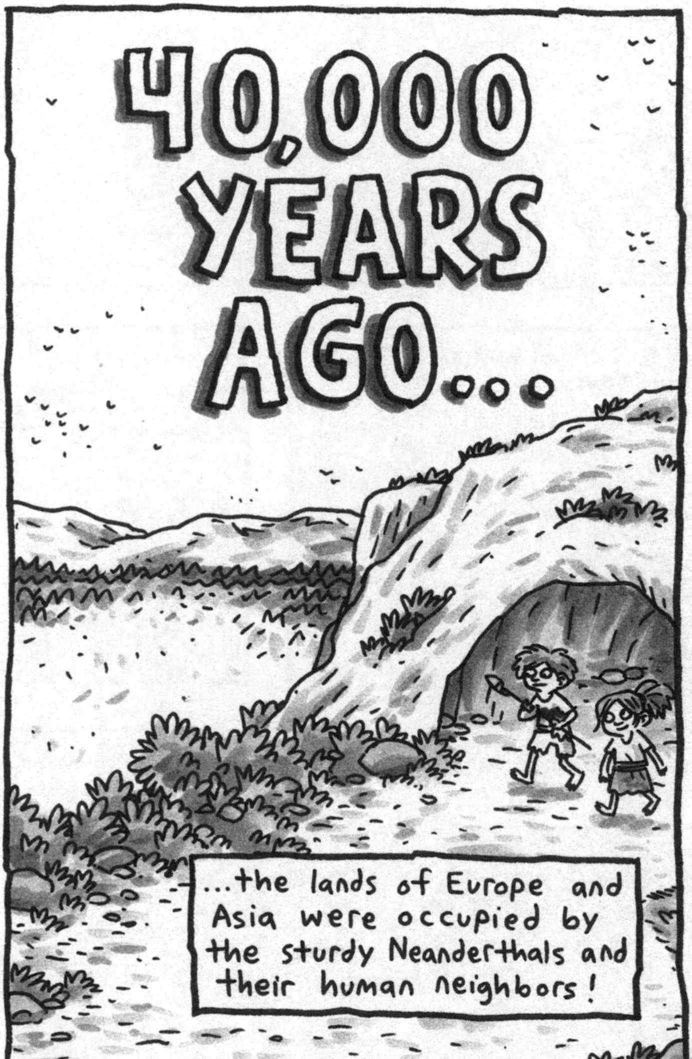
40,000 YEARS AGO...
...the lands of Europe and Asia were occupied by the sturdy Neanderthals and their human neighbors!

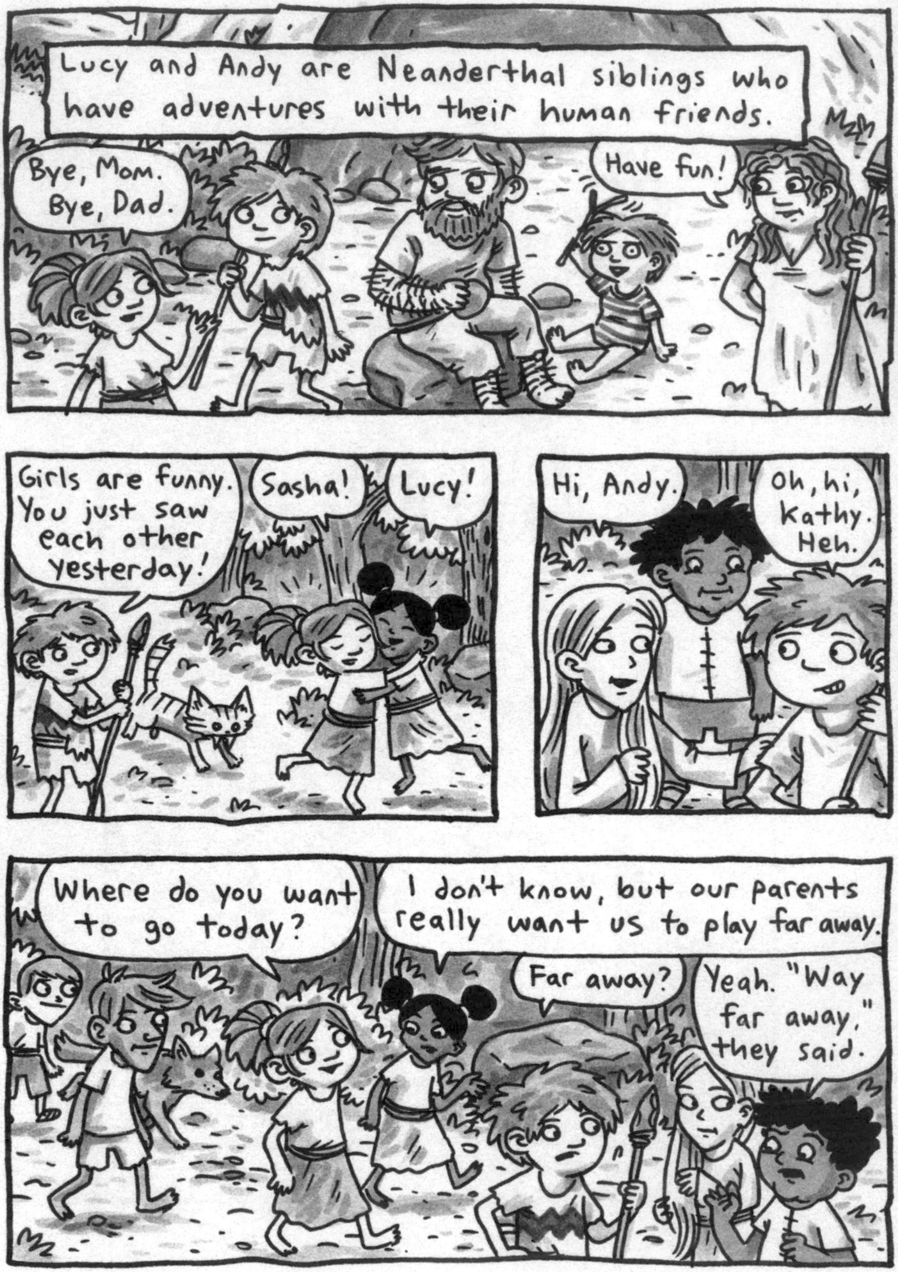
Lucy and Andy are Neanderthal siblings who have adventures with their human friends.
Bye, Mom. Bye, Dad.
Have fun!
Girls are funny. You just saw each other yesterday!
Sasha!
Lucy!
Hi, Andy.
Oh, hi, Kathy. Heh.
Where do you want to go today?
I don't know, but our parents really want us to play far away.
Far away?
Yeah. "Way far away," they said.

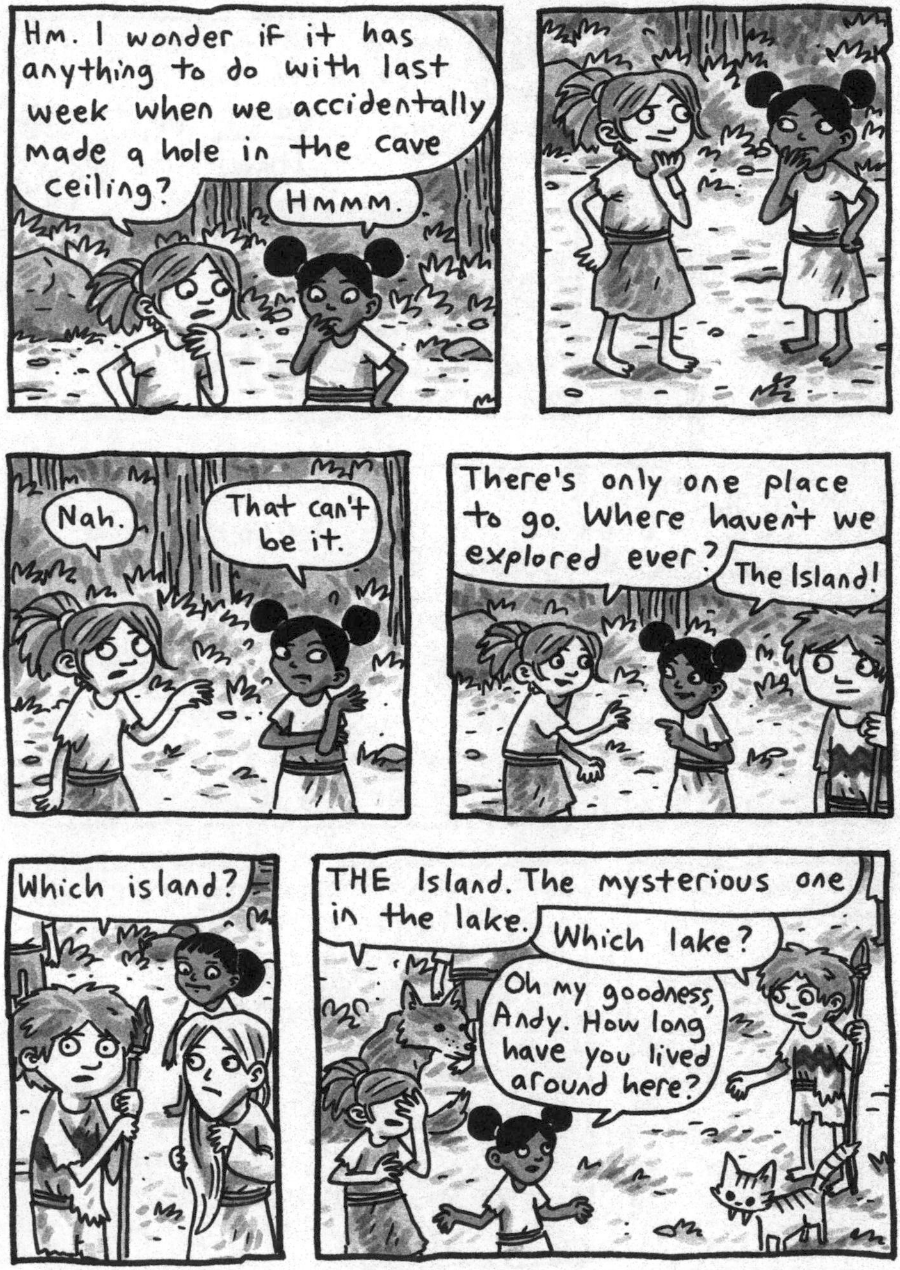

Hm. I wonder if it has anything to do with last week when we accidentally made a hole in the cave ceiling?
HMMM.
Nah.
That can't be it.
There's only one place to go. Where haven't we explored ever?
The Island!
Which island?
THE Island. The mysterious one in the lake.
Which lake?
Oh my goodness, Andy. How long have you lived around here?

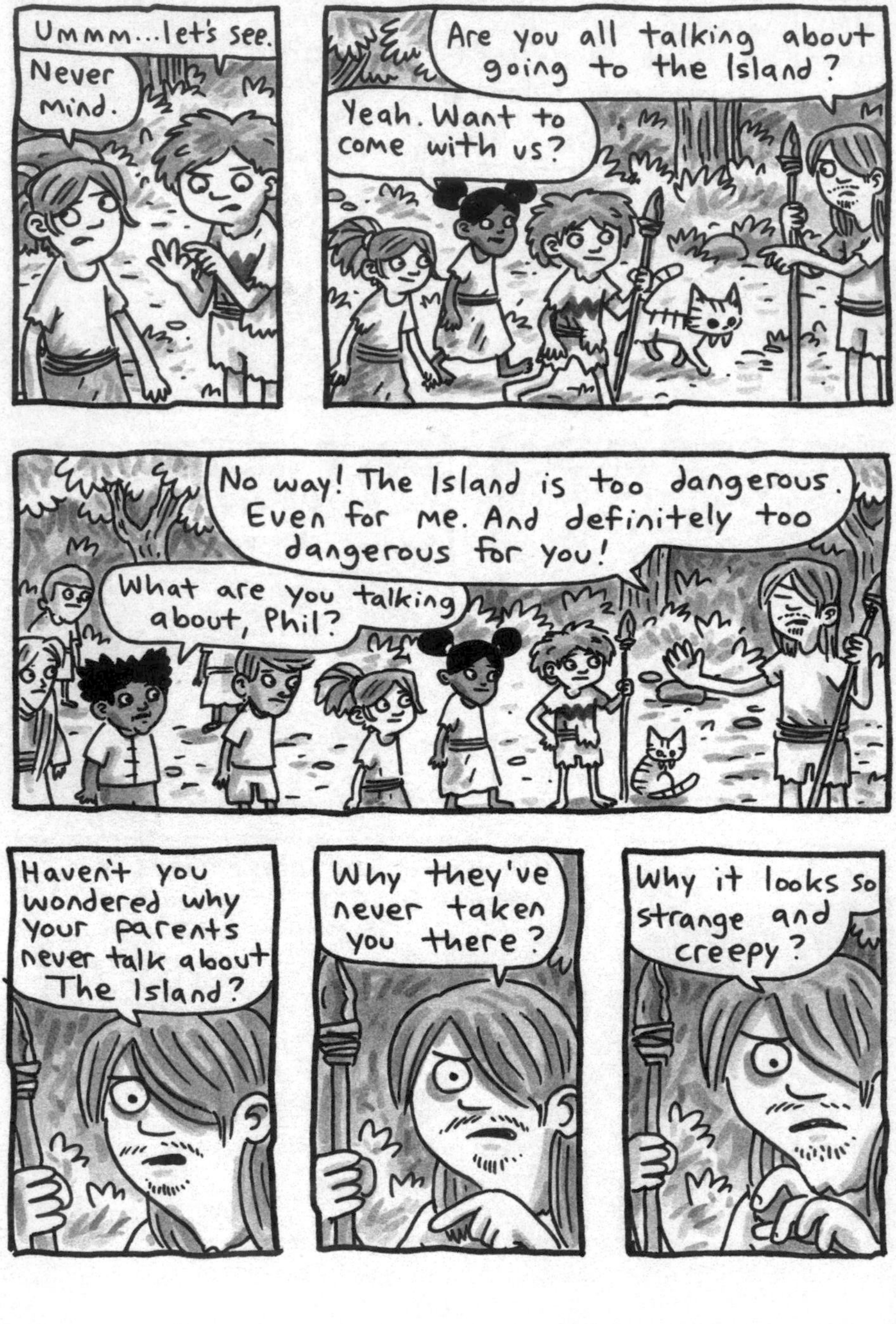
Ummm...let's see.
Never mind.
Are you all talking about going to the Island?
Yeah. Want to come with us?
No way! The Island is too dangerous. Even for me. And definitely too dangerous for you!
What are you talking about, Phil?
Haven't you wondered why your parents never talk about The Island?
Why they've never taken you there?
Why it looks so strange and creepy?

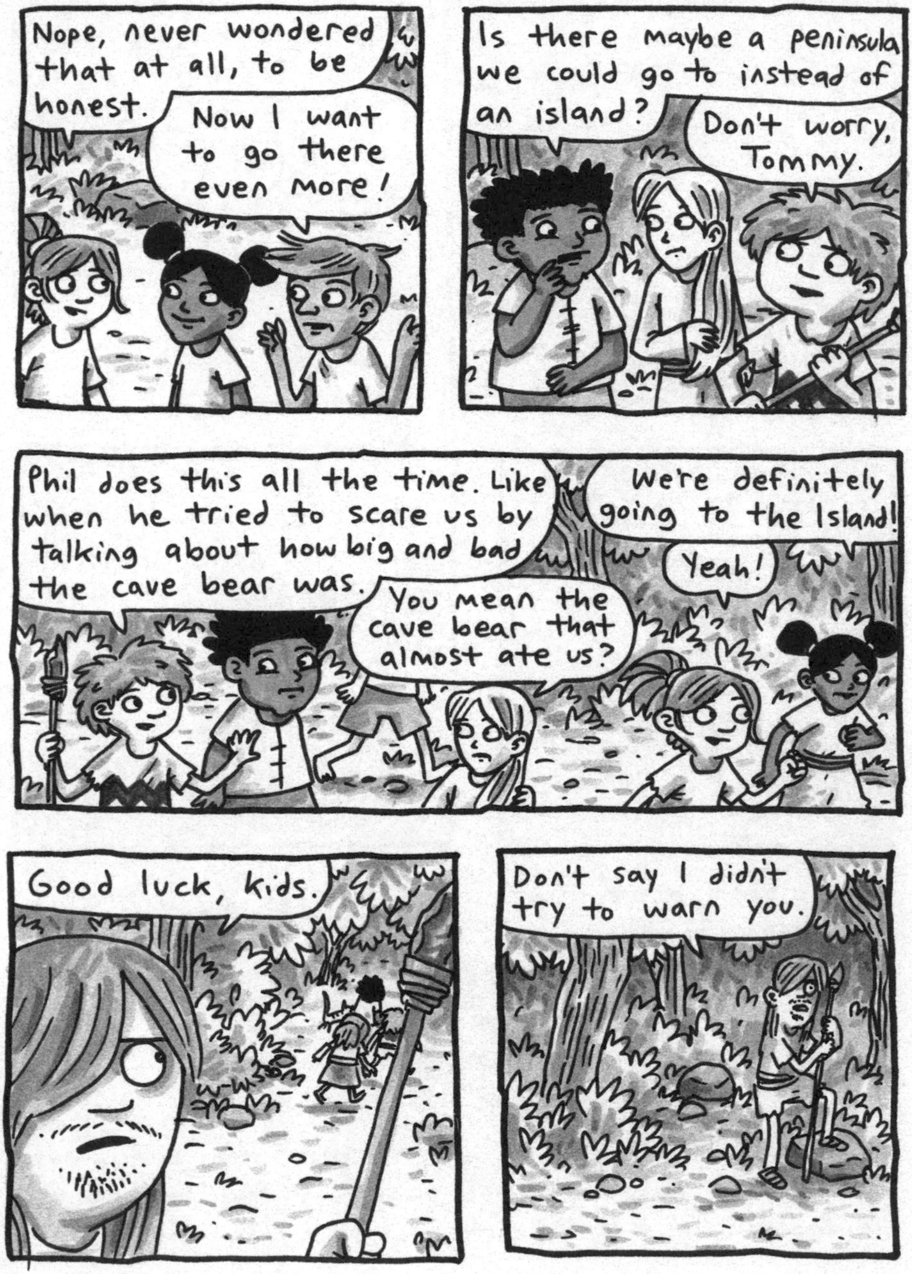
Nope, never wondered that at all, to be honest.
Now I want to go there even more!
Is there maybe a peninsula we could go to instead of an island?
Don't worry, Tommy.
Phil does this all the time. Like when he tried to scare us by talking about how big and bad the cave bear was.
You mean the cave bear that almost ate us?
We're definitely going to the Island!
Yeah!
Good luck, kids.
Don't say I didn't try to warn you.

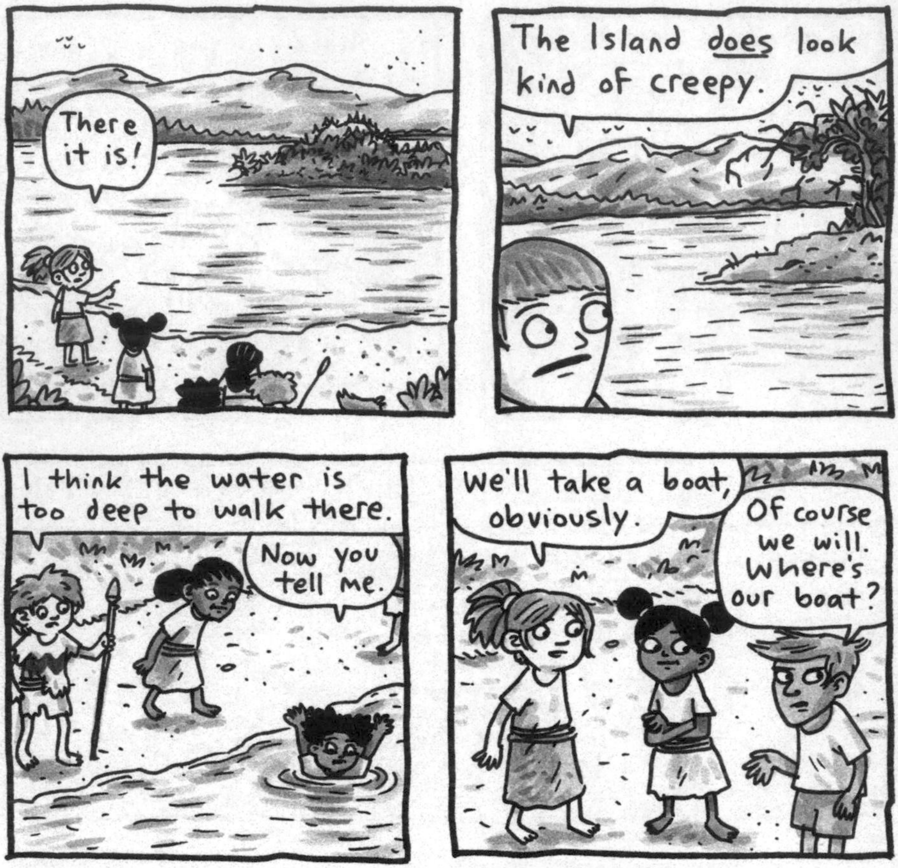
There it is!
The Island does look kind of creepy.
I think the water is too deep to walk there.
Now you tell me.
We'll take a boat, obviously.
Of course we will. Where's our boat?

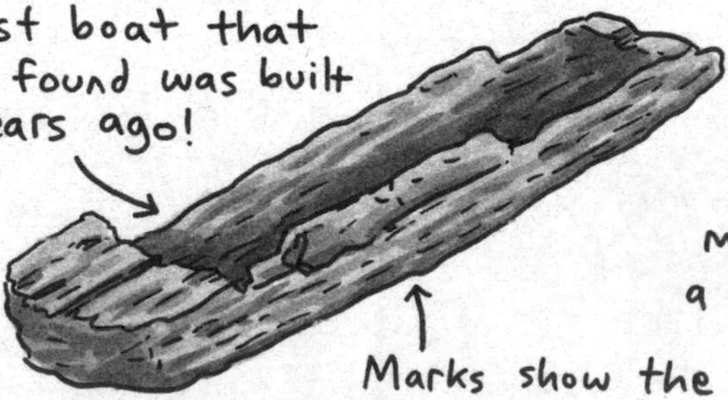
The oldest boat that has been found was built 10,000 years ago!
The Pesse Canoe was made out of a pine tree.
Marks show the canoe was carved out by an ax, but they don't tell how many times people tipped over and fell into the water.

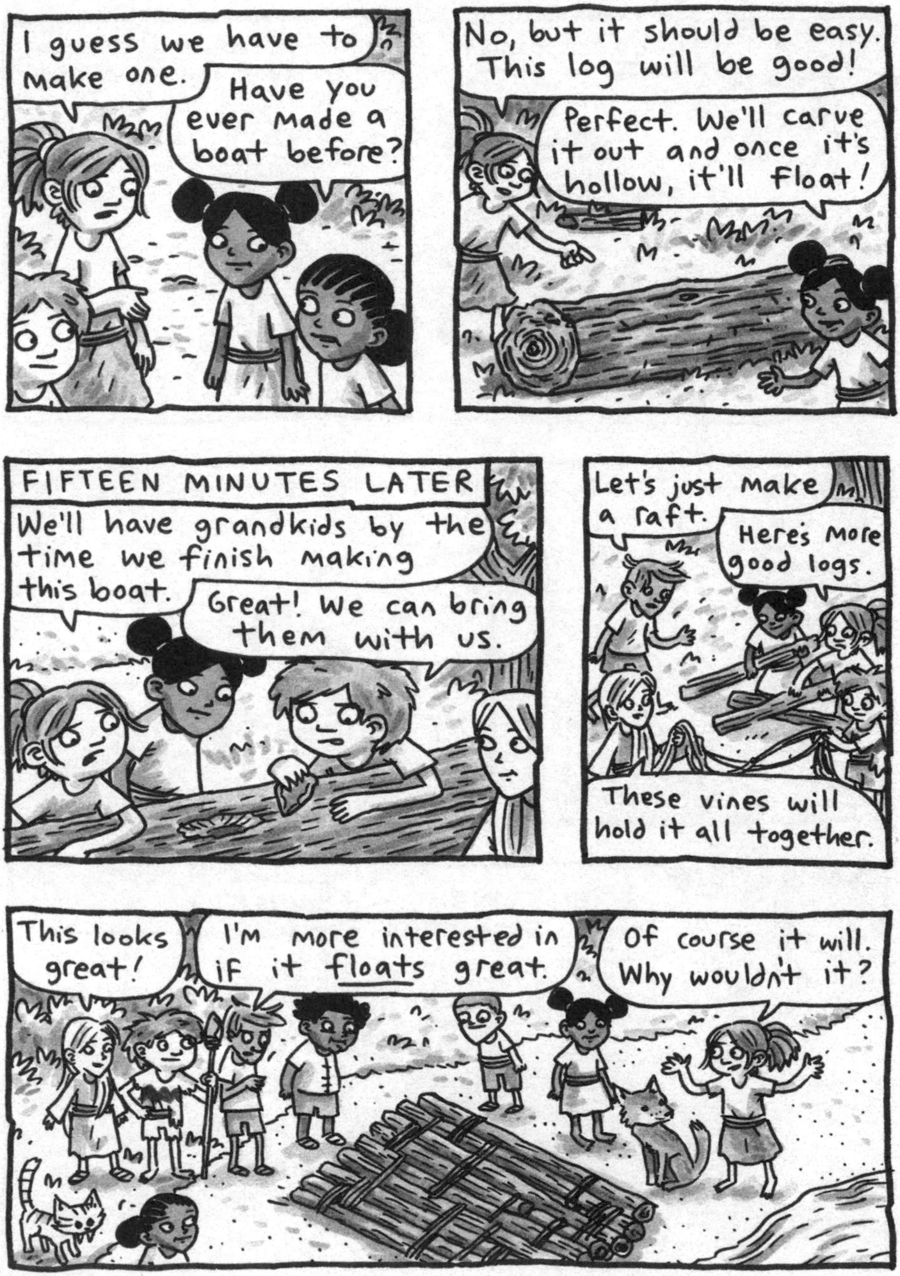
I guess we have to make one.
Have you ever made a boat before?
No, but it should be easy. This log will be good!
Perfect. We'll carve it out and once it's hollow, it'll float!
FIFTEEN MINUTES LATER
We'll have grandkids by the time we finish making this boat.
Great! We can bring them with us.
Let's just make a raft.
Here's more good logs.
These vines will hold it all together.
This looks great!
I'm more interested in if it floats great.
Of course it will. Why wouldn't it?

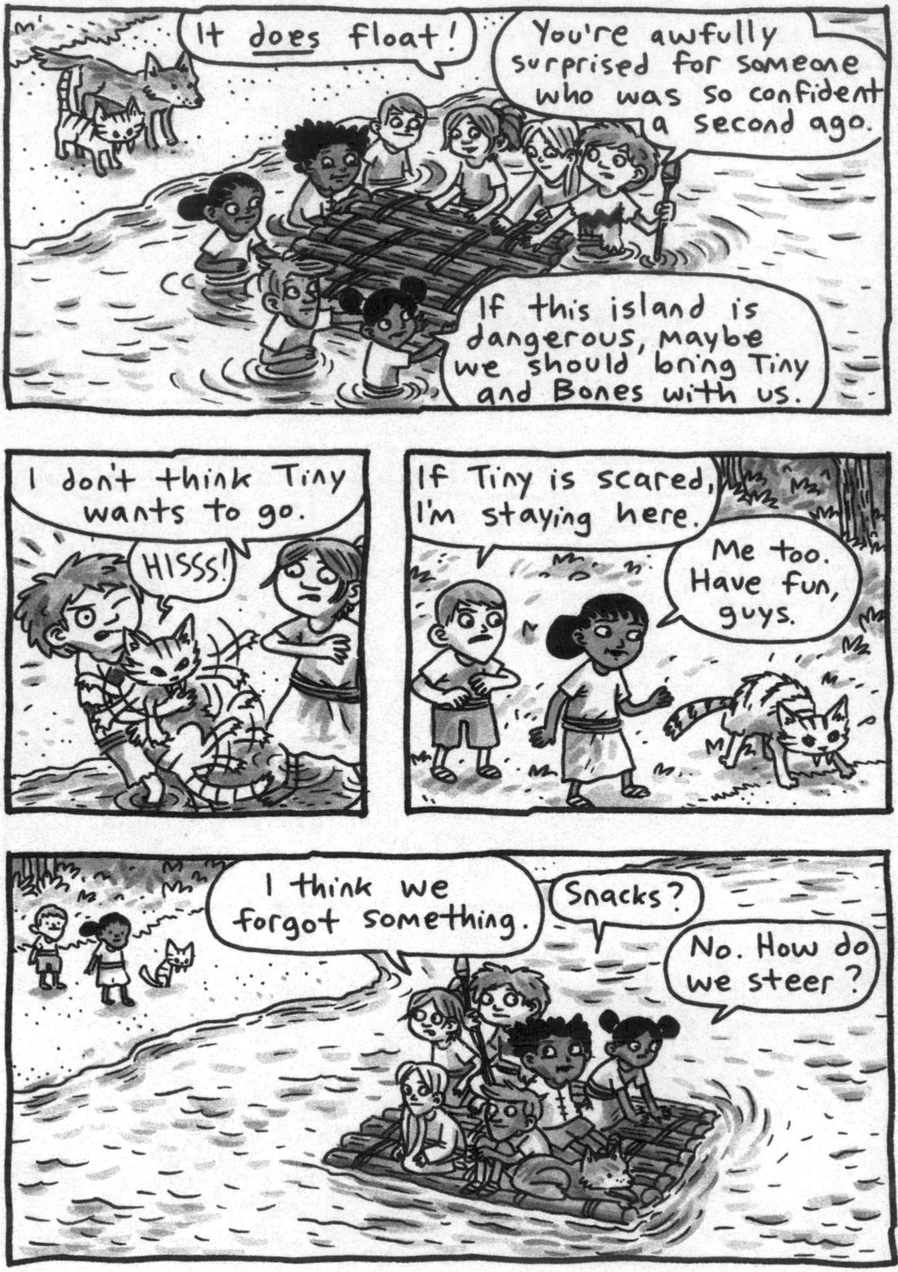
It does float!
You're awfully surprised for someone who was so confident a second ago.
If this island is dangerous, maybe we should bring Tiny and Bones with us.
I don't think Tiny wants to go.
HISSS!
If Tiny is scared, I'm staying here.
Me too. Have fun, guys.
I think we forgot something.
Snacks?
No. How do we steer?

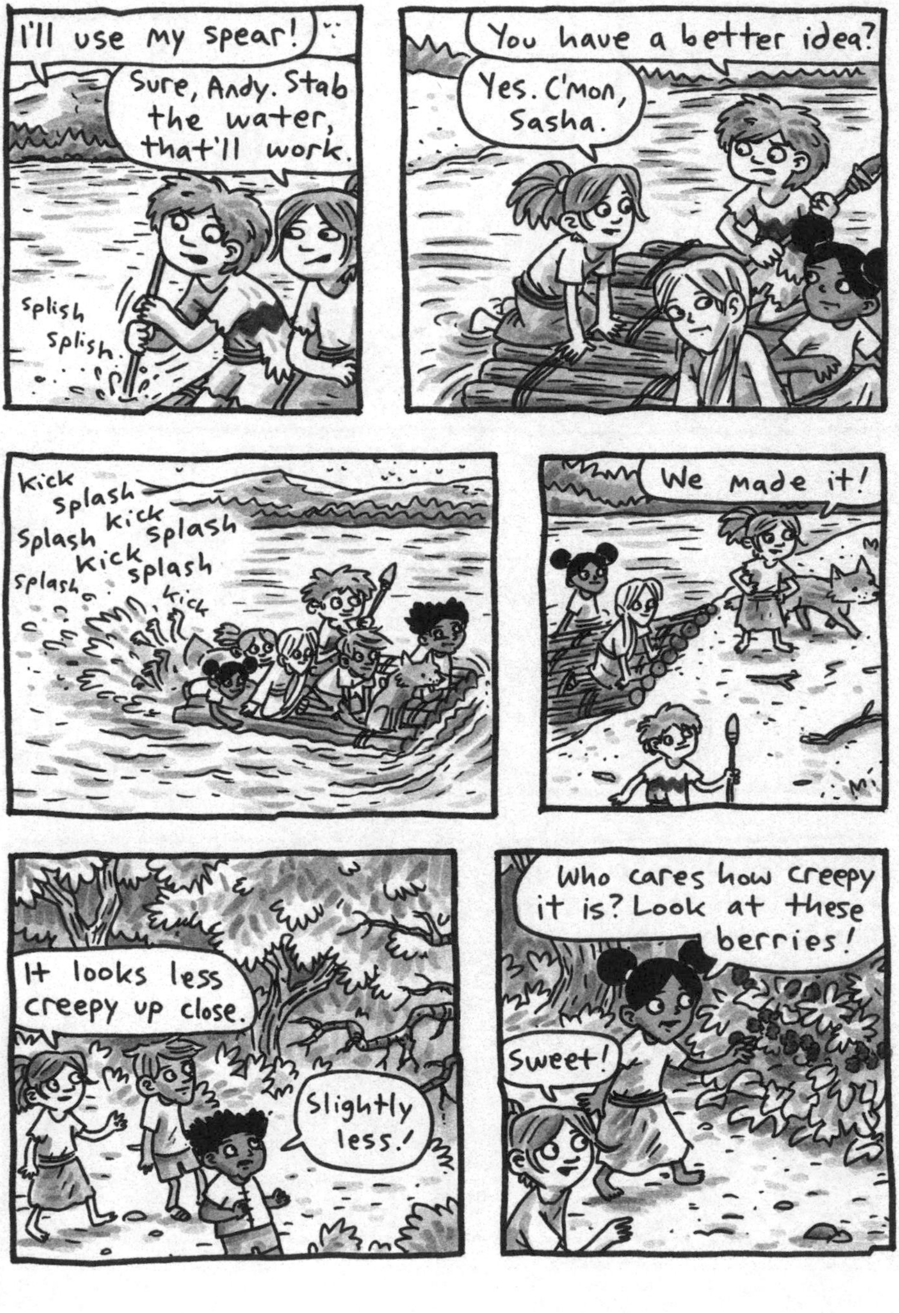
I'll use my spear!
Sure, Andy. Stab the water, that'll work.
splish splish.
You have a better idea?
Yes. C'mon, Sasha.
kick splash kick splash splash kick splash kick splash splash kick
We made it!
It looks less creepy up close.
Slightly less.
Who cares how creepy it is? Look at these berries!
Sweet!

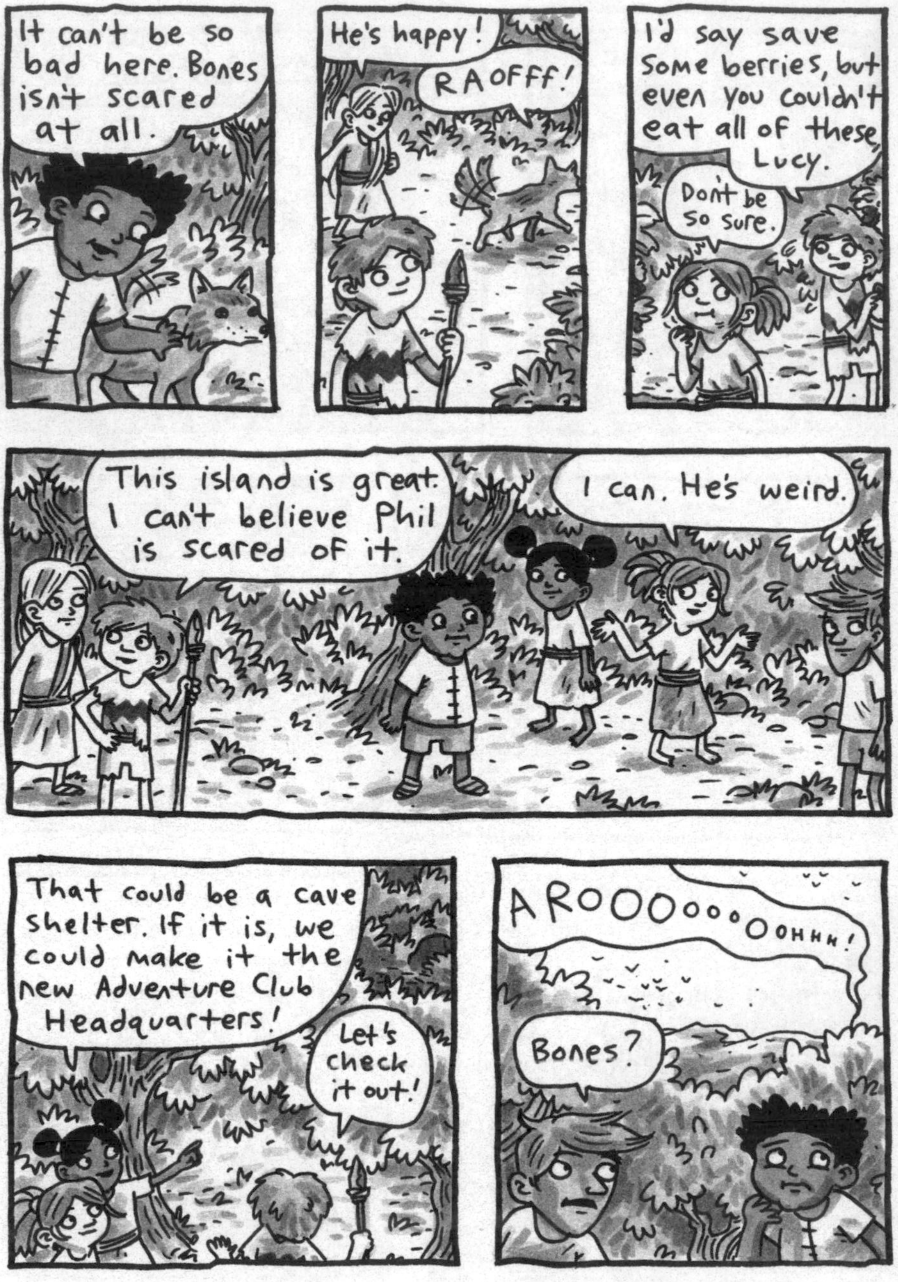
It can't be so bad here. Bones isn't scared at all.
He's happy!
RAOFFF!
I'd say save some berries, but even you couldn't eat all of these, Lucy.
Don't be so sure.
This island is great. I can't believe Phil is scared of it.
I can. He's weird.
That could be a cave shelter. If it is, we could make it the new Adventure Club Headquarters!
Let's check it out!
AROOOooooOOHHH!
Bones?

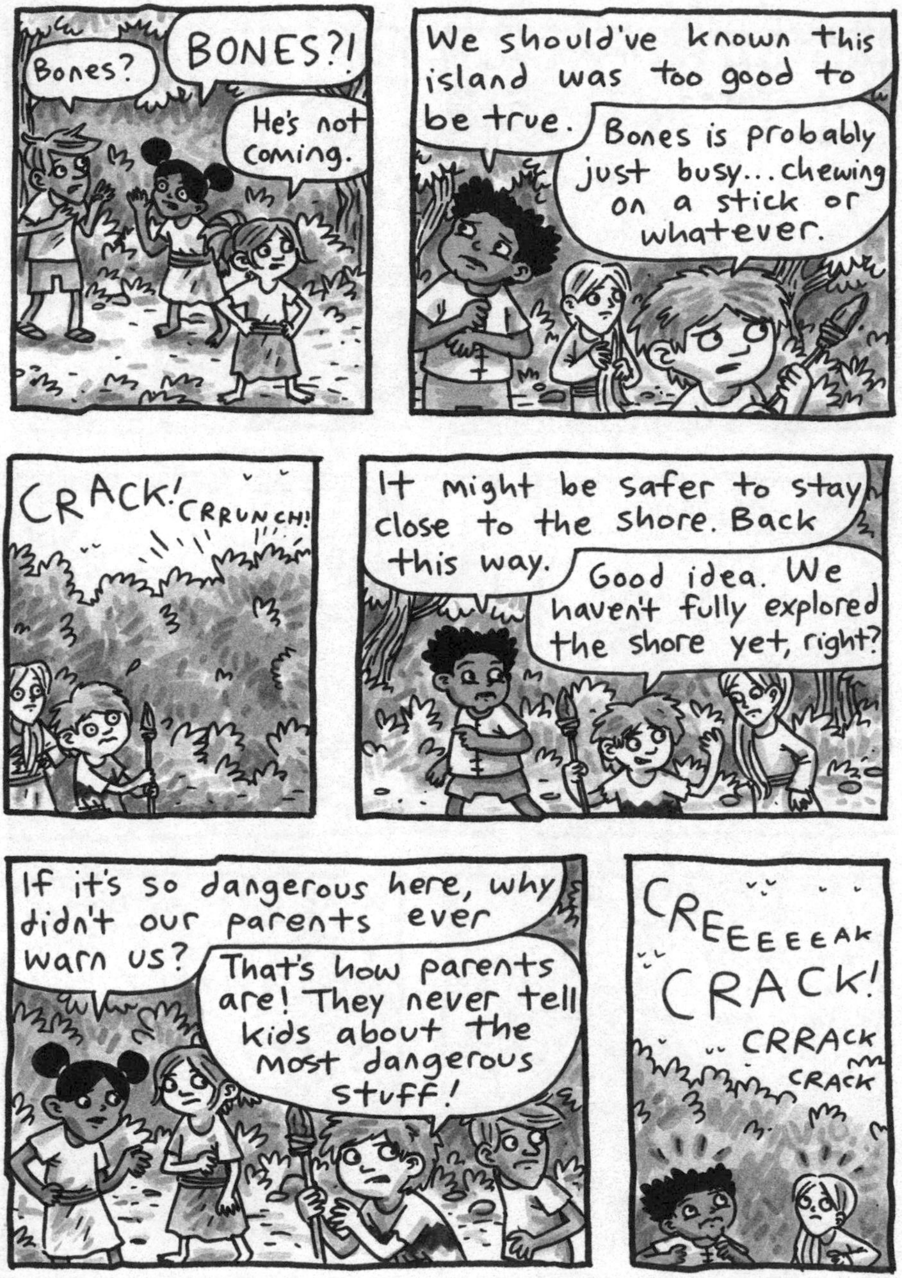
Bones?
BONES?!
He's not coming.
We should've known this island was too good to be true.
Bones is probably just busy... chewing on a stick or whatever.
CRACK!
CRRUNCH!
It might be safer to stay close to the shore. Back this way.
Good idea. We haven't fully explored the shore yet, right?
If it's so dangerous here, why didn't our parents ever warn us?
That's how parents are! They never tell kids about the most dangerous stuff!
CREEEEEEAK
CRACK!
CRRACK
CRACK

Let's get out of here!
CRACK! CRACK!
What about Bones?
Do you really want to stay and find out what ate him?!
What's happening!
It's breaking apart!
Our raft!
What do we do?!
Hey! There's another boat over here!
What if it's a trap?
I prefer this trap to any trap that might eat us!

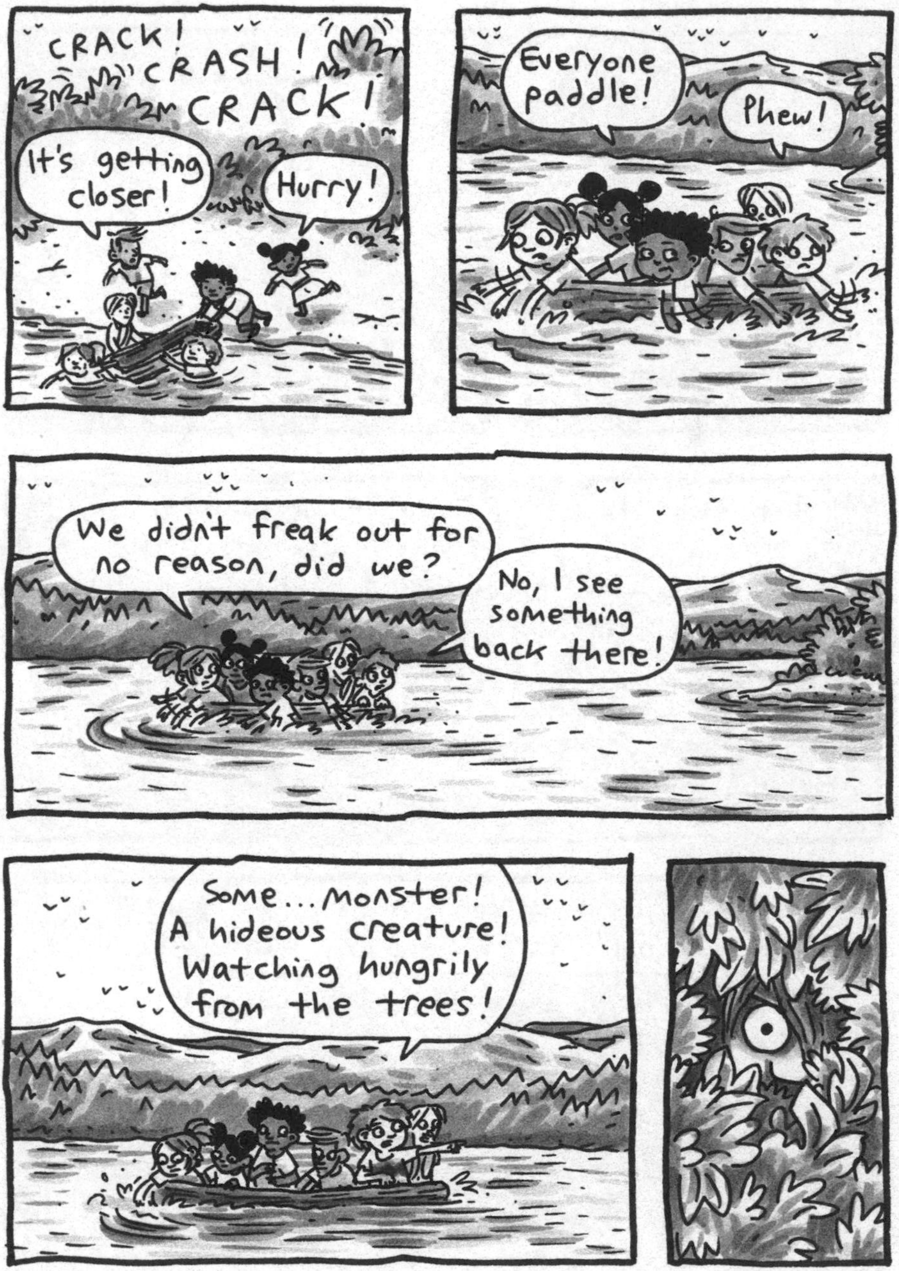
CRACK!
CRASH!
CRACK!
It's getting closer!
Hurry!
Everyone paddle!
Phew!
We didn't freak out for no reason, did we?
No, I see something back there!
Some... monster! A hideous creature! Watching hungrily from the trees!

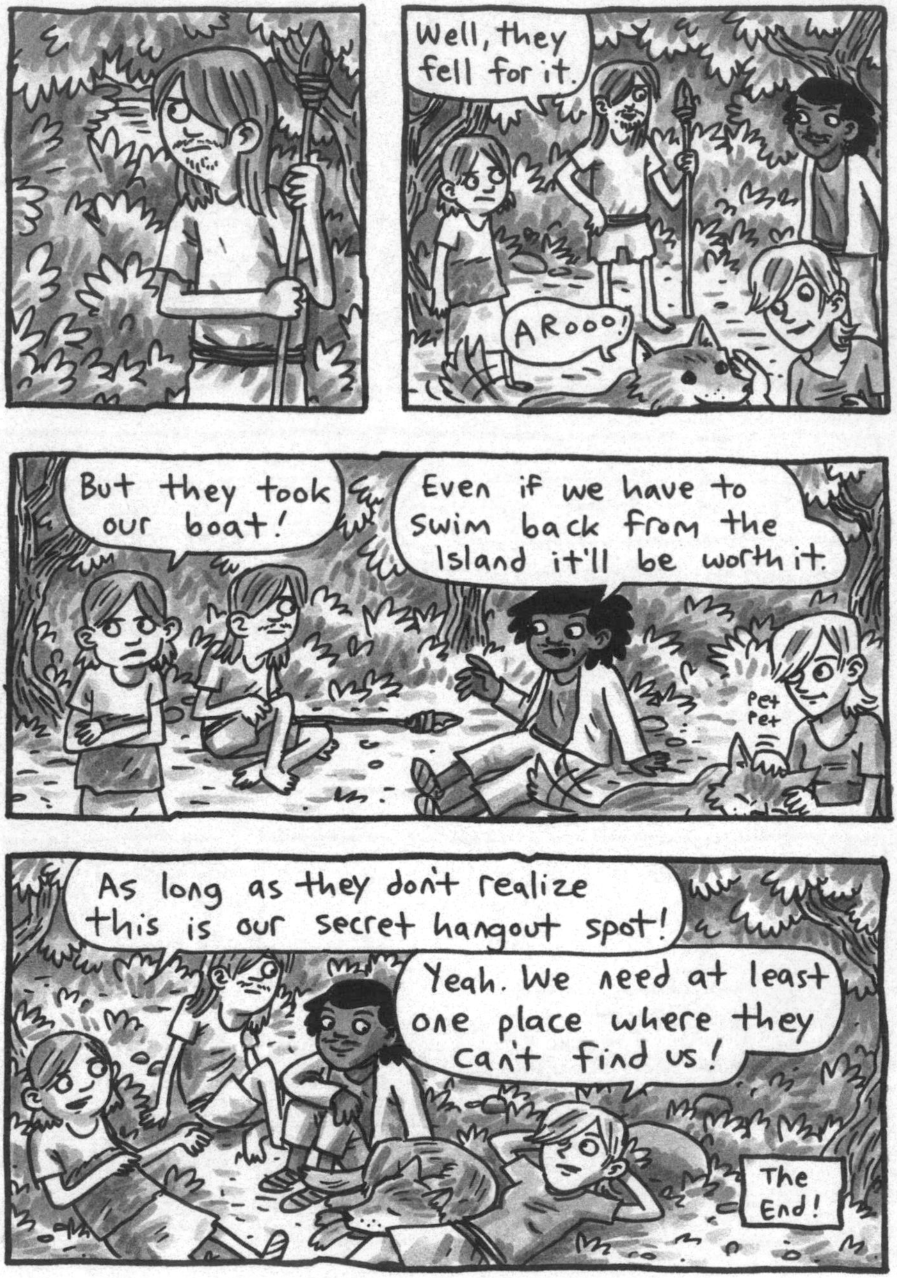
Well, they fell for it.
AROOO!
But they took our boat!
Even if we have to swim back from the Island it'll be worth it.
Pet Pet
As long as they don't realize this is our secret hangout spot!
Yeah. We need at least one place where they can't find us!
The End!

The oldest boat we've discovered is only 10,000 years old, but people have been making and using boats for as long as 800,000 years!
Rock carvings show what some early boats may have been like, but since they were constructed from organic materials, the oldest boats haven't survived.
Evidence of where early human populations lived and how they migrated shows us they must have crossed large bodies of water.
We can even construct boats using the tools and resources available to early humans. Ready to test the one I made?
Hm. You can come back and pick me up if it doesn't sink first!

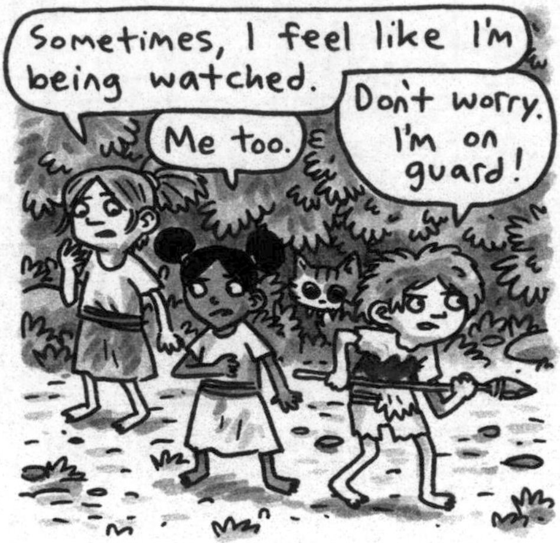
Sometimes, I feel like I'm being watched.
Me too.
Don't worry. I'm on guard!

DIG INTO MORE PREHISTORIC FUN WITH

LUCY & ANDY NEANDERTHAL

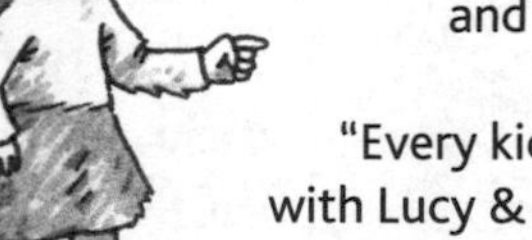

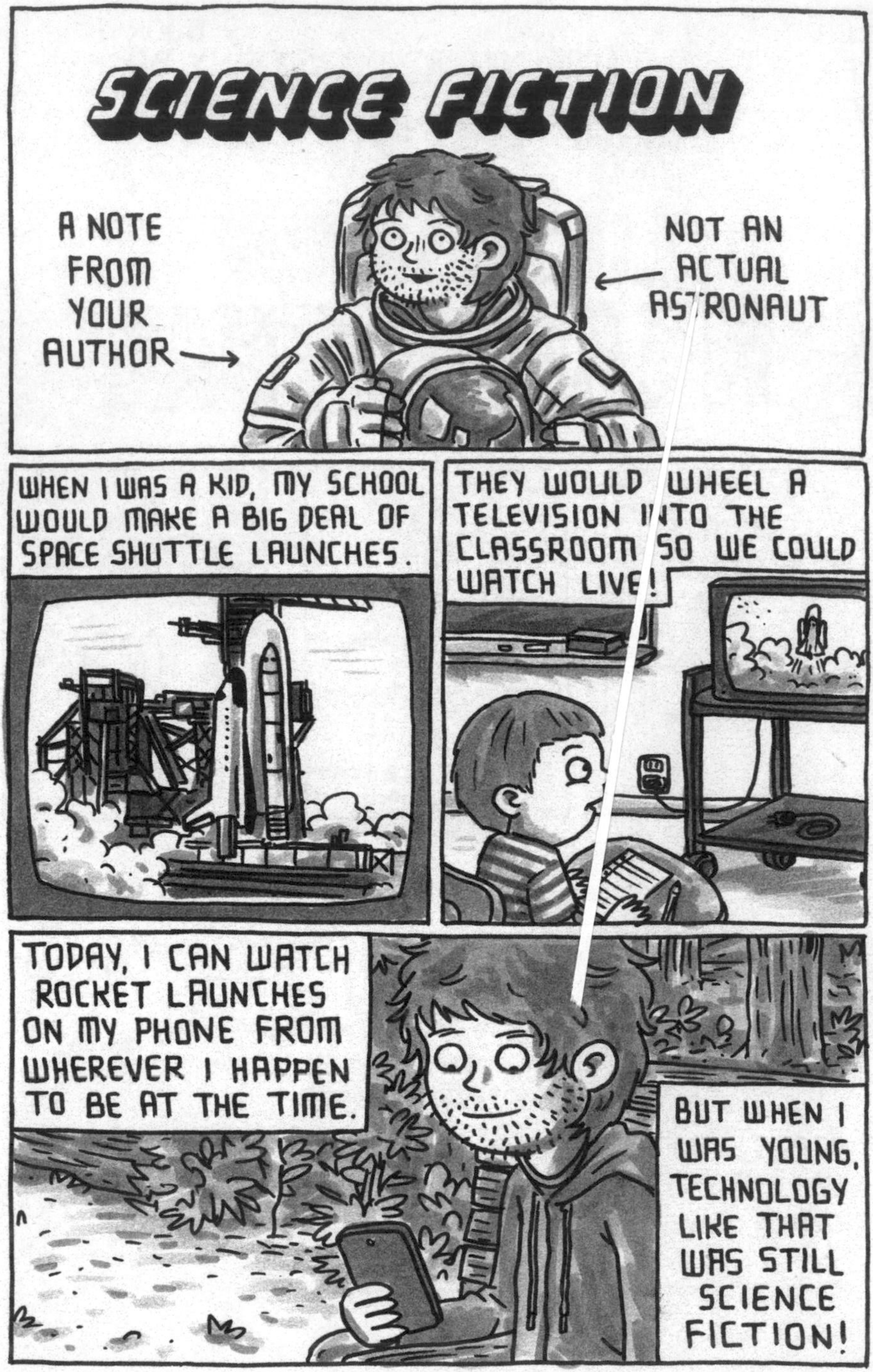
SCIENCE FICTION
A NOTE FROM YOUR AUTHOR
NOT AN ACTUAL ASTRONAUT
WHEN I WAS A KID, MY SCHOOL WOULD MAKE A BIG DEAL OF SPACE SHUTTLE LAUNCHES.
THEY WOULD WHEEL A TELEVISION INTO THE CLASSROOM SO WE COULD WATCH LIVE!
TODAY, I CAN WATCH ROCKET LAUNCHES ON MY PHONE FROM WHEREVER I HAPPEN TO BE AT THE TIME.
BUT WHEN I WAS YOUNG, TECHNOLOGY LIKE THAT WAS STILL SCIENCE FICTION!

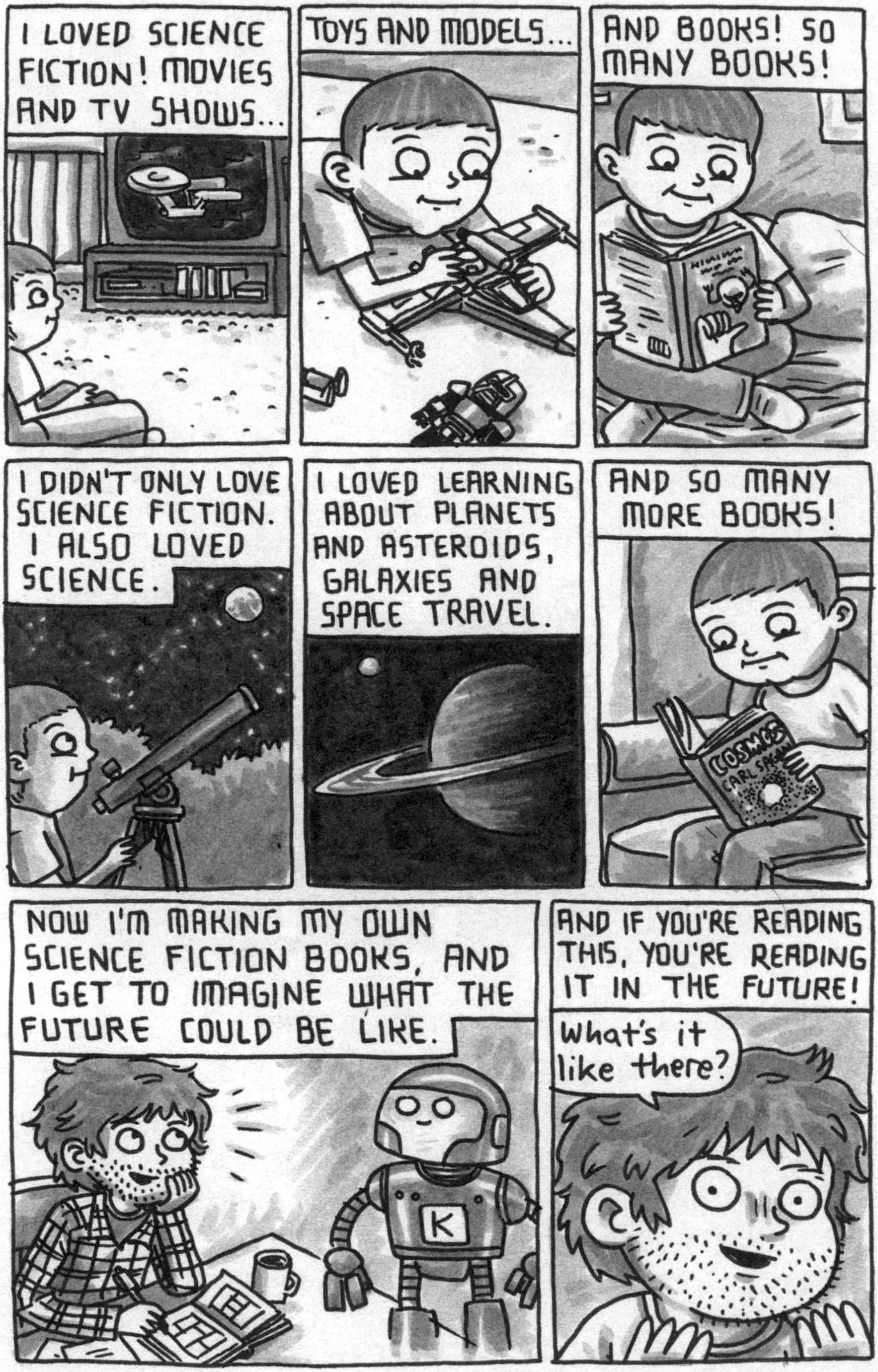
I LOVED SCIENCE FICTION! MOVIES AND TV SHOWS...
TOYS AND MODELS...
AND BOOKS! SO MANY BOOKS!
I DIDN'T ONLY LOVE SCIENCE FICTION. I ALSO LOVED SCIENCE.
I LOVED LEARNING ABOUT PLANETS AND ASTEROIDS, GALAXIES AND SPACE TRAVEL.
AND SO MANY MORE BOOKS!
COSMOS
CARL SAGAN
NOW I'M MAKING MY OWN SCIENCE FICTION BOOKS, AND I GET TO IMAGINE WHAT THE FUTURE COULD BE LIKE.
K
AND IF YOU'RE READING THIS, YOU'RE READING IT IN THE FUTURE!
What's it like there?

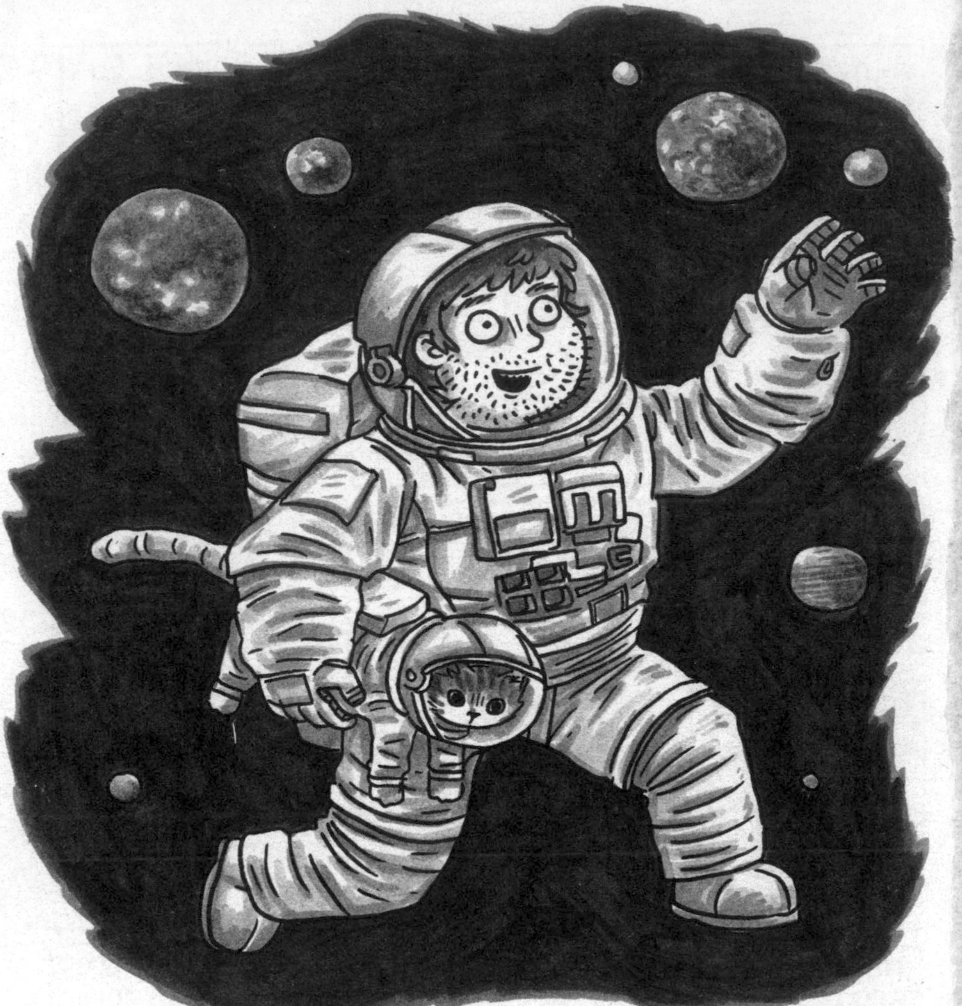

JEFFREY BROWN IS THE AUTHOR OF THE LUCY & ANDY NEANDERTHAL MIDDLE-GRADE SERIES, AS WELL AS THE BESTSELLING DARTH VADER AND SON AND JEDI ACADEMY SERIES. HE LIVES IN CHICAGO WITH HIS WIFE, TWO SONS, AND CAT. JEFFREY WOULD PROBABLY MAKE A TERRIBLE ASTRONAUT, BUT HE STILL LIKES TO IMAGINE TRAVELING INTO OUTER SPACE....

VISIT HIM ON EARTH AT JEFFREYBROWNCOMICS.com
P.O. BOX 120 DEERFIELD, IL 60015-0120 USA